faking cinderella

Pippa Grant

USA TODAY BESTSELLING AUTHOR

PIPPA GRANT

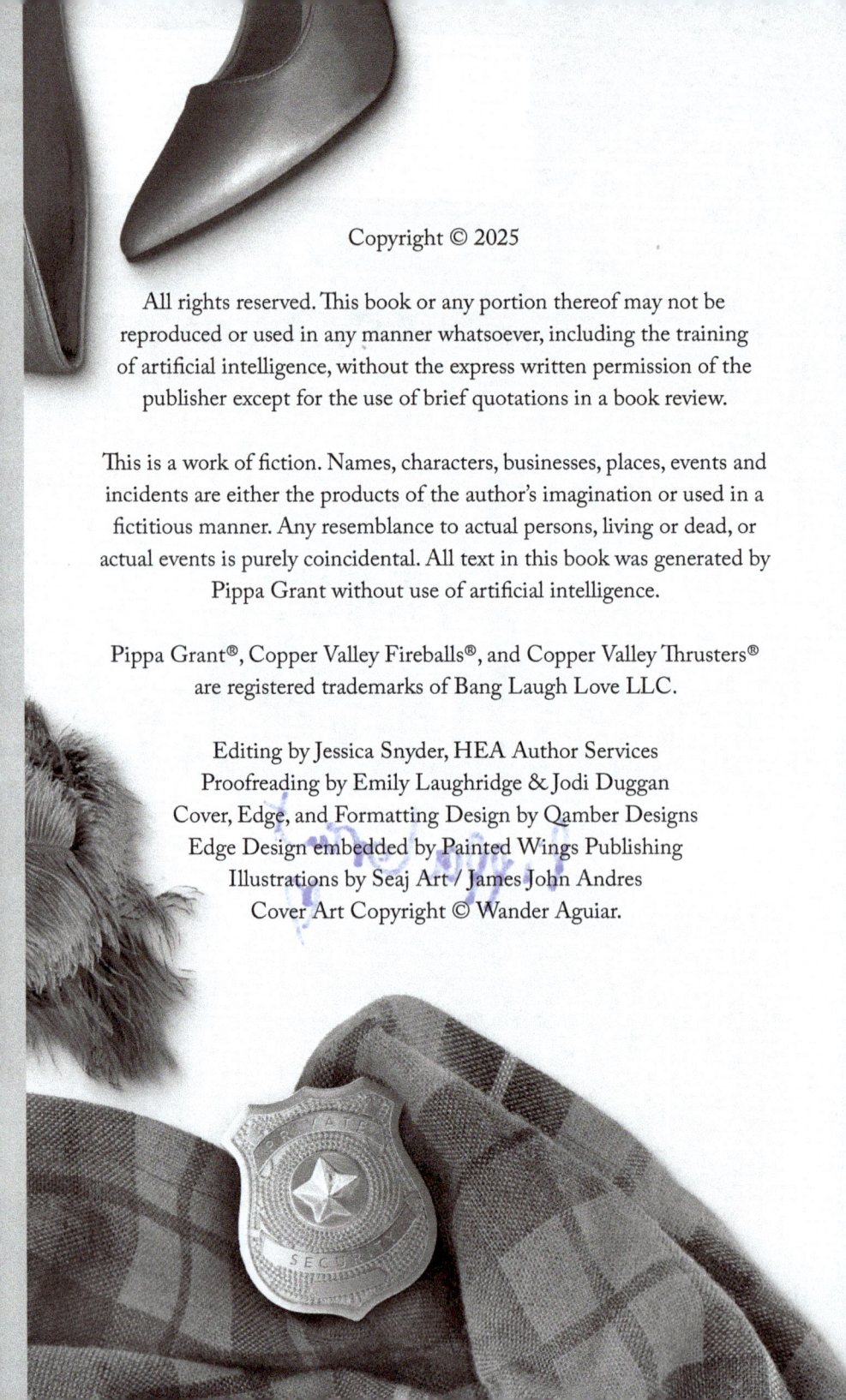

Copyright © 2025

All rights reserved. This book or any portion thereof may not be reproduced or used in any manner whatsoever, including the training of artificial intelligence, without the express written permission of the publisher except for the use of brief quotations in a book review.

This is a work of fiction. Names, characters, businesses, places, events and incidents are either the products of the author's imagination or used in a fictitious manner. Any resemblance to actual persons, living or dead, or actual events is purely coincidental. All text in this book was generated by Pippa Grant without use of artificial intelligence.

Pippa Grant®, Copper Valley Fireballs®, and Copper Valley Thrusters® are registered trademarks of Bang Laugh Love LLC.

Editing by Jessica Snyder, HEA Author Services
Proofreading by Emily Laughridge & Jodi Duggan
Cover, Edge, and Formatting Design by Qamber Designs
Edge Design embedded by Painted Wings Publishing
Illustrations by Seaj Art / James John Andres
Cover Art Copyright © Wander Aguiar

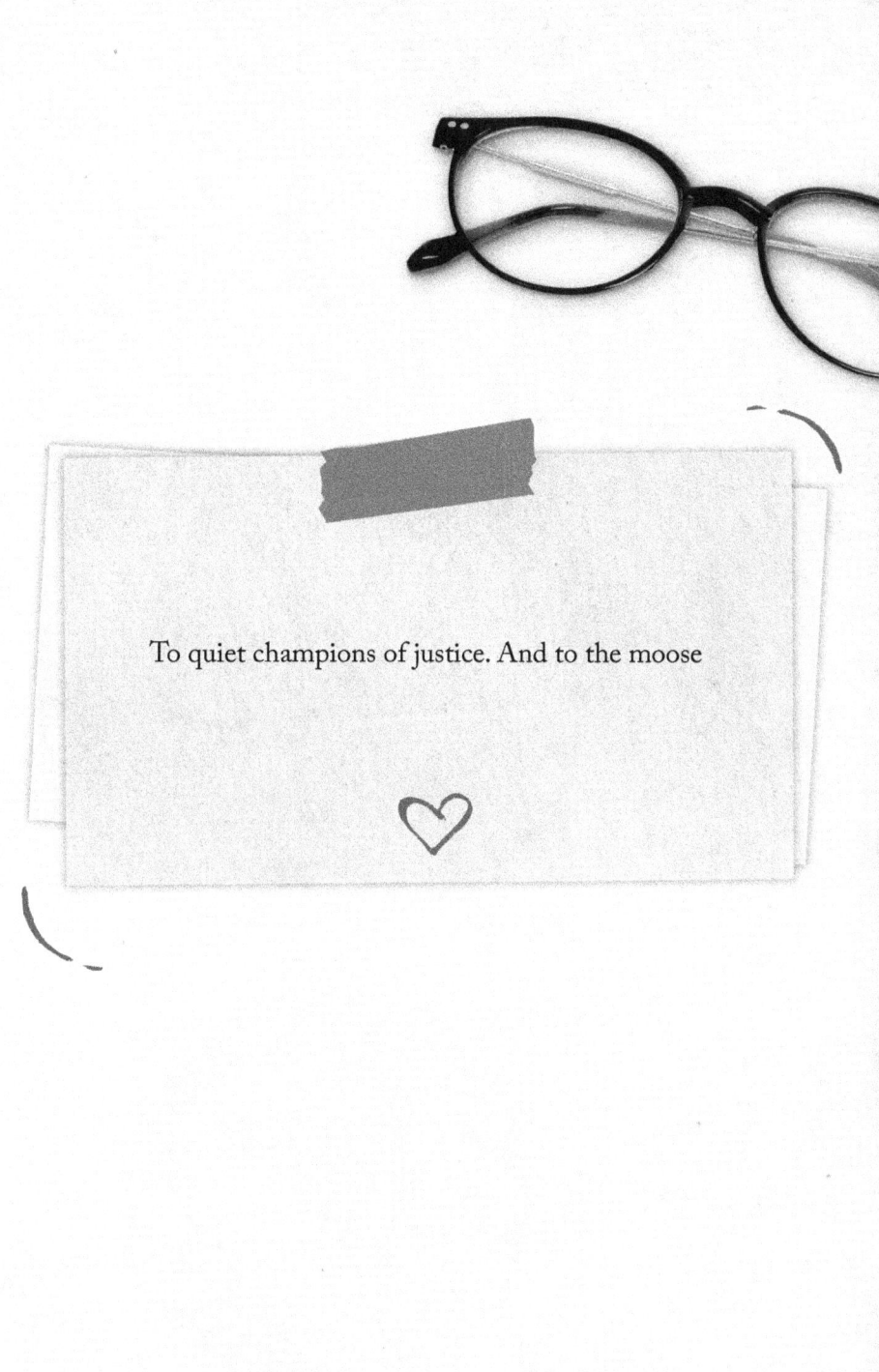

To quiet champions of justice. And to the moose

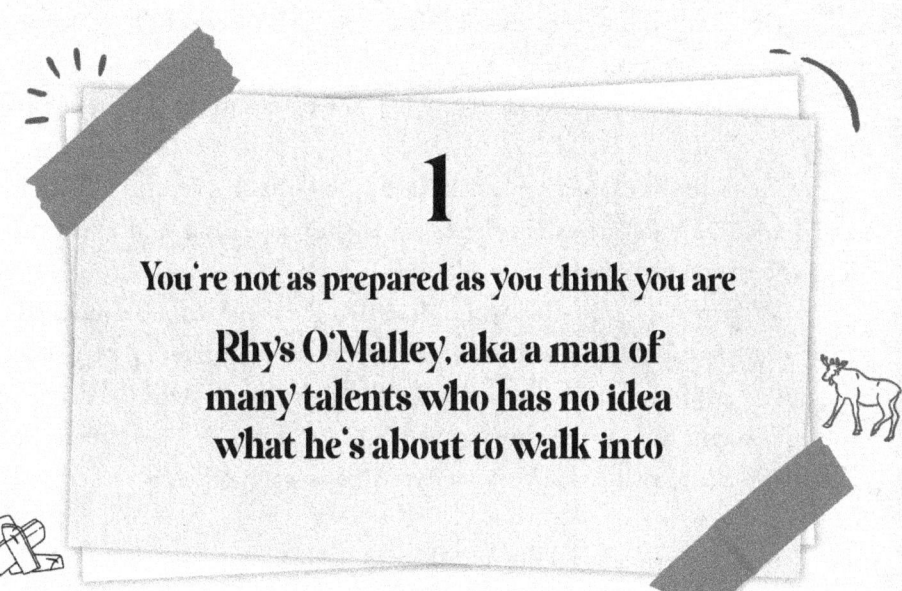

1

You're not as prepared as you think you are

Rhys O'Malley, aka a man of many talents who has no idea what he's about to walk into

I f there's one thing I learned growing up in the private security world, it's to be prepared for anything.

Tonight, that means watching for deer, elk, and bear on the dark, winding mountain roads on my way to the cabin that my buddy Decker Sullivan shares with his two identical brothers.

Usually, being on high alert is my default.

Right now, though, I'm more tired than I should be, and it's my own fault.

Should've stopped a few hours ago and finished the drive tomorrow.

But the idea of getting here first, before the triplets' newly discovered half sister arrives tomorrow, was appealing.

Settle in early. Have time for a hike to decompress in the morning. Get firewood prepped if I need it. Never know what Colorado Septembers will bring.

Breathe for the first time in a few months. Solidify a few more plans for the private security firm I want to open on the West Coast.

Do a little more research on this woman who seems to have absolutely no internet presence.

Practice my surprised face for when she comes to stay in the cabin too.

That's the story Decker asked me to use—that his secret half sister and I are accidentally both at the cabin at the same time, and I had no idea she would be there.

We're playing it like it's an accident that the triplets double-booked their getaway cabin because, unlike his two brothers, Decker's pretty suspicious of anyone claiming to be family through that MatchDNA site.

Though, they're the three guys who took the DNA test there in the first place to make sure they were related to each other.

Yeah.

Identical triplets, taking a DNA test to make sure they were related to each other.

I'm ninety percent certain they did it as a joke, but it had serious repercussions—they found out the man who raised them wasn't their biological father. They've been keeping that secret from him for a few years now, which means they don't know if he knows, or if he doesn't know they know, or if they all know but they're just not talking about it.

Hence having a surprise half sister—presumably they share a biological sperm donor somewhere—is not the best news for my buddy, and he wants to know more about this woman without her knowing he's looking into her.

And since I didn't have anything better on my calendar—being chronically unemployed after being blacklisted in the private security field by my stepfather's been a trip, let me tell you—here I am.

I steer my truck onto the winding driveway that leads to the remote log cabin that Decker and his brothers inherited from some relative on their mother's side. My shoulders are tight, my eyes are dry, and my ass is ready to be out of this seat. After a couple switchbacks on the long dirt driveway, the cabin comes into view.

The moonlight cuts through the trees, adding to the illumination from my headlights.

All is dark.

Just as it should be.

I park beside the door, kill the engine, and grab my phone.

I'll text Decker to let him know I'm here early once I've made sure the place is secure and I'm inside.

Like I said.

Always be prepared.

I'm too young for my joints to creak and pop the way they do when I climb out of the truck, but they care less about my age—I'm barely in my mid-thirties—and more about what I've put my body through in those years.

I grunt through the aches and head on foot to make a sweep around the log cabin in the chilly September night.

Moonlight's bright enough tonight to detail the exterior log walls, dark windows, and the pinecone wreath hanging on the front door. Single-car detached garage door is closed.

Nothing looks out of place.

Not much out of place, anyway.

Decker told me he crashed here a few nights last week, which explains the work gloves on the unsplit wood pile and the maul left out in the elements.

The dude always bitched about having to pick up after himself.

Annoyed the shit out of me when we were in the Marines together, but he's a good guy regardless of his sloppy habits.

I shove the gloves in my back pocket and grab the maul, then finish the circle of the house. I retrieve my bag out of the back of my extended cab and sling it over my shoulder, weariness taking over with every step up the small porch to the front door.

It's time for my head to hit a pillow.

I hit the code on the key panel, and a bright green light flashes in the darkness while the lock snicks open.

Finally.

Here.

Time to rest.

It's habit to slip inside silently, so that's what I do.

I'm on high alert still—seriously, so fucking hard not to be—but apparently not high enough, because when I hear a click and the subtle sound of string snapping, I don't move fast enough.

And even if I did, it wouldn't have been in the right direction.

Because my instinct is to duck, but gravity has already won for the opponent I didn't know I have, and I get a cold, wet spray of water that rains down on top of my head.

I'm so startled at being startled here that I do the dumbass thing and look up as part of my visual sweep of the room, maul gripped and ready, but when I look up, a drop finds its way into one of my eyeballs, and fuck me, that's not water.

Water doesn't burn.

What the actual—

Fuck on a flatbread, my eyeballs are on fire, and the scent of—fuck me again.

Whatever's burning my eyes smells like my ex when she'd touch up her roots in the bathroom.

Bathroom's too far.

Kitchen's on the right.

Kitchen sink.

Need to get to the kitchen sink, rinse this shit out, and then I need to sweep this place and find out if Decker has a crasher or if Decker's playing a prank on me, in which case I need to decide how long he has to live.

I take a step in what I think is the right direction, and a cloud of dust explodes in my face, going right into my mouth and nose and making me cough.

And then the voices start.

So many, many voices. Male voices. Female voices. Indeterminate voices.

"Intruder! Intruder!"

"I told you to get the hell out of here!"

"Where are your manners?"

"Bear! There's a bear!"

I spin, dropping my bag but holding onto the maul, both of my eyes stinging now and my throat choking itself with the fucking dust. Flour.

Tastes like flour, shit shit shit, why is this place booby-trapped?

Where's the kitchen?

I need a sink.

What the fuck is in my eyes?

"Detonation in one minute," a mechanical female voice says.

"You're gonna regret the day you were born," an older dude's voice growls.

"What the fu—" I cut off my own question as I cough again, maul handle gripped tight, poised to attack if necessary, while I try to squint through the pain in my eyes.

This.

This is why my body aches.

Because I take assignments guarding people who do shit like booby-trapping their own fucking homes.

"Decker?" I rasp.

And that's the last thing I get out before a shadow looms in my peripheral vision and something thick and hard smacks me in the stomach as I'm twisting toward it, making me bend double.

"Get down," a woman shrieks.

As if I have a choice.

Fuck me.

Can't breathe.

Can't see.

Can't stop coughing, but also can't breathe.

"Jesus fuck." I grunt.

"Get down," she repeats, voice high with panic. "How do you know Decker?"

The other voices have stopped, and I realize this one's different.

This one's here.

The others were recordings.

Shit.

Shit.

I don't get my days wrong.

So either someone broke into Decker's cabin, or his half sister showed up a day early too.

And she's also paranoid as fuck.

Best-case scenario. Could be others. Crazy exes. Squatter. The third triplet invited someone to use the cabin too.

"Friend," I gasp.

"That's what anyone breaking in would say. Do you really know Decker, or do you just know he owns this place?"

The tremble in her voice is the only thing keeping me on the defensive instead of the offensive.

"Gave me—" I pause and cough my lungs out again, the burn still burning my eyeballs, before I finish. "Door code."

"Decker gave you the door code?"

"Yes," I wheeze. Fuck on a kumquat, how did I ever call myself a Marine? This is embarrassing.

Her voice is farther away. Still shaky, but growing more commanding by the moment. "Drop the fucking axe now or I'll bash your brains in."

I don't believe her, but it doesn't matter what I believe.

Have to quit coughing.

Eyes need to quit stinging.

Paranoia's gonna fucking suck for the rest of this trip.

If I don't bail.

Which I won't, because this gig comes with a side gig that should be my way back into the personal security world, and I desperately need that.

Need a job.

Need to get back to my roots.

I drop the maul and hold my hands up in an I'm harmless gesture. "Found—outside—should be—put—away. Not weapon."

"Who are you?"

"Friend," I rasp again. "You?"

"Why are you here?"

"Decker—said stay."

"Decker told you that you could stay here?"

"Yes."

"Now?"

"Yes."

"Did he consult a calendar first?"

Wait.

I know this voice.

Don't I?

Or does she just sound like every other woman I've annoyed in my life now that the terror is leaving her voice?

It's still lingering—there's some squeaking in her words—but she's clearly getting a grip.

My eyes are stinging a little less, but they still burn.

I can still see.

"Who—you?" Fuck me, I need to quit coughing.

"Until you're the one holding a cast-iron skillet, you're not the one asking questions. Ever been a woman in this world? Stay down."

A cast-iron skillet.

She socked me in the gut with a cast-iron skillet.

Wonder what size.

I wheeze and cough while my eyes water. "Decker—prank—me."

"Decker pranked somebody," she mutters. "Hey, Lucky. So sorry to bother you this late, but I was just falling asleep when, ah, this makeshift home security system that I set up went off? And there's a guy here who says Decker said he could stay?"

Okay.

Definitely the newly discovered half sister. Lucky's one of Decker's two brothers, and the brother who's most excited about meeting a new family member.

She's on the phone with him.

And she's not supposed to know that I know she's going to be here, but it would've been nice if Decker could've told me she was the kind to booby-trap a house.

Also, she probably took the bedroom.

Goddammit.

I start to rise. My eyes are back to being on fire.

"Get down," she orders again, voice still high and tight and this side of shaky.

I cough out what I'm fucking determined to make my last cough of the night, and I squint through the fuzzy haze of my burning eyeballs. "What the fuck did you put in the liquid?"

"What's your name?"

Despite the lingering fear in her voice, I'm starting to hate this woman. I hope she has deep, dark secrets that I can find and ruin her with.

And yes, I also have an unfortunate level of respect for this home security system she rigged.

Like, boner-level respect.

At least, I will in the morning.

If my eyeballs survive. And if a few hours is enough time for my pride to recover from being beaten so very thoroughly at my own game.

No one gets the jump on me like this.

Not physically.

Mentally and emotionally—shit.

Nope.

Not thinking about my stepfamily. They can suck the stinging end of a jellyfish for the rest of eternity.

"Rhys O'Malley," I wheeze out. Gonna have a cast-iron-shaped bruise on my torso tomorrow. "Decker offered the cabin. Needed a getaway. Start a job here next week."

"His name's Rhys O'Malley," the woman reports.

She's somewhere in the room close enough now that I can hear Lucky burst out laughing on the other end of the phone. "No shit? Rhys is there?"

"That's who he says he is."

"Ask him how his fiancée's doing."

"Tell Lucky to suck my nutsack," I rasp.

"Yep, that's him," Lucky's tinny voice reports. "Sorry about this, Margie. I'm texting Decker, but he's not answering. Because he's an asshole. I know Rhys. You can trust…"

The rest of what he's saying fades away, but the lights flip on.

And my cohabiter of this cabin—Margie Johnson, she says her name is—mutters a thanks, and then—

"Oh, fuck."

It's reverently whispered, like she knows she's created a massive problem, but she's also impressed with herself.

That makes two of us, Margie.

That makes two of us.

2

Purple dye and red eyes

Margot Merriweather-Brown, aka a billionaire heiress undercover on a secret mission to destroy her father to avenge her disinherited sister

English is the worst language.

We don't have specific words for grief bacon, and we don't have specific words for I'm simultaneously proud of myself for not freaking out and calling my security agent immediately and also horrified at the carnage in this cabin and also holy fuck, that dude is big, and I took him down all by myself, and I'm a badass, or I will be once the adrenaline leaves my system and I can take a deep breath without wanting to cry, and oh my god, do I want to cry right now, and I never cry.

Maybe I'll just call it Friday night.

That'll do.

For the rest of my life, whenever I think Friday night, that's what it will mean.

And maybe my heart will try to beat out of my chest the same way it did when I was woken out of a dead sleep when the alarm started squawking, and the way it's still thumping too fast right now.

I thought I was being overly paranoid when I rigged the homemade burglar alarm.

That I'd wake up in the morning and call Daphne, my sister, and tell her how ridiculous I was, and we'd both laugh about what might've happened if someone had walked under the bag of hair dye and gotten flour all over their face.

But instead, the fucking thing went off, and nothing about this is funny.

Someone broke into the cabin in the middle of the night, on the first night of my entire life without a security team within a hundred yards, and as I stare at the man hunched over and still coughing softly, I need a paper bag to breathe into and a place to go have a panic attack, which is what I'm pretty sure this is.

Rhys O'Malley's identity will be verified for me shortly, because I texted my head of security his picture and name and told Cyril to look into him.

But right now, Rhys is blinking at me as I hang up with Lucky, the only one of the triplets I've spoken with so far. Lucky's confirmed that Rhys is a family friend and that this isn't the first time Decker's messed up the cabin's calendar.

It feels very convenient.

Especially since Lucky slipped in one of our email communications and clued me in that his brothers—Decker especially—were worried I'd say something I shouldn't to someone I shouldn't be near while I'm here.

I should be more suspicious of Rhys, but it's hard to not feel increasingly more in control when he has dark purple hair dye dripping down the top of his face and flour all over his nose and short beard.

His eyes are blood red and leaking tears.

I mean, they're actually a lovely shade of blue—the irises—but the whites of his eyes are as angry as the twist of his lips.

Hopefully the dye and flour and red eyes don't make it too hard for my security team to identify him from the picture I sent them.

faking cinderella

I huddle closer to the short hallway that leads to the bedroom, ready to sprint. I can lock myself inside, then crawl out the window when Cyril gets here, which will likely be within the next three minutes, but I don't think that'll be necessary.

I hope it's not necessary.

If I wasn't worried about blowing my cover before I've even gotten to meet the other two triplets, I would've already ordered my security agent here to handle Rhys, because who the fuck breaks into a secluded cabin in the middle of the night?

But what I'm here to do—to finally put my father in his rightful place after everything he's put Daphne and me through, but especially her—is too important to blow it on the first unexpected turn of events.

"I need to rinse my eyes. Can I move without you flinging the skillet at my head?" Rhys says.

His voice is deep and raspy in ways that remind me I haven't had sex in at least six months, but then I remind myself that Margie Johnson, my cover identity, hasn't had sex in two years, and that doesn't actually help.

Also, I'm clearly on the downhill slope of the adrenaline rush if I'm thinking of sex and not just survival.

I nod to him. "Yes. Move slowly and go to the kitchen sink."

I don't ask if he's been here before.

Lucky's reaction on the phone made it clear Rhys is a known entity to him, so it's possible Rhys knows the floor plan and can find the kitchen on his own.

Provided this really is Rhys.

I text his picture to Lucky too.

Is this the guy you know?

Rhys finishes rising slowly, and did I say the man was big?

That was an understatement.

He's six five if he's an inch, and he could fill a doorframe and a half with how wide his shoulders are. He stretches his fingers on one hand, then balls them into a meaty fist. Thick veins trail up from his hands, disappearing beneath his leather jacket, which hangs open to reveal a tight black T-shirt, also covered with flour but clearly outlining thick pecs and a solid stomach underneath.

A wisp of fear takes hold in my gut again.

Can you blame a woman who's used to having personal security for going overboard with the self-protective measures when that's what was looming in the shadows?

"Who are you?" he asks while he makes his way quickly to the kitchen, one wincing bloodshot eye trained on me.

I trail him from just the right distance that I can still get to an exit path if necessary.

"I'm Margie Johnson," I announce.

The lie is easier than it should be.

While I pride myself in overachieving the hell out of everything I do—apparently now including makeshift intruder alerts—this is the first time I've tried to overachieve being someone else, and it's weird.

Rhys bends over at the kitchen sink. It's an old porcelain single basin that fits perfectly with this mountain cabin vibe, which I'm purposely focusing on so I don't stare at his ass.

My phone buzzes in my hand—the hand not still holding the cast-iron skillet—and I look down at a note from my head of security, who's staying in a cabin a mile down the road.

The text includes an image of some kind of building access or security badge bearing a picture that's strikingly similar to the man in front of me, along with the quick info on Rhys.

Rhys O'Malley. 34. Formerly private security for Technique Group Inc. Unknown if terminated or quit. Ten years in the Marines. No criminal history. No known current employer. Immediate threat assessment is relatively low. Use code word if situation changes.

Translation—Cyril is not, in fact, a mile down the road, but is now right outside the window that I cracked open after I smacked Rhys in the stomach so that my head of security could hear me if I needed to say the code word.

Cyril doesn't congratulate me on my security system working right.

Probably because if he'd had his way, this guy never would've made it through the front door, because Cyril would've been outside waiting instead of me relying on a homemade booby trap.

"How do you know Lucky?" Rhys's voice bubbles a little through the water rushing over his face.

Guilt threads through my belly at the knowledge that I assaulted an innocent man—even if I didn't know he was innocent at the time, because honestly, who arrives at a remote mountain cabin after midnight?—and the guilt isn't assuaged by knowing that I'm about to drop lie number two.

It's good to practice on real people instead of myself in the mirror. And the one thing I promised Lucky—that I wouldn't tell a soul that we share DNA—is the most important piece of my job here.

It's how I intend to earn my brothers' trust before I confess my real name and ask them for a favor.

Plus, god knows I've seen families destroyed. Theirs seems functional and healthy.

The lies about the man who raised them being their biological father aside.

Which are actually admirable, if you ask me.

I'd do a lot of morally ambiguous things in the name of protecting my sister, and keeping a secret that she doesn't need to know and that could hurt her would be the easiest of those things.

And finding out that they're related to my father is definitely something that could hurt them.

"We met in nursing school and kept in touch after I dropped out," I tell Rhys.

He briefly angles his face to look at me like he doesn't believe me.

He shouldn't. I come from a long line of liars, even if I prefer to operate with the truth until I can't anymore.

Like right now.

I've known for years that my father has other children besides Daphne and me. I've known for years I'd only find out who they were if I managed to locate the legal paperwork detailing the payoffs and the nondisclosure agreements. My mother probably knows too, but she's always looked the other way because she likes the billionaire lifestyle. It's far more comfortable than the way she grew up.

But then I took a DNA test under a fake name on the off chance he'd missed any, and now here we are.

Not only did the Sullivan triplets of Snaggletooth Creek, Colorado, slip through the cracks of my father's otherwise meticulous cleanup processes with his mistresses, but there are three of them.

Triplets.

My father missed that he fathered triplets about the same time I was born.

"You dropped out of nursing school?" Rhys says while my phone buzzes again.

This time it's Lucky. Yeah, that's him, and I'm gonna need the story about what's up with his face.

I'll text him back later. For now, I look back at Rhys, debating if that internal whisper of *you need to apologize to your brothers' friend* is right or not. "Yes. I fainted dead away the first time I had to stick someone with a needle."

Lies, lies, lies, more lies. At least this is one that Lucky and I agreed on beforehand.

I'll help you find a better job and you can stay in my cabin while you get on your feet, but you can't tell anyone who you really are because my dad doesn't know we know that we're not genetically his, is what Lucky said three weeks ago when I told him I wasn't happy in Iowa, where Margie Johnson was raised by a single mom who passed away two years ago.

"And you didn't know before nursing school that that would happen?" Rhys says.

The man is highly suspicious of me.

Not surprising.

If Cyril's info is correct—and Cyril's info is nearly always correct—then Rhys is in the same line of business as Cyril, who would also be questioning my story. And I'm sure the military time didn't help the paranoia.

Good thing Lucky prepped me fairly well with what to say about dropping out of nursing school. And that I love research. "Did you know there's this thing where you can do all of the normal things like get your shots and give blood at blood drives and have it taken for medical tests, but you have a panic attack when you have to stick someone else with a needle?"

He twists his neck so that he can peer at me again, the water rushing over his forehead now.

Doubt that solves the dye problem though.

His face will have purple streaks and smears for days. The dye's been on too long for it to completely wash off on the first try.

I gesture to my hair, once again fighting an urge, this time to offer to help him. Now that the adrenaline has fully left my body, the guilt is seeping in harder. "You probably want to rinse your entire head. The dye's permanent, and the longer you leave it in, the darker it'll get."

"The—fuck."

It could be a question.

Or a statement.

I shrug one shoulder. "My mom always told me to make sure intruders could be identified later. And Lucky told me—well, he said no one else was using the cabin, which I interpreted to mean no one else would be showing up. Logically. And especially when we're talking about someone arriving at one in the morning."

Say sorry, Margot. Say the words. Say you're sorry.

I grimace while I swallow the urge.

I am sorry, and also, I was justified in setting up a warning system, and I've also been working hard for the past few years to be the type of person who apologizes, despite the way I was raised.

But I don't know if this is an I'm sorry situation.

Exactly.

What if he'd been a real intruder?

His face is granite as he fishes his phone out of his pocket.

He lifts it, but I'm certain he's not taking a photo of me, which suddenly has me freaking out a little as I realize I forgot to put on my glasses, which are part of my Margie Johnson disguise.

His growl confirms for me, though, that he's using his phone's camera as a mirror to check himself out.

He's a mess.

He really is.

His face will be streaked purple. His hair will be streaked purple.

I did a good job of defending my castle all on my own.

My father stripped Daphne of her security detail when he disinherited her over four years ago.

I wondered while I was setting this up tonight if she ever did the same. She refused my offer to keep paying for security for her—actually, she refused every offer of any kind of assistance I made—out of sheer spite. Not against me, but to prove she could make it on her own despite having absolutely zero preparation on how to live life without a trust fund.

I've always loved her, but my level of admiration has hit peak levels these past four years, and she's the reason I decided to learn to be someone who apologizes when I'm wrong.

"Fuck on a waffle." Rhys's voice is still rough, but it has a strangled quality to it now too.

I make myself set the cast-iron skillet on the Formica countertop as I realize I'm still gripping it hard enough that my hand is aching, and I push this conversation with Rhys just a little further. "So now that you know why I'm here, why are you here?"

He lowers his phone and glares at me, then buries his whole head under the faucet for a long time, scrubbing his face and his beard and his hair.

Is it brown, or is it a deep copper red? I can't tell.

I need to see him in the sunlight.

No, correction—I need to not see him at all.

Margot Merriweather-Brown, future CEO of the Aurora Gardens international hotel conglomerate, would have already seen him out the door.

Actually, Margot Merriweather-Brown would've bought a house to serve her needs while here and wouldn't have to set up Christmas-movie style booby traps because she has a security team that would've stopped him long before he got to the front door, and I might not have even heard it happen.

But Margie Johnson, the current role I'm playing as a daughter of a deceased single mother from Des Moines who's looking to connect with half brothers that she never knew she had while working a temporary job in housekeeping at a new local retreat center, wouldn't have the same poise and command of any given situation.

The crashing adrenaline is probably helping me play the role as I ask questions that Margie Johnson would definitely ask. I don't feel badass and in control right now.

I feel tired.

Ready to go back to bed, where I hope I can fall asleep, but where I'm worried my brain might keep me up.

Rhys finishes scrubbing his head and grabs a towel hanging off the dishwasher handle beside the sink.

He doesn't ask me if he's gotten it all—he hasn't—but instead rubs the towel all over his face and head.

Then he straightens and looks at me.

Really looks at me.

His eyes are still bloodshot, and he's squinting like he's still dealing with the effects of the dye in his eyes, but the man's staring me down as if he thinks he's in charge here.

Like he got here first, which he clearly did not.

Daphne and I used to play that game when we'd go to the Hamptons. Our parents let us pick which bedrooms we wanted, and inevitably, Daphne would always beat me to the room with the balcony overlooking the water.

I'd play the older sister card and demand that she hand it over to me because I was an asshole.

She'd relent, and I'd wake up with seaweed in my bed because she's Daphne and I deserved it.

All of the best stories about my life involve Daphne.

I wish she were here to see this. She'd be laughing her ass off.

Instead, she's in upstate New York, living her best life as a normal person, newly madly in love with my ex-fiancé.

It's fine.

Really, it is.

At some point in the past four years since he broke up with me—it happened around the same time Daph was disinherited—he both grew a spine and decided he hated CEO life, which really wouldn't have worked for us long-term.

Plus, after Daph was disinherited, I started taking a long, hard look at who I am. How many of my values were formed at the hands of parents whose values suck if they're willing to disinherit someone they viewed as embarrassing instead of helping her find more constructive ways to channel her energy toward saving the world.

How many of my life choices were my own, and how many I'd been manipulated into by my parents.

Who I want to be and what I want to do with my life.

How completely inadequate I am at loving people.

"Why are you here?" Rhys asks me.

"I told you. Lucky said I could stay here. And I'm not the one breaking in in the middle of the night."

Margie Johnson has pluck, even if she's not attempting to command the room.

"Had the door code," he reminds me.

"But no one knew you were coming."

"Decker told me to come."

"He told you to come?"

"Said I could stay here until I find my own place."

Good. This should be temporary. A few days at most. A few very awkward days if the way we've met is any indication. "You're moving here from somewhere?"

"Yes."

"Where?"

"None of your business. I'm leaving this room, getting my bag, and going to the bedroom. Don't hit me again, or I'll defend myself this time."

"I'm in the bedroom."

"Of fucking course you are," he mutters to the ceiling.

I channel my inner Margie Johnson, the housekeeper. "But if they'd told me you were coming, I would've left a blanket on the couch for you. Lucky told me the pull-out sofa is surprisingly comfortable."

He doesn't ask me again why I'm here.

Doesn't ask me to repeat my story about how I know Lucky so he can find holes in it, which is what I'd expect of any halfway adequate executive protection specialist.

Instead, he does exactly as he said he'd do, and he moves intentionally toward me.

A behemoth of a man, moving like a glacier, with streaks of hair dye running down his forehead and disappearing into the beard on his cheeks, but still so large and poised that he's probably intimidating the paint on the walls in here.

And I like it.

Deep, deep down, somewhere way inside me, a bone-deep respect and appreciation for this beast blossoms.

He's unknown. He's danger. He's a challenge.

Large enough that he could've hurt me when I attacked him, but he didn't fight back.

He's your brothers' friend, and this is already too messy, I remind myself.

He gets closer, and ohhhh shit.

His eyes are gonna be dyed too.

I step gracefully out of the way, remember Margie would be less composed, make myself scramble, and I slip on the flour on the wood floor behind me.

"I'm not cleaning that up," Rhys informs me as I right myself without any assistance from him.

Cyril would've helped me even if he was mad at me, even if I told him not to, that I'd clean up my own mess. But Cyril can't be spotted. Especially by a guy who's apparently done security too. "I'm a housekeeper. I've got it."

He slides another look at me as he grabs his green duffel bag from where he dropped it beside the door.

I don't like it.

The look he's giving me, I mean.

I don't care what luggage he chooses to use.

I care that the man's obviously suspicious of me.

"I'm booby-trapping the living room," he informs me.

"I—I won't be in the living room while you're sleeping unless it's to get to the kitchen."

More side eye.

I'm torn between wanting to offer to help him dye his hair back to its normal color and puffing my chest up and glaring at him like I'd glare at any of the usual men who walk into my office thinking they can order me around.

Ultimately, I decide on a sigh. "I thought I'd be here by myself, and a woman can't be too careful. Especially in new places. If I'd known you were coming, I really wouldn't have...done all of this."

He grunts, then disappears down the short hallway to the bathroom.

Which has one door into the hallway, and one door into the bedroom. Just like you'd expect of a cabin built for one. Or for one happy couple. Which, clearly, Rhys O'Malley and I are not.

And that's when I let myself look at the carnage.

The axe that he dropped by the dining room table, at this end of the living room near the front door and kitchen.

The boot prints in the flour and then across the room and down the hallway.

The rug that I'll need to replace since it's splattered with hair dye.

Daphne gave me the rundown on using thrift stores. She's become an expert since our father left her broke. I'll find a new rug at a thrift store.

Play the part of the penny-pinching housekeeper until I'm ready to confess my real identity and replace the rug with something better.

A door clicks shut down the hallway.

I sag against the wall between the living room and the kitchen and quickly text Cyril back.

All is well. I think.

His response is immediate.

I'll be outside.

I make a mental note to give Cyril a raise for all of the extra tasks I'm assigning him while it's just him as my security detail here.

And then I get to work practicing my new day job since I won't be getting back to sleep easily anytime soon. I won't get it all done before Rhys is out of the bathroom, but I can tackle the worst of it.

While I don't think about how nice it is that there'll be a mountain of a man sleeping on the couch.

Being the security I'm used to.

He might be a stranger, but he's a stranger who's passed all of the tests.

So long as you consider not murdering me immediately for what my intruder prevention and tagging system did to him passing all of the tests.

Guess we'll see if I survive until morning.

3

It's nice to meet you

Margot

Nerves are usually something that motivate me.

I get nervous, I use that as fuel to step up and own whatever situation I need to own.

Today, as I'm standing over the kitchen sink, rinsing out the rags that I used to clean up the carnage of my homemade security though, they're making my stomach hurt.

Rhys, Decker's friend, grunts in my direction from the doorway. "I'll be back. Don't booby-trap this place again."

"I—" I start, then hear the door click shut.

"Won't," I finish on a sigh.

I slipped into the kitchen to rinse the rags when I heard him go into the bathroom fifteen or twenty minutes ago, after I'd already showered for the day, since I didn't get to finish cleaning up last night.

And in five minutes, I'm meeting a brother I never knew I had.

In person.

Face-to-face.

That's when my plans get real.

And when I discover if I'm enough all on my own for three guys who share DNA with me to want to call me family, and if so, if they're the kind of family who'll help you get justice for another sister they also didn't know they had.

Only one of those is truly terrifying, and it's not the part about justice.

I'm wringing out the last of the rags that I need to replace—these are spotted with purple hair dye—when there's a knock at the door, and then it swings open. "Hello? Margie?" a guy calls.

I suck in a fast breath through my nose, then wipe my hands on a towel and turn toward the doorway into the living/dining room. "In the kitchen."

A tall man with well-trimmed brown hair, warm blue eyes, and a smile peers in at me. He's in slacks and a polo, with a short beard. "Hi. I'm Lucky."

My heart tumbles all over itself and my eyes get hot and my stomach twists and a little voice in the back of my head whispers please please please please please like me.

I've been communicating with Lucky over email for about three months now. He was working late yesterday, so he sent me the code to get into the cabin with instructions to text him if I had any issues.

So this is the first time we've met in person.

My half brother.

Someone I'm related to.

Someone I share genes with.

Someone who'll help me answer the question of is everything wrong with me nature or nurture?

I take a big gulp and smile, because oh my god, I have a brother.

"Margie," I say, walking toward him and extending a hand. "It's nice to meet you."

He looks at my hand, then quirks a brow at me. "Not a hugger?"

"I—" Crap.

My eyes are already watering and my nose is already twitching with the urge to cry.

Hugs have been in short supply in my life, but I love when Daphne hugs me, so I nod. "I am."

He grins, and then I'm being swallowed in a giant bear hug that has my eyes even wetter.

"This is so cool," he says as he lets me go. "I've never had a sister. My cousin Sabrina's close, but it's not the same."

I manage to get the emotions under control, and I'm almost steady as I reply, "I've never had a brother either. Or anything close."

"Well, now you have three." He winces. "Kind of."

"Decker's suspicious," I say. Can't help it. Tackling elephants is what I do.

He winces harder. "It's not you. It's him. He's not a people person. He's a people-he-knows person, but not a people person in general."

"It's okay. I know it takes more than blood to make family."

"Yeah. Good thing too, because my dad—" He pauses and gives me one of those awkward looks that I've gotten very familiar with since I started making an effort to get to know as many people as I can in my department at work, not just my direct reports, but as many people as I can. "My dad's fucking awesome, and there's no other way to put it. He's family, no matter what's in our veins. We don't want to hurt him."

"I'm good at keeping secrets," I tell him. "If your parents find out we share a little DNA, it won't be through me. Promise."

I'll lie to him about other things, but not this.

Honestly?

I think his mother was smart to keep the truth from them, even if the lingering question is if she's kept the truth from their dad too.

And much as I want the triplets' help, I won't lay who I really am, and also the favor I'd like to ask, at their feet unless it's clear they're open to it.

Not having their help will make finishing the job of destroying my father harder, but not impossible.

Nothing's impossible.

But I've been looking for a smoking gun for four years, and they're it.

If they ultimately don't want to help—nope.

Can't even think about facing another four years of pretending to be happy every time I see my parents, that I love working beneath my father, that I'm not ready to take his position by force and do to him what he did to Daphne.

Or as close as I can come to it.

Lucky blows out a breath. "I appreciate it. We all do. It's just—"

"Family's complicated, and I don't want to make it worse."

"Yeah. That. That's how we feel too. Speaking of complicated… Rhys here?"

"No, he left a few minutes ago."

"Everything okay there? I'm really sorry—"

"Oh, don't be sorry. Honestly. I appreciate you letting me stay here. And if sharing a cabin for a few days is what it takes, that's fine. Rhys was—ah, he was understandably grumpy. But I guess I don't have to set up any more home security systems while he's here, huh?"

Lucky grins again. "Unless you want to have some fun. Decker and Jack and me might have set up a few booby traps in our time."

My eyes burn again.

Daphne's always channeled her energy into things like saving the polar bears or stopping climate change, but if we'd grown up in a less high-pressure environment, she absolutely would've channeled her energy into something fun like this.

Lucky lifts his brows at me. "You okay?"

"Yes! Yes." I rub at my eyes. "Dust. Bad thing to be reactive to for a housekeeper, but it's fine."

"It's okay. Finding out you have family you never knew—especially when you're all out of your own—that seems like wet-eye territory."

I suck in a breath that's all too real. "It—it is."

"You hungry? My cousin's coffee shop is legendary around here. And she's not supposed to be working today. Which is good. Sabrina sees all, hears all, and knows all, if you know what I mean."

My breathing evens out, and my gratitude for Lucky being so kind grows infinitely. Would he have been as kind if he'd been raised how I was? "Town gossip?" I ask.

"Kind of. She doesn't share what she knows unless it's harmless or unless she has to. And she's awesome, but like…we want some time before we have her in the know about you. But if you like lemon scones and coffee, there's nowhere better in the world."

I like coffee, but today? On this stomach? It's settling the longer we talk, but everyone's always on their best behavior for a first meeting.

And the part of me that's had my family ripped apart the past few years can't help the desperate craving for Lucky and his brothers to like me.

To want to be my family too.

I do know DNA doesn't make family. But god, I swear I see Daphne's smile in his, and how can I not want to be family with that? "Any tea?" I ask.

He grins. "Oh, hell yeah. Tea too."

"Sounds wonderful."

He slings an arm around my shoulders. "Then let's go get some breakfast, and then I'll show you Snaggletooth Creek. Ever been to the mountains?"

I grab my phone on our way out the door, breathing in the cool morning air.

So far, this is easy.

Comfortable.

All credit to Lucky—he's easy to warm up to. Friendly and kind.

"I have. I came once with my mom," I tell him, which isn't a lie.

Exactly.

I've been to many mountains, many times with my mother, even if my mother isn't who Lucky thinks she is. So technically, I've been once.

And a few other times too.

"Girls' trip?" he asks.

"Gotta do special things every now and again, don't you?"

"Nah. Gotta do special things at every opportunity."

Honestly, how could I not want to be related to a guy who looks at life that way?

He opens the passenger door of his blue sedan, and I climb in.

While he circles the car, I quickly text Cyril that I'm headed to town with Lucky, then tuck my phone away before Lucky opens his own door.

"So is Lucky your real name or a nickname?" I ask him as he starts the car.

"Real name." He grins. "I was supposed to be a Michael, but I was youngest and smallest and clearly headed for the most time in the NICU when we were born, so when one of the nurses called me a lucky little fella, my parents shifted and decided I needed to be a Lucky."

"It seems like it fits you."

"So much better than Michael." He shudders. "I must've known what they were planning, so I fought hardest to not be born until they'd reconsider."

That makes me laugh.

He grins, steering his way down the driveway with ease. "Tell me about this home security system you set up. We've talked about putting cameras up since it's vacant a lot, but homemade security systems are really more our style. We clearly share genes."

And there go my eyes getting hot and stinging again. "I'm not usually quite that creative. The mountain air must've inspired me."

"Mountain air's the best." He gestures ahead of us as we round a curve in the road and a range rises before us.

The peaks are likely at least five to ten miles away, maybe farther, but they're majestic, already snow-capped despite fall not officially starting for a couple weeks still, with the sun shining down on them while a brilliant blue sky stands behind them.

"Beautiful," I breathe.

"Nothing on earth like it."

"It must be amazing to have this view every day of your life." It's funny—I've seen mountains all over the globe.

But every set of mountains is unique, and they're all gorgeous in their own way, and they still take my breath away.

Daphne loves camping.

I love hiking, especially in places with towering natural scenery.

It makes me feel connected to the world in a sobering, grain-of-sand kind of way.

And then I go back to Manhattan, and I love that too. I love working on something bigger than myself, even if I feel disjointed at not loving the roots of Aurora Gardens anymore.

Lucky quirks another grin at me, this one holding a slight wince again. "If you decide to stay, we'll have to address the elephant."

I was hired as extra help for a month—apparently there's a big conference being hosted at the retreat center and it's nearly full in the weeks leading up to that, and they're still figuring out staffing requirements, which, clearly, I could be helpful in assessing, if I were admitting to who I really am.

But it means that we know this is a trial. A short-term run to see if Margie Johnson would like it here enough to fight to keep the job and settle down.

Be close to the brothers she's just met now that her mother's dead.

And honestly?

My mother might as well be dead.

While I'd suspected Daphne was with Oliver, my ex, on a cross-country road trip last month when my executive assistant brought me a picture linked to an article about a mystery couple who'd been giving money away all over the Midwest, the rest of the world found out for sure when they were arrested together in a town a few hours north of where I am now.

My father apparently saw the same photo I had.

He'd been making noise about me getting back together with Oliver, and I'd been playing along since that's what you do when you don't want your enemy to know how close you are to destroying them.

So as far as my parents knew, I was interested in Oliver again.

And when Daph and Oliver were arrested, my mother called—not to ask how I was doing, but to talk about how dreadful it was that Daphne was still smearing the family name.

Being dramatic in a fashion only Daphne could manage.

Causing all of my mother's friends to be horrified once again that my parents could've raised someone like Daphne.

My parents don't call to ask how I'm doing.

They don't check in.

If it's not adding to the bottom line of the family's reputation or holdings, then they don't care.

Fuck that.

Daph hasn't talked to our parents since they disinherited her, and I'm close—so close—to being there too.

"We'll worry about elephants when we have to," I tell Lucky. "Until then—can you pull over? I want a picture. But only if it's safe."

He brakes instantly, and a moment later, we're on the side of a mountain road, with me leaning out the window, taking a picture of the morning mountain view.

I'll send it to Daphne later.

And hopefully, Daph will get a chance to come out here and meet Lucky and his brothers herself sometime soon.

If all goes well.

"If Rhys starts to be a problem," Lucky starts again as I settle back in the car and strap in, "just let me know. Decker's a disaster with calendar management. But we can find another situation."

"I'm sure he and I will figure things out."

"He letting you have the bedroom?"

"Do you really think a guy who's walked into a human mousetrap made of hair dye, flour, a squawking phone, and a woman armed with a cast-iron skillet is going to make a fuss about having the bedroom?"

Lucky hoots. "No."

"I'd be happy to share. I mean, take turns." No, you meant share, my libido whispers.

The man is attractive in a big, broody, scowling, grumpy, exact-opposite-of-everything-I've-ever-looked-for-in-a-man kind of way.

"Nah. Couch is comfortable enough. I should know. Decker always claims he needs his inspiration sleep when we're both there, and Jack says he's allergic to the pull-out mattress when he and I are both there, so I know firsthand about the couch."

"What do you do when all three of you are there?" I ask.

"Me? I go home after dinner and crack up at the arguments they're probably having."

My heart swells in my chest.

I don't think it's instant love of my brother, given that I don't think I know how to love someone.

I think it's a desperate desire to have the kind of relationship with him—and his brothers—that they have with each other.

To belong.

To know that even when we disagree, we'll still have each other's backs.

If I hadn't already known from my text and email conversations with Lucky the past few months that the triplets have that, this morning on its own would solidify it.

Daphne and I are close, but we've lived such different lives, in such different places since I left for college, which was almost half her lifetime ago.

The triplets—our half brothers—are still tight.

Lucky told me they each went different places after high school—Decker to the Marines, Jack to Colorado School of Mines, Lucky to nursing school in Denver, not far from Jack, but still far enough away that they didn't see each other often.

But they all made their way back to Snaggletooth Creek within five years of high school graduation.

They have what I'd love to have with Daphne.

What I'm still working on having with Daphne as much as we can when I live in the city and she rarely travels back there.

It's not where her heart is, and everyone she knew growing up basically abandoned her too when she was cut off.

I don't blame her for staying in Athena's Rest, where she was kicked out of her last college and then disinherited, where she'd made tight friends with a woman who took her in and helped her figure out her new life path, and where Oliver's settling now to be where she's happy. So they can be happy there together.

Lucky turns onto a road that opens us up to a main street with more mountains standing proudly in the distance, and I draw in a steadying breath.

"I can see why you moved back here after nursing school," I tell him.

He grins again. "Nowhere else I'd rather be."

He points out various things as we drive down the street—city hall behind us with a statue of a miner that he tells me has quite the history—"Both" being his answer to the miner or the statue?—and a baked pretzel shop and the hair salon where he says Sabrina's mom works, a pub and a chiropractor.

"Oh, a bookshop too?" I ask as we pass another shop.

"Yep," is all he says to that.

Interesting.

Considering Decker's job is writing books, I would've expected him to say a little more about a book store.

I'll wonder about that later.

"Best Indian restaurant ever right there," he says, pointing out a place called House of Curry and making it subtly clear that we're not discussing the book store. "And—no, I'll save telling you about that for later."

"Telling me about what?" I ask.

He ignores the question with a grin as he points out an art gallery, and finally, the corner building on the left where a large bee hangs over the door.

Bee & Nugget.

The coffee shop, and our destination.

"I'm not saying it's the best just because my grandparents ran it ever since my dad was little and it's almost always been in the family," he insists while he parks behind the building in a spot between a classic Cadillac convertible that weirdly looks like a bee and a truck that I'm almost positive belongs to Rhys. "It really is the best, and it keeps getting better."

Exactly what I'd like my entire life to be.

And what I'm nearly at.

I eye the truck once more.

"You see the bee-mobile?" he asks, hooking his thumb at the car on the other side.

"It's adorable."

"I helped restore it. We all did."

"You and Decker and Jack? It's yours?"

"Us and some friends. And nope, not ours. It's a communal car for my friends. Long story. Oh, hey, that's Decker's truck," he says, pointing across the lot. He grins at me. "Ready to meet one more of us?"

My heart thumps.

Ready to convince one more of us that you're worthy of love?

"Absolutely," I say. "Can't wait."

And I hope, on some level, that Decker feels the same.

Guess we're about to see.

4

Scones and suspicions

Rhys

The Bee & Nugget coffee shop, as I understand it, is an institution in Snaggletooth Creek. It's a corner building at the end of the main drag in downtown, with a large fiberglass bee hung over the door on the outside. Inside, there's a massive central wood fireplace, a smattering of tables and booths, one large picture window overlooking the mountains and the lake in the valley below, and another window made of bee hives between glass.

And people.

So fucking many people today.

I hate crowds.

They're where problems always started on the job.

While the bells on the door jingle behind me as I step inside and into the crowd, I scan over everyone's heads until I spot Decker waving at me from the bar.

Dude's in his normal hiking pants, long-sleeved performance tee, and puffy vest. His brown hair is shaggy and his face is its normal scruffy.

The only thing different is the horrified way his eyes go round when I get closer to him. "Dude. The fuck happened to your hair? And your face?"

I take the stool beside him, wishing the damn thing faced the door instead of putting my back to it. I hate having my back to the door. "My unexpected roommate booby-trapped the place because someone failed to tell her she wasn't the only one borrowing your cabin and she's… paranoid. Clearly."

He stares at me briefly, then looks past me.

I turn to look at whatever he's looking at too, but he grabs my arm. "Don't look," he hisses. "Do not look."

"Is she here?" I mutter.

I want a cup of coffee and one of those scones he's always talking about. And to figure out why Margie feels familiar.

There's something nagging the back of my brain about her, and I can't decide if it's irritation that she got the better of me or if it's something else.

Like we've met before.

"Yes. No. Not her. Other her," Decker says. "We need to—"

"Morning, Decker," a short, curly red-haired woman says on the other side of the bar. "Who's your friend?"

"Shit," Decker whispers.

And one more thing about this place clicks.

Bee & Nugget is his cousin's coffee shop and kombucha bar.

His cousin.

Sabrina.

Gossip.

Knows all. Learns all. Decides when and where to tell all.

And I'm sitting here with an uneven dye job in my hair and faded purple smears all over my face and in my fucking eyeballs.

The mirror and I had a conversation this morning.

I lost.

It's still laughing.

No idea what my roommate thinks of my face. I saw her just long enough in the kitchen to grunt something that she might have interpreted as good morning before I left the house.

I was halfway to town before I realized why the cabin felt weird.

It was because the entryway barely had any evidence left of the way she ambushed me.

I'm fucking slipping.

A year off of daily private security, doing random-ass shit for friends here and there while trying to replan my life after it imploded, and I failed to notice that she'd mopped up all of the flour and removed the rug.

"He's not my friend," Decker says to the redhead. "I don't know him. There's nothing interesting about him and no reason for you to know him."

I reach across the bar, holding out a hand despite Decker's nowhere-near-subtle warning. "Rhys O'Malley. And you're Sabrina?"

Her green eyes sparkle with the kind of mischief you'd expect of someone who's cousins with the Sullivan triplets, even if biologically, they don't share any genes.

"You've been here before," she says to me while she shakes my hand.

"Time or two." Decker used me as inspiration for a popular main character in one of his early novels, and insisted I come visit not long after he got out of the Marines. Said thank you for letting him use me by treating me to a mountain getaway.

Most guys leave the Marines with a bestie who saved their life.

I left the Marines with a friend who'd immortalized me in a litRPG novel and who still sends me a case of my favorite beer every year on the anniversary of its publication.

"Kombucha's new, isn't it?" I say to Sabrina.

"We've had it a few years now. My husband and his best friend make it. What happened to your face?"

"It learned the hard way not to piss off a hairdresser."

"My mom's a hairdresser, and she takes her dye responsibility very seriously. She would never."

"If only they all did."

"Coffee?"

"And a lemon scone, please."

"Fresh batch is in the oven. I'll get you one as soon as they're done."

"Why are you working on a Saturday?" Decker asks her.

She grins. "If I didn't know better, I'd think you were disappointed to see me."

"Always happy to see you," he grits out.

"You're a worse liar than Lucky. So, Rhys, what brings you back to the Tooth?"

"Work," I tell her, my brain catching up and remembering that the locals call Snaggletooth Creek, the town, the Tooth for short.

"That's so specific."

"Leave him alone, Sabrina," Decker says. "He's doing security for Spruce Creek."

"Permanently or just for the big event?"

I don't call her out on the lack of specificity on the big event because I'm glad she's not specific.

The fewer people who know the purpose and guest list for the upcoming private conference at the new center, the better.

"To be determined," is the only answer I'm willing to give her.

If I have my facts right, she's married to one of the guys who invested in turning a nearby formerly private ski retreat for some old billionaire into Spruce Creek Retreats, so she could technically be one of my bosses, but she's not on any of the paperwork I've filled out for the retreat center, so I don't offer any more information.

The doorbell jingles, making me instinctively glance around for a mirror or reflective surface to see who just came in.

Can't find one.

Don't like it. Dealing with crowds was—is—part of my job, and I dislike both having my back to the door and not having any way beyond obviously turning around to keep track of what's happening behind me.

Sabrina looks past us, her brows drawing together the slightest bit as the two customers next to me side-slide off their stools. "Who's that with Lucky?"

"You weren't supposed to be working today," Decker says again.

I don't need to turn around to know who's here with Lucky.

It'll be Margie.

Probably. My body's as tense as it would be if it's Margie, and it makes sense that they'd be hanging out together.

Selling her cover story about being a failed nursing major who needed a housekeeping job in the mountains.

Sabrina snorts at Decker. "You know I was going to hear that you showed up for breakfast with a guy whose face had a fight with hair dye and that Lucky showed up for breakfast with a woman, so what difference does it make if I'm here to see it myself or if I hear about it later?"

"All the difference," Decker tells her. "It makes all the difference."

Understandable.

The best, most reliable information comes from the nuance, and you don't get the nuance if you don't see it.

From what Decker's told me, Sabrina gets the nuance. And that will make her my new best friend.

I want to know everything. Helps me do my job better.

"Lucky, look who's here," Sabrina calls. She points to the empty seats beside me. "And look! I saved you a space."

Decker sighs and rubs a hand over his face.

Not like I have much to report to him yet other than that Margie's freakishly strong to be able to wield a twelve-inch cast-iron skillet—and yeah, I have a bruise, but I don't think any cracked ribs—and that she's definitely related to him if her idea of the best way to jerry-rig home defense is to use hair dye, flour, and a recording of various people threatening to kill you.

That's a Sullivan-triplet-level security system.

"Oh, hey, you two meet in the daylight yet?" Lucky Sullivan asks me as he drops into the seat beside me, Margie at his side.

The triplets are identical except for the way their personalities shine through and their style choices. Decker's a scruffy-faced hiker type, whereas Lucky's vibe is best described as former high school golden boy.

Brown hair short and styled, beard neatly trimmed, shirt a button-down, and his jeans look like they were pressed.

"We've met," I tell him while Margie gives me a lopsided grin and says, "Not really."

"Meet in the daylight?" Sabrina asks. "What does that mean?"

Lucky hooks a thumb at his half sister, who has curly dark brown hair, glasses that she wasn't wearing last night, and is dressed in jeans and a green flannel open over a simple T-shirt bearing a smiley face.

She's familiar.

And pretty. Her blue eyes have a glimmer of a sparkle, and her skin reminds me of a peach.

But the familiar part is what I need to concentrate on.

Why the fuck is she familiar?

"This is Margie," he says. "Old friend from nursing school. She needed a job, so I hooked her up doing housekeeping at the retreat center and staying at our cabin. And Decker offered Rhys here a place to stay in our cabin while getting him a job in security at the retreat center, so they're accidental housemates as well as coworkers for a bit, and since Decker's an asshole who didn't fucking tell us, Margie had a bad scare when Rhys showed up last night."

Sabrina nods. "I'd be terrified too if a streaky-faced mountain of a man showed up at my house in the middle of the night."

"You live with a mountain of a man," Decker reminds her. "Married him. Had his mountain-sized baby who loves to cuddle with your mountain-sized dog. Ring a bell?"

Sabrina ignores him and leans over the bar toward Margie, scooping away the dishes from the previous customers. "You poor thing. You want some coffee? Tea? Breakfast? Kombucha? I have lemon scones in the oven. They're legendary. And we harvest our own honey here for the biscuits. New secret family recipe. Oh, wait, let me back up. Hi. I'm

Sabrina. I'm Lucky's cousin. Decker's too, but he's on my shit list. If they haven't told you, there's a third who looks just like them, Jack. He knows I'm working today, so he's definitely not coming in, but don't let them pull the triplet swap thing on you."

Margie's smile grows the more Sabrina talks, like she has no idea Sabrina probably knows exactly who she is.

Margie shakes her hand. "It's lovely to meet you, Sabrina."

"Samesies. So. Breakfast?"

"Could I please see your tea selection?"

"Coming right up." Sabrina grabs a dark wooden tea case and sets it on the now-clean counter, then pours me a cup of coffee. "Back in a few."

Lucky and Decker share a look around me, and I take an opportunity to glance at Margie, who's studying the tea packets in the wooden organizer.

Swear to fuck, I know her from somewhere.

"Sabrina didn't take our orders," Lucky says.

"You know she knows," Decker mutters back, jerking his head at Margie.

Margie slides a look at them, half-friendly, half-forehead-furrowing. "About...how we met in nursing school?"

Lucky winces.

Decker winces.

"I meant it when I said Sabrina knows everything," Lucky tells Margie.

"She's chaotic good," Decker says. "She won't do anything to cause problems."

Lucky nods. "She uses her skills responsibly. She actually swore off gossip a few years back, but it's in her blood, so she's just a lot more..."

"Smart and strategic about it now," Decker finishes. "Not that she wasn't smart and strategic before. But she's more honed."

"Expert-level," Lucky says.

Margie's eyes pinch the barest amount as she selects a tea bag and closes the wooden case. "That's good."

If this woman doesn't have a secret, I'll pour hair dye into my own eyes again on purpose.

Where the fuck do I know her from?

Decker leans around me to nod at Margie. "Oh, hey. Hi, Margie. I'm Decker."

The stress lines fade, her eyes crinkle when she smiles at him, and the way she leans closer, hope and a smidge of desperation touching the way she's looking at him—fuck.

I know that feeling.

That's longing.

Longing for a family.

The number of times I felt that after my mom married Xavier Yates, when his teenage sons would be at the house, boys who could've been my brothers but wanted nothing to do with me, then the way they all treated me like I was a problem to be dealt with after my mom died—

Yeah.

Yeah, I know something about wanting to belong.

Something about wanting to have a family.

"I thought that was you," Margie says. "You look like your official author photo."

"That's actually me." Lucky puffs his chest. "His assistant booked the photographer for him since he was overdue for new headshots, but he didn't want to do it, so I grew my hair and beard out and posed for the photo shoot. I make him look good."

"We're identical, dumbass," Decker says.

"Only in the outside stuff. On the inside, my vibe sparkles, and that's what makes your author photos so magic. The camera loves my sparkly vibe. Just like all of the people at that litRPG con loved—never mind." He looks at me. "Speaking of sparkly vibes, you're rocking those lavender streaks on your face."

I blink at him.

It's a slow, intentional, shut the fuck up blink.

Margie purses her lips together like she's hiding a smile.

I shift my glare to her.

"What'd you say you used? To make the streaks?" Lucky says to Margie.

"Purple hair dye," she tells him. "I got the idea off the internet. A girl can't be too careful, you know? The internet said if you mark the intruders in some way, the police can find them easier later."

"Wouldn't have worked against a bear," I tell her.

She lifts one brow at me like I've proven a point.

Shit.

Right.

The man and the bear thing.

She probably would've rather a bear broke in last night.

What the fuck is wrong with me? I'm off my game.

"I'm a little sorry about your face this morning." She says it to me like it's a confession, and she accompanies it with another smile that would be charming if I wasn't certain she's hiding something.

"Just a little? And only about my face?"

"I had a friend once who knew someone who knew someone who said their sister came home to find a guy jacking off in a box of her favorite cereal. You really can't be too careful these days."

All three of us stare at her.

"That's so for real," Sabrina says as she delivers a cup of hot water to Margie, then sweeps the tea box away. "Totally something Theo would've done to Laney back in the days when they hated each other. Maybe. Though that might've been too far even for Theo. Maybe. Then again, he did some pretty messed-up stuff…"

Now we all turn to stare at Sabrina, who shrugs, flips two mugs up onto the counter in front of Lucky and Decker, grabs a coffee pot from behind her, and pours for both of them, then disappears again.

Lucky breaks the silence. "Decker should be more sorry about Rhys's face," he says to Margie before glancing at me. "If he could read a calendar and communicate, you wouldn't be wearing hair dye streaks on your face."

Decker rolls his eyes. "I'm working on a book that happens in May. You know I lose track of shit when I'm in the groove. Especially when I'm writing a book in the wrong season. In my head, the aspens are just getting buds, and then I walk out the door, and they're turning golden. It's fucking with me."

Lucky squints at him like he knows Decker's fabricating excuses. "I'm pinging Nell."

Decker groans. "Don't ping Nell."

"Who's Nell?" Margie asks.

"His virtual assistant," Lucky replies. "She keeps his life running. She wouldn't have let this happen."

"Do not ping Nell," Decker repeats.

Lucky shakes his head. "Dude. Until you can read a calendar, you can't lend out the cabin without checking in with Nell."

"This is a good accident," Decker says. "Margie apparently needs a security system. Rhys is a security system. Problem solved. Everyone's happy."

Margie eyes me.

I eye her right back.

She's wearing that expression again. The one that says *someone please love me.*

I don't like what it's doing to my chest. Not when I'm supposed to be suspicious of her.

"Are you sure he'd be happy?" she stage-whispers to Lucky.

"He always looks like that," Decker says. "I mean, not the leftover dye streaks, but the scowly thing. It's why he's good at his job."

"Hey, you two could even carpool since you're both working at the retreat center," Lucky says. "Margie, didn't you say your car was making a weird noise?"

"It hasn't since I got here."

"Have you driven it since you got here?"

"Well, no, but I'm sure rebooting it solved the problem."

Why am I suddenly picturing her with blond hair? Dark blond. The kind that's dark enough that it could be brown but that people still call blond. Full. Straight.

Am I losing my shit, or am I onto something here?

"You don't reboot cars," Decker says.

Margie flicks her wrist. "Reboot. Restart. Same thing. I didn't get enough sleep last night."

"Dude, lighten up," Lucky says to Decker. "Cars are half computers anyway these days."

"Not the parts that make weird noises."

"What kind of car is it?" I interrupt.

I didn't look in the garage, but I'd bet that's where it was when I pulled up last night.

"It's an old Toyota minivan," Margie tells me.

"Wait, it's a minivan?" Lucky says. "Do you have kids?"

She dips her tea bag a few times. "My mom's friend sold it to me cheap when my last car died. Her kids had grown up, and she'd already been thinking of upgrading to a Lexus."

She's lying.

She's lying through her teeth.

It's a feeling. A sixth sense.

There's something too rehearsed in her answer.

"Remember when Jack wanted to get a minivan?" Lucky says to Decker.

Decker smiles for the first time all morning. "For his band equipment."

"That he didn't have."

"Didn't have the bandmates either."

"Only because you were terrible on the guitar."

"You were terrible on the guitar. I was pretty decent."

Margie props her cheek on her fist, watching them with a soft smile while they bicker about the band that wasn't.

The steam off of her tea fogs her glasses, and she wrinkles her nose, one eyeball rolling slightly toward the sky as she does it.

Like she's not used to having steam off of tea fog up her glasses, and it's an annoyance she doesn't want.

A memory flashes so hard and fast, my brain almost cramps.

Hoteliers Association dinner.

My last assignment with Technique Group.

I was tasked with staying close to Imogen Carter, the ancient matriarch of the family who operate Carter International Properties. First time we'd worked for the family in any capacity.

I'd been shocked Xavier gave me the assignment. Figured he would've put one of his sons on someone whose family would've made great long-term clients, but I started thinking he'd finally figured out I was better than they were. Didn't realize he was setting me up to fail so that he could blame me for losing business and fire me.

Before things went to shit, though, midway through dinner, some other late middle-aged dude approached Imogen Carter, and whatever he said to her got her so agitated that I had to step in.

But I wasn't the only one.

While I was leaning over to ask Ms. Carter if she wanted to step outside for air, another guest arrived at the table and intervened so smoothly with the dude that he didn't realize it was happening.

She made that same nose wrinkle, with one eye rolling upward, right before she got his attention.

I didn't know if she was an assistant or family member or executive, but I knew I appreciated her enough to look twice.

"Big plans for the day?" Sabrina asks the four of us, pulling my attention away.

"Margie's never been here before, so I'm gonna take her on a tour," Lucky says.

"I drove around the lake and saw the train station when I got here," Margie says. "It's so quaint and cute. How do you live here every day and not just stare at the mountains?"

"Oh, the people are much more interesting," Sabrina says. "They—"

A clatter explodes behind us.

I leap to my feet and spin around.

A young man's squatting near a table, gathering a tray full of shattered mugs. "Sorry, Sabrina," he says.

I don't hear Sabrina answer.

Because Margie's suddenly next to him, carefully helping pick up the broken porcelain pieces among the liquid all over the floor. "You okay?" she asks the kid.

He flashes an awkward smile. "Oh, I've got this, ma'am."

"Was that my coffee?" someone at a nearby table says. "Dammit, I've been waiting for that for ten minutes."

The kid cringes.

"Shit happens," Decker says.

"Never seen Cedar drop a tray before," Lucky adds. "Someone bump you?"

"All an accident," Cedar says while Margie keeps helping move broken mug pieces onto the tray and out of the walkway.

Sabrina appears with a mop. "We'll get you a replacement coffee right away," she says to the guy who's glaring from the table, then drops her voice and adds, "but it's not like you need it because you had a toddler who woke you up at four-thirty this morning like some of us did."

Margie rises and reaches for the mop. "I'll get this."

Sabrina squints at her. "You sure?"

"You're very busy today."

"No, I got it, Sabrina." Lucky slides in between the women and snags the mop before Margie can take it. "Margie's right. You're busy. We'll handle it."

"Make room, people," Decker says. "Slippery floor. Don't want more of you spilling coffee. That'll wreck your day."

Other than the one unsatisfied customer, everyone's pretty chill, though there are a lot of people in here.

Every booth and table is full, and more people are in line.

"Fucking tourist," Decker mutters to me while Lucky and Margie help Cedar finish the cleanup.

My shoulders tighten as I study the people around us.

A lot are dressed like Decker, mountain casual, like they're all headed off for hiking or backpacking after coffee.

Some are more casual.

There's a table of women all in sweatpants or leggings and hoodies or sweatshirts. A table of older dudes having an animated conversation. Some people in line are checking their phones, others are staring at the menus.

The doorbells jingle again, and I flinch.

Too many people.

If I were running security here, I'd tell whoever I was guarding that we were leaving. I gesture to Sabrina, who seems to be everywhere but is currently behind the counter again. "Can I get mine to go?"

Decker eyes me.

"Too crowded," I mutter.

It's not a lie.

But also, I need to get back to the cabin.

Solo.

Pull up my computer.

Find pictures of that last security gig I worked.

Identify the woman I'm thinking of so I can verify for myself that I'm hallucinating in thinking Margie looks anything like her beyond making a similar facial expression.

I know what the problem is there.

The problem is that it wasn't the only time I saw the woman that night, and I liked her the first time, even more the second.

Not liked her.

I was still engaged to Felice.

Planning to marry her the week after that night.

But I appreciated that woman at the event. Noticed her for the kindness.

Because the second time I saw her, when a server hit the ground and started having a seizure, the same woman who'd easily saved Imogen Carter from the annoying older man was the first person dropping to the ground next to the server, calling for help and clearing the server's dropped tray away to make room for someone like me—security with medical training—to get there and assist.

She was calm, collected, and compassionate in a place where everyone else was ego and arrogance, and I wanted to know who she was.

I wanted to know who she was and why she was there with that crowd.

And then, when my world imploded not twenty-four hours later, losing both my job and my fiancée in practically the same breath, I wondered if that woman would've shown me the same kindness if I'd wanted a shoulder to cry on.

I shake my head.

Definitely need to go for a hike too. Touch some nature. Relax.

Pull up my computer and confirm for myself that I'm hallucinating and need to get out more and worry less.

"Coffee to go for me too," Decker says to Sabrina. "And two more scones." He jerks his head at Lucky and Margie, who are finishing up with Cedar. "Put theirs on my tab too."

Margie squints again, this time at me, and fuck me sideways.

It's that little lift in her eye.

That's too distinct.

And I'm losing my fucking mind because how the hell would a housekeeper from Des Moines have been in the same place with the world's most important hospitality dinner in Manhattan?

And why is the idea that it's her making my hidden-in-stone heart flutter unevenly?

"So I guess I'll see you at home?" she says to me.

"I'll announce my presence."

Lucky grins. Decker grimaces.

"If I'd known you were coming—" she starts, then shakes her head and smiles at me. Full-on beams, actually. With white teeth flashing and eyes bright and cheerful, her lips smooth and plump and the perfect shade of pink. "Thank you. I appreciate the thoughtfulness. A girl can't be too careful."

"As you've said." I look at her once more, a good long look, then turn and leave without another word.

I don't tell Decker I'll meet him outside.

He knows. He's seen me bail on crowded restaurants before. This won't be fully weird.

What would be weird is if his half sister was in New York as a guest of some kind at my last security event with the company that my stepfather stole from me.

And she couldn't have been.

I just need a reboot, and then I'll get back to normal.

5

I didn't know I'd want family this much

Margot

Long hours and high stress are basically my life as the marketing VP for Aurora Gardens, and I generally thrive in it.

I'm built for it.

I've spent much of the past four years questioning everything about the belief system my parents raised me with and whether they would still treat me the same if I were more like Daphne.

What if I hadn't wanted to go into the family business? What if I'd pushed more boundaries? What if I'd forged a separate life for myself beyond being a Merriweather-Brown working at Aurora Gardens?

And I always circle back to the same answer, that I know to the depths of my soul that I wouldn't be happy if I didn't have a job that pushed me hard to excel at the highest levels.

That part is me.

But since Daphne was disinherited, I've realized that there's another part of me that's been starving.

And that's the part of me that wants to be loved unconditionally, when I fuck up and when I'm having a bad day, when I'm underperforming expectations and when I just feel off.

The part of me that knows that I need to learn to give that kind of love if I want to receive it too.

I've nearly told Lucky who I really am half a dozen times this weekend as he's been showing me all around Snaggletooth Creek and the surrounding area, telling me stories about his friends and brothers and parents while Decker's retreated to work on a book that's on deadline and Jack's apparently off camping.

I want Lucky to like me for me, not for the persona I'm playing.

But I can't tell him. Not yet.

Not when Decker still doesn't trust me—yes, I see the irony—and when I haven't even met Jack yet.

And all of it has me exhausted by Sunday night.

On top of my fake identity, I generally prefer to live alone with security nearby, not on top of me, so having a cabinmate, even a cabinmate who's supposedly safe and would be helpful in the event of a situation arising, is complicating the situation, regardless of how he feels about me.

Especially with the living room being his bedroom, and neither of us broaching the subject of one of us moving out if temporary isn't as short-term as I hope it is for Rhys.

I can't go stay somewhere else without making Lucky and his brothers wonder where I got the money for a hotel or other rental house—my broke-as-hell housekeeper story really sold him to the point that I couldn't turn down his offer to stay in the cabin and take a job out here, especially when Lucky insisted on paying for my gas money too.

Clearly, I'll pay them back and then some, whether or not they ultimately agree to go to the Aurora Gardens board of directors with me to prove once and for all that my father and his cheating are a liability for the company and that the board needs to boot him.

And then I'll amply pay my half brothers back for every bit of their trouble.

faking cinderella

But, on the other side of the spectrum, if I decide I can't trust them, or if there's some other reason I can't tell them, I'll disappear and send cash anonymously.

Either way though, right now I can't tell the triplets I don't want to share their cabin with one of their friends.

So I'm being agreeable Sunday night when I leave my room after sneaking a few hours of answering emails from my executive assistant and find Rhys in the kitchen, stirring something that smells so good I almost drool.

The dye streaks are still on his face, even if they've faded to the kind of lavender-blue that makes it look like he has thin skin showing off odd veins.

While he hasn't said a word about his stomach, I've seen him wince a few times, like when he got off the barstool at the coffee shop yesterday, so I think I probably left a mark there too.

"Looked at your van," he says. "Drive belt's shot. Jack's on his way with a new one and the tools to replace it."

"Oh. Thank you."

He grunts.

I open my mouth, then close it.

Margot Merriweather-Brown would just buy a new car. Or tell my staff to do it, except my staff is so good that I never know when there are car troubles.

Or possibly even when I get a new car. They're functional tools to me, not hobbies, so my staff handles making sure there's one available wherever I am, with a driver in the city or a full tank of gas when I arrive at one of my vacation homes—if it's a home in a location where I want to drive myself around.

So what, exactly, does a normal person say to I'm fixing your car besides thank you, which I've already said?

Am I supposed to offer him a blow job?

My research into how to live frugally and take a job as a housekeeper didn't extend to this exact situation.

"Smells good in here," is what I settle on.

"Beef and barley stew," he says. "Grab a bowl if you want some."

"I—yes. Thank you." I pause again. "Can I give you money for the ingredients?"

"No."

"Okay. Thank you."

He slides a glance at me like he too has noticed that I'm overusing the words thank you.

"Oh, I should get a bowl right now?" It's a legitimate question on my part because he's still stirring, and he hasn't served himself anything yet.

"Yes."

He doesn't move when I slip around him to grab a bowl from the upper cabinet to his right.

I like the cabinets. Someone painted them a dusty blue, and it adds a charming touch.

I like the bowls too.

At home, my bowls are fine china.

These are hefty. Thick, brightly colored porcelain that reminds me of the dishes at Daphne's apartment in the Hudson Valley.

And I'd enjoy them more if I were enjoying them without this heavy dose of awkward hanging out in the kitchen with us.

"This isn't poisoned, is it?" I ask him, going for a joke to cut through the tension.

He slides me another unreadable look, then makes a show of lifting the cooking spoon to his mouth, blowing on it, and taking a very large bite.

"Ah. So if it is, we'll both be dead."

"If I wanted to kill you, I'd return the cast-iron skillet favor and leave your body somewhere that the bears could get it."

"Comforting."

"Someone would probably notice you were missing though."

I almost do a double take because I almost think he's talking about Cyril, or my sister, or god forbid, my parents, but I make myself stay breezy and calm, forcing a friendly smile.

He can't be talking about Cyril.

No one here knows about Cyril or who I really am, and this is all fine.

He takes the powder-red bowl from me and fills it with soup, then hands it back. "Oyster crackers are on the table."

I hesitate before leaving the kitchen for the shared dining/living room. "Are you eating too?"

"Made it, didn't I?"

"I meant at the table."

"Yes."

"Will I be in your way?"

And there's another glance from him. An *is this chick for real?* kind of glance. "Invited you, didn't I?"

"If you were just being polite—"

"Don't really suffer from that."

I almost smile for real, but I squelch it.

I've never been into the gruff, cranky type, but I'm oddly appreciative of having Rhys and his absence of manners here with me.

Unlike me, he doesn't have to pretend to be someone he's not.

And I like that he's not afraid to be who he is.

If I let my manners drop around my father, I pay for it in the form of his passive-aggressive warfare.

But not for much longer.

Soon, I'll be free to be just as real as Rhys.

But not until after I've pretended I'm someone completely different from me for another little while.

I take my bowl to the table in the dining room half of the front room.

Rhys joins me as I'm taking my first bite. Rich, salty stew floods my mouth, lighting up my taste buds, and I barely stifle a whimper of appreciation.

I can cook—I used to love watching my parents' chef in the kitchen when I was young, still watch cooking shows interspersed with home improvement shows today, and I like my own space enough that it's been necessary to keep up the basics in the kitchen in the name of both nutrition and privacy—but I can't cook a simple stew like this.

Not enough time to truly hone it to perfection.

If Rhys notices my reaction, he doesn't respond.

He dumps a bunch of oyster crackers straight out of the bag and into his own bowl, then digs in like it's a race to finish.

And honestly?

I like that about him too.

For as much as I know I'm a badass in business, I also know I've worried so much in my life about how every action, every word, every thing about me will be scrutinized and studied for possibly being used against me that it's taken a lot of work the past few years to figure out who I want to be and how to just be me without second-guessing.

So despite all the reasons Rhys and I will likely never be friends—didn't exactly start on the right foot, and we've hardly seen each other all weekend—I appreciate him.

I appreciate him being unafraid to be exactly who he is.

It's inspiring.

And also, this stew is unreal.

How can a guy not be attractive when he can cook like this?

"So you and Decker have been friends for a long time?" I ask between my own bites.

He grunts.

Then he sighs and looks up from his bowl. "Yes. We've been friends for a long time."

"Are you this enthusiastic about all of your friends?"

"Yes."

"Good to know." I wince to myself. Is this awkward or is it just me? "Look, I really am sorry about…" I gesture vaguely to his face.

"It's fine."

"The mountains are a lot different from where I grew up. I'm… more cautious here…because it's so different."

He slides one of those unreadable looks at me while he shovels a spoonful of stew into his mouth. "Yeah. Mountains are a lot different from…other places."

Other places?

Why is he saying that like he knows what other places are?

"Very," I agree.

"Worlds apart. Depending on where other is."

The tiniest amount of sweat starts gathering at my hairline. Is he—is he trying to talk in code, or am I being paranoid tonight?

I swallow another bite of soup. "Have you spent much time out here with Decker?"

"Some."

Such a solid, definitive answer.

Which I don't observe out loud, even if I want to.

Gotta play the Margie part. Especially since I start my housekeeping job at the retreat center tomorrow.

Rhys drops his spoon on the table. "Look, I know who you are."

Every muscle in my body seizes. I don't know how I manage to not choke on my food, but I manage to not choke on my food.

Which is good.

Margie would, by default, know exactly what he meant.

Unfortunately, I'm not only Margie. "You do?"

The man stares at me like he can read the code of all of my past lives that have imprinted somewhere in my soul. Like he knows every identity I've had in every incarnation of my life back to the beginning of time.

And like he knows that Margie Johnson is a lie, and Margot Merriweather-Brown is not to be trusted.

And then he picks up his spoon again and looks down at his stew. "Decker told me about the DNA thing."

Thank.

Fucking.

Fuck.

I shovel a spoonful of stew into my mouth, then swallow without hardly tasting it, which is a shame considering how good it is.

"He did?" I ask after I swallow.

"You didn't tell any of your friends you have unexpected half brothers?"

I'm actively sweating now when I shouldn't be.

He doesn't know who I am.

He thinks my only secret is that I'm related to the triplets, which, clearly, I suspected he knew anyway.

"Of course I told my friends. But they're not here. Where it could get uncomfortable for their family if their parents find out."

That's the story. That they don't know if their parents know that they know that their dad is not their dad, and they don't want me to blow it.

It's a good story.

Even if I suspect that the triplets' cousin who runs the coffee shop knows who I am too.

In the related-to-the-triplets sense.

Once a secret's out, you can't put it back. They're playing with fire.

And that means that even if I never tell another soul, I'm still at risk of being blamed. So I have to stay squeaky-clean and stick to this story in public no matter what.

"You meet them?" Rhys asks me. "The parents?"

"No. I don't—I will if all three of the triplets want me to, but I get the impression they'd rather I just remain an old friend of Lucky's who washed out of nursing school. And I'm aware that not all of them are happy I'm here."

"You really go to nursing school?"

I shake my head, reverting to the story I told Lucky. "College wasn't for me. Any kind of school, really. After high school. Which was hard."

"Where'd you grow up?"

"Des Moines."

"Iowa?"

"Is there another one?"

"Yes."

"Oh."

"Had a buddy who went to high school there. How old did you say you were?"

Fuck. Here we go. "I'm twenty-nine." Thirty-one, actually, but I'm fine fudging the truth here. The triplets haven't asked, so right now, it doesn't matter.

"Huh," Rhys says. "So was he. Where'd you go to high school?"

"You know all of the high schools in Des Moines?"

"Know my buddy's."

"You must be very close. Where did he go?"

He stares at me.

I stare back.

I'm not often questioned by strangers, but I've had a lifetime's worth of being questioned by my father.

Rhys O'Malley is getting nothing out of me.

Except a gnawing anxiety in the pit of my stomach as I question if he's grilling Margie or if he knows more than he's letting on.

If Cyril had been dyed, dusted, and smacked with a frying pan upon entering a room, he would've absolutely not rested until he found every hole in their story.

Good thing I really love research.

Because I can pull off being Margie Johnson like a boss.

Even if I'm well and truly sweating now. Can he smell it? Can he smell my sweat?

"I hope it wasn't Piedmont," I say, naming a real high school in Des Moines. "They were assholes in football. Though Northview wasn't much better."

"You didn't go to either of those two then?"

I force a smile. "I didn't say that, now did I? Where did you grow up? Was football a big thing there? You probably get this a lot, but you look like you could've been a linebacker."

More staring.

More eating stew.

"I gather your high school experience was as fantastic as mine then." I take another spoonful of stew too.

"What wasn't great about yours?"

"The usual. Not part of the in crowd, didn't like half my teachers, and with being raised by a single mom, I needed to work to help pay the bills."

This is my favorite part of my fake life history.

The part where I was tight with my mom and we worked together to raise me, even if I was a misfit who just wanted someone to understand her.

My original plan to tell anyone who presses is that she got married once to a man with two daughters, and my stepsisters hated me for those few years, and one of them even stole the captain of the football team out from under me for a prom date when I thought a miracle was about to happen.

Yes, fine, I'm twisting Cinderella a little, but it was my favorite when I was little. I'll never be Cinderella, but playing housekeeper for a few weeks while pretending to be basically broke and alone is as close as I'll ever get.

But I don't like the way he's staring at me, and I'm starting to think the Cinderella thing might be overkill in my fake story.

It's like he doesn't believe even the little bits that I've told him. Or I've triggered something with my story that's making him even more suspicious of me.

Do I need to make up more details? Tell him a fabricated story about somewhere that I worked in high school?

More likely, I need to shut up and ask more questions of him than I give answers in return.

Or maybe tell him the fucking truth? my conscience whispers.

As if I wouldn't in a heartbeat if I thought I could trust him.

Sleep in the same cabin when he's passed the basic security checks from both Cyril and the triplets?

Fine.

Outright tell him who I am?

There's not a world where that makes sense, no matter how much I'm sweating under his scrutiny.

"So where did you grow up?" I ask him with as much of a smile as I can force.

He lifts his eyes and stares at me with the slightest smirk playing on his lips. "Connecticut."

My stomach bottoms out.

I'm not overly worried about being recognized here. My father loves the limelight, so while I'm known in some circles, I'm not famous famous the way some of my friends from childhood are because dear ol' dad takes all of the attention from Aurora Gardens and the family for himself and rarely shines it on anyone else.

But I'd still prefer that an unexpected roommate had grown up somewhere much, much farther from New York.

Much farther from where I'm occasionally on local news channels.

An engine hums outside, saving me from having to come up with a quick follow-up question that I don't want to know the answer to.

Like, were you living there before coming here? or how much do you pay attention to the New York scene?

"Jack's here." Rhys takes one last spoonful, finishing his bowl of soup, and rises, heading toward the front door.

My belly flutters.

The one thing I didn't expect when I decided to come out here to meet my half brothers was how much I'd like them.

I hoped I would, but you never know what you'll find on the other side of a DNA test. See also, my father is an asshole, and while my mother doesn't like him much, she likes the life he provides enough that she does what he tells her.

Neither of which I appreciate having in my DNA.

But here, Lucky's been so very kind.

Decker might be suspicious, but I respect that about him.

Listening to them talk at the coffee shop yesterday—it was like watching Daphne in action. I can see the family resemblance, even if they likely don't see it back in me.

No matter how hard I play at being Margie.

It doesn't escape my notice that Rhys checks above the door before he opens it.

Like he has concerns that I've constructed more booby traps just for fun.

I hear a voice outside, but the door shuts before I can filter out the words.

After two more rushed bites of stew—seriously, you wouldn't think beef and barley and some random vegetables could taste this good, but they do—I head outside too.

Jack doesn't spot me immediately. He and Rhys are pulling tools out of the back of Jack's truck, so I get a second to take stock of my third half brother while my heart speeds up and my eyes sting a little.

He's real.

There truly are three of them.

And this third brother of mine has his hair military-short, with his face clean-shaven. He's in jeans and a T-shirt, and there's a mid-size black-and-brown mutt poking his head out of the truck with a happy grin.

All three of the triplets have distinctive styles.

If Daph and I shared a face, people still would've been able to tell us apart based on our haircuts and clothing choices, so that makes sense.

I'm almost to the car, debating pausing to meet the dog first, before Jack notices me and does a double take.

"Hi." I extend a hand. "I'm Margie."

"Jack." He shakes, his grip warm and friendly without being weak, and I instantly like him too. His smile's not as golden retriever-ish as Lucky's, but also nowhere near as skeptical as Decker's. "So weird. You have my brother's eyes."

I blink at him as my eyes sting harder.

I have brothers.

Family.

Ties that go beyond just Daphne and me.

People that maybe, if all goes well, might accept me for all of who I am and want to spend more time with me someday.

I swallow back the instinctive answer of *and you have my sister's love of chaos* as Rhys grunts and shuts the tailgate on the truck.

"All three of you have the same eyes, dumbass," Rhys mutters. "Hers are blue. Same as yours."

"But they're the same shape as Decker's."

"If you say so." Rhys jerks his head toward the car. "And that's Bandit. He'll be your best friend if you let him."

"He's beautiful." I rub the short black-and-brown-spotted fur on Bandit's head between his two floppy ears, and he licks my hand, prompting an even bigger real smile from me. "And I'm happy to be his new best friend."

My life doesn't easily lend itself to having a pet, but I've been thinking more and more that I'm missing out. And god knows I could spoil a dog silly.

Once everything's settled with my father and I've taken his position at Aurora Gardens.

"Just give him back when you're done," Jack says.

"Of course. Thank you for your help with the van. I can scrub a toilet until you can see your reflection in it, but I don't know much about what goes on under the hood of a car."

"You know a little something about rigging a home security system though. Call me next time you do it. I can help."

"Do not call him," Rhys mutters.

"Of the three of us—me and my brothers, I mean—I'm the one with a degree in explosives engineering, which makes me the best for high-impact results for homemade security systems."

"Stop talking," Rhys says to him.

"Don't mind Mr. Grumpy Butt," Jack says to me while I keep loving on his dog enough that he lets Bandit down out of the truck. "Some chick painted his face with hair dye and he can't see it for the gift that it was."

A startled laugh rolls out of me. "That was me, and it was a gift?"

"You've given him the gift of seeing who likes him for his personality instead of his face."

Rhys lifts a middle finger, which makes me like him even more.

I want to be that unfiltered all the time.

I really, really do.

And Jack has a point. Now that the streaks are fading from Rhys's face, I can see that he's likely one of those guys who's regularly being hit on.

Not just for his size, but because he's classically handsome too.

The jawline. The nose. The cheekbones. The beard.

The intense, hooded blue eyes that seem to see everything.

Stop it, I order myself.

"Can we get to work?" he says.

Jack and I share a grin, and I get a little misty-eyed again.

Daph and I might have some family who are people I'd want to hang out with when all of this is over.

Unless they no longer want to see me when they find out who I really am.

Fuck, this is complicated.

But necessary.

Because no matter how much I might like my new half brothers, I still have an amazing life back in New York, with more goals and hopes and dreams for all of the places I still want to take Aurora Gardens.

After I force my father out.

See how much he likes having his family and his life taken away from him like he took it away from Daphne.

The cheating fucker.

"You want to watch and see how this is done?" Jack asks me as he trails Rhys to the open garage and I rub all over Bandit's belly.

"She's not going to need another belt anytime soon," Rhys says.

"Doesn't mean it's not interesting," Jack replies.

Rhys looks at me—the intensity, holy damn. "You ever need to replace a belt on a car before, Margie?"

My lungs freeze at the way he says Margie.

There's definitely lingering suspicion in that question.

"Ignore him," Jack says again. "He's had a shitty year and isn't done taking it out on everyone around him."

Rhys holds eye contact with me for another moment, then shakes his head and pops the hood on the beat-up old van. "Whatever. Let's do this."

My current motto.

Right behind please like me.

The dog grins up at me.

I smile back at him.

If only people were this easy too.

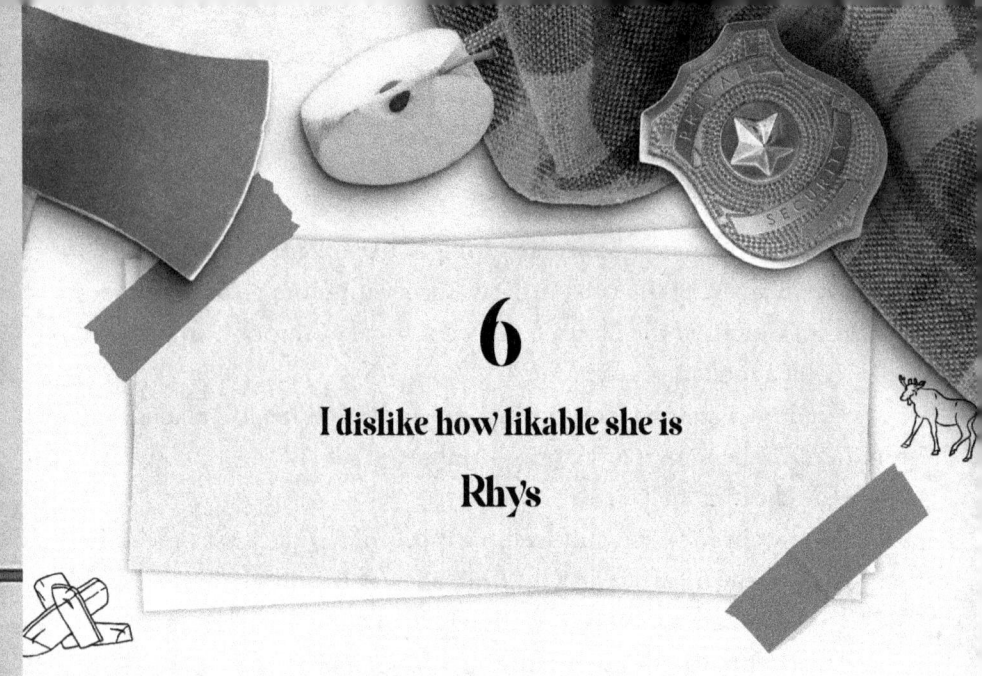

6

I dislike how likable she is

Rhys

Margot fucking Merriweather-Brown.

The woman who behaved like a low-key assistant in a fancy dress on my last assignment for Technique Group is Margot fucking Merriweather-Brown.

Billionaire heiress to the Aurora Gardens hotel chain conglomerate.

Rumored to eat sharks in her sleep.

And my buddy's secret half sister, who brought me a jar of honey and a box of lemon scones from Bee & Nugget on Monday.

To thank you for dinner and fixing my car, she said.

The woman who's kept the bathroom we're sharing meticulously clean and free of the face creams and hair products I'd expect to have scattered all over the limited counter space, and who stood at the kitchen window staring in awe at a small herd of elk who passed through the yard shortly before we both left the cabin for work yesterday.

She's good at pretending she's not Margot Merriweather-Brown.

I'll give her that.

It's been five days since she caught me off guard and left me marked with the results of her makeshift intruder deterrent system, and we've spent the past three days getting up to speed in our respective jobs at Spruce Creek, the retreat center in a valley beneath what used to be private ski runs for some billionaire who bought himself a mountain, and one day since I became absolutely certain she really is Margot Merriweather-Brown operating with a fake identity at work.

If it weren't for the hundreds of pictures I've stared at of her since I started digging up photos from that association dinner where she caught my eye, and then finally spotting the security agent that I knew she had to have somewhere around here, I'd still think it was a coincidence that Margie Johnson, the triplets' unexpected half sister, looked just like a billionaire heiress and businesswoman that I crossed paths with once at a gala where I wasn't supposed to be working.

Where I had no idea who she was, just that she seemed kind in a place where I didn't expect kindness, in a time when kindness would rapidly become in short supply in my life.

But now—now, after my research and spotting the agent and finding her real driver's license in a box under her bed, I have no doubt.

The only question is, why?

And that question of why is the full reason that I haven't yet told Decker what I know about his half sister.

I told him I'd find out if he can trust his newly discovered half sister.

The quick and easy answer is of fucking course he can't because she's lying about who she is.

Except I've been around and worked for enough celebrities and CEOs in my lifetime—first watching my mom do her thing when she and my grandpa founded Technique Group, then joining the firm myself after the military—to know that the quick and easy answer isn't always the right one.

I need to learn more about this woman.

Who she really is.

What she wants.

And to do that, I've taken to spying on her. Including now, mid-afternoon Wednesday, as she delivers fresh towels to a guest in one of the chalets.

"Are you sure this was washed with non-GMO chemical-free organic detergent?" the older man asks her as she stands on the chalet porch in her black uniform pants and shirt, offering him the stack of towels.

"Yes, sir," she says smoothly. "I checked the detergent myself this morning because I knew it mattered to you. Would you like to see a picture?"

"Yes."

She slips her phone out of her pocket and holds it out for him to see.

He leans in close—too close, in my professional opinion—and pretends to squint at the screen.

Fucker's really squinting at her chest. I'd bet my entire month's salary on it.

"Are you sure this is from the laundry room here?" he says.

"Yes, sir."

"You didn't take this picture somewhere else?"

"Sir, I've been at work since seven this morning, and I don't have industrial washing machines at my house. See the timestamp? Just after eight."

He straightens, still staring at her chest.

I feel a growl start low in my own chest.

It's far more protective than it should be, and I don't want to contemplate why.

She's lying.

She's lying about who she is, but because I've seen her show basic human decency to multiple people, she's getting under my skin in the worst way.

The way that makes me vulnerable and stupid.

"Fine. Come in and put them in the bathroom," the guest says.

"I'm not allowed to enter occupied rooms, sir."

"I just told you to come in and put them in the bathroom."

"Thank you for your generous invitation, sir, but rules are rules, and I can't afford to get fired."

He reaches out and grabs her elbow. "I'll tell them not to fire you."

Fuck.

Much as I want to watch her lay him out flat—and given what she did to me Friday night, I have zero doubt she could—I have a job to do as well.

So I stroll around the corner and clear my throat loudly. "Johnson, stop fraternizing with the guests. Sir, is this woman bothering you?"

I look pointedly at his hand, then back up to his face.

He's a couple decades older than me, more gray than black in his beard, carrying himself with the arrogance that comes with a lifetime of not having his place in the world ever questioned, and he's in a white retreat center robe and possibly nothing else.

It's high-end here. They have a spa and a wine tasting room featuring wines from all over the state, both at the top of the mountain, accessible by either trails or a gondola.

"She won't bring my towels into my room like I told her to," he says to me.

"Because she'll be fired." I climb the two steps and take the towels from her, getting a whiff of lavender and lemon and sunshine as I do. "Where do you want them?" I ask him.

"He requested the bathroom, sir," Margot—Margie—says to me.

I look at the guest. "Where's the bathroom?"

"I—she—fine. I'll do the damn work myself." He grabs the towels and slams the door in my face.

Margot's face twitches in annoyance.

It's not a large sign that she's not who she's claiming to be, but it's one of the very, very few times I've seen her irritated to any degree since she got here.

Why the actual fuck is she pretending to be a housekeeper?

What's she up to?

Are the triplets a convenient cover story for her to scope out retreat center competition to her hotel chains?

Is she really related to them?

"Thank you," she says to me.

"You didn't have your skillet. Someone had to do something."

She purses her lips together, but a small laugh still slips out. "That wouldn't end well for my job either."

I slide another look at her.

She doesn't need this job.

But I'll give her credit. These past three days since we both started, she's efficiently cleaned every room or chalet she's worked on spotlessly, without complaint, though I did hear that she's taking too long sometimes and had an incident with a spray bottle.

At home, I haven't seen her much in the cabin. She's frequently out later than I am after work, and when she's there, she keeps to herself aside from the occasional meal we share, where I've been pushing limits to see if she'll crack with her cover story.

But while she's been there, I've heard her moving around in the bedroom, and she's not making the noises I'd expect of a pampered heiress who doesn't generally do manual labor every day like she's doing now.

It's like she has the same boundless energy as the triplets.

Figures.

If I had to play housekeeper with all of the running around and bending and straightening and dusting and bed-making and towel-delivering, I'd be moaning and groaning and living in Epsom salt baths every night, and I say that as someone who keeps himself in good shape.

She moves back to the housekeeping cart on the sidewalk. "How has your first week been?"

I fall into step with her as she makes her way up the sidewalk. My job is to patrol the grounds and be available via radio if anyone needs anything. It's cushy compared to my last security gig but more active than the occasional tasks I've been doing for another former military buddy who went into private detective work when he got out. That's been mostly computer-based research or sitting in a car conducting surveillance.

Boring as shit.

"Quiet," I tell her. "It's been quiet."

"One of the triplets said you used to do private security? Like that's different from what you do here?"

Fuck.

She probably knows why I left Technique Group.

She probably knows more about me than I know about myself by now, actually. Or else she needs a new security team.

I'd hope they know everything they can about me since I'm living with her.

"It's different," I confirm while she pushes the cart. I can see her notes and know she's headed to nearly the end of this row, to a cabin on the left instead of on the right.

She slides another look at me.

I don't explain different.

"I heard the boss say there's a big event next week," she says.

"Yep."

"Wonder who's coming."

"People."

She glances at me, doing that half-squint thing that gave her away the other day. "Are you still mad about Friday night?"

"No."

"Did I do something else to offend you?"

"No."

"You're simply always this aloof?"

"Yes."

I could tell her at any time that I know who she is and demand to know what the fuck she wants with the Sullivan triplets, but I haven't had a good puzzle in too long.

I want to see if I can figure it out on my own before I confront her.

And then there are the other things that keep rolling through my mind.

Like that she's normally in a position of power.

She can make things happen.

Very specific things.

Like saying the right thing to the right people to ensure that no one in her circles ever hires anyone related to Technique Group ever again.

Essentially blacklist them among her colleagues and friends the way that Xavier had me blacklisted in the industry.

Not that I've decided I want to be that kind of asshole.

Yet.

The idea of destroying what my mom built with my grandpa—that hurts.

But it won't ever be mine again.

So yeah, revenge is in the back of my mind.

As is my memory of her knowing exactly what to do and not hesitating during a medical emergency for a member of the staff at that dinner that first night I noticed her, and then how quickly she leaped into action to help the kid at the coffee shop who'd dropped his tray last weekend.

I spent far more time in the Marines than I did doing private security for the company my mom built that my stepfather now runs, but the time I spent in private security was working for celebrities and CEOs who didn't jump in with assistance while wearing a cocktail dress.

"If I do something to offend you—something else, I mean, besides accidentally giving you a makeover—please just tell me," she says. "I can handle it, and I dislike when people don't communicate. Especially people who live together. Even accidentally and unwantedly."

I make a noncommittal noise.

"Such a guy," she mutters.

I shift my gaze her way as she stops the cart and locks the wheels.

It's honestly astonishing how good she is at this housekeeping thing. Those little details, like locking the cart wheels—I'd expect them to trip her up.

Though I still want more details on her incident with a spray bottle.

"The occupant in this room is a seventy-year-old woman who came here because she wanted to write her first novel, and I'll break the rules for her to put her towels into her bathroom because the thinner oxygen at this elevation has been giving her a little trouble," Margot-Margie tells me. "If you could stay right here as a witness that I'm not behaving inappropriately, I'd be grateful."

"Sure."

She smiles at me. "Thank you."

It's a pity she's actually a hotel chain heiress that I hear makes sport of making grown men cry in board meetings.

As Margie Johnson, she's pretty likable.

As a person.

Not as a woman.

I stifle a growl.

Fine.

She's honestly fucking gorgeous. She came home wearing jeans late last night, and I couldn't stop staring at her ass.

Then she offered me half of the cinnamon-sugar soft pretzel she picked up at a store downtown.

Said she saved it for me because it was so good that she wanted to share it with someone else who might enjoy it.

Like I'm not leftovers.

Or a problem.

But someone she actively thought about including.

She's putting a human face on her reputation, and it's made her undeniably likable.

Which I'm actively trying to ignore.

After what happened with the last woman in my life, I'm fucking over them and have entered into a committed relationship with my fist instead.

No matter how much the part of me that craves a place to belong is lapping up every bit of her thoughtfulness this week.

She knocks on the cabin door, calls, "Housekeeping. I have your towels, Mrs. Pinsley," and waits.

And waits.

And waits.

And waits some more.

"You can knock again," I tell her as I start to wonder if I need to be prepared for a medical emergency here too.

But at that moment, the door cracks open, and a weathered old face peeks out.

"Hello, dear," the grandmotherly woman says. She's roughly the same height as Margie-Margot, a little plump, a little wrinkly, and a lot smiley in her purple T-shirt and baggy sweatpants. "You brought company."

"Afternoon, Mrs. Pinsley. I have your towels. Would you like me to bring them inside?"

"Oh, yes, please. That's so sweet of you."

"My pleasure." Margie-Margot steps into the room, sliding a doorstop beneath the door to keep it from shutting her inside without a witness. I know the rules here are for the protection of the staff more than for the protection of the guests, and I'd assess Mrs. Pinsley as low threat, but rules are rules, and while Margie-Margot's breaking them, she's doing it smartly.

And kindly.

"How's the novel coming?" Margot-Margie asks Mrs. Pinsley while she disappears deeper into the chalet.

"Good. I wrote three hundred words yesterday."

"That's amazing! Good for you."

"But then I got to a scene where I needed a strong man to arrive, and I wasn't sure what he looked like, so I got stuck."

"That's the story of my dating life."

Mrs. Pinsley giggles. "Don't tell me you've never seen a handsome man."

"I'm ridiculously picky."

"What about him?" The older woman points at me as Margot-Margie comes back into view inside the cabin with an armload of used towels that make me wonder how many showers this old lady takes in a day. "It takes a confident man to wear my favorite color in his beard."

Margot-Margie smiles in my general direction. "He doesn't talk enough for me to know if he's handsome or not."

"Ooooh, that's so smart to not decide if he's handsome until you've heard him talk. My Peter was a talker. A talker. You couldn't get him to shut up, and he had opinions on everything from baseball to tampons. As if the man ever used a tampon in his life. But oh, he had opinions. And no idea how much he talked. He used to talk nonstop about how much I talked, and if that doesn't say it all, I don't know what does."

"They never really know how much they talk," Margot murmurs.

"But you found one who doesn't talk enough?"

"He's not mine. The retreat center loaned him to me for the day."

"Because of the handsy guy in chalet three?"

I straighten. Chalet three—that was the guy who was throwing a fit about Margie not putting his towels in his room. "Is one of the other guests being inappropriate toward you, ma'am?"

Both of the women look at me, then at each other.

"Well, if he's saving his words for sentences like that, you might want to look into the loan-to-own program," Mrs. Pinsley says.

Margie-Margot smiles at her. "You should use that phrase in your book. Did one of the other guests make you uncomfortable?"

"No, no, all's fine. I just see things, you know? It's easy to notice things when no one notices you."

My heart tugs.

My mom used to say the same thing, first about how not being noticed was an asset when it came to private security, but later about how my stepfather took her for granted.

I didn't realize her meaning had shifted until she was gone.

That he didn't really notice her.

That he didn't pay attention.

That he just wanted to take over the business she started with her father while getting a mother for his two sons, and she did a kick-ass job.

The younger of my two stepbrothers graduated high school a few months after she passed.

It sometimes feels like they got her longer than I did, even if I had her first. I was seven when she married Xavier, so a lot of those years are years I don't have clear memories of her.

"If you do see anything, or if anyone makes you uncomfortable, please tell me," Margot-Margie says. "Or you can tell Rhys. As you can see, he's a vault. But he's also obligated to keep things safe here. That's what he's paid for."

"There's a lot of security here," Mrs. Pinsley says, dropping her voice. "Are they doing mobster stuff? Is that why?"

There's not a lot of security here.

Just the right amount. Possibly a man or two more than necessary, in fact.

For this week.

Next week's another story.

I watch Margie-Margot closer as she answers because I suspect she knows it too.

"No, ma'am," she says. "Apparently this much security is normal at luxury resorts and retreat centers."

"Do celebrities come here?"

"I have no idea, ma'am. I just started."

"I'll keep watching even more then. Just in case."

"Don't neglect your book though. And you should take advantage of the spa while you're here too. Anything else I can get for you today,

Mrs. Pinsley? Coffee or tea supplies? Would you like your trash taken out?"

"No, no, dear. I don't need to hold you up."

"If you need anything, you know the number for housekeeping."

Margot-Margie steps back off the porch and joins me again at her cart, where she dumps the dirty towels into a bin. "Either someone's bothering her or she saw someone bothering someone else," she murmurs.

"Picked up on that."

She pinches her lips together and doesn't say anything else as she unlocks her cart wheels and continues down the sidewalk.

Doesn't ask me to look into what's happening with Mrs. Pinsley.

Doesn't ask me not to either.

Probably because she's been at this hotel-retreat-hospitality thing her entire life. She knows you can't fix a problem if you don't know exactly what it is, and a vague I see things isn't concrete enough.

But she'd have to out herself for us to have that conversation.

"Last stop of the day?" I ask her two chalets later after she's dropped off fresh towels for one more guest, this time without incident or chatting.

"Just vacuuming the dining room before dinner, and then I'm off."

She says it like she's looking forward to vacuuming.

So. Fucking. Weird.

"Huh," I say for lack of any other appropriate statement.

She squints up at me. "Are you sure I haven't offended you in some way?"

I squint back at her.

I'm not ready to let her know I know who she is yet.

Drop hints and see if she'll squirm?

Yes.

Outright tell her?

No.

So I can have some fun.

And fun's been distinctly lacking lately. Partially my own fault, partially not.

"I don't like women," I tell her.

Her brows lift. "Did women do something to you?"

"My fiancée left me a week before our wedding to run away with my stepbrother."

She gasps.

But she doesn't just gasp.

Her eyes almost fall out of their sockets, her mouth gapes so far open that I could probably see her tonsils if I looked at the right angle, and she hunches in on herself as if I've punched her.

Finally—finally—she's cracked.

Not just a little. Not in a way that makes me question if I'm imagining things.

But fully, completely cracked.

"Oh my god," she whispers.

I shrug one shoulder. "So I don't like women."

"I—" She stops herself, staring at me like she's debating what to say next.

I know what I'd say if I were her because her personal life has been in some corners of the news lately.

"It's not you," I tell her, even though it is, in fact, partially her. She's lying to a guy who did one of the coolest things anyone's ever done for me, and I do take that personally.

"No, I know. It's just—I have—had—a friend who just hooked up with my ex, so this is…weird. That we both…have that."

Her friend is her sister. And the news is reporting that Margie—Margot is taking a sabbatical for personal reasons, which is being covered by gossip sites as Margot Merriweather-Brown is having a breakdown over her sister and ex-fiancé betraying her.

A few gossip sites.

Not many.

Liv Daniels apparently had a bigger scandal this week, and she's actual Hollywood royalty, so no one really cares much about a hotel chain heiress who's had relatively little reason to ever have press coverage.

They're more excited about her wild-child sister—Daphne—who went on some road trip with Oliver—the ex, who just fucked over his own family after saving the family's convenience store corporation—and how the two of them apparently got arrested together after giving away millions in the Midwest.

The details were more than I cared to know.

"I'm not saying we have to be besties over it," Margie-Margot says, recovering her composure. "But you're…not alone."

I grunt.

She sucks in a breath through her nose. "Right. Sure. You don't want to talk about it. I get that. I'm having dinner with the triplets at some secret place tonight, so I won't be home until late."

I grunt again and nod.

I'm invited tonight too, which I don't tell her.

"Just didn't want you to be startled if you hear the door late."

Right. So I don't booby-trap the house back on her.

It'd serve her right.

But probably also get me a personal visit from the security guy that I spot again lingering in the rock garden down the path from the chalets.

Margot-Margie notices him too.

I almost miss the subtle nod she gives him, so subtle that I could be imagining it.

"I'm sorry they did that to you," she says. "My situation wasn't quite the same, but I still know how much it hurts to be dumped and betrayed."

I study her.

That feels like possibly the most honest thing she's said to me.

I look back at her security guy, planning to ask if she knows which cabin he's staying in just to watch her squirm, since I don't like feeling this connection with her, but he's disappeared.

My radio squawks to life. "O'Malley, Fornier, and Gustav, front desk please."

I nod to Margie-Margot, answer the radio call, and turn down the path leading to the main lodge.

"See you tomorrow," she calls after me. "And I'm not calling it a secret place because I want to keep it a secret from you specifically. I honestly don't know what it is. Lucky said they might have to blindfold me to take me there."

I lift a hand in acknowledgment and keep going.

Soon—very soon—I'm going to figure out her goal here.

And then I'll decide what comes next.

7

Oh, fuuuuuuuuucccckkkkkk

Margot

I text Cyril before I start vacuuming because I want to know if Rhys's story about his stepbrother and his ex is true, or if he's figured out who I am and he's using my own story to manipulate me into giving myself away.

What are the odds?

Very slim. That's what the odds are.

Cyril's deeper research this week into Rhys's past revealed that his stepfather owns the security firm Technique Group, which was founded by Rhys's mother and grandfather, and around the time Rhys quit, they each filed lawsuits against the other and have very different stories in their filings about the circumstances of Rhys leaving the company and what financial obligations Technique Group failed to meet.

Both suits were dropped, but that's all Cyril has found.

So this new story about his stepbrother and ex?

That's an avenue to explore.

With my request for more information sent to Cyril, I pop in earbuds and get to work vacuuming.

Once I get my father removed as CEO of Aurora Gardens and the dust has settled, assuming all goes well with every part of my plan, we should have our next corporate retreat out here.

I'd get to see the triplets, and the setting couldn't be better.

Between the chalets and other lodging options, there's room for around eighty guests, plus independent and group work spaces scattered through several various-sized buildings on the property. The dining room, kitchen, and staff offices are in a single log building, and the mountain views are spectacular nearly everywhere.

Add in the hiking trails and the gondola that will take guests the rest of the way up the mountain to more work areas, a wine tasting room, and the spa, and it's pure magic.

It's not something I'd want to invest in—given the pricing sheets I've seen and what I know about real estate and wages in this area, I suspect this is a tax write-off venture, or even a passion project, rather than a profit-generating model, which is unsurprising considering what I know about the owners—but the center here is speaking to my soul.

Soothing the parts of me that I didn't realize were agitated by city life.

Don't get me wrong—I'm absolutely returning to New York in the next few weeks, once I've done what I need to do here—but I like this place as a getaway.

It reminds me of my house in the Sierra Nevada.

I always feel an extra bit of peace there too.

And then I happily return to the city when the quiet gets to be too much. Because the quiet sometimes is too much.

That's what I'm contemplating—my own private vacation retreat in California and how it's different from the constant hum of a busy city—when I realize I'm not alone as I vacuum the dining room.

Two men have entered as well, one of them with heavily tattooed arms who's gently bouncing a tiny bundle of a baby against his shoulder.

Fine on its own, except I personally know the non-tatted of the two men, and what the actual fuck?

Why is Jonas Rutherford here?

Yes, he's one-third owner of this place, but Cyril told me that he wouldn't be here.

That Jonas was on a vacation with his family for a month. Something about a major anniversary or a retirement with not just his wife and kids, but also with his parents and his brother's family.

I know his entire family.

They run the Razzle Dazzle movie and entertainment conglomerate, and while I've had more face-to-face time with Jonas's older brother than I have with Jonas himself, we aren't strangers.

My skin starts buzzing and my pulse shoots into the heavens and I reach up to double-check that I'm wearing my glasses.

He won't recognize you, I tell myself, and I sincerely hope I can manifest that into reality. Considering he wouldn't expect to see me here, I'll have the advantage of being out of place while also being someone easily overlookable.

Just have to keep my head down and keep doing my job.

I haven't met the other man, the tattooed one bouncing the baby, but I know who he is. Theo Monroe, former GrippaPeen star and one-third owner of the retreat center. Also someone who, according to Sabrina at the coffee shop, would have possibly jerked off in a box of cereal once upon a time.

One of the other housekeepers pointed him out to me yesterday, as if I wouldn't have researched the hell out of anywhere I intended to work to be able to recognize the owners on sight, which clearly, she doesn't know.

But I'm not worried Theo will recognize me.

Theo didn't sit on the board of directors of one of the largest arts endowment charities in the Northeast with me for five years.

Jonas Rutherford, however—who's starred in half the movies his family's entertainment conglomerate makes, and who married Theo's sister, Emma, last year—did.

I turn my back on the men, flip the vacuum off, and get busy winding up the cord.

I'm not done, but I'm done enough. Not getting fired if someone notices the back part of the carpet didn't have a vacuum run over it today, even if it low-key annoys me to leave a job incomplete.

"This has clusterfuck written all over it," Theo's saying to Jonas, who laughs.

"It was your idea."

"I didn't think they'd go for it. I just wanted them to leave me alone."

"Too late now."

"It's not too late. Cancel."

Jonas cackles while I hustle through pulling the vacuum closer and closer to the plug in the wall so I can completely bolt out of here.

Later, I'll wonder what Theo got into that has Jonas cackling—I'm not sure I've ever heard him cackle—but right now, I don't care what's prompted it.

Right now, I need to get out of here.

When the damn vacuum cord is plugged in three feet from where the men are standing.

Maybe I should ditch the vacuum and pretend I have a personal emergency and come back and get it later.

I can fake food poisoning.

From the lunch I brought from home. Definitely would have to clarify I didn't get food poisoning from eating here at the retreat center.

"Excuse me, miss," Jonas says.

Fuuuuuuck.

He's not talking to me.

Please, please, please tell me he's not talking to me.

"Miss?" he repeats.

Dammit.

A quick glance around confirms for me that no one else is in here. By default, he has to be talking to me.

I angle more in his direction, not looking up, and make my voice higher-pitched than it normally is while I adjust my glasses. Like he makes me nervous.

Unfortunately, he really does right now.

"Me, sir?"

"Yes. Do you know how long it takes to break down the tables in this room after a meal?"

"I'm new, sir, but I can get someone who knows."

"Too long," Theo says. "Just tell the man it takes too long."

The baby in his tattooed arms makes an adorable little cooing sound, like she has an opinion on table break down.

"I'm not in the business of moving tables, but I could do this myself in under an hour, which means a crew can undoubtedly clear it in fifteen minutes or less," Jonas says. "Does that sound about right to you?"

Goddammit, he's talking to me again. "I'm sure you're right, sir."

"No, he's not right," Theo says. "If we needed to flood this room to make it unusable, like with water, or maybe even soup or something, how long would that take?"

I yank the plug out of the wall, still not looking straight at either of them. "I'm afraid that's not my area of expertise, sir."

"You're not flooding the dining room," Jonas says to him.

"Watch me," he replies.

"We'd have to shut down."

"Worth it."

"Again, you're the one who invited them—"

"You sound like my high school principal."

I need to text Cyril and have him get me out of here, but I can't stand in front of my bosses and pull out my cell phone if I want to keep my job.

Were I in their shoes and a housekeeper wasn't answering my questions and instead pulled out her phone—yeah, I know how that would end.

And while I don't need this job, it's such a convenient cover story, and I'd have no excuse for doing something stupid enough to get me fired on my third day.

"Miss, do you have a moment? I'd like to time something," Jonas says to me. "I'm sorry. I missed your name."

I glance up at him and instantly regret it, because the smiling, brown-haired, warm-eyed, friendly Jonas Rutherford goes from all is well and I'm enjoying my brother-in-law's discomfort to that wrinkle-nosed, paused, do I know you from somewhere? expression.

Daammmmmiiiiittttttt.

I drop my gaze to the floor again. "Would you like me to operate the stopwatch or do the thing that needs timed, sir?"

"He doesn't need any help," Theo says. "Quit making the staff nervous, asshole. And read her name tag. Margie? Margie. You can go. Don't mind him."

"There's nothing to be nervous about," Jonas says, but he's not as jovial as he was a minute ago.

"Dude," Theo mutters.

"What?"

"How many times do you have to make the staff nervous before you remember you're a fucking movie star?"

"Maybe she's an old fan of yours from your own…glory days."

"Which we also don't talk about," Theo mutters.

Jonas giggles.

Giggles.

Then he clears his throat and addresses me again. "Apologies for taking your time, Margie. It's not often I get to turn the tables on my favorite brother-in-law and torture him instead of being the subject of his pranks. This is a fun twist."

I nod at the floor and angle toward the vacuum again. "Not a problem, sir."

"But—have we met somewhere before?"

This is it.

I'm busted.

Caught.

Made.

And I know my half brothers hang out with him, which means they're going to hear about this from Jonas before I can explain myself, and before I know if I can trust them and if it's worth asking for their help.

If I find out something I don't like about the triplets, something that puts my plans—or them—in danger, I leave here, cut off all communications, and go back to my life.

Without the final bullet I need to blow up my father's control of his personal and professional life.

When I've spent four years investing in understanding why I felt so personally betrayed by Daphne being disinherited, and then concocting a plan to pay him back for what he did to her, when he's so very, very meticulous about everything that it's taken this long to get so close.

I can't lose it now.

I need to be in control here.

And I'm suddenly not.

I shake my head. Should've gone for bangs too. Maybe I'll add them tonight. "No, sir."

He's squinting at me. I can feel it even as I'm not looking directly at him. "Are you—" he starts, only to be cut off by a rough voice.

"Johnson, what are you doing?" Rhys barks. He strides into the room like he—not the other two men in here—owns it. He nods to them before scowling at me again. "Cynthia's looking for you. Coffee pot exploded in one of the chalets, and they want you on cleanup."

"Yes, sir," I say. I catch myself before I curtsy—fucking curtsy, what the fuck?—and lunge for the vacuum.

Cynthia's head of operations here. Rhys's boss, and my boss too. Likely reports directly to Jonas and Theo and the third owner, who's married to the triplets' cousin, Sabrina.

"Sorry to interrupt," Rhys says to the two others. "Sounded important. Carpet stains and curtain damage or something."

"Anyone hurt?" Theo asks.

"Chalet was empty. Window open. Bird turned it on or something."

I rush through finishing wrapping the cord and lift the vacuum, murmuring a soft excuse me as I step around the men.

"You're the triplets' friend," I hear Theo say to Rhys behind me.

"Knew Decker in the Marines."

"You're the one," Jonas says. "The one Decker based Rip Tide off of."

Rhys grunts. "Yeah. Excuse me. Need to take care of something."

"I see it," Jonas says.

"Unmistakable," Theo agrees. He nods to Rhys. "Thanks, man. We'll catch up later."

Rhys didn't say which cabin, but I've never been so glad for an incident with a bird and a coffee pot.

I hustle down the hallway and stash the vacuum in the housekeeping closet outside the kitchen. When I turn to dash to the lobby and the exterior door, Rhys is right behind me.

I stifle a shriek, my hand flying to my heart.

Fucker's quiet.

And that's not the worst of what he is.

Oh, no.

The worst of what he is?

Smart.

That's the worst of what he is.

Because while I'm standing here catching my breath, he's smirking.

He looks back at the dining room.

Then down at me.

His blue eyes twinkle.

His lips curve up higher.

The fading dye marks on his face taunt me. The not-fading purple streaks in his beard taunt me more.

And then the bastard drops the bomb.

"Almost got made, didn't you, Margot?"

8

Is it hot in here, or is that the fumes?

Rhys

"There's no cabin emergency," I say as Margot gapes at me. "And you're welcome."

I start to turn away, but the woman grabs me by the front of my shirt and yanks me into the closet.

I let her.

The room descends into complete blackness for a split second before she switches the light on. It's a lone lightbulb hanging from a cable that swings in response to the cord being pulled. The light beams bounce around us like the bulb is dusty, and I notice the whir of electronics and catch sight of a row of internet routers and cables on the shelves, along with far fewer cleaning supplies than I'd expect.

Must be a secondary closet for this level, since there's a much larger storage area in the laundry room in the basement.

"Who do you think you are, and why are you calling me the wrong name?" Margot demands.

Yeah, this is Margot.

No Margie in sight.

She's tall and confident and the set of her jaw and the flash of her eyes telegraph that she knows what to do with my body if I say the wrong thing, and she has me pushed against the shelf of cleaning supplies, making ammonia and lemon and a bit of dust tickle my nose.

I step forward until our bodies line up when she refuses to budge an inch. Doesn't matter that I have her by at least eight inches and probably a hundred pounds.

She's not backing down from staring at me, and she doesn't retreat.

She also doesn't shove me back when her hands land on my chest, though we're both aware that she could.

Absolutely, undoubtedly, no questions, this woman thinks she runs the whole world.

But she's fucking kind too.

And I don't like that contradiction in her.

"Why are you pretending to be someone you're not?" I reply.

"I don't know who you think you are—"

"You were at the Hoteliers Association dinner. Saved Imogen Carter from your father's drunk ass."

"He wasn't—I don't know what you're talking about."

Victory. "You're right. He wasn't drunk. Just checking."

Her pretty blue eyes narrow. "What do you want?"

"For my silence?"

"Yes."

"The truth."

"So that you can tell Decker because he asked you to come here and accidentally be my housemate so that you could spy on me and find out all of my secrets?"

"You're very suspicious."

She arches a brow and glares up at me. "What part of that was wrong?"

"Irrelevant. How long do we have before your security agent realizes you're trapped in a closet?"

Her cheeks take on a subtle pink stain. "Two minutes at most."

"He didn't intervene Friday night. When you ambushed me."

"He understands the delicate situation, and he knew I had things under control."

"Why's it delicate?"

"That's none of your business."

"You're lying to a guy who saved my life once. I'm making it my business."

"He saved your life," she repeats.

No. Fuck, no. We were barely at the same duty station long enough for that to happen, even if we did make fast friends. Back when I could make fast friends. When I trusted the whole fucking world as much as a Marine can trust the whole world.

"Yes."

Her gaze slides to the door. "By making you into a character in a book?"

"People can do more than one thing in their lives."

Margot's lush pink lips pinch together.

Voices drift through the door.

Theo Monroe and Jonas Rutherford.

From what Decker's told me about Theo, I suspect he wouldn't blink at two people being in a broom closet together unless he thought one was harming the other.

As for Jonas, I don't know how he'd react to two people in a broom closet, though I do know who's renting out the retreat center next week, and the bits of the conversation I overheard just now suggest he's okay with that, so he probably wouldn't blink either.

Margot's gaze shifts to the door again. Her hands are still resting on my chest, and if I were a betting man, I'd bet she's calculating the odds she'll feel the need to fling herself at me, climb me like a tree, and kiss me to put on the show that we're secretly fucking around while we're working.

My damn dick decides he likes that idea and lifts to half-mast.

I could make noise.

Rattle a shelf.

Something subtle enough that she'd have to throw herself at me, and I could see if she tastes like a shark, or if she tastes like a complicated, red-blooded woman who might want some stress relief between the sheets while she's here.

Knock it off, dumbass, I tell my libido and the more Neanderthal half of my brain.

I'm not sleeping with Margot Merriweather-Brown.

I'm not sleeping with anyone.

Ever.

For the rest of my life.

Not after what Felice did to me.

The voices outside the closet fade.

I open my mouth, but Margot lifts a hand and holds up a single commanding finger.

Be quiet. Don't talk yet.

I know that finger well.

Used to get it from my stepfather.

Two seconds pass.

Three.

Five.

Eventually, ten or so seconds later, she drops both of her hands and takes the smallest step back. "I won't discuss this with you here."

"Here in the broom closet, or here in the state of Colorado?"

"Don't be obtuse."

"Skillet, I've been around your type in one way or another most of my life. I know to be specific."

"Skillet?"

"It's that or Margot. Which one do you want me to call you?"

Her lip curls, flaring one nostril with it. "Skillet is fine. But don't presume I'm a type. You know nothing about me."

"I know you're on a sabbatical from your life because your little sister's shacking up with your ex-fiancé."

That one's annoying.

I don't like having things in common with people like Margot.

And by people like Margot, I mean people who lie about who they are and claim to be related to people I care about.

The Margot who helps clean up spilled coffee in a café and makes friends with elderly novelists and has her fellow housekeeping staff talking about how nice she is—if it's real, I could not dislike that about her.

Which isn't the same as liking something about her.

It's simply not disliking her.

She smirks right back at me. "They have my blessing. I'm actually happy for them."

"Right."

"Aren't you happy for your ex and your stepbrother? Assuming they're both happier now? Which I'm not saying was your fault. Sometimes people just don't match. And sometimes people change. The world is rarely black-and-white, right-and-wrong, good-and-evil."

"We're talking about you. Are you actually related to the Sullivan triplets, or are you scamming them for something?"

"What the actual fuck would I scam them for?"

"You tell me."

"We share DNA. There's zero chance my mother would've given birth to triplets without the world knowing about it, and they insist their mother remembers giving birth to them, and that they accidentally found out their dad isn't their biological dad, which means my father and their father must be where we get the common genetics."

"Maybe their existence is inconvenient for you and you need to learn the best way to take them out."

"Oh my god, are you serious? No, stop. We are not discussing this here."

"We're discussing it somewhere if you want me to not tell Decker immediately who you are and what you're doing."

She's a pacer. You can tell she wants to pace, but this room is approximately the size of one and a half of me.

There's no room.

And the look she gives me suggests it's my fault the room is this small.

She picked it.

She can deal.

"I'm going to tell him," she grits out. "I'm going to tell all three of them. But not yet. There are things—"

"There are always things. When? What date and time are you telling them?"

"Three weeks from this Friday."

She made that up on the spot. I don't know how I know, but I know. "Why then?"

More voices drift in from the hallway. Can't tell if it's guests or staff, but it's not Theo and Jonas again.

"I have to get back to work because I have a job I've committed to and I'm going to fucking do it," she hisses. "I'm off in thirty minutes. Think about what you want. We'll discuss it at the cabin. Also? If you tell a single soul who you think I am before we discuss exactly how we're going to ride out this situation, you will regret it every single day for the rest of your life."

I swallow the ooh, so scary retort that's at the tip of my tongue.

Because I, too, have to get back to work.

Decide what I want in exchange for my silence.

And I can think of two different things to ask for.

Two very, very different things.

One will get me closer to the future I want to live in, even if there won't be any guarantees it will work.

One will give me satisfaction about the past, but possibly destroy part of my soul—the part of my soul that knows I've always behaved in a way that my mom would be proud of—to do it.

Question is, which strategy am I going to take?

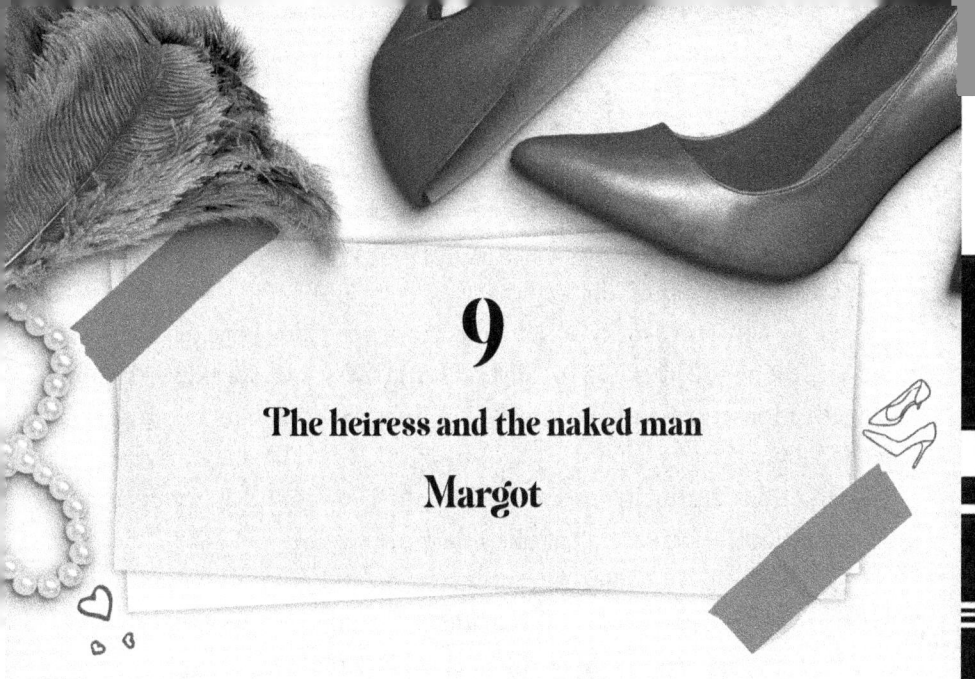

9

The heiress and the naked man

Margot

I dislike when I only have two options, but I can only see two options right now.

The first is to just drop the bomb on the triplets—our father is the second-generation CEO of Aurora Gardens and I'd like your help to take the bastard down to avenge our sister—and the second is to negotiate with Rhys for his silence while I continue to get to know them so I can feel out their willingness to help me once they know me.

It took me two years to build up the kind of relationship I need with three-quarters of the board to trust they'd vote on my side when I propose forcibly removing my father from his position, if I can bring them enough proof that he's a liability.

Building enough trust with the triplets to convince them to forgive me for my hesitation to be fully honest with them about my identity from the beginning, and then to also be the final nail in the coffin of my father's career for Daphne's sake?

I knew I wouldn't have two years, but I thought I'd have more than five days.

Between Jonas spotting me and Rhys knowing who I am, though, the clock is ticking.

Rhys's truck is already back at the cabin when I arrive, which is fine.

Let him think he has some power by being here first or whatever.

He clearly wants something, or he wouldn't have told me he knows who I am before telling the triplets.

I texted with Lucky to let him know I'd had a long day at work and still hoped to make it to Silver Horn, the secret speakeasy hiding beneath House of Curry in downtown Snaggletooth Creek, but that I needed a nap first.

Nothing in Lucky's response—totally get it, my days are like that too sometimes—suggested that he's suspicious of me yet.

I park my van, which is running so much better now than it was when it was delivered to Cyril outside of Boulder last week so that he could be prepared for me here, and I check my phone.

Just a message from my lead security agent.

I'm coming up through the woods. Open the window.

He's not pleased that I'm having this conversation either.

I text back an ok emoji, click the button on the garage remote to shut the door, and heft myself out of the van.

Garage doesn't smell much better than the van does, though the garage at least has more garage smells and fewer children-spilled-milk-in-this smells.

I would very much like the smell of my van to be the biggest problem in my life right now.

Since the garage is detached, there's a short walk from the side door to the house, and I pause when I'm halfway between the two.

It feels like something's watching me.

Something rustles in the forest behind the house, the opposite direction Cyril should be coming from, and the hairs on the back of my neck stand up.

"Just the wind," I whisper to myself as I hustle the rest of the way into the cabin, texting Cyril to watch for wildlife on my way.

When I step inside, Rhys isn't immediately in sight.

He's not in the kitchen, nor is he in the dining-slash-living room serving as his bedroom either.

Good news, though, is that there are no obvious booby traps.

If I were him, I'd absolutely be plotting the revenge of a lifetime against me right now. Though it's hardly like he's personally damaged by me protecting my identity from relatives I didn't know I had until I took a DNA test online a few months ago in a last-ditch effort to find something that I could use to prove that my father had illegitimate children who could one day cause problems for him, and therefore Aurora Gardens too.

"Hello?" I call.

No answer.

I study the room for anything out of place, then step carefully through.

He didn't have time to plant anything here.

But then, I'm not sure how long he's known who I am.

Was it a test, telling me that his bride ran away with his stepbrother? Cyril hasn't gotten me the full dossier I asked for on that yet.

Apparently some things take more than a couple hours, which is annoying as hell. Though I do appreciate Cyril's text back that he's at the cabin and there's no visible wildlife or other problems for me to worry about.

I know he's only one man, and while he's good, he can only work so fast solo.

But solo is necessary.

The more people who know where I am and what I'm doing, the more people who might slip.

"Is anyone home?" I call again.

I peek down the hallway to the two doors and find the hallway bathroom door closed, with the sound of running water behind it.

I knock. "I'm back. Don't scream."

"Are you coming in?" is the response I get.

Not exactly what I would've expected, but then, every day seems to be full of surprises.

"No," I reply.

"Your loss."

My brain betrays me and flashes images of a wet, naked Rhys, chest broad and soaped up, his large hands reaching down to—

Shut up, brain.

"Such a fucking man," I mutter.

"Heard that."

I flip the door off, more out of agitation with myself for fantasizing about someone who's undoubtedly about to blackmail me than irritation with his comment, which was absolutely made just to bait me.

"Saw that too," he announces.

Does he have the hallway bugged?

I leave him to his after-work shower and head into my bedroom, where I drop the knock-off Louis Vuitton bag that Margie carries on my bed and check that nothing in the room has been disturbed.

Computer and my real ID are still locked in their case beneath my bed.

Bed's still made meticulously the way I left it this morning with the moose quilt.

The sliding closet door is exactly as I left it too, hanging halfway off of its hinges, which Lucky told me was something they'd all been waiting on each other to fix, but none of them had yet.

They've had the cabin for about a year, and according to Lucky, they're still debating if they want to expand it into something the three of them can fully enjoy together, if they want to turn it into a vacation rental, or if they want to keep it as is.

Apparently Decker likes to use it for a nearby writing retreat when he needs a change in scenery. Jack likes it as a spot close enough to his favorite trails that he doesn't need to find parking to use them. And Lucky likes it because Lucky seems to like everyone and everything.

There's a rustic wooden dresser that I found empty when I got here, where I hid a stash of cash inside a box of tampons beneath some clothes in the third drawer down, and that's undisturbed too.

If Rhys searched in here, he left no trace.

Not that he'd find much unless he picked the lock on the safe holding my computer.

A presence looms in the bedroom doorway.

I turn and find my housemate half-naked, still wet, wearing just a gray towel around his waist. "Forgot to grab my clothes," he mutters.

You'd think being stripped of nearly every stitch of clothing would make the man seem smaller.

Instead, his broad chest, thick abdomen with the subtle outline of a round bruise, and wide, muscled shoulders, bare except for his skin and the hair on his chest, seem to have expanded in the shower, which has my brain giving a very large, very loud *even better than we imagined.*

How does he even fit in the doorway?

Is he this big everywhere?

And yes, I mean *everywhere*.

I'm back in the closet at the retreat center, my hands on his chest, trying desperately not to notice how solid the wall of muscle was beneath my palms and fingers, and even more desperately not to like it.

Seriously. Brutes have never been my thing.

But Rhys O'Malley—the man is getting to me.

I force a swallow and a no-nonsense glare at him. "Are you going to get dressed for this conversation?"

He rubs his beard and puckers his brows together like he's contemplating the question. Then—"No."

I occasionally visit Daphne in her adopted hometown of Athena's Rest in upstate New York. It's a couple hours' drive from the city, and she swears bad things happen whenever she comes back near where we grew up, plus she hates our parents and reminders of them, which—legit.

But something she always says to me when I go see her and remark on basically anything charming in her small town is drifting in the back of my mind now.

Margot, you need to get out more.

She doesn't mean to shows and dinners and drinks with friends.

She means to see more of the world. To get out in nature like she does regularly. To have a broader variety of experiences beyond work and city life, and according to her, it doesn't count as getting out more when I hide away in any number of various mansions that I've bought or that our family has owned for decades in another city where I don't often leave the property and instead treat myself to gorgeous views while sipping wine or coffee or occasionally hiking close to my property, most often solo, because the solo life fits me these days.

Being interrogated by a nearly naked bear of a man in a remote cabin in the Rockies qualifies to me as getting out more.

And honestly?

I don't hate it.

The view for this interrogation isn't bad.

Could definitely be worse, in fact.

Shut it down, Margot. You're not here for a romp in the sheets.

I step aside and gesture to my bed, since my brain so kindly suggested it. "Did you want to sit?"

He studies me for another minute, intense blue eyes searching my face, the purple streaks fully gone from the whites of his eyes now, even if it's lingering the barest amount on his face, then takes three steps into the room, turns, and plants his wet-toweled ass on my quilt.

His thighs spread, and the towel gapes.

I keep my eyes trained on his face like the professional I am, absolutely certain that if I looked down at that gaping towel, he'd have it positioned just right for me to see nothing, and also absolutely certain that he'd smirk at catching me looking.

This game is so obvious.

He wants to throw me off by having a conversation where he's nearly naked. Probably thinks his body is one of the world's most magnificent wonders, and he's probably had women fall for this *I'm naked and inherently vulnerable now, so you can trust anything that comes out of my mouth* psychological bullshit.

But god, I want to look.

And it's making me tingle in places I can't be tingling during this conversation.

"You gonna sit too?" he asks.

"No, thank you."

He lifts a shoulder, drawing my attention to a long, thick scar across his still-damp skin. "Whatever makes you happy."

What would make me happy is not having this conversation. But since that's not an option now— "What do you want?"

"How much are you going to give me?"

"You want a number?"

He scowls. "I'm not for sale. I want information."

"About?"

"Why you're here."

This week has been interesting. I prepped myself well to work in housekeeping—I can make a bed, clean a bathroom, and I take an odd satisfaction in dusting, even if it's taken a few days to realize I'm being too meticulous and need to work faster, not deeper—but more than the job itself, more than this opportunity to experience the hospitality industry as low-level staff interacting with guests, walking around more or less invisible in a housekeeping uniform is a good way to hear things.

I was under the distinct impression that Theo Monroe and Grey Cartwright, two of the triplets' best friends here locally, were the more hands-on owners with the retreat center and that Jonas Rutherford wouldn't be anywhere in the vicinity. And that a substantial part of the staff would know the triplets.

That's proven true.

I hear things. File them away. Slowly so far, but it's happening.

And I definitely haven't heard anything about Rhys other than that half the housekeeping staff thinks he's hot.

But my body's still a little worn down from the nonstop physical activity, and I'd like to fling myself onto the couch in the living room with a pint of ice cream and binge-watch home renovation shows instead of having this conversation.

Not that I can when the couch is his bed.

I rub my brow and frown at him when I'd like to pace the room. Don't pace, Margot, it shows weakness, my father always said. "I have no intention of causing harm to the triplets."

"Don't you?"

"No. I don't. Why would I want to hurt them?"

"Because they could destroy your family."

I roll my eyes. "Oh, no, a rich and powerful man cheated on his wife and has secret grown children squirreled away somewhere. Don't let the news know, or his life will be over."

The man has the decency to cringe, and I don't think it's at my flat sarcasm.

And let's be real.

That's exactly why I'm afraid my plan won't work.

It's why I need the triplets' help.

They need to convince the board that they'd be a problem and make my father look like a problem. Without that—without that, I need a new plan.

And I don't like my options. Not when it's taken four years and a dose of luck to get this close.

"They might want money from you," Rhys says.

"I have plenty. I also have the capacity and proper positioning to make plenty more. Why wouldn't I share with siblings who didn't have the same financial advantages I did?"

"If that's true, why are you lying to them about who you are?"

"Seriously?"

"If you're not worried they'll ruin your family, and you're not worried they'll want money, then why lie?"

"I have trust issues in personal relationships."

"No shit. What else?"

"Trust issues are enough of a reason where I come from."

"Like you didn't have them investigated to dig up all the skeletons in their closet before getting within a hundred miles of them."

He's not wrong. "Do you like your stepsiblings, Rhys?"

His eye twitches. "We're not talking about me."

"So long as you're threatening to blackmail me, we are. Do you like your stepsiblings?"

There's something delectable about making a man's jaw go tight and his lips flat. "No."

"Do you have any family that you like?"

"No."

"Do you ever wish you did?"

"You don't like your family?"

"I adore my sister. Fucking adore her. She's funny and unpredictable and strong as hell and she has the biggest heart of anyone I know. Why wouldn't I want to get to know more people who might be like her?"

"While lying about who you are. Great way to build a relationship."

He shoots, he scores.

I spent too many hours debating if I'd tell them who I really am while I was laying the foundation to come here and meet them. If there was a way to be fully honest from the start where I wouldn't be at risk of tipping my hand on what I'd ultimately be asking for or freaking them out at where their genes came from.

Of my father finding out where I am.

In the end, I decided it was better to risk the triplets hating me forever when they find out who I really am than it was to risk that it would get back to my father that I was with sons he didn't know he had.

The only way my hostile takeover works is if he doesn't see it coming, so I have to do this the slow and steady way.

But god, I like them.

It's impossible to not like Lucky. And Jack—bringing his dog and fixing my car? Even Decker—I appreciate the hell out of how much he looks out for the people he cares about.

That's admirable in my book.

So yes, I want them to like me. All three of them.

It's a bone-deep, soul-deep, desperate desire to have more family that likes me for me.

Not for my money. Not for my name.

But for the person that I've been trying to be.

I shrug at Rhys though. "They already know we're related. I'm lying because I have trust issues and I want to get to know them, to know if they can like me as a broke housekeeper who has nothing to offer them, before I tell them that their biological father is worth billions of dollars."

His eyes flicker over my face. "You wanted to call him an asshole. Their asshole biological father."

He's not wrong. "Relationships are complicated. Now. What do you want?"

"You seriously expect me to believe you want more siblings like the sister who stole your fiancé?"

I rub my brow and sag against the wall.

People are so annoying sometimes. "Oliver dumped me several years ago when his family was having legal issues. Told me he didn't want to sully my name when he was also overwhelmed at the position he'd been thrust into unprepared, and he couldn't handle both me and the job he had to do. So yes, I was initially pissed and hurt, because that's a natural reaction to being dumped, but I've also had a lot of time to get over it."

"Rumor is—"

"Wrong. Rumor is wrong." I know, because I started it. Margot Merriweather-Brown wants her ex back. They were going to combine their businesses and be the world's biggest power couple, but then her sister stole him.

I didn't want Oliver back. I never wanted Oliver back.

Aside from being unwilling to put myself in a position where the same person could hurt me twice—see again, trust issues—I'd seen enough of him the past few years to know that he's changed from when we were involved, and while I have the utmost respect for who he's become after all he's been through, I'm not attracted to him anymore.

Not like that.

Also?

Oliver's a good person. He deserves to be loved by someone who can put her entire heart and soul into it in a way I never could.

But I had to play the role that I wanted him back so my father would think I was complying with his wishes, and his wish was that I marry Oliver so that I could facilitate a corporate merger that would've actually been a takeover of Miles2Go, Oliver's family's gas station and convenience store corporation.

That I was still the same heartless, aggressive, business-first daughter that he raised me to be.

People don't think about you as much when you're agreeable as they do when you make waves.

So my father has no idea I'm about to destroy him.

He still thinks I'm his good daughter when I've had a rage slowly burning hotter by the day every day for the past four years that he'd classify me and Daphne as the good one and the bad one.

Rhys is frowning at me again. "That's all you're going to give me? Rumor is wrong?"

"He changed, I changed, Daphne changed. Though, in retrospect, I should've known they'd be good together. They've both always been softhearted and cared more about the bigger things in the world. Oliver needed more fun in his life. Daphne needed someone who's loyal to a fault. Especially now, after what my parents did to her. Congratulations, you now know more about how I feel about this than anyone else in the world, with the exception of my sister and her boyfriend."

I should stop talking.

I really should.

The more I tell him, the bigger his request. The more he has to hold over me.

The more he can leak to the press.

But the more I tell him of the parts I want him to know, the more likely he is to see me as less of a bad guy.

And I need him to know I'm not a bad guy.

Parts of me are. It's impossible to be positioned where I am in business and not make decisions that occasionally—or sometimes even regularly—make me the bad guy to someone.

But I don't want to hurt the triplets.

I will bend over backward to not hurt the triplets any more than my necessary lies about my identity will hurt them.

"The rumor was your cover story for your sabbatical," he says slowly.

"Yes. I wanted a way to anonymously get to know my brand-new siblings without all of the pressure that comes with the expectations people have when they find out who I really am."

I love pressure.

I thrive with pressure, and I love thriving.

But since Daph was disinherited, I've discovered an appreciation for other things too. Simpler things like kindness and patience and forgiveness.

The way Rhys's eyes are narrowing while he studies me—I wonder if he knows.

He's seen people who fit my profile before. Worked for a lot of them in his previous job. Technique Group does security for very wealthy clients, and you don't get wealthy without having some of the same character flaws—quirks—that I have.

And considering Rhys's mother founded the company, he's likely been adjacent to my world his entire life.

Which means he probably knows there's more to a lot of us than a bloodthirsty desire for more, more, more.

"And now that you know my side of the story, you have two minutes to tell me what you want before I have my protection agent take care of you for me," I tell him.

"If I disappear, I have an email scheduled to go to Decker telling him who you are."

I lift a shoulder and feign indifference like the idea of having to face Decker and Lucky and Jack this soon with my truth doesn't send fear slithering through my chest.

I haven't proven to them yet that I'm a good enough person. That I'm worthy of being someone they call a sister.

Hell, I haven't proven to myself yet that I'm a good enough person. "I'll deal. Are we negotiating or not?"

"You know half their friends are almost as filthy rich as you are. They're not going to blink at who you are or how much money you have."

"Friends aren't the same as secret family. And how much longer will the triplets be able to protect their dad when they're carrying around the secret that they're related to the Merriweather-Browns? Lucky said the story he's told himself is that their parents found out their dad's swimmers didn't work, so they used a sperm donor and didn't want to talk about it. I can promise you, my father wouldn't have ever donated to a sperm bank, and for all of his faults, I don't think he would've forced himself on a woman either. I'm doing them just as much of a favor right now as I'm doing for myself. One minute, Rhys. What do you want?"

My favorite part of any negotiation is that moment when I know I've won.

And this is that moment.

I have the upper hand.

He cares about Decker. Doesn't want to hurt him.

Hell, I don't want to hurt him either. I don't want to hurt any of them.

The idea of hurting them—that's the worst.

But the seconds are ticking down and he's glowering at me, and I suddenly don't know that I've won.

That Rhys might not actually have a price for his silence.

That this was all in vain.

That he's going to tell them anyway because he's a truth is always right person.

Fuck.

This isn't how I wanted the triplets to find out.

It's truly not.

"You'll do whatever I ask?" he finally says, low and slow.

"If it's not the wrong kind of illegal."

He snorts, clearly disgusted. "Fucking rich people."

"Illegal is still occasionally ethical and moral, and my sister has an arrest record to prove it. What do you want?"

He holds my gaze, swallowing and making his Adam's apple bob.

There is something he wants.

Something big.

I wonder if I'll be building a center for veterans. An arboretum in his mother's name. She died when he was in his early teens. Cyril found the obituary.

A string of curses rolls through my mind as another angle he might be after pops into my head.

What if he wants his ex back? What if he wants my help with that? I don't know how or why I could help with that, but I don't know who she is.

Maybe she knows people in my circles. Maybe she'd listen to them.

I've decided I've made a tactical error when he finally speaks, his voice low and gravelly and hesitant. "Hire me."

"What?" That is not what I expected him to say.

There's something haunted in his eyes that says he wants something more than a job.

"You only have one man here."

I blink at him. "Do I?"

Better question—how long has he known who I am that he's been able to figure out I'm operating with only one security agent?

"You do. Let me be his backup. I want to start my own security firm, and an endorsement from someone like you would go a long way to getting me up and running."

I fold my arms, a clearer picture forming in my mind as I piece together what I know about his background.

His unemployment for the past year.

The lawsuits between him and Technique Group.

Him not being involved in the company his mother founded anymore but still wanting to work in the industry.

"That's not what you want," I say softly.

His brows lift just enough to make the fading dye streaks on his forehead wrinkle, but it's the haunted look in his eyes that convinces me I'm right.

"You're an expert on what I want now?" he says.

I stare at him.

He stares back.

There's definitely something else that he wants.

Something he's not asking for.

And if it's what I think it is—if it's what I'd want to ask for—my respect for him is honestly growing.

It takes character of the kind that I'll never have, no matter how much I try to be a good person, to have an opportunity to ask for revenge and not take it.

"You already have a security job," I say. "With people like Jonas Rutherford to endorse you."

"Resort security isn't the same as executive protection."

"You have all of the connections to get hired on Jonas's personal team."

He flinches.

Just barely, but enough that it's noticeable.

So either he already asked and they said no, or he didn't ask at all for some reason.

"What are your qualifications?" I ask.

"Experience and proximity."

"Experience didn't stop me from taking you down the night you got here."

"I wasn't on the clock." He gives me a flat stare. "And normal people don't hang bags of hair dye and rig flour explosions inside their front doors. Or have the strength to manhandle a cast-iron skillet as a weapon."

I barely suppress a smile. "Girl's gotta do what a girl's gotta do. It worked, didn't it?"

He grunts an acknowledgment.

And is that a modicum of respect shining in his eyes?

I do believe it is.

Dammit.

Yes, dammit.

His respect for my methods makes me like the man more.

Much like my respect for his balls in attempting to blackmail me makes me like him more too.

I'm complicated like that.

"Why did you leave your last job in private security?" I ask.

"Personal reasons."

"I don't hire people without checking references, and I've dug enough to know it wasn't that simple. So why don't you spare both of us the trouble of me having to go the roundabout way of finding out what you don't want to talk about?"

His jaw tics. "You already know my stepfather runs it, or else your team is shit."

"Paper tells a different story from the human angle that's always an element. Did he fire you, or did you quit?"

His jaw works back and forth for a moment. "Both."

I can actually believe that. "Your stepbrother works there?"

"Both of them."

Well.

That's awkward.

Can't imagine it would've been comfortable to stay and work at a place with the guy who stole his bride.

"Was the part where they fired you when you quit performance-related?"

"That's the story they'll tell you."

I'm getting a very clear picture of what he's likely been through in the past year.

And honestly, I have very little to lose if I give him a chance and this fails. "So you want my endorsement when you start a competing firm in exchange for your silence about who I am?"

His eyes flicker with something that speaks to the bloodthirsty parts of my soul. "Yep."

"And that's all you want?"

"For now."

There it is.

I almost smile again, but this one's different. It's not joy and pride at rigging a damn good human mousetrap. It's bone-deep appreciation for what my gut is telling me about this man.

I'm not the only one in this room who wants to see justice done.

Who knew one of my unexpected half brothers would have a friend that I could relate to so very, very much? "Your stepfather raised you after your mother died?"

He flinches. "Off-limits."

Good lord.

I'm here faking Cinderella, but he's the one with the evil stepfamily. "Any other skeletons I should know about before I put my people to investigating you thoroughly?"

"No."

"And what are you going to tell Decker when he finds out you lied to him in exchange for a job with me?"

"He'll understand."

"Will he?"

"That you blackmailed me into silence? Yep."

The unspoken other half of that message is clear.

He'll believe me because he trusts me, whereas he has all the reason in the world to not trust you.

He's not wrong.

My research on Decker revealed that he left the Marines when his third book came out, though I missed the part where his most popular early character was based on Rhys. That little detail came from the conversation I overheard this afternoon.

Decker had been self-publishing for fun, but then suddenly, his books were making him more than his military salary.

But his career has hit a new level of success lately that I suspect makes new personal relationships hard for him. And a broke-ass, previously unknown half sister showing up right as he's first hitting bestseller lists and getting mentions in national publications?

Yeah.

He should be suspicious of me.

"How'd you make me?" I ask. He mentioned the Hoteliers Association when I saved Imogen Carter from my father, but that event is typically in the fall, so it's likely been around a year.

Maybe more.

Long time to remember someone.

He gestures to his face. "You have a distinct way of squinting at people."

I catch myself narrowing my eyes. What the fuck is he talking about? "That's a very specific thing to notice about a person."

Is it my imagination, or are his cheeks going pink? Not the way the rest of his skin's been fading from the pink that suggests his shower was scalding hot either. "It was a very specific look when your father wasn't aware you were making faces behind his back."

"Quite the memory for one night."

He scowls. "You also helped the staff member. With the seizure."

Oh.

That night.

"You resent me for that?"

"I liked you for that. Thought you were some rando personal assistant. Not the big girl boss who's lying to my friend."

It's like he flipped through a card deck of what's the most terrible thing I could say to Margot right now? and found whatever's worse than worst.

I saw you for who you want to be and I liked that about you, but now I hate you since I know who you actually are.

I swallow hard. "Good thing you realized you hate women." And then I lift my phone and open my texts to the message thread with Cyril. "Please interview my roommate to be your backup for the duration of our stay in Snaggletooth Creek," I dictate after noting he's mentioned once more that there's nothing in the woods around the house.

"Can I put some clothes on first?" Rhys says.

"No."

"You gonna stay and watch?"

"Also no. My turn for the shower, and then I have a date with my brothers. I hear they're fun."

"If you hurt them—"

"I told you. I don't want to hurt them. Are you done trying to intimidate me, or do I need to change my mind about giving you a chance to prove you can handle me?"

"I can definitely handle you." His blue eyes flicker over my face, and something warm tingles low in my belly.

I'm not the only one lying here.

He still likes me.

And I like that about him.

It's brave.

And unusual.

Few people in my life see me as anything more than a bloodthirsty boss bitch.

Finding a complete stranger unafraid to go toe-to-toe with me?

A stranger who recognized me at my best?

Who's now making something flutter in my belly at the recognition that he has a little bit of a taste for revenge too, even if he's not saying it out loud?

This could be fun.

As long as he doesn't fuck up my plans. It's taken me four years of meticulous planning to get this close to taking my father down.

God help the person who gets in my way.

No matter how much he might have once liked the person I want to be.

10

Speak easy and carry a bag of Chex Mix

Rhys

She knows.

Margot knows what I'm not asking for.

My mom would be horrified—vengeance isn't the answer, Rhys—but fuck, it feels good to let myself daydream about a world where everything goes right enough that I manage to destroy my stepfather.

To think about the man who gave the barest shit about me unless I was useful having a taste of his own medicine, yeah.

Yeah, it feels like claiming back some of who I am.

Like defending the teenage kid who needed a parent who still loved him but got stuck with fucking Xavier Yates instead.

But it's not an idea without cost, which is why I haven't asked for it.

Once I go there—I can't take it back.

Revenge is messy. It comes with unexpected consequences. And I don't know if that's how I want to restart my life when I take my place back in the security world.

I rise from my spot on her bed, hand on the towel where it's tucked in on itself. "Good talk. Don't fuck me over."

"I rarely fuck people over unless they deserve it. Don't blow my cover."

"Don't make me have to."

She's standing just to the side of the open bedroom door, tracking my movements as I head out of the room.

I'm nearly past her when she reaches out and touches my stomach, which promptly breaks out in goosebumps like an asshole. "Did I do that?"

I look down at the round purplish bruise and ignore the visible shivers on my skin. "Yep."

"I wouldn't have if I'd known you were coming."

I lift a brow at her. "Wouldn't you?"

She smiles, her expression a mix of mischief and kindness, and I feel like I've been socked in the gut all over again.

This time, though, the sensation is accompanied by a distant, hazy memory of my first high school girlfriend.

She was a pain in the ass, but she was cute.

Fun too.

I don't want to believe Margot knows the meaning of the word fun if it doesn't come with flaying someone alive.

And I don't believe for one second that her only motivation in lying to the triplets is that she has trust issues and doesn't want to complicate the lies they're telling their families.

She's up to something else. I can feel it in that part of my gut that's never steered me wrong.

"Have fun tonight," I say as I saunter out of the room like I don't want to touch her back just to see if her skin would also be the kind of asshole that would pebble up with goosebumps under my fingers. "Hear Jonas is gonna be there."

She doesn't reply, but I swear I can hear her thinking a solid motherfucker.

Also, I didn't hear anything at all about Jonas Rutherford, and even if I had, I doubt it would've been that.

Decker said since their friends who co-own the retreat center started having kids, they don't hit town after naptime much anymore.

And Jonas's security team would probably have a fit at an underground speakeasy.

No easy second exit route.

Margot's security guy seems none too pleased with it either as he interviews me for a position as his backup after I get dressed in the living room while Margot's showering.

He tells me he's running my references and will be in touch.

I don't wait for her to finish getting ready, and soon after my informal interview, I'm happily strolling into Silver Horn myself after giving the password at a nondescript door in the alley behind an Indian restaurant downtown.

I've heard of this place, but it's the first time I've seen it in person. Dim lighting, lots of low, curving furniture in reds and blacks. Old-fashioned paintings of mountains and gold mines hang on the brick walls between red velvet curtains that can be drawn around various sections for more privacy.

Fucking swanky for a small town in the mountains.

Decker and Jack are at a seating area tucked in a back corner beyond the glossy wood bar with a curtain mostly closed around them, so I make my way over the Turkish rug-covered wood floor to join them. Decker's in the same clothes he was in the other day—or maybe his pants are green instead of tan today?—and Jack's wearing a PAC-MAN T-shirt that makes me want to hit an arcade. Their hair is polar opposites—Jack's military-short, his face shaved, while Decker's as shaggy as I've ever seen him in both hair and beard.

Jack's dog is on the floor beside him. He lifts his head, pants, and wags his tail a bit, but otherwise doesn't react to my presence.

"Margie with you?" Jack asks as I take a seat in the chair farthest from the door with my back to the wall and a view out of the parted curtains.

I shake my head. "She was showering or napping or something."

"How's her van?"

"Seems to be running fine now."

"Good."

Decker eyes me, and for some reason, that makes Jack sigh.

I look between the two men. "You doing some kind of silent triplet communication?"

Lucky drops into the seat beside me, dressed in dark blue nurse's scrubs that aren't dissimilar to the housekeeping uniform at the retreat center, just a different color.

"Dude, why are you having Rhys investigate Margie?" Lucky says to his brothers.

"That's exactly what I was just asking," Jack says.

I glance back at the bar.

Bartender's occupied, and clearly, they feel comfortable talking about their business here.

Curtains must be effective, because I can't hear any distinct words from the conversations of the other groups of people here.

"Just watching out for all of you," Decker says.

"You've been writing too much suspicious crap," Lucky tells him.

"Look, if she'd shown up five years ago? Before Theo got accidentally famous and Emma fell for Jonas fucking Rutherford and Sabrina hooked up with the guy who made a fortune inventing those self-sealing cereal bags, I'd have been like, cool, whatever, don't tell Dad who you really are, but now? Now, we're too close to people who are people, you know?"

I have no clue how I keep a straight face through that.

Margie could buy the whole town and have enough left over for dessert.

"I heard Margie met Jonas and went basically catatonic at work today," Jack says.

"Can confirm," I say. "Firsthand witness."

And it's mostly true.

She freaked the fuck out.

I know they say she eats sharks for breakfast, but the woman has a soft side. She's not all steel and meticulous business calculations.

She also makes friends with old ladies and delivers peace offerings to guys she hit while defending herself.

And don't tell me she has to be doing the housekeeping work she was hired for herself, though I'm still not certain that's not some angle related to her real day job.

Maybe she's also undercover to look for an angle for a hostile takeover of the retreat center.

Who knows?

"You almost went catatonic when you first met him too," Lucky says to Jack.

"I did not," Jack objects.

"Didn't you though?"

"I was changing his kid's diaper the first time I met him. It was the smell."

That doesn't make any sense to me initially until I remember that Jonas didn't know his oldest kid existed for the first almost two years of his life.

Not Emma's fault, the triplets have told me on more than one occasion. She apparently tried to get in touch with him, but his team didn't think her messages were real.

Decker looks at me. "So? Find anything?"

Yeah, your sister's a liar and she's still hiding something.

She's also someone who could get past my defenses if she wasn't lying because I fucking like her. Appreciate her. Respect her. Something. "She makes terrible coffee, but she's a damn good housekeeper."

Decker's eyes narrow like he knows I'm selectively telling the truth. "And?"

"And I'll keep digging and watching. She made friends at the retreat center with some old lady who's writing her first book."

"Dude, yeah, she texted me about that yesterday." Lucky kicks Decker's shoe. "She probably would've texted you directly if you weren't so Judgy McJudgypants."

"She knows Mom and Dad don't have any money, right?" Decker replies. "That staying in our cabin for a few weeks is all she's getting?"

"Knock it off," Jack mutters.

"Taking her side?" Decker mutters back.

"I'm fucking Switzerland, okay?"

Lucky sits straighter. "You have a new girlfriend named Switzerland, and you didn't tell us?"

"Don't be a literal asshat," Decker says. "You know what he meant."

Movement near the door catches my attention, though I probably would've sensed her even if I hadn't seen her.

The woman radiates the energy of a squirrel and the tenacity of a bulldog.

Don't think that part's genetic.

The triplets don't have it the way she does, at any rate. They're good dudes, all motivated in their own ways, and they get their shit done, but they can't touch Margot and her capacity to tackle the world.

Maybe all three of them together could get eighty percent of the way to her determination and drive.

And if that's all she was—a businesswoman with drive and tenacity and an endless capability to keep going until she gets what she wants—I'd be telling Decker right now who she is.

But I'm still stuck on remembering the way she helped the server at that dinner, and the way she's smiled at my friend and his brothers, and the unexpected ways that she's not the high-maintenance spoiled rich woman I would've expected.

There's more to Margot Merriweather-Brown than meets the eye.

Jack and Decker notice she's here too.

Lucky can't see the door with the angle of the curtains and his seat, so he's slower to realize something's shifted, but as soon as Bandit leaps to his feet and makes the softest woof of greeting I've ever heard a dog make, Lucky turns too.

faking cinderella

Margot sails through the speakeasy like she owns the place, and based on the way Decker slides another look my way, I think he thinks so too.

Like he hadn't expected his secret half sister to have the poise and confidence she does.

I shrug at him.

His cousin's a barista from a small mountain town, raised by a single mother, and she'd walk through a building like that.

He sighs again and slouches back in his seat like he's thinking the same thing.

"Seriously, lay off researching serial killers," Jack mutters to him while gesturing for Bandit to sit, which he does, though he's still panting excitedly. "You're getting stupid paranoid."

"You can't write a dystopian novel where serial killers are the only people who survived without researching serial killers," Decker mutters back.

"Bad move, switching away from litRPG," Lucky says.

"Dumb decision," Jack agrees. "Keep doing what's working."

"Maybe they'll both work," Decker shoots back. "Won't know if I don't try."

"Or you're afraid you've peaked and you're running away."

"Hi, guys." Margot—Margie, I remind myself—stops at the edge of our circle, bending to love all over Bandit as she smiles broadly like she wasn't glaring at me an hour ago. "Have room for one more?"

Lucky leaps up and pulls an extra chair over for her, so she's across the little circle from me, her back firmly to the door, the dog within reach.

Other than a brief nod, she doesn't much acknowledge my presence. Irritating.

No matter who I am and what I know about her, I'd appreciate a little reciprocation to the way I'm distracted by how her soft lavender T-shirt hugs her breasts under a darker purple flannel.

I swallow and make myself look away.

She's a shark, I remind myself.

With a heart, myself answers back.

Great.

Now I'm arguing with myself in rhyme.

Should've stayed home, except I get to show off how I can be places it's not as easy for her security guy to get into by being here.

A server drops by and takes orders from the three of us who've basically just arrived, then disappears to get our drinks and appetizers.

"Did you come straight from work?" Margie asks Lucky once we're alone again.

"Yeah."

"He usually does," Jack says. "Dude's a workaholic."

"Like you can talk," Decker says.

"Hi, kettle," Jack replies.

Margie—sure, she's still Margie tonight—smiles more while scratching Bandit's head, and I wonder if she's feigning that hunger in her eyes.

Not ruthless hunger.

I want to belong hunger.

Could that honestly be most of what she wants? To have more family? Because hers is shitty but she still believes in the power of genetics making family?

"So all three of you love your jobs and work hard," she says. "Got it."

"How's your job going?" Lucky asks her. "Everyone being cool?"

"Yes. It's good. Nicer than my last job. Thank you."

I stifle a snort.

She doesn't look in my direction, but her shoulders seem to tighten beneath her flannel.

Decker glances at me, then at her. "Heard you ran into a movie star."

She tucks a strand of dark, curly hair behind her ear, then adjusts her glasses. "That was very unexpected."

"He's one of the owners," Jack tells her, which I'm certain she already knew.

"I didn't run into the owners much in any of my previous jobs. Nor were they ever famous."

I don't react to that lie either.

Mostly.

And even if I did, she's charging ahead. "So, again…unexpected. Jack, I didn't realize when you mentioned it the other day that explosives engineering is a real thing and not a joke? That sounds dangerous and fascinating. I have this friend back home who'd basically kill me if I didn't demand to know how often you touch TNT."

Lucky winces. "Here we go…"

"Dammit," Decker adds.

Jack, though, has straightened and is grinning. "I blow shit up all the time."

Bandit makes another soft woof in agreement.

"He has to do a lot of math and boring stuff to do the blowing up. The math is most of his job," Decker says.

"But he never talks about that, so we banned him from talking about his job in public for at least like, five straight years," Lucky tells Margie. "Maybe six or seven at this point."

"He goes on and on and on," Decker agrees.

"Because it's fucking cool," Jack says.

"I've sometimes wished I could blow up a few things some of my exes left behind," Margie says.

"Oh, we have a potato gun for that," Lucky says. "Anything you want to destroy, we shove it into a potato and launch it into the mountains."

"Very cathartic," Jack agrees.

"Until your neighbor gets pissed that you're littering," Decker says.

"Is your neighbor that far away, or is your potato gun a little… impotent?" Margie asks him, sending Lucky and Jack in howls.

"My neighbor's that annoying," is Decker's only response, which makes Margie smile bigger.

"No girlfriends for any of you?" she asks.

"Jack's fucking Switzerland, but he won't tell us if that's her real name or if she's undercover," Lucky reports.

Jack flips him off. "We took a vow of bachelorhood. All three of us. No real girlfriends."

Margie's brows go up, and I don't think that's an act. "Whoa. Really?"

The three brothers share a look, then all three shift their gazes to her.

"We don't talk about this in public—" Lucky starts.

"And we're not talking about it now," Decker mutters.

"Think we should, bro." Jack tilts his head at Margie. "She might be collateral damage."

"Are you fucking serious?" Decker replies.

"Two against one here," Lucky says. "We have to tell her. Jack's right. It might've hit her too."

I sit straighter.

Margie sits straighter. "Something genetic?" she says quietly.

All three of them shake their heads.

Lucky's as serious as I've ever seen him. Jack's grim. Decker's clearly annoyed.

"No, it's not genetic," Decker says.

"It's a curse," Lucky whispers.

"You met Sabrina?" Jack says. "She doesn't even know about this."

"She knows about this and does us the favor of not mentioning it anywhere," Decker says.

Lucky sweeps a glance around the room and leans in closer. "But she doesn't know it's real."

"You're…cursed?" Margie whispers.

The three of them share another look, then nod at her.

She blinks once.

I'm doing a little more than blinking. Might involve my lips twitching in a telltale manner and having to clear my throat to keep from having a verbal reaction.

Decker glares at me. "Not funny. It's fucking real."

"If any of us ever fall in love, our sibling connection will go ka-boom," Jack says.

Margie opens her mouth, then shuts it again.

Credit where credit is due—I believe this is an honest reaction.

Mine is too.

I'm almost laughing for the first time in—actually, I don't remember how long.

Decker shoves me. "Don't make me rewrite your character, asshole."

Jack and Lucky are leaning so close to Margie that I almost can't hear what they're saying. But Jack's dog has returned to his side, snout on Jack's knee like he's saying it's okay, buddy, I'm here. I got you.

"Back in high school, there was this chick who was Wiccan," Jack's saying.

"I thought Wiccans generally did no harm," Margie murmurs.

"They're not supposed to, but she was like, still learning," Lucky says. "And Jack pissed her off."

"You helped," Jack replied.

"I walked into a landmine, dude. I didn't know you were telling her witchcraft isn't real."

"Biggest mistake of your life," Decker says.

"Witchcraft is so real," Lucky agrees.

Jack winces. "It…is."

"So you pissed off a witch and she cursed you with having to choose between your brotherhood and finding true love?" Margie says.

"Yes," all three of them answer together.

Once more, Margie—Margot Merriweather-Brown—does a fish impersonation for a moment, and fuck me if it's not the cutest thing I've ever seen.

"So you all—you never date?" she says.

They share a look.

"We all…have fun…on occasion, but never let it get serious," Lucky finally says.

"Don't want to risk it," Jack agrees.

"Fuckin' right," Decker says.

"If we didn't date at all, people would get suspicious," Lucky adds. "But it's all good. We're happy this way."

"Wow," she murmurs as Decker and Jack both nod.

"You've never been cursed?" I ask her.

She looks me square in the eye. "It would explain a few things, but wouldn't it for everyone?"

I lift a shoulder.

"I didn't think it was real," Jack says, "but then…"

"Then," Decker and Lucky agree, both nodding.

"It's definitely real," Jack concludes.

"And she bought the damn house next to mine," Decker mutters.

"And she won't lift the curse," Lucky adds.

"We've asked," Jack says.

Lucky nods. "She'd probably consider it if Decker would give her the greenhouse, but he's being stubborn."

I look at Margie.

She slides an I have no idea what they're talking about either look at me, then turns back to the triplets. "So you think I got hit with the side blast because it was related to siblinghood?"

"Possible," Jack says. "You ever had back luck in love?"

Margie does her one-eyed squint. "My best friend just hooked up with my ex, and it was…messy."

And there she goes telling another lie that's almost the truth.

The triplets share another look.

"She got hit with the blast," Lucky says.

"Sorry, Margie," Jack adds.

I clear my throat. "Did I too?" I deadpan, since they all know about Felice and my stepbrother.

"No, you just have shitty luck," Decker replies.

Margie chokes on a giggle, then clears her throat. "Maybe I can talk to your neighbor about an uncursing. Since I'm innocent—"

"Are you though?" I ask.

All four of them look at me.

So does the dog.

I pause just long enough to get a look from Margie, then I gesture to my face, where there's still the barest hint of evidence of how Margie and I met. My hair has a little more, but I've been wearing hats all week to cover it, and I'm about to shave my beard down to scruff to get rid of the purple streaks in it too. "This doesn't reek of innocence."

"Wasn't her fault," Jack says.

"Agreed. Decker fucked up," Lucky says.

They both look pointedly at him.

They know he did it on purpose.

Margie undoubtedly knows he did it on purpose too.

"Hey, Margie, are you allergic to macadamias?" Decker says, prompting snorts from his two brothers.

Smooth transition away from a loaded conversation, that was not.

But Margie goes with it. She shakes her head. "No, are you?"

"All three of us," Lucky says. "We thought for a hot minute that our friend Laney's dad was our dad because he is too, but she took a test, and we went back to square one. Until you popped up."

She purses her lips and nods. "I'm not. And neither—neither was my mom. We used to eat them as a special treat."

"We got to eat frog guts for a special treat," Lucky says.

"Frog guts?"

All three of them grin.

"That's what our mom calls Chex Mix."

"Dude, she hated making that stuff."

"We wanted it all the time."

"Shit, I want some right now."

"You think we can find somebody to run to the grocery store and bring us some?"

I watch Margie watching them, her smile softening with every word of praise that they utter about Chex Mix.

Is she faking?

Or is she really enjoying watching the three of them in their natural element?

They're entertaining as hell on a normal day—clearly—and I doubt she sees this kind of behavior in the boardrooms and offices of her real life.

Which isn't to say I'm softening toward her.

It's to say I'm trying to understand her.

There's a difference.

"Does that one app work here?" she asks them. "What's it called? MunchieGoGo?"

"Nah, the only driver we had retired after less than a year because people tipped like crap and he made more money flashing his junk on GrippaPeen," Jack says.

"I didn't know Theo was the MunchieGoGo guy," Lucky says. "Why don't you tell me this stuff?"

"He wasn't. Derrick Swayman did GrippaPeen too. He made money. Just not Theo-level money."

"Theo—is that the retreat co-owner with the tattoos and baby?" Margie asks.

Again, like she doesn't know.

"Yeah, he's like, super famous in some circles, but he retired from GrippaPeen too when he hooked up with Laney. His wife. They hated each other in high school. You know how it goes. He was her best friend's bad boy brother, she was the good girl in line to take over the family company…"

"Yeah, Margie knows how that goes," I agree, since she's also clearly the good girl in line to take over her family company.

I'll probably hear about this later, but apparently I'm in a mood for fun too.

Or possibly a mood to keep her on her toes.

She slides me a flat look before rolling her eyes at the triplets. "A man catches you reading a romance novel and thinks he can mock you for life."

"I'd never mock. I know what you can do to a man who pisses you off."

She gestures to her face, her smile not reaching her eyes. "Honestly, that's just the start, now that I know I have a brother who's an explosives engineer."

Jack beams at her. "I can hook you up, Margie. Just say the word."

"Still want Chex Mix," Lucky says, and I can't tell if he's missing the undertones of my conversation with Margie, or if he's just stuck on thinking about his stomach. "They should serve it here."

"Rock paper scissors for who goes to get it," Decker replies.

Jack rears back, no longer happy. "Fuck you."

Margie and I both glance at him.

Decker snickers.

Lucky grins. "He always loses."

"Every time," Decker agrees.

"Usually over changing diapers for our friends' kids," Lucky adds.

"I can go make a Chex Mix run," Margie says.

All three of them immediately object.

Dumbasses.

They're getting played.

"Rock paper scissors for it?" Margie says over my soft snort.

The triplets once again share a look.

"Whoa," Lucky mutters. "This changes everything."

"She's not our quadruplet, dude. It doesn't change everything," Decker says.

Jack frowns at them. "What if she is, and Mom and Dad just didn't tell us they didn't want a girl?"

Margie pinches her lips together, but the giggle still slips out. "They let you use explosives?"

Lucky busts up laughing. Even Decker cracks a real, broad smile. "Hell, yeah. Rock paper scissors for the Chex Mix run. She might be worse than you, Jack."

All four of them put their hands in.

And fucking Margie—fucking Margie—blinks fast and hard.

Because her eyes have gone shiny.

Either she's one hell of an actress, or she meant that part she said about wanting to get to know her family.

I need to find out more about her sister and parents.

Her relationship with them.

If she might actually be that poor little rich girl looking for a place to belong.

Because that sad little boy that I was twenty years ago when my mom passed—he relates hardcore to wanting a place to belong.

To wanting a real family.

I should've had a family, but Felice decided my stepbrother was more her speed.

She wanted me to leave the military and move back home.

She wanted to get engaged, but then couldn't pick a wedding date.

We finally picked a wedding date, and then she couldn't find the right venue or the right flowers or the right cake.

But it wasn't the wedding.

It was me.

She didn't want me.

She wanted my stepbrother.

The stepbrother she's already married to, barely a year after she was supposed to finally marry me. The stepbrother whose baby she's expecting early next year.

The stepbrother she was probably cheating on me with for most of our prolonged engagement.

Margie and the triplets shake their fists three times before picking their plays, and then Decker, Lucky, and Margie all play paper while Jack plays rock.

Jack howls in outrage while Decker, Lucky, and Margie dissolve into laughter.

"You planned that!" Jack bellows.

"Dude, no," Decker gasps.

"Couldn't have—not that good," Lucky agrees.

"I'll still go get the Chex Mix," Margie says. She's laughing so hard she's wiping her eyes.

And she does exactly what she's offered.

With a smile on her face still, even when she gets back twenty minutes later.

Glowing.

Happy.

With a bag of Skittles that she offers to me, like she's noticed that I always grab myself a bag from the staff vending machine to eat on my way home.

Fuck me.

I know it's equally likely that she ran to the store herself, or that she had her security guy bring her the Chex Mix and the Skittles, but the way her entire body softens as she watches the triplets grab their own bags, and then the way she includes me in her smiles when I take the bag of Skittles—I can't deny even to myself anymore how much I think I like this woman.

Lies and secrets and complications and all.

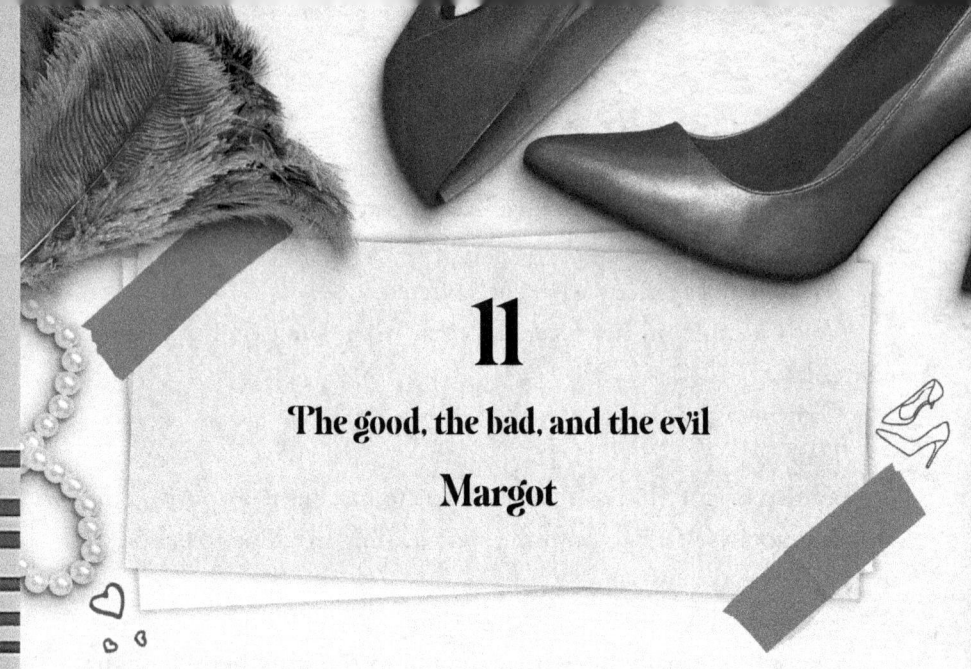

11

The good, the bad, and the evil

Margot

Aside from Rhys's occasional little murmurs or pauses or looks at opportune times to remind me that he could destroy me at any point if he decides he no longer wants my endorsement, this evening is everything I've wanted.

Needed, if I'm being honest.

Laughing with my half brothers? Being let behind the curtain with their cursed dating lives and Jack's bad luck with rock paper scissors and the new direction Decker's going with his novels?

Snaggletooth Creek, Colorado, will never be home for me. My heart belongs in New York.

But the thirsty part of my heart is taking a long, deep gulp of cool water after living in a love-parched desert.

"If someone handed you a million dollars tomorrow and told you that you could do whatever you want with it, what would it be?" Lucky asks as we sip our drinks and eat the Chex Mix beside the assorted appetizers that they ordered from the bar.

Rhys clears his throat across from me.

All three of my half brothers shift a look at him.

He pounds himself on the chest. "Swallowed a little wrong."

Once again, I'm torn between wanting to throttle him and respecting his courage.

Lucky looks back at me. "No thinking. Gut answer."

"I'd donate it to a cause to help save the polar bears," I say.

That's been Daphne's mission since she learned in elementary school that the polar ice caps are melting. So I can confidently speak to the importance of my biggest cause, even if it's technically not mine.

"Dude, did you hear that there's a new kind of bear?" Jack says. "A polar bear mated with a grizzly bear. Isn't that terrifying?"

Lucky grins. "Evolution in action. It's a beautiful thing."

"Until you stumble across one on the trail."

"Polar bears aren't this far south," Decker says. "Pretty sure you're fine unless you're going somewhere way far north for a trip you're not talking about."

"Or unless they migrate south," Rhys says.

All three of the triplets gape at him.

He sucks in a grin as they each start protesting, and once again, he's both irritating and intriguing.

Who was he before his ex shredded his heart?

And don't tell me she didn't.

You can hear it in his voice and see it in his eyes when he talks about it.

"You ever see a polar bear in the wild, Margie?" he asks me over the triplets' continued insistence that polar bears aren't migrating this far south.

"I have not," I reply, because Margie Johnson most definitely hasn't left the lower forty-eight to go far enough north to see a polar bear in the wild.

We're not talking about the things Margot Merriweather-Brown has done.

Especially since Daphne doesn't know about that one trip I took to the northern parts of Alaska and would basically die if she knew I'd seen a polar bear in the wild when she hasn't.

"Huh," Rhys says.

Like he knows I'm lying.

I hold his gaze for a moment, getting an innocent stare right back.

"When would she have seen a polar bear?" Lucky says to him. "Dude. You really so insecure about her getting the better of you when you met that you're acting like she'd lie about that?"

Rhys breaks eye contact with me and shrugs at Lucky. "Never would've guessed by my history that I've been to all seven continents, but I have. So you never know."

"All seven?" Jack says, and they're off again, demanding to know how and when and which continent is Rhys's favorite.

It's fun watching them interact.

The triplets, I mean.

Studying their relationship with each other. Spotting the places they have inside jokes and shared stories, and the places where they've done their own things.

Daphne and I have more stories of doing our own things, especially the past decade or so, than we have together.

But she's still my favorite person.

Just like you can tell the triplets are each other's favorite people.

The evening passes too quickly, with me liking my brothers more and more with each passing minute, and before long, Decker's asking for the bill.

I reach for my wallet in my back pocket—for cash, of course—but he gives me the annoyed look of a man who doesn't want to have to tell me he's got it for me to know I need to put my wallet away.

And that makes me suck in a smile.

Not because I can afford to pay for dinner and drinks tonight, but because I swear that's likely how I look every time Daphne has offered to pay for lunch out or the bill at her favorite cheese shop in Athena's Rest when I've gone to visit her.

"Thank you," I murmur instead of any of the number of other things I'd like to say.

Like *no, really, it would be an honor to get this tonight.*
Or *I'd like to pay rent for your cabin.*
Or *can we do this again every night?*

"No rock paper scissors for the bill?" Rhys asks.

"We let Mr. Big Bucks handle it and pay him back in other ways," Jack replies.

Lucky grins. "Like being on call when he has a hypochondriac moment."

"Which is all the time," Jack mutters.

Decker flips him off. "Is *not*."

"*Lucky, look at my big toenail. Is it a different color from my other toenails?*" Lucky replies, falsetto, sounding nothing at all like Decker.

"*I dropped a kettlebell on it,*" Decker shoots back.

"How do you pay him back?" I ask Jack, who's rolling his eyes at the other two.

"Research assistant when he gets super geeky in his novels, sometimes indulge his never-gonna-happen plans about accidentally shooting a firecracker at the neighbor's house."

"So… I should offer to clean his house?" I ask.

"Only if you want to learn more than you ever wanted to know this fast," Lucky replies.

Jack nods vehemently. "On top of the wall of fan mail that's honestly embarrassing, he has some weird collections that you don't want to stumble upon without actually liking him for who he is and also hearing the backstory, which he won't share until you pass like seventeen more tests."

"Thanks, guys," Decker says. "Appreciate knowing who I'm sacrificing dating for."

Jack and Lucky both grimace.

I glance at Rhys, who's glancing at me, a little bit of *yeah, they're sometimes a little far gone* in his expression, which makes me swallow another smile of my own.

"If you want me to talk to her—" I start, but all three jump in with instant *nos*.

"You'd have to admit why it mattered," Lucky says to me.

"And she won't believe someone as hot as you would be asking because you wanted to date one of us," Jack adds.

Decker pulls a face. "Seriously? I just ate."

"We only just found out we're related," Jack says. "How many times have you passed an attractive woman on the street and thought, *oh, she's pretty*, and then wondered if you thought that because she looks kinda like you, which, duh, is attractive because we're hot ourselves, but not knowing who our dad is means that maybe we would've been related?"

"Don't ever say any of that out loud again," Decker says.

Jack grins at me like he's irritating Decker on purpose, which makes me once again suck in a smile.

Daphne will love these three.

Lucky looks at Rhys. "As someone who's not related to her and someone who probably has reason to actively dislike her, would you say Margie's hot?"

Thoughts of my sister flee my brain as my stomach dips and my heart goes for a run without permission.

I lock eyes with Rhys again.

He makes a show of looking me up and down, getting a shove from Jack and a glare from Decker and a soft growl from Lucky.

"You asked," Rhys says to Lucky.

"I didn't mean mentally strip her while we sit here, asshole."

Rhys shrugs. "She's all right." He tilts his head at me. "Maybe if I picture her as a blonde…"

Jack shoves him again while I stifle a twitch at one more of Rhys's little pokes at knowing who I really am, then all four men go still and silent.

A second later, the server pops into our little curtained area with a point-of-sale machine. Decker hands her his credit card without looking at the total, then signs the machine and takes his card back.

"Whatever you're up to, make sure it's memorable," she says to the group of us as she departs with a grin.

"Sometimes I hate living in a small town," Decker mutters.

"Dude. Sometimes you hate everything," Jack replies.

"If too many people figure it out—"

"Your dad has no idea, does he?" I ask softly.

All three of them, plus Rhys, look at me.

"Why would you think that?" Jack says.

"He took a DNA test himself, didn't he? Why would he do that if he knew it would make a record for you to link with—or not link with—later?"

The amount of silent communication going on between the triplets is telling.

"We got it for him for his birthday," Lucky tells me.

"I did the log-in. He doesn't have it," Jack adds.

"Hates computers," Decker says.

"*Hates* computers," Lucky agrees.

"He mostly wanted to know where his ancestors came from," Jack says.

"Your mom didn't object?" I ask.

All three of them shake their heads.

"We don't think she knows it can be used to find other people you're related to," Decker says. "Both of our parents—they mostly use computers to play Frenemy Crush or pay their bills or look up what the neighbors' houses are selling for. And even if they hear their friends talking about MatchDNA, they don't know we took the test."

Maybe it's the margarita, or maybe it's feeling like they're letting me into a closer inner circle, but I don't school my face fast enough, and all three of them give me matching embarrassed smiles.

"It was mostly a joke," Lucky says. "Us taking the test. One of my patients kept telling me I should make sure we were related—"

Jack picks up the story. "And then we got tipsy on eggnog while we were talking about it—"

"And a few weeks later, our entire world got turned upside down," Decker finishes.

Lucky shakes his head. "All because of eggnog and a joke."

I swallow.

Then swallow again.

"For what it's worth," I say quietly, "I'm sorry it turned your world upside down, but I'm not sorry we had an opportunity to meet."

Lucky smiles at me.

Jack does too.

Even Decker softens.

"And I still won't tell anyone," I add. "Any of it."

Rhys eyes me.

I ignore him.

I *won't* tell anyone else. Daphne deserves to know, but she can keep the secret.

She and I both know what my father would do if he found out about the triplets.

But I also know what I'd do if he found out.

And I'm glad I have an attorney on retainer who has no loyalty to or business with my father. If the triplets—if my brothers—ever need her, they'll have her.

When I tell them my full truth, when they understand why it matters, when they agree to help me, *then* I'll have her already in their corner, ready for whatever my father might try to retaliate with.

He'll have to go through me and every ounce of firepower I can summon to get to them.

"Never know what life's gonna bring," Lucky says. "Curses aside, always tends to be a little good with the bad."

"Not always," Decker says.

"Pessimist to the end." Jack rolls his eyes. "You need someone to walk you to your car, Margie? Bandit and I would be happy to help."

"I've got her," Rhys says.

All three of them look at him again.

"What?" he says. "Can't let her get there first and booby-trap the place again."

Lucky grins at me. "Never let it be said nature doesn't rule over nurture."

And there I go, getting misty-eyed once more.

If I had to pick surprise brothers, I'd pick these three.

But I don't have to pick.

I just get them.

And hopefully, they'll still pick me back when they know who I am.

12

Wood and other wood

Margot

My body is so fucking tired.

It's a good thing Cyril's following me as I leave work on Thursday, because I'm so exhausted that I shouldn't be driving this van.

I don't get it.

I'm up late all the time in Manhattan. I work out five days a week and use a treadmill desk in my office. I regularly have a glass or two of wine, and I only had a single margarita last night—a light one at that—with the Chex Mix and other appetizers at the speakeasy.

But today—oh my god.

I make it to the cabin, then to my bedroom, and that's where I faceplant.

The next thing I know, it's almost seven, and there's a regular thumping outside my window.

I roll to my side and stifle a grunt as I peek out the window, noting two things at once.

First, something smells amazing.

And second, Rhys is splitting firewood.

He's in a short-sleeved black T-shirt that's stretched over his broad chest and thick arms, dark jeans that hug his hips and thighs, with a black ball cap on his head and scuffed brown work boots. I watch him methodically grab a piece of thick, round firewood, place it upright on a wooden chopping block, and then swing his axe to split it into smaller chunks.

The sun's dipped low and the sky peeking through the trees is a deep orange tinged in pink. I have the best show in the universe.

What is it about watching a big, bulky, grumpy man split a chunk of wood into smaller pieces that has my clit humming and my breasts tingling?

Competence porn, my brain answers for me.

Rhys might have taken every opportunity to subtly barb me about knowing my real identity last night, but he was also watching the door every time someone came in, and all day at work today, he showed up right when I needed a hand, either because a guest was getting too comfortable—like robe-and-towel guy in chalet three—or when I needed to move a piece of furniture to clean a spill on the carpet, or when I needed a task to escape being part of the photos my boss wanted to use on socials of the staff for staff appreciation day.

In some ways, him knowing my real identity is incredibly helpful.

He also helped me locate Mrs. Pinsley's water bottle, which she'd left in the dining room at breakfast, and he pretended he didn't hear one of my fellow housekeepers calling him a stud as he helped move tables for a workshop for a small group of children's book authors.

He's good at his job too.

And that's also attractive.

But not as attractive as this brute show of force as he splits firewood like it's warm butter.

I absently rub one of my breasts as I lean closer to the window.

Rhys grabs another piece of unsplit wood, balances it on one end on a chopping block made of a thick tree stump, and then makes one smooth, easy arc of the axe, bringing it down precisely in the middle of the log and making it fall off in two relatively even pieces before grabbing the next unsplit log from the pile behind him.

I lean closer to the window, prop my elbow on the ledge, and it promptly slides off, propelling me forward and making my face smush into the glass.

He pauses and looks my way as I straighten.

Our eyes meet, and I realize I'm still rubbing my breast, and that has me bolting up off the bed and out of sight.

I hover against the wall beside the window, silently chastising myself.

Don't get turned on by your roommate chopping wood. Your roommate who could blow your cover at any minute. Your roommate who clearly wants more from you than just a job.

This is too complicated, and you know better, Margot.

Cyril has reservations about taking Rhys as backup, but it's a concern born out of the awkward situation more than a concern based on Rhys's employment history and demonstrated competence.

There's a knock on the window.

I rub my eyes, stretch my limbs, and then step back into view. "What?" I say through the glass.

Rhys holds up the axe. "You want a swing?"

Whatever I expected, it wasn't that. "Are you serious?"

"Saw you staring at my…axe. Looked like you wanted to use it."

I wasn't staring at his axe, and we both know it, but using it—

Oh my god.

Yes.

Daph wouldn't hesitate. She'd already be in the yard by now.

I don't know why I'm hesitating, because while Daph would do it for the fun, I'd do it to feel like a powerful beast.

I start to smile. "Can you teach me?"

He grunts, then nods.

I fly through changing into jeans and a flannel shirt, and then into my hiking boots, and I take off outside, leaving my fake glasses in the bedroom.

Rhys has flipped on one of the outdoor flood lights so that we can see what we're doing as the sun dips lower and lower in the sky, and he's also stacked most of the wood he's split on the pile near the back of the garage. The temperatures have dropped, and there's a chilly wind blowing through that doesn't seem to faze him at all in his T-shirt.

He hands me a pair of work gloves. "Only other pair," he says when they swallow my hands. "Here. Put on safety glasses too. Then grab a log."

I slide the safety glasses onto my face, then pick up a log off the unsplit pile.

He sighs. "Not that one."

"What's wrong with this one?"

"See the knots? Harder to split."

He rustles through the pile and selects a different log, this one so gray it's almost blue, with nary a knot in the sides of it anywhere. "Ever do this before?"

"Nope."

"Harder than it looks."

"Is that a challenge?"

He smirks. "Of course not."

It's totally a challenge.

But if he's expecting me to try to prove something right off the bat, he's wrong.

I know I can.

I also know I need to learn how before I can.

"Any tips or tricks I should know before I start swinging?" I ask with a nod toward the axe.

He grabs it at the end, then flips it in the air and catches it just beneath the head. "Don't hit yourself with this part."

"Don't maim myself. Got it."

"Don't get cocky."

"Have to log a few hours at the chopping block first?"

The man blinks at me in slow motion. "Did you just—"

Make a terrible joke? Yes, and again, Daph would be proud.

I smirk at him. "I'm smart, I'm pretty, I'm rich, and I'm funny."

He pinches his lips together.

And then he does something far worse than telling me I'm not any of those four things I just smugly proclaimed to be, and he lines his body up behind mine.

He wraps his thick arms around my shoulders and slides his hands down my arms until he's guiding the axe into my hands with me, gripping the handle at the bottom with one hand and near the top with the other.

"This is a maul," he says, his voice low and silky in my ear. "Goal is to get the sharp, pointy side square in the middle of the log with enough force to split it."

No, I'm fairly certain the goal is to use his body to intimidate me into not making any more bad puns about logs.

And it's working.

My mouth has gone drier than the desert and my pulse is inching into so this kind of wood is sensual too territory.

I make a noise of acknowledgment.

"You can use various techniques. Beginners will often do this, here." He lifts my arms straight above my head, so the maul head is high, but not in danger of falling on my head if I drop it, sliding my higher hand lower as we raise the axe—the maul, I mean. "You want to be holding it like this when it reaches its pinnacle. Then swing it down hard. But first, let's make sure you're lined up properly."

We lower the axe—maul—and test how far I am from the log that needs to be split. The heat radiating from his body cuts through the chill of the night and makes me warm everywhere.

And I do mean everywhere.

"Good, just like that," he murmurs.

My nipples turn themselves inside out and my vagina pulses to life.

Not that she's regularly asleep.

It's more that she gets bored easily.

Don't catch a crush for a man who's using you, dumbass, my brain whispers.

Shut up, I whisper back. They're all using me.

Rhys's breath tickles my ear, his voice teasing my eardrums. "Now, lift the maul—just like that, good—and when you bring it down, squat instead of bending. Like so."

One hand strokes down my arm over my flannel, down to my hip, and he hunches lower, single-handedly guiding the maul down slowly while he aligns my body with his into proper form.

His thighs are beneath my hamstrings.

His crotch against my ass.

His chest to my back.

Still holding my hands in just one of his meaty paws, helping me through the motion two more times, a bulge against my ass telling me I'm not the only one affected, even if he's not rubbing himself all over me. "Got it?"

"Mm-hmm," I croak out.

"Whenever you're ready then."

He releases me and steps back, the heat of his body replaced with cool night air, and I falter as I swing the maul down, completely missing the log.

Well played, Rhys O'Malley.

Well. Fucking. Played.

And you know what?

I laugh out loud at how terribly bad my swing is.

Is it bad because this truly is harder than it looks though?

Or is it bad because his personal demonstration has every carnal nerve ending in my body sitting up and asking why he's still sleeping on the couch?

Either way, this lesson is highly enjoyable.

I reach into my back pocket for my phone, but my gloves are too big, so I have to pull them off before I can get a grip on it. Then I hold it out to Rhys. "Take a video of me trying again? My sister will laugh for days."

His brows briefly pinch together, but he pulls his own gloves off and takes my phone, our fingers brushing, and it's only a lifetime of practice being poised that keeps me from visibly shivering—in the good way—at the contact.

"You honestly like your sister," he says, aiming my phone at me while I line up on my own to swing at the log again after putting my gloves back on.

"I do."

"Why?"

"Because she's the absolute best." I swing the maul down, and this time, I hit the log.

Not in the middle though.

I hit it right at the edge, sending a small chunk flying one direction while the rest of the log teeters, then spins, then falls off the splitting block.

"Well done," Rhys says.

His dry delivery cracks me up.

And me laughing earns another squinty stare.

"What?" I ask.

"Who are you?"

"Seriously?"

He lowers my phone. "The internet says you're going to own half of Manhattan someday."

"I've heard that rumor. Pretty sure my ex-fiancé started it."

"You don't want it?"

"I'd take it, and I'd be good at running it all."

He lifts a brow.

I grip the maul in both hands and face him. "You have dinner in the oven inside."

"So?"

"So security isn't your entire personality. You like to cook, and you like to cook food that tastes good too. It's obviously more to you than a necessary function. Business isn't my entire personality either. I also adore my sister, and I've realized sometime in the past few years that there's more to a successful life than a business ledger. So I can absolutely rule Manhattan someday, but I will also make time to be a kick-ass aunt when Daph has kids, and I'll make time to walk along the beach and feel the sand between my toes, and I'll stand on a mountain and laugh at myself when I'm terrible at chopping wood. I want to be a person, not a robot."

The wind blows through again, carrying a few yellow aspen leaves and the subtle scent of woodsmoke while Rhys studies me.

I get it.

Powerful women get reputations for being completely heartless.

Thank fuck for Daphne, or I probably would be. She inherently understood her own humanity from the time she was born, and she taught me mine. I might be older, but she's wiser in so many ways.

I grab the log and straighten it while Rhys watches, then I line myself up.

Daph talks about a weekend every year back in Athena's Rest, her home in upstate New York, where she and her best friend, Bea, head out to Bea's brother's farm to help him split wood for winter.

Maybe I'll get good enough that I can participate this year.

Or next.

I don't know when wood-splitting weekend is. Maybe I'm missing it by being here now.

But I know that when I fling that axe—maul—down on the wood, and it splinters and cracks apart under the strength of my blow, I feel a different kind of power course through me.

It's primitive and raw and thrilling.

I bounce on my toes and grin at Rhys. "I did it!"

He's still staring at me like I'm a puzzle. "Good job."

I barely hear him.

I'm digging into the log pile for another log without many knots.

When I find it, I set it on the chopping block, and I picture my father's face on the top of the log when I swing the maul down.

And fuck, it feels good.

So I do it again, picturing my father's face and all.

And again.

And again, until I'm huffing with the effort, until my arms ache and my eyes are unexpectedly wet.

I pull off my gloves and swipe at my eyes.

"Who'd you imagine?" Rhys asks.

If he's said anything else since I got in the groove of pick, picture, split, I haven't heard him.

I give him a wry smile. "As if you'd get it out of me that easily."

"I imagine my stepfather."

I look at the pile of wood left to split.

It's mostly knotty and gnarled.

And then I look at Rhys, broad and thick, and I hold out the maul. "Need a few whacks? I left you the hard ones."

He's been stacking while I've been splitting, so there's not much for me to do besides watch while he takes powerful swings that easily split through the knotted wood.

Watch and get turned on.

Beefy displays of testosterone have never done it for me. Give me an intellectual man who can debate economic policies with me, and I'll be planning a strategic wedding in my head before I can stop myself, mostly because the lesson of Merriweather-Browns marry for business was drilled into my head so young that it's instinctive and I have to actively argue back against it now.

But this?

Contemplating where the wood came from, knowing there's a big wildfire risk in this part of the country, that these logs won't be fuel for any wildfires, but useful in heating the cabin instead now that we've split them down—there's something magic about that.

And something even more magic about watching Rhys use his power and strength to do the work efficiently and quickly.

Purposefully.

With enough vigor in his swing that I believe he really is picturing his stepfather the same way I was picturing my own father.

He checks his watch, then steps back from the pile. "Gotta check dinner," he grunts.

"I'll stack."

Once again, he looks at me.

Just looks at me, like he wants to ask me who I am again.

I smile. "Princesses can't stack firewood?"

He shakes his head and turns away. "Stack it fast or your dinner will be cold."

But even as he says it, he grabs five split logs and tucks them under his arm.

Not to stack.

He carries them inside, me watching his ass and getting warm in the cheeks.

I hustle through stacking wood, and I'm nearly done when I feel the same sensation I had when I left for work yesterday.

Something's off.

Like, hair-raising, adrenaline-pumping, off off.

Something snorts nearby in the thick brush with the browning leaves.

I'm facing the wood pile, but I turn slowly, so slowly, certain I'm about to come face-to-face with a mountain lion, when I spot something entirely different.

And holy fuck.

That's not a deer.

It's not one of the elk I saw wandering through the yard either.

It's much larger.

The rustling in the brush is coming from a full-blown daddy moose with daddy moose antlers.

Staring at me like I'm in his territory.

Wow.

He's beautiful.

Large as a horse—probably larger—with dark brown fur and a big bump between his shoulders and the most massive antlers I've ever seen, those fathomless dark orbs staring directly at me while he slowly chews something in his huge jaw.

But also—didn't one of my brothers make a comment last night about not fucking with moose?

And that is a moose. Like, the moose.

If there are bigger moose, I don't think I want to know.

It snorts at me again, big brown eyes narrowing.

I creep closer to the back of the house for lack of a better idea.

It lowers its head.

I'm contemplating making a mad dash for the front door when a window clatters open beside me, screen launching away from the house, and a long, thick arm reaches out.

"Inside," Rhys barks.

And that's the last warning I get before the moose charges as Rhys hauls me into the house through the window.

He flings me onto the bed and slams the window shut, then throws himself on top of me.

All of the air wooshes out of my lungs, and every muscle in my body tightens while I wait for the moose to sail through the window and maul us.

But there's no thud.

No glass shattering.

No shouting.

Just me and the mountain of a man pinning me to the quilt-topped mattress.

"Is it gone?" I gasp with the little air that's left in my lungs.

"It's staring," Rhys whispers.

And that's when I'm reminded that the firewood isn't the only wood at the cabin.

That solid lump against my right butt cheek is definitely not a leg, and if I thought that was a bulge against my ass earlier, I was mistaken.

Holy shit.

Is that real, or is he pranking me?

"Rhys?" I squeak out.

"Fuck on a rice cake, he's huge," he breathes.

"I'm noticing."

The rest of his body goes as stiff as the thick steel rod against my ass, and then he rolls off me, but he flings an arm out. "Don't move."

I twist my head enough to look at the window, and oh my god.

He's not kidding.

That moose—he is huge.

Huge and staring at us with a special kind of contempt.

Like he knows what Rhys is doing as he adjusts himself, and like the moose also knows that my clit is tingling and aching, and that if we didn't have a chaperone, I'd be seriously considering pulling the man back onto the bed.

But also— "He's majestic," I whisper.

"Rare," Rhys murmurs.

"Magnificent."

Rhys shifts closer to me, still angling himself between me and the moose at the window.

And that's when I notice his arm.

"You're bleeding."

He looks down, then back up at the moose, who snorts at us through the window, then saunters away. "Just a scrape."

It's fresh. I lean closer and touch his arm, twisting it to get a better look. "Did you cut it on the window?"

"Must've."

"There's a first aid kit in the bathroom. Stay here."

"I can—"

"You almost broke through a window to pull me to safety. Let me bandage your boo-boo, okay?"

His blue eyes finally lift to mine, and once again, I feel like he's studying my soul.

Like he wants to know every thought I've ever had, every happy moment, every sad moment, and everything in between, so that he can line it up with his own life's triumphs and tragedies and make sense of why we're here, together, now.

I lick my lips.

I haven't hired him yet.

He's not off-limits yet.

So I could kiss him.

I could kiss him and run my fingers through his hair and explore his broad chest and see if his hard-on is as notable as first impressions would suggest.

Sure, he's more or less blackmailing me, but I am definitely okay with kissing people who blackmail me.

It's a benefit to knowing I'll never fall in love.

His gaze flickers to my mouth, then back to my eyes, and fuck it.

Just fuck it.

I move slowly, giving him all the time in the world to push me away as I slide a hand up his chest and around his neck to the back of his head.

He's pliable and easy, his gaze flitting back and forth from my mouth to my eyes as I pull his head down to mine.

"I know better than to fuck people I want to work for," he murmurs.

"Maybe I can simply endorse you for…good behavior."

"I can't decide if you're the nicest evil person or the evilest nice person I've ever met."

"Let's just say I'm complicated."

His lips brush mine. My eyes drift closed, and I let myself feel.

The scratch of his short beard against my mouth.

His large hand sliding down my spine to linger just above my ass.

The scent of sweat and pine and something else intriguing but just out of reach.

The swipe of his tongue across my lower lip.

The desperate need tightening and twisting deep in my center.

I should be tending to his wound. It's the kind thing to do.

But I'm enjoying the way he's teasing my lips, the taste of his lips on my tongue while I thread my fingers through his thick hair.

There's no hurry.

No desperation.

Just a game of slow, languid kisses on a cool mountain night.

Exploring.

Learning.

Indulging.

His hand creeps lower on my back.

I angle closer, my legs parting wider to straddle his thigh.

He grabs my hip and pulls me tighter against his thick quad, his solid muscle right under my aching clit, and I barely stifle a whimper of satisfaction at the friction.

I deepen the kiss, my tongue wrangling with his while my hips start an ancient rhythm against his leg.

God, I miss physical touch.

Holding someone's hand.

An arm casually draped around my shoulders.

Stripping someone out of his shirt and fumbling with his pants.

Chopping wood is good.

Riding wood is better.

And I miss—

"Hello? You guys here?"

Rhys and I break apart, me panting, him drawing a deep breath as he swipes his thumb over his mouth.

His eyes are dark.

Hungry or haunted, I can't tell.

"Margie?" one of the triplets calls again. "Rhys?"

Definitely one of the triplets, but I can't tell them apart by voice yet.

Calling for me first suggests Lucky, but it could be Jack.

Definitely not Decker.

"Yes, we're in the bathroom," I call back, hearing the frantic desperation that comes from interrupted kissing in my voice.

I shove Rhys in that direction.

"Ahhh…" answers me from the direction of the living room.

"First aid!" I call, my voice higher and tighter. "Giving first aid!"

"Is that a euphemism?"

Rhys doesn't smirk.

Just watches me, quiet, poker-faced, while he lets me push him into the bathroom.

"What?" I whisper.

"I don't like how much I like you."

One more thing we have in common. "Everyone has issues. Happy to be yours."

He stares at me for another beat, and then he does the best-worst thing he could possibly do.

The man has the absolute audacity to smile back at me.

Eyes crinkling at the edges. The barest dimple appearing in his stubbled cheek. Front tooth just a little crooked.

He's fucking beautiful when he smiles.

And I don't know what to do with that.

I just know it's not good.

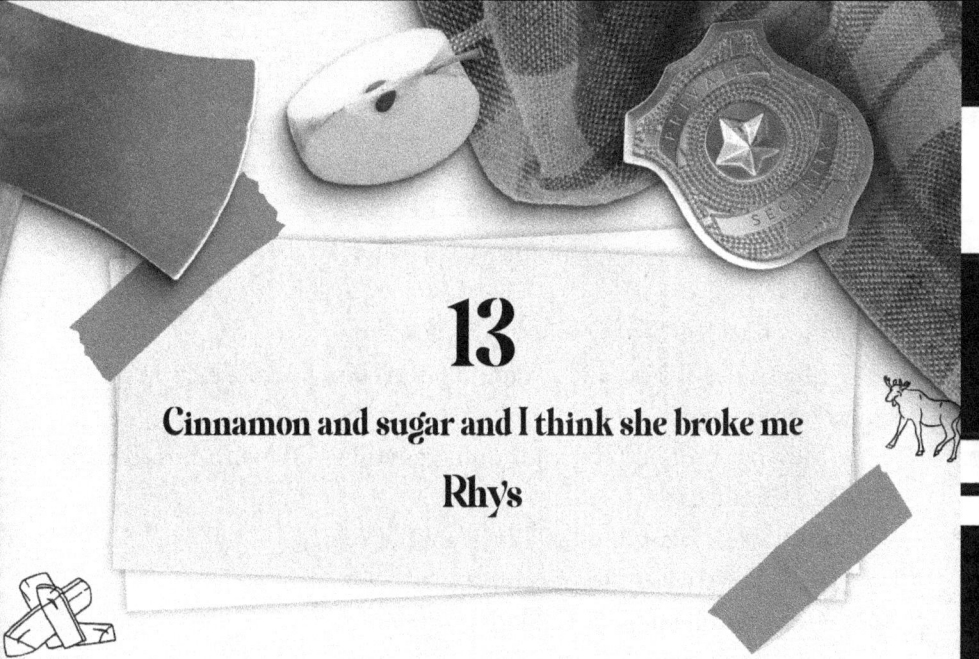

13

Cinnamon and sugar and I think she broke me

Rhys

L ucky, who showed up under the pretense of checking the propane tank, stays for dinner, which is good.

I need someone else here to keep me from doing anything stupid.

Like grabbing Margot and hauling her into the bedroom and tearing her clothes off and devouring her mouth and her skin and her pussy and basically any part of her that I can touch and lick and suck on and then some.

Fuck on a cupcake, she tasted like cinnamon and chocolate and temptation, and one kiss is not enough.

Especially after watching her split that wood.

It was equal parts funny and beautiful, and I'm just fucking gone.

I can barely keep my boner under control beneath the table, while she's carrying on as if we're practically strangers instead of two people whose tongues were wrestling twenty minutes ago.

"You don't have a dog like Jack does?" Margot—Margie is asking Lucky as we eat roasted potatoes and carrots and balsamic-glazed chicken that I barely taste for being distracted by everything about her.

"Nah, I work too many hours," Lucky says. "So I get to be a dog uncle instead, which is even better than being a real uncle, because real uncles have to change diapers. Plus, dogs don't have opinions the way almost-four-year-olds do. Ask me how I know."

"So that's why you chose geriatric care? Because it's easier than pediatrics?"

He chuckles. "Nah. Honestly, it picked me."

She smiles at him, and I want to punch him for stealing one of her smiles from me.

He's her brother. She's not doing anything else with him. This is platonic. Family-ish.

And I still want to punch his stupid face in.

And I rarely want to punch people.

Get a goddamn grip, O'Malley, I order myself.

"You like working with older people then?" she asks.

"Are you serious? I fucking love it. Seasoned people tell the best stories. They've seen things."

"And you have no stories of your own?"

The way the dude's eyes twinkle leaves no doubt. "Might have a few. We have fun around here. How about you, Rhys? Accidental face and hair dye job aside, you have any stories?"

I look at him, then at Margot, almost forget the question, remember it when she stifles a smile that should've been aimed at me, then look back at Lucky. "Yeah. I have a story or two."

"Anything about Decker?"

Focus, idiot. "I don't sell out my friends."

"Probably already heard it," Lucky says.

"Then you tell it."

"He's no fun," Lucky says to Margot.

"He taught me to chop firewood," she replies.

"Split," I correct, latching on to the one thing I have at ready disposal in my brain. "Split firewood."

Lucky smiles at her. "No shit? You any good?"

"I girlbossed it." She flexes a bicep.

He holds out a hand for a high five while my dick reacts to Margot Merriweather-Brown pretending to be Margie Johnson pretending to be a badass.

Yes, she did a decent job, but it's not like I gave her hard wood to split.

And it's not like she's not a girl boss in her real identity.

Fuck.

Now I'm thinking about how I've always been a sucker for girl bosses and how I currently have very hard wood.

"But then the moose showed up—" she says, pausing when Lucky's eyes bug out.

"You saw a moose?"

"He was in the backyard, and—"

"You saw a moose here?"

"Called nature, my friend," I interject.

Yeah. Yeah, that's good. That sounds normal. I'm getting a grip on myself.

Not the way I need to, but at least mentally.

Lucky looks at me. "I've lived here my entire life and I've never seen a moose here."

I shrug. "Maybe you don't have the moose touch."

Margot smiles, and I suddenly want to be the asshole.

I want to be the asshole who's been assuming the worst of her because she's an heiress lying about her identity, when I should want her to be the asshole so I quit liking her so much for all of the little things I've seen her doing for the people here.

Lucky looks between us.

Then looks closer between us, then starts puffing up his chest as he settles on staring at me.

Or, more appropriately, glaring.

Like he's just noticed me looking at his sister wrong even more than he thought I was last night, when I wasn't looking at her wrong at all.

And like he's enjoying having a sister to defend.

As if she needs anyone to defend her.

Goddammit, why won't this boner chill the fuck out? Why am I getting harder over the idea that I get to defend my territory?

She's not my territory.

I just want her to be.

Because you didn't learn your lesson the last time, dumbass? an intelligent part of my brain finally says.

"So I met this fascinating guy at the retreat center today," Margot says. She taps Lucky on the hand, getting his attention. "He said that he raises cows back home, and one day he decided to write a children's book about them as if they're actually matchmaking grannies setting up other farm animals. Isn't that adorable?"

Lucky angles another look at me before smiling back at her, suspicion still etched in his expression. "Yeah. That's cute."

"I love the retreat center," she says. "It's so neat to meet so many different people with so many different stories. You probably get the same thing at the nursing home?"

That fully distracts him.

Lucky launches into story after story about his patients and the things they've told him, including a few about his grandfather, who's not a patient but still a seasoned citizen and also in a committed relationship with Lucky's cousin's husband's grandmother.

My dick finally starts listening to the part of my brain reminding us both how dangerous dating high-powered women is.

Maybe just women in general.

One kiss and a few kind gestures don't make her any less dangerous to the heart I'm never offering on a chopping block again.

By the time Lucky's left after dinner, I feel like I have a hangover from the effort it's taking to fight my attraction to this woman.

The attraction that's one-sided.

Or if it's not, it's on a different page. Singing a different tune.

Definitely not a compatible attraction.

Margot orders me to let her do the dishes since I cooked.

I should go out to the garage just to not be near her, but instead, I linger in the doorway, watching her be domestic.

Lying to myself.

Telling myself that I'm fully back in the game of looking for holes in her story so I can tell Decker what she's up to before she decides to share herself.

"Something on your mind?" she asks as she scrubs the glass dish that I baked the chicken in.

Entirely too much, in fact. "You do dishes at home too?"

"Yes."

"Always?"

"If I cook, I clean."

"You cook?"

She glances over her shoulder at me.

The curl in her hair has tamed this evening, but the dark dye job and the glasses are an oddly effective cover still.

"I'm a human, not a robot," she says, parroting what she told me outside. "What have you been doing since you left your last job?"

"This and that. It struck me—if you're here pretending to be someone you're not, your parents don't know about the triplets either, do they?"

Her spine stiffens.

It's subtle enough that I wonder if I've imagined it until she looks over at me again.

The blue of the cabinets behind her makes her eyes brighter and prettier. "I don't like to ruin people—I much prefer to build them up—but I will do what's necessary to protect the people in my life, and yes, that includes my half brothers. My father would make their lives hell if he knew they exist."

I shift in the doorway, crossing my arms while she goes back to the dishes. "Why haven't you told him?"

"I'm sure you can imagine a thousand different scenarios, and whichever you want to settle on for your peace of mind is fine with me."

"Are we playing poker here? You trying to bluff me?"

"I will tell the triplets the truth when it's time. And then they get to decide what to do with that information. But that time is not yet."

Yes, I'm poking her.

But it's for a good cause.

And the cause is to trip her into saying something that makes me not like her.

Something that will get through to my dick the next time she does something attractive.

But every time I think I'm close to getting her to slip and tell me something horrible, she says the only thing that could possibly appease me.

It's not annoying though.

It's dangerous.

I'm done letting my heart convince me someone might love me and not leave me or betray me.

And it unfortunately knows no other way to be interested in a woman.

It's all or nothing with me.

I shove away from the doorframe with a grunt. "I'm gonna go watch TV."

"Which show?"

"Something gory and horrible." I'm turning on something fluffy that I'd deny watching if anyone ever asked me if I'd seen it. Mostly because of who I'm shipping on the show.

Stupid romantic heart.

But at least it's safe to ship fictional characters since I only watch the shows where they get their happily ever afters.

"You like popcorn?" she asks. "I learned how to make this amazing cinnamon-sugar popcorn off a food show."

And there she goes again.

Saying the exact right thing that shouldn't be the exact right thing but is.

I swallow, studying her closely.

Does she know?

Or is this a coincidence?

She lifts her brows, a silent please answer the question, Rhys.

I clear my throat and break eye contact. "My mom used to make cinnamon-sugar popcorn."

"So…is that a yes or a no?"

The right answer is no.

If Margot's cinnamon-sugar popcorn is better than how I remember my mom's, I'll hate it. If it's worse, I'll hate it.

But I don't have to eat it, so I just shrug at her. "Whatever you want."

I head into the living room without waiting for her to decide what she wants, closing up the hide-a-bed and shoving my blanket off the couch in case she does make popcorn.

Being a shithead is my only current defense against how much I like her.

When I met Felice, I was enamored with how smart and successful she was. She was a junior vice president at a marketing firm in Virginia not far from where I was stationed with the Marines, though she had aspirations for opening her own firm someday.

Just like my mom had opened Technique Group with my grandfather.

Grandpa was me—the muscle—but Mom was the brains. She had a knack for seeing through bullshit, and she made a name for herself by finding and hiring disciplined protection agents with good instincts. She worked hard, and she loved me fiercely, and there's no way I could've had a single mom like her and not grow up into a man who had an appreciation for badass women.

Hence me bending over backward to make Felice happy.

Because I wasn't going to be one of those twatwaffle men who took a partner for granted. I was going to be one of those men my mom taught me to be—before she fell for Xavier's bullshit—who meant it when he said partner.

One of those men who celebrated my partner's success.

One of those men who respected what she built and pulled my share of the weight at home and treated her like the intelligent, amazing woman that she was.

Because she was.

Felice was intelligent and independent and funny and driven, and I was so fucking in love with finding someone like her who said she loved me back that I missed all of the warning signs that lingered in the background for years.

And now here I am again, with what can only be described as a crush on an even more successful woman, who's keeping secrets but kisses like some kind of angelic vixen and who does small things like the dishes and making popcorn that you'd think someone who could afford household staff wouldn't do herself.

Wouldn't even know how to do.

I grew up in the Technique Group offices.

Stories about the rich and famous and the outrageous things they did, along with the outrageously simple things they often couldn't or didn't do themselves, were part of my childhood too.

I cue up the sitcom I've been watching late at night—some goofball thing about a haunted manor where one of the owners can see ghosts—but I don't start it yet.

I should.

I should start without her, distract myself with falling into the plot, and not put myself in a position to entertain any fantasies whatsoever about Margot Merriweather-Brown.

But I can't help myself.

When she's talking to her brothers, she lights up. She compliments her fellow housekeepers' hair and asks the retreat center visitors how their projects are coming and if the mountain air has been good for their creativity.

She's right.

She's not just a robot.

But that doesn't mean she's the right not-just-a-robot for me.

Even if I want her to sit a little closer when she arrives on the couch with fresh-popped cinnamon-sugar popcorn, napkins, and the reusable water bottle I didn't realize I left in the kitchen.

And even if I want to slip my arm around her shoulders.

Tug her next to me.

Smell her hair.

Tangle my fingers in it.

Kiss her until I can't breathe.

All because she's done the bare minimum to be a kind human being.

More than the bare minimum, my conscience whispers.

I hit play on the episode and watch out of the corner of my eye as she reaches into the popcorn bowl, resisting every urge to touch her to the point that I wait until her hand is gone before I sample a bite myself.

And fuck me.

I teeter on the edge of losing all control as I grab another handful of cinnamon-sugar popcorn.

It's exactly the kind that takes me back to childhood.

To watching movies at home while Mom and I lay in a blanket fort, eating cinnamon-sugar popcorn for a Saturday night dinner after a long work week for her and a long school week for me.

To celebrations after the school year was over, whether I'd had an easy year or a hard year.

To picnics with friends where Mom's popcorn bowl would be empty before the main dinner dishes were uncovered.

"Is it just me, or would the neighbor and the guy who died in the suit of armor make the best couple? Like, why can't the neighbor see the ghosts too?" she says midway through the episode.

I stop the show and turn to stare at her.

"What?" she says around a mouthful of popcorn.

Her blue eyes are a little wider. Forehead a little wrinkled. One brow slightly higher than the other.

"Are you fucking serious?" I ask her.

"About shipping two characters on a TV show?"

"I ship them."

"Obviously. They'd be adorable."

"No one else on the forums is shipping them."

Shit. That slipped out.

Didn't mean to confess to being that level of invested.

But she doesn't react to me being a forum geek.

Instead, she stares at me with horror. "No one? No one?"

"Maybe five other people. Most of the forums want him to hook back up with the princess ghost."

Margot makes a face like she tasted spoiled cottage cheese. "I don't like to say negative things about women in general, but the princess ghost is getting on my last nerve. She's been dead for three hundred years. I think she can learn how to be nicer to the ghosts who smell like toast."

I'm sweating.

I'm getting harder by the minute, and I'm sweating, and Margot has a dusting of cinnamon sugar in the corner of her mouth, and I want to lick it off her, and then haul her into the bedroom and make her scream my name.

All because she's all in on seeing my favorite show the same way I do. "How fucking much did you investigate me?"

One side of her lips curves up in a half grin. "If my team investigated your TV preferences, I didn't get a dossier on it, if that's what you're asking."

I want to kiss her.

I want to kiss her while she's smiling, and I want to feel every inch of her body, and I want to—

I want to protect myself from making the same stupid fucking mistake twice, so I turn back to face forward and hit play on the show.

She's watching me.

I can feel it and half see it out of the corner of my eye.

The show keeps playing, not that I can process a single word that's being said.

She laughs at something that I completely miss.

I reach into the popcorn bowl to distract myself, and inadvertently grab her hand instead.

Everything inside me freezes.

I'm not a freeze guy when it comes to fight or flight.

Except right now.

Right now, I'm frozen with my hand on hers, having an internal panic attack because she kissed me.

She kissed me, and I can't get out of my own way to read the signals about if she'd kiss me again, and I can't get out of my own way to decide if I want her to or not.

"Are you okay?" she says softly.

"You remind me of my ex, and she fucked me over so badly I wasn't sure I had a heart left after she was gone, and no, I'm not okay."

Shit.

Shit.

I just said that.

Margot shifts her hand, turning it to wrap it around mine and squeeze softly. "You ever talk about it much?"

"No."

"Want to?"

"No."

"Probably should."

"Yeah, everyone wants to hear about how I was picking out baby names for nonexistent children the week before our wedding while she was fucking my stepbrother in the back of the SUV the company assigned me for work."

"Want me to destroy them?"

I start to laugh—one of those not-funny laughs—and rub my eyes with the hand that hasn't been in the cinnamon-sugar popcorn. "You'd enjoy that, wouldn't you?"

"Honestly? Probably not. I generally—not always, but generally—get far more satisfaction out of helping people reach their best than in tearing them down. But I do have resources, and I do recognize the value of occasionally assisting karma."

I squint at her. "People call you a shark."

"I'm smart. I'm strategic. I see opportunities. That doesn't mean I'm unkind. Especially—" She sucks in a big breath, squeezes her eyes shut for a minute, and then sighs as she blinks her eyes open at me again. "Especially since my parents cut Daphne off. And how. She was—is—all heart, and what they did to her was cruel and callous and unnecessary. What they did to her forced me to face some truths I'd been conveniently ignoring about how I felt about the way my father runs the ship."

"So you're not a shark?"

"I'm a lioness. I lead the pride. And the pride is more powerful when every lion in it is getting what they need to thrive. Not when they're being pushed past their breaking points and taken for granted and abused."

I swallow hard.

Then again.

I haven't even started the fire with the wood I brought in for that very purpose, and I'm sweating.

The woman shouldn't be this attractive. She shouldn't.

Being in the Marines? Got it. Hard work, sometimes scary, but I've got it.

Personal security? Same thing.

Relationships? Being attracted to a woman again?

I'm a fucking baby bird, exposed to the elements and completely unable to handle my shit.

"Forgot something in the garage," I mutter.

I upend the popcorn bowl when I bolt to my feet, but I don't stop. I just retreat.

Because if I don't, I'm going to fall head over heels for Margot Merriweather-Brown, and that's the last thing I have space for in my life.

Now or ever.

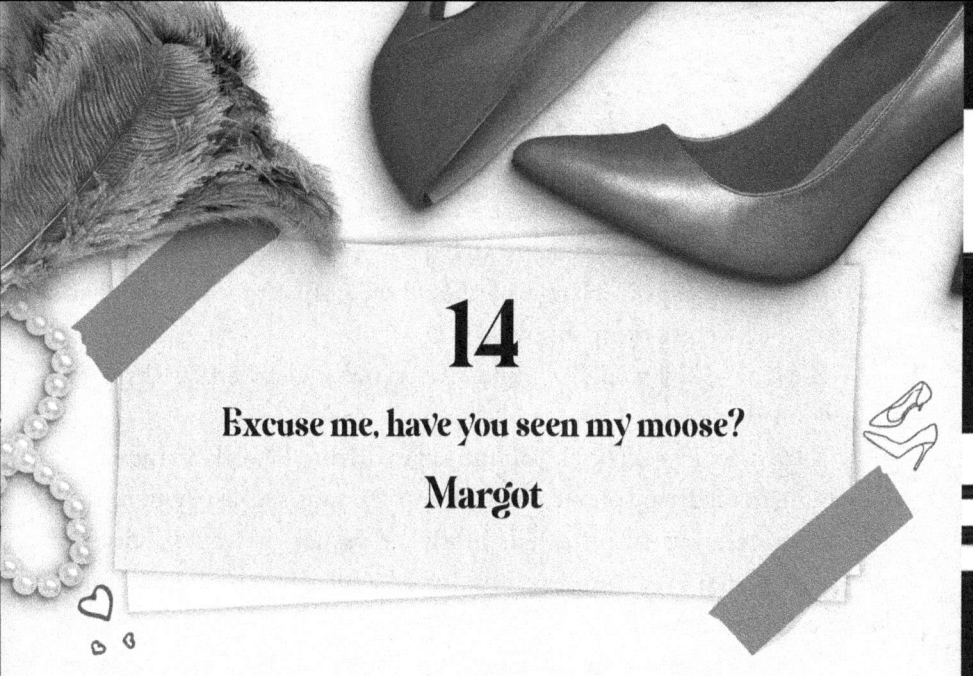

14

Excuse me, have you seen my moose?

Margot

Rhys doesn't come back to the house from the garage until after I've cleaned up the popcorn and gone to bed, and he's quiet—not grumpy, but quiet—as we both get ready for work Friday morning.

It's not my business to find out more about his relationship with his ex, but I want to know.

And honestly?

I do want to destroy her.

He's gruff and grumpy and suspicious, but I'm starting to suspect it's all a protective measure.

You can't tell me that a guy who ships two of the clearly most emotionally wounded characters on a goofball sitcom isn't some level of emotionally wounded himself.

That he hasn't been hurt.

That he didn't deserve to be hurt.

I meant what I told him—unless we're talking about my father, I'd rather build people up than tear them down, and that's the reason I have the lowest staff turnover rate in my department back home, and it's the reason my department has the highest productivity rate and job satisfaction ratings on surveys.

For the past three years, anyway.

Since I decided to take charge of who I want to be instead of blindly following who I was raised to be.

As soon as I'm in charge of the whole corporation, I intend to replicate that success company-wide.

But I low-key wouldn't mind five minutes alone with Rhys's ex and stepbrother.

To distract myself, I call Daphne as I'm driving to work on the curving mountain roads, my phone plugged into the van's speaker system.

"How are our surprise half brothers?" is her first question. She and I have texted over the week, but our schedules haven't aligned for a phone call until now.

"Clearly related to us," I reply. "I'm so pissed. They got the same fun genes you have, and I'm just over here being the boring businesswoman."

Daphne laughs. "You are not boring."

"The other night, they invited me to a speakeasy—"

"A speakeasy?" Daph shrieks. "No!"

"Don't act like you've never been to one."

"I've never been to one," Oliver says in the background.

"How have you never—no, never mind. Add it to the list of things we need to do," she says distantly, obviously talking to Oliver, before her voice comes back more clearly on the phone. "I thought you were in a dinky little mountain town. Did you go into Denver or something?"

"No, they have one here," I tell her.

"With a secret door and a password?"

"Yes."

"Are there animal antlers all over the place?"

"No. It's like…castle-chic. Old brick walls, old paintings, Turkish rugs, lots of red velvet in the furniture."

"Ooh, I officially will need the password once you've completed your secret mission so that I can go meet them too. Tell me who's who. What are they like? If we weren't related, would you hit on any of them?"

"No."

"This is where I remind you that you called her," Oliver says.

"Fair enough," I reply as she laughs.

"Are they seriously as fun as I am, or are they actually just a little more fun than you, so you think they're as fun as I am?"

"Feeling the love this morning, Daph." I'm smiling as I say it, because she has a point. "But I think they might be more fun than you. They play off of each other, so it's like watching a perpetual game of one-upmanship, except it's hilarious instead of annoying."

"Tell me more."

"Apparently, Jack always loses at rock paper scissors, so when we were at the speakeasy, Decker and Lucky demanded they play to determine who had to leave and go get Chex Mix from the grocery store."

"Lame," Daph says at the same time Oliver says, more distantly, "What's rock paper scissors? I've never heard of that before."

She cracks up. "Stop, you have too," she says to him.

"Not if it's a game. I'm boring. I don't do games."

"Oh my god, you're in a mood." Daph's still laughing.

"A good mood," he replies.

I miss my sister.

And oddly, I think I miss Oliver too.

He's annoying as hell right now—he's being intentionally obnoxious—but that's Daphne's problem, and she clearly likes this new, outspoken, annoying version of him, so I'm happy for them both.

Provided Oliver never hurts her.

Then I'll break my own rules about not tearing people down.

"Lucky—he's the nurse—grew his hair out to pose as Decker—he's the novelist—for Decker's official author photos," I tell Daphne and Oliver. "And then they argued about who's more handsome."

"Aren't they identical?"

"It's a seriously good thing they have different styles. I couldn't tell them apart based on face alone. Body either, honestly."

Daphne snickers. "I'd totally do that if I were a triplet."

"I know. There are some inside jokes I still don't get, but they told me that Jack was fucking Switzerland, like Switzerland is the name of his current hookup, and even though I know they were talking about how Lucky likes me, Decker's highly suspicious of me, and Jack's playing it neutral, it was really, really funny. Oh! And get this—they don't actually date, because supposedly Decker's neighbor cursed them when they were in high school and if any of them falls in love, then it'll splinter their triplet brotherhood."

"No."

"Yes. At first I thought they were messing with me, but honestly? I think they're completely serious. I got a vibe like they truly believe they're cursed."

"If I didn't have a job, and if I had any money, I'd be on a plane right now to meet these guys," Daph says.

Oliver makes a noise he never would've made when we were dating—a growly, irritated, overprotective grunt that we all know means quit your job because I can take care of you and you know I'll pay for you to fly to Colorado to see your brothers anytime.

As if I wouldn't beat him to it.

Or try to.

The Oliver I dated was a complete pushover, but this one throws punches and gave my father a black eye a few weeks ago when dear old Dad insulted the fuck out of Daphne.

It's possible Oliver's even more protective of her than I am now.

And while he's on a mission to give away his own fortune now that he's stepped away from his family's corporation, he's still the kind of guy who'll make sure he has fallback money so that he can do things like guarantee neither of them ever has to work again if they don't want to and put Daphne on a plane to Colorado to meet our half brothers anytime she so much as thinks about them.

"I need another couple weeks," I tell her. "If my cover doesn't get blown. Or if I don't get eaten by a moose." I tell them about running into Jonas Rutherford and about the moose, and then finally get to the other reason I'm calling. "And I mentioned Decker's suspicious? He asked an old military buddy to come check me out. And the military buddy figured out who I am."

"Oh, shit. Do you need help burying the body?" Daph asks.

Oliver snort-laughs. "You think she hasn't already taken care of it?"

"He's fine," I tell them, which is a complete lie. Rhys is way better than fine. In all of the ways a man can be better than fine, which also makes him the complete opposite of fine. "If I disappeared him, Decker would notice, and my cover would absolutely be blown. Instead, we're…compromising."

"Is this a naked kind of compromising?" she asks.

My god, I wish. That kiss—and then Lucky interrupting it— "No."

Silence lingers on the other end of the phone like she doesn't believe me.

"No," I repeat.

"I don't understand what there is to negotiate. He's a problem, so you have to eliminate him."

"I'm not that kind of ruthless."

"Aren't you though? Don't you want to be?"

"No."

I wasn't lying when I told Rhys I wanted to get to know my family. After watching Daphne settle into her life without money, I swear she's happier than I am some days.

Probably most days, in fact.

Somewhere in the past few years, I've realized too many of my friends are the type who are friends with you because it's better than being enemies.

Or they're the type who only wanted to talk about work and strategy and success, like your whole worth is determined by how hard you work instead of the sum of all of who you are.

Not all, but enough of them.

And honestly? I've been just as bad.

But Daph—when she was disinherited, she moved in with a friend she'd met there at her last college, and I watched their friendship blossom into something that hit my envy buttons in ways that even Daph dating Oliver hasn't.

She's so tight with Bea, I sometimes worry Bea's going to replace me as Daphne's favorite sister.

Or only sister.

I'm not here getting to know the triplets because I'm afraid she'll replace me though.

And I'm not here only to ask if they'll help me.

I'm here partially because they're completely untouched by my world, but still family, and after watching Daphne form a small family of friends, I've realized there's never too much of a good thing.

When family's good.

And so far, I think they are.

"So if there's no naked negotiations going on, and you're not hiding his body…what's the deal?" Daph asks.

"He's blackmailing me," I reply, even though I'm almost positive Rhys will keep my secret because of the nuance of the situation and all the ways being related to me could fuck up Decker's life.

Daphne gasps.

Oliver mutters something that could be a whoa, or possibly he choked on his coffee.

"It's fine," I say.

"Margot. It is not fine. What aren't you telling me?"

"I actually respect his nerve."

"And?" she prompts.

I start to smile. "And I'm the reason he's been walking around all week with lavender streaks on his face and in his eyes. So I feel like I owe him a little leeway."

"What did you do?" Daphne whispers reverently.

"Homemade personal security system involving hair dye. I told you I was going to set it up. It worked."

"Margot," she squeals. "I'm so proud of you!"

"His eyes?" Oliver asks.

"Apparently hair dye can stain the whites of your eyes if you don't rinse it out fast enough," I say. "I nailed him in the gut with a cast-iron frying pan too, which I regret more than the dye. That was overkill. I was running on adrenaline. Probably I need to spend a little more time without security and tackle a paranoia issue. But my roommate and I have come to a kind of compromise, and now he's teaching me how to split firewood and saving me from mooses—mooses? Meese? Wait, it's just moose, isn't it?"

My sister's still cackling on the other end.

"It's just moose," Oliver says.

"Aw, you haven't changed in some ways," I say.

Daph cackles harder.

"But about this compromise," I say, "Oliver, I need a favor."

"Does it involve working?" he asks.

"Tangentially."

"Then no. I already have a job, and I'm only working one job at a time, so there's no room left for me to do anyone work-tangential favors."

I shake my head while I keep my eyes peeled for moose and deer and elk.

He's managing a drive-in movie theater and making popcorn, doing a fun job instead of the high-stress chief executive role he left behind a few weeks ago.

"Maybe between making batches of popcorn, you could make one or two phone calls for me?" I say. "I don't want my hands directly on this."

Especially since Rhys hasn't asked me to do this, and I'm operating on a gut feeling that it's what he wanted to ask. I could be wrong about it.

"I can do it," Daphne says. "I love phone calls."

"No," Oliver and I say at the same time.

He sighs heavily. "Fine. What do you want?"

"Anything you can find out about the security firm Technique Group. Rhys—my accidental roommate—worked for them, and my instincts are screaming that everything's not okay there. I have copies of court filings they made against each other when he left the company, but there's always more to it than what they spill in legal paperwork."

"You can't have your security detail do this?" he grumbles.

"I don't want it linked back to me."

"And yet you're asking me to do the phone calls..."

"The entire world believes I hate you right now. You're actually the best person for the job."

"Why do you have to be so logical?"

"Does he whine this much all the time, Daph?"

"Instead of answering that the way I want to, I'm just gonna say no," she replies. "And you're welcome. Because my real answer is full of innuendos and details that you don't want to hear."

Oliver snickers.

"Gotta go," I tell them as I pull into the parking lot. "I'm at work."

"Figure out if you can trust the triplets or not soon," Daph says. "I want to meet them too."

"I'm not sure the town's ready for a fourth of them."

She giggles.

I smile.

Daph and I aren't very much alike. We have our own goals and dreams and brands of fun.

But I still adore the shit out of her.

I pause in my van to put on my name tag and unplug my phone, and when I look up, there's a freaking bull moose standing right in front of me.

I shriek.

He snorts.

With Daphne's voice still in my head, I lift my phone and pull up the camera app and snap a few photos, my heart beating a little too fast and the hairs on my neck standing up too.

Why are moose so big?

And why is this guy so close?

Rhys pulls into the parking spot next to mine in his truck, and I look over at him, then point to the moose, like what the fuck?

He shrugs.

Then he honks his horn.

The moose startles, then snorts at the truck, and finally meanders away.

I turn another what the fuck? look at Rhys.

Mostly because honking was a little rude.

He could give me any number of responses in his expression.

He could be like what, you needed help?

Or he could be like don't give me shit for doing what you could've done.

But what does the man do?

The man who haunted my thoughts all night with wanting to make his life easier, with wanting to make him hurt a little less, with making him want to trust a little more?

He smiles.

He smiles at me again, a broad, uninhibited, tooth-baring grin of yeah, that was fun.

And my stupid heart melts just a little more for a man who's clearly unavailable.

Not that that's what I'm here for.

But apparently the cost of choosing the path where I take Daphne's side over my parents also means choosing the side where my own heart works harder, and my own heart working harder means I feel more for the people around me, especially the people who wear their damage on their sleeves.

I burst out laughing, shake my head at him, wait a few more minutes to be sure the moose has fully left the area, and then I climb out of my car and get to work.

He's still in his truck.

Watching me.

Waiting to make sure I get to work safely, but at a safe distance for his own heart.

Freaking man.

He's entirely too likable.

15

She's playing with fire

Rhys

It's a slow day at work. Yesterday was a heavy turnover day, and today's almost as busy, but everyone's behaving themselves.

I avoid Margot in the staff room by having an early lunch, even if I find excuses to spy on her from a close distance when I know she's working the chalets since Mr. Robe-and-towels is here for one more night.

Mrs. Pinsley, the elderly woman working on her first novel, is checking out today, and I spot her hugging Margot as another of the security guys loads her luggage onto the retreat's golf cart, which will transport her up to the main building and the shuttle to the airport.

"Now, no arguing. The tip I left is exactly what I meant to leave, and it's for you, understand?" Mrs. Pinsley says.

"That's not—" Margot starts, then catches herself, and smiles at the older woman. "Thank you, Mrs. Pinsley. Getting to know you has been reward enough in itself, but I appreciate your generosity."

"Bah. It's the least I can do."

"Keep working on your novel. I'm going to check your website to make sure you did it."

Mrs. Pinsley beams at her.

And even though I know I shouldn't, after the old lady has been loaded up in the golf cart, and after Margot's had enough time to switch out the bedding and towels and gather the trash and clean up the rest of the room, I circle back to the chalets.

She's pushing her cart back toward the robe-and-towel dude's room.

"How much did she leave you?" I ask as I fall into step with her.

"Two hundred dollars."

"Holy shit."

"It's going in the communal tip jar."

I grunt in acknowledgment.

Not surprised.

I'm starting to believe she really is nice.

Or at least has an unexpected level of self-awareness.

"You really gonna look up her website?"

"Already have it saved on my phone with a reminder in my calendar to peek at it every other month."

I don't want to believe her—it's safer not to—but I do.

She locks the cart outside the chalet one door down from robe-and-towel guy, whom I spot peeking through his windows. "Gimme his towels," I say on a sigh.

"Maybe I should just slip you the big tip instead," she says with a cheeky grin.

My face gets hot as the phrase *I'd like to slip you my big tip* runs through my head. I'm able to control my dick today, but only barely.

"Not necessary," I mutter.

"Many thanks." She hands me a stack of towels.

I deliver them to the dude that I'm going to suggest management should blacklist, who stares at Margot when he's not scowling at me.

She needs to quit this job.

It's not necessary, and she's interacting with too many people.

Too many people who might figure out who she is.

Too many people who see an attractive woman and start looking at her the way this guy's looking at her.

The dude shuts his door in my face, and I head back to Margot's cart.

She's disappeared inside the empty chalet. "You need anything else?" I call to her in the doorway.

She peeks out of the bathroom door. "Nope. Got it. Thank you."

I linger as long as I can without drawing attention, but then I get a call about a deer that's looking at someone wrong, then about helping move some tables. I'm pausing in the staff room for a drink when the other two housekeepers on staff today come in.

"I'm just saying, if I were married to Jonas Rutherford, I'd be here every day, not just one Friday a month. You know the whole reason he had the spa installed was for Emma to be able to use it whenever she wants," one's saying.

I pretend I'm scrolling my phone and not listening as the other one opens the fridge. "It's so sweet. And did you see the baby?"

"So. Cute."

"Her smile!"

"And the little coos!"

"And the way he's holding her and managing Bash too so Emma can just enjoy the day…"

They both sigh.

I glance up then, because my brain has fully caught up to the conversation they're having, and this is going to be a problem for Margot. "Boss is here?"

Identical giggles answer me. "Hey, Rhys," the younger one says. Zelda. Her name is Zelda.

"If you were married to Jonas Rutherford, would you be taking spa days every day instead of once a month?" the other—Louisa—asks.

I flip through my mental list of where the staff should all be right now based on the schedule I saw, and Margie—and yes, she has to be Margie right now—should be up at the spa helping with the laundry.

If Emma Rutherford's headed that way—then Jonas might be too.

"Depends. We talking couples massages or getting facials and seaweed wraps with the girls?" I ask.

They both giggle again.

"Oh my god, he's had spa treatments," Zelda whispers to Louisa.

"They can't do couples massages," Louisa replies. "They didn't bring the babysitter."

"But they brought a driver so they can have a nice lunch with wine."

"I'd be having wine lunches every day after spa time."

"You don't think that would get boring? I'd have to keep working. Not like, here, but like…something."

I don't have Margot's number—that's an oversight—so I text her security guy.

Jonas Rutherford is headed Margie's way.

No immediate answer.

Doesn't surprise me.

Dude doesn't owe me a response.

I grunt something to the two housekeepers and head out of the room.

Have to get to the gondola and get up to the top of the mountain and figure out how to get Margie off the top of the mountain without it looking suspicious, like she's hiding from someone.

And that's when inspiration strikes.

Laundry room is right down the hall.

I sneak in, grab the dish soap refill from the retreat center's main supply closet down here, pour a shit-ton into one of the machines holding sheets ready to be moved into the dryer, and I restart the cycle.

And then I'm on the move.

I pass Jonas and Emma in the lobby, just as the housekeepers said. Jonas is holding the baby and also the preschooler's hand while Emma, his perpetually happy wife, squats to talk to the little boy. I think I heard he's about four, and he's staring at the brightly colored origami swans hanging from the ceiling and demanding to know how to make them himself.

No one notices me as I head for the gondola to the top of the mountain, but I notice that Jonas and Emma are just a couple cars behind me on the lift.

Margot's security guy still hasn't texted me back.

I head immediately to the spa when the gondola car opens at the top of the lift.

Been about seven minutes. The washer should be about to overflow, shouldn't it?

No one blinks at me walking into the staff entrance on the lower level behind the spa, where I know they have laundry facilities too. I heard they almost put a kitchen in here, for spa lunches, but decided to keep the food at the winery tasting room on the other side of the lift at the top of the mountain here.

Storage rooms are empty. Just shelves of lotions and oils and rocks or stones or—actually, just all kinds of things I can't identify despite knowing the words seaweed wrap and facials.

Laundry room's empty too. Which leaves a small locker room— also empty—and a single stall bathroom with the light off and the door wide open.

I'm about to head to the main floor, knowing I'm at risk of running into Jonas and Emma again, when the door to the back stairway opens, and Margot steps through with her arms loaded down with towels and sheets.

"Hey," I say.

She shrieks.

I hold up both hands. "Just me."

"Oh my god, I thought you were the moose."

I look down at my clothes.

Huh.

Moose-brown uniform shirt today. Didn't do that on purpose.

I shake my head. "Jonas Rutherford is here. Here here. In the spa here. With his wife."

"Oh, fuck. Seriously?"

I grab the laundry. "Don't worry. Got you covered."

"I have to wash those."

Not grinning at that is impossible. She trails me into the laundry room, where I shove the towels and sheets into a single load. "You're about to be banned from laundry duty."

"Towels and sheets separate, Rhys," she hisses, which is a question I wonder if she's ever thought about before in her life.

"Oh, don't worry, this isn't the worst you'll do to get banned from laundry duty."

"What are you talking about?"

"I—"

My radio squawks to life. "Situation in the main laundry room," Cynthia says. "Someone locate Margie Johnson. She needs to clean up her mess."

Margot looks down at the radio clipped to my hip.

Then back up at me.

"What did you do?" She whispers the question with a cringe, but her voice holds an air of reverence.

I toss a normal amount of the right detergent into the washing machine and start the cycle for her. "You used dish soap instead of laundry detergent in the washing machines."

Her blue eyes flare wide.

And my grin keeps growing as I lift the radio. "Just ran into her," I report to our boss. "I'll bring her down."

"You're evil," she whispers.

"You're fucking welcome." I hustle her toward the back door at the exact instant the stairwell door slams shut again behind us. "Dada, we get mama a tweat?" a little voice says.

"We're going on an adventure," Jonas Rutherford replies.

Margot's shoulders stiffen as I grab the door and open it for her. I glance back at Jonas, give him a brief nod, then follow Margot out.

"One minute, please," Jonas calls to me.

Margie inhales sharply and keeps walking out the door.

"Yeah, boss?" I say.

"Are there...s-n-a-c-k-s down here?"

I shake my head. "Mostly s-o-a-p and l-o-t-i-o-n."

"Ah. Then we've gone the wrong way. Thank you."

I nod and head out the door.

Margot's already halfway to the gondola. I catch up with her as she reaches the platform.

Once we're inside a car, she takes a seat and sags, her head hanging over her knees.

And then she starts laughing.

Which is, unfortunately, fucking beautiful.

16

Revenge is hot

Rhys

Margot's still laughing when my radio squawks to life again. "O'Malley, how far out are you with Margie? This laundry room is a disaster."

"On the gondola down," I report.

"My sister would love you," Margot says when I've clipped my radio back to my hip.

"Thought she already took one of your exes. You want to give me to her too?"

She cracks up again, and something cracks in my chest.

Something that I don't want to crack. Something I'd prefer to keep hard and impenetrable around my heart.

I haven't been able to laugh about anything related to my stepbrother stealing my bride, but here Margot is, weeks after her sister started dating her ex, light and happy about it.

I want that.

I crave that.

Maybe not the part where I'm happy for them, but the part where I can be happy for me.

And the part where I feel whole enough to enjoy being in a little gondola car on a lift with a woman who lights up every room she walks into and who's kind to strangers. She has secrets, but she keeps showing me sides of her that are so far from the cutthroat businesswoman heiress she's rumored to be that I'm starting to reconsider my entire worldview.

"Apologies," she says, eyes sparkling and smile wide. "I don't mean to make light of the horror that is a sibling hooking up with an ex."

I shrug like my entire world isn't having an earthquake just below the surface of my skin. I can't be around this woman and not want to kiss her. "If you're fine with it..."

"At the risk of being that person who protests too much, I repeat—I'm happy for them."

My face says a few things for me, and her joyful laughter rings through the gondola car.

I watch the trees move beneath us as we make the short trek down the mountainside, soaking in the sounds of happiness.

They've been in short supply for far longer than the past year.

I just hadn't been paying enough attention to realize it was missing.

She eventually wipes her eyes and lets loose a deep, happy sigh. "You know, there are no winners if you let them make you quit living," she says softly. "Grieving time is important, but don't—don't make yourself the loser in your own life."

And there she goes, doing it again.

Slipping little bits of wisdom and perspective into my life when I least expect it but most need it.

I shift a glance at her.

She spreads her hands, palms up. "Not calling you a loser."

"I know."

"Someone had to tell me something similar a few years ago. It was helpful."

"You needed to be told not to be the loser in your own life."

Her spread hands go jazzy. "Surprise! All the money and power in the world can't buffer you from childhood trauma, messy emotional stuff, and questioning everything you've ever known about the world."

"Few years ago—before your sister stole your ex, then."

"She didn't—you know what? Fine. For simplicity's sake, yes. Yes, before she stole my ex."

I lift my brows at her, wondering if she's going to tell me more, when the gondola screeches to a halt.

I stumble forward, still in motion when the car is not, and almost lose my balance against the front glass.

Margot sucks in a breath as she braces herself with the railing beside the door. "Are you for fucking real?" she mutters.

We're maybe a hundred feet or so from the bottom platform, and the mountain is steep enough here that we're dangling at least thirty feet off the ground.

I peer down at the base of the lift, and then swipe my hand over my mouth.

"What is it?" Her voice is smaller now.

"Can't tell."

She scoots back on the bench, putting her hands out when the gondola sways a bit, then tucks her knees up by her chin.

Her face has gone pale, and all of the amusement has left her eyes. "Think it'll be long?"

"Shouldn't be." I call on my radio to ask what's up with the gondola stopping, but don't get an immediate answer beyond my boss saying they'll look into it if it's still not running in a few minutes. It stops on occasion whenever anyone needs extra time getting in or out of one of the cars. This isn't unusual.

Not yet anyway.

She blows out a slow breath.

"You good?" I ask her.

"Yes."

"Liar."

"Perception is reality."

"So if you believe hard enough that you're good, you're good?"

"Yes."

I peer down again.

No obvious movement on the platform, so it doesn't seem to be stopped because of an issue with anyone getting on or off on this end.

Margot's staring straight ahead, breathing slowly.

As if I wasn't already fucked with thinking about her as a human being. A vulnerable human being whom I'm realizing might be lonely in her own way.

I move slowly across the short distance to sit beside her, the instinctive need to protect taking priority over the need to shield my own exposed heart. "Tight spaces or heights?"

"Being trapped without an exit plan."

Relatable. "Ever go skiing?"

"Not for a few years."

"Too cold, or you got stuck on a lift?"

"It didn't come naturally to me, so I got frustrated and quit."

"Ah." I settle farther back on the bench. The gondola sways slightly.

She sucks in a shallow breath through her nose and keeps staring straight ahead. "I don't usually give up when it's hard."

"Sure."

"I don't."

"Can't be a badass boss lady if you give up when it's hard. Gotta know when to pick your battles against your own nature."

"So it wasn't a lift incident."

Her knee brushes my arm as she shifts, then she temporarily freezes as the car sways a bit. But she still draws a deep breath and answers me. "No. Not a lift. I got stuck on a stalled subway train during a power outage once. Close to two hours in a dark space with dozens of strangers squished all around me. I was trying to understand how our normal guests lived and what kind of experiences they had when they stayed at our hotel."

I jerk a glance at her. "That's what you're doing here too."

Her lips twist in a wry smile. "Busted."

"You do stuff like this often? Get a different view of how your hotels run?"

"As often as I can, but not as much as I used to. Especially after the subway incident. My security thought taking the train was overkill for the experience, but they went along with it, and then the train stopped, and…yeah. They were right. I didn't need that to understand more about what someone wanted in our hotels."

"You get recognized?"

"No, it was just—just highly uncomfortable. Being so far from control. Unable to fix it in a high-risk situation."

"You think you're in control pretending to be a housekeeper?"

"I can walk out of here anytime I want." She grimaces as her eyes flit about the enclosed car. "Except for right now."

Distractions tend to help in these situations, so I change the subject instead of hugging her like I want to. "So how do you know Jonas Rutherford?"

She blows out a slow breath and keeps staring straight ahead while she answers me. "We are—were both on the board of a nonprofit that provides funding to bring humanities studies to low-income schools. Art supplies, musical instruments, instructors, things like that."

"See him often then?"

She shakes her head. "Maybe a half dozen times in the few years before he moved here. I see his brother more now."

"You seemed surprised to come face-to-face with him the other day."

"He was supposed to be out of town for a family thing. When Lucky said he could get me a job here, I had Cyril look into it. I might have timed things differently if I'd known our intel was wrong. Maybe. Other things lined up to make this excellent timing. Things I couldn't plan but could very easily roll with."

Her breathing is staying relatively steady despite her face remaining pale. Good sign.

Not that I'd expect someone like Margot to freak out over a small inconvenience.

Like she said, she can will herself into believing whatever she wants. And she has to know we won't be here long.

I shift beside her, leaning back to plant my hand on the bench behind her, the closest I'll let myself come to touching her.

Fuck me, she smells good. Like lemon and pine trees with that little hint of cinnamon and coffee lingering beneath it.

I clear my throat. "Speaking of Lucky and family, how'd you find out about the triplets?"

She slides me a look, but it's not as suspicious as it probably should be.

"I assume people in your zip code aren't doing DNA tests on ancestry and matching sites regularly," I add. "Prefer to keep the skeletons in the closet, right?"

"You think you're getting confessions out of me since we're stuck in the air?"

"I think family's complicated. The one person I told about my own family troubles went and started fucking the family member I complained about most, so whatever your reason for wanting to find more family, not my place to judge. Just curious."

She studies me, color coming back into her cheeks. "This conversation is about seven left turns and a boat ride away from the don't you fucking dare hurt my friend that we started at a few days ago."

"I watch you."

Her eyes stay focused on mine in a way that makes my heart speed up and my fingers tingle in anticipation.

We're alone.

No one on the cars ahead of or behind us.

I could kiss her.

I could kiss her again right now.

"I've noticed," she says softly.

Focus, dumbass. "You look like you want to fit in. To my very simple brain, that means either you have a natural talent for acting, or that you don't feel like you belong in the family you have now, no matter how much you say you love your sister. So maybe you do still have an extra secret agenda or two, but life's complicated."

She's completely lost track of the fact that we're trapped in a gondola thirty feet off the ground, or if she hasn't, she's clearly not uncomfortable with it anymore.

Not with the intensity of the attention she's aiming at me. "Life is complicated," she agrees.

"Wish it wasn't."

"Will starting your own security firm really be enough for you?"

I'm such a fucking sucker for a smart woman.

Even more so for a woman who'd give half a thought about what I want beyond what I say out loud.

"Would be nice," I reply.

One corner of her mouth hitches up. "Would be nice to start a security firm? Or would be nice if starting a security firm is enough for you?"

Another thing I like about this woman.

She sees me too.

Will my own success be enough if I know my stepfather and stepbrothers are out there in the same world, succeeding with what my mother built? When I first joined the Marines, I did it to get some real-world experience with hard things, always planning on going back to take my rightful place in my mom's company eventually.

I stayed as long as I did because it fit.

And I went back planning to be more mature and intelligent about my issues with Xavier than I'd been when I was eighteen.

But it didn't work out the way it should've because he had no morals or ethics and never truly loved my mom at all.

I swallow hard. "That's a complicated question."

"I made a phone call," she says. "Asked someone to do some digging into Technique Group. On a hunch."

My ears get hot and my heart gives a loud, painful thump that echoes through my abdomen and makes my stomach drop.

She did that for me.

Someone who barely knows me did something for me.

Without me asking, but because, I suspect, she understands more about me than I want to admit.

"What—" I clear my throat again, suddenly feeling thick and awkward and vulnerable. "What hunch?"

"That you want something more than an endorsement for your own security firm."

"You're asking someone else what I want?"

"No, I'm asking someone else to find out if there's dirt on your stepfamily. But I can also ask them to stop if you'd like me to."

I blink quickly and shake my head.

Answering out loud is impossible.

I suddenly don't trust my voice.

I don't know if I can actively seek vengeance.

But I don't want to stop her from digging up dirt on Xavier and my stepbrothers either.

"You're right," she adds softly. "I do have an extra agenda in being here. But I'll bail if it'll hurt anyone. It's one thing to destroy someone who deserves it. It's another to cause collateral damage. My sister was collateral damage in the vision my parents have of their reputation and image in their social circles. I won't cause that harm to anyone else. So if there's anyone who could become innocent collateral damage as my friend is asking questions about your former employer, please let me know."

Moral revenge.

She's talking about moral and ethical revenge.

Being karma.

Being consequences.

Being justice.

Doing it for me, but without hurting people who don't deserve it.

And fuck me, more than just turning me on, it makes me feel seen.

Recognized.

Cared for.

Honored for who I am, what I want, and where my principles lie.

Don't do it, a voice whispers in my head. Don't trust her. Don't fall for this again. You know it'll hurt.

But she's right.

I do want Xavier and Colt and Hayden—and Felice too—to pay for what they did.

For the way they cut me out.

The way they used what my mom built—used me too—until they set me up to fail so that they could force me out.

And she's the first person I've met who gets it.

Who understands.

Who can see the pain and help me get the justice.

"My mom and grandfather founded the company." Shit, I'm hoarse, and I can't fix that.

"I know," she says softly.

"Grandpa died when I was twelve. Mom when I was fourteen. I think she'd just started realizing my stepfather was a narcissist in sheep's clothing when she got sick, and since he could see what he stood to gain when she was gone, and how fast she was going downhill, he stepped up and played the part of the perfect husband. Fooled her again. As soon as she was gone though—I was a problem to be dealt with."

"People aren't problems." She rolls her eyes. "Until they make themselves problems. But you were fourteen."

"I joined the Marines the day I turned eighteen. Had to get away. Grow up some on my own. But I still owned part of the company. It was in my mom's trust. So when I met Felice—my ex—and she wanted me to get out and settle somewhere, I thought I could handle as an adult what I was moody about as a teenager, and I went back. Claimed my place in a business I still half owned. Four years ago now."

"But it was a different business then," Margot guesses.

"He changed everything. Mom was picky about clients. Xavier wasn't. Mom had procedures. Xavier didn't."

"Was it profitable?"

I snort. "Of course not. Then he would've had to cut me a check."

She makes a low, aggravated hum.

"Yeah."

"You still own half?"

"No."

She lifts a brow, and I realize she dyed them too. Her real eyebrows are lighter in the pictures.

"I'm assuming you didn't voluntarily sell to him," she murmurs.

"He set me up. He knew Imogen Carter didn't like bulky guys on her security squad, so when I had to more or less manhandle her into the car when she got rushed by some nutjob when we left dinner—"

"Imogen Carter got rushed by a nutjob?"

God, I like this woman.

She's smart and sexy and multi-faceted.

I nod. "Called her name and came running directly for her with something in his hand that I couldn't see clearly but knew wasn't good."

"She's pissed a few people off over her decades in the business, but she's not exactly relevant in the industry now. That's...unexpected."

"Like I said. He set me up."

Her hand lands on my thigh. "Do you have proof?"

I grimace. "We didn't make it far enough in our mutual lawsuits against each other to force document production."

She winces. "Court's never fun."

"It is not," I agree. "Especially on the tail end of being told I no longer belonged at the firm my mother founded. Where she would've wanted me to have the option on my own to stay or go. It was a family firm. I was family. Except not to him. Add in that that's the night I got home and found Felice packing up to leave me. Week before our wedding. Said I was making her choose, so she was choosing him. Life's kinda sucked."

Margot's grip tightens on my thigh. "Had she—had she participated in planning the wedding?"

"Fuck knows every opinion I had about it was wrong, so yeah. Yeah, she participated. Planned the whole thing when she clearly didn't want me."

She stares at me with wide eyes. "You have very bad taste in women."

I snort out a laugh.

Fucking worst moments of my life, and this woman has me cracking up about it. Cracking up and wanting her to inch her hand higher on my thigh.

"You know I think you're sexy as hell?" I say to her.

She grins. "Like I said, terrible taste."

"Why'd your ex dump you?" I need a distraction before I kiss her.

"He gave me the line that since his father had been sent to prison, he didn't want the dirt on his family's name to sully mine, but really, he couldn't handle filling his father's shoes at his family's company and also having a relationship with me."

"He couldn't do both?"

"In all fairness, his business situation and mine were vastly different. My father's unlikely to go to prison, and his father had run their company to the brink of bankruptcy. I'm sure you've seen the articles."

Is she serious? "And now you're being fair."

Her eyes crinkle as her smile widens, making me hope they never fix this lift. "Now, yes. Then, no. Then, I was furious and hurt, but my parents cut my sister off about two weeks later, and suddenly the world looked very different."

"Seriously? You got over being dumped because your sister was hurt?"

"It was eye-opening to realize how much I've always been rewarded by my parents for not being her, and how much she's been punished for not being me. I sometimes wonder if they timed destroying her to take the attention off of my ended engagement. They could've…handled what they thought was a problem…without putting her in the position they did, but they chose to actively hurt her the worst way possible. Suddenly no one in our social circles was talking anymore about how Oliver called off the wedding. It was more fun for them to talk about how terribly Daph must've fucked up and how funny it was that she was suddenly broke with nowhere to live and no functional skills about how to survive in the world without security and household managers and assistants."

My respect for this woman is growing exponentially, helped by the clear offense she feels on her sister's behalf. "Hence you want no collateral damage."

"Exactly. So. Would you like me to take care of your stepfather, or do you want to be involved?"

I look her straight in those pretty blue eyes, and I say the thing I've wanted to say for over a year.

The thing I can't take back once it's out.

The thing I might regret later, but the thing that makes me feel like I have a voice again. "I want him to know it was me."

She smiles, but it's not a friendly smile.

It's a wicked smile.

A wicked smile, with her eyes going dark and her lips parting and her gaze dipping to my lips, like she's turned on by revenge.

Revenge is no basis for a solid relationship, that voice in my head whispers.

Fuck a relationship though.

I just want to have fun.

And fun—fun is kissing Margot Merriweather-Brown.

My new partner in crime.

My soulmate in executing justice.

I lean in.

She leans in.

I finish what I started, wrapping my arm around her, and settle my hand on her hip.

Hers glides up my chest.

And then everything jolts, and we're thrust backward as the gondola starts moving again.

I block her head from hitting the glass at the back of the car, and she grabs onto my shirt as an anchor while the car sways with its new movement.

"That couch can't be comfortable," she murmurs as the car begins slowing almost as quickly as it got up to speed. We're almost at the end of the ride.

"Slept on worse."

"Maybe we can find a way for you to sleep better tonight."

So I'll be walking around with a boner for the rest of my shift.

Fabulous.

Her smoky blue eyes sparkle. "Provided you help me clean up a mess I apparently made."

"I cook or clean, Skillet. I don't do both."

"Are you offering to make me dinner?"

"Yes."

"I can cook too."

"You can prove it tomorrow."

The doors start to slide open as the car enters the terminal.

I rise and help her to her feet.

Adjust my crotch.

And then get the pleasure of watching her ass as she exits before me, passing by a group of dudes who don't even look at her.

Fucking idiots.

And I'd say that whether she was a housekeeper or a billionaire hotel heiress.

No relationships, just fun, I remind myself. Fun and revenge.

So long as I don't contemplate that she's the first person I've told this much about Felice and my stepfamily, and how much I genuinely like her as a person, I can keep believing that.

17

Bubbles are the new black

Margot

I never knew I could be grateful for not having a penis, but here I am, massively relieved that no one can outwardly tell how turned on I am after that discussion with Rhys.

For the past four years, anytime anyone would ask me what I was looking for in a man now that I was single, I'd say the same thing.

Someone pliable who takes orders well.

I like them meek and subservient.

But here I am, lusting after a giant of a former military man who's both vulnerable and dangerous, agreeable but only to a point, with a strong mind of his own and the added bonus of a massive case of the grumpies.

Grumpy has always been inconvenient to me. There's an extra layer of work to manage someone who's grumpy.

But Rhys's brand of grumpy—it's understandable.

Sympathetic, even.

I was a bear that first year after being single again, when I was also absurdly worried about Daphne, who was refusing all of my attempts to help her get set up after the disinheriting.

That's what I'm contemplating—how much I like Rhys and how turned on I am by him admitting he wants justice in his life—when I walk into the laundry room.

And gasp.

No, I choke on a gasp.

A knee-deep ocean of bubbles has flowed almost to the doorway, stretching across the room, the occasional sud-peak piled as high as the countertops where we fold the towels and sheets. A thin line still drizzles out of the open washing machine.

Cynthia, my boss, rounds the corner to the laundry room and shoves a mop at me. "Do this again, and you're fired."

"Yes, ma'am," I reply, despite every instinct yelling at me to deny that this was my doing.

I would never.

Never ever.

But when my options are being blamed for a room of suds or getting made by Jonas Rutherford, I'll take responsibility for the suds.

And for real—my lady boner isn't getting any smaller at the respect growing for how large of an issue Rhys managed to cause me.

He hasn't followed me down here, so I don't know where he is, but I get to work, head down, apologizing anytime any other staff attempts to enter the room while I'm cleaning.

Playing the part.

Equally impressed with how Rhys saved me and irritated at the pile of work he made for me.

We owe each other payback.

I'll take mine in bed. With his sweaty, broad body over mine, his beard tickling my skin while he—

"You know not to put the sheets back in the washing machine, right?" Louisa, one of my fellow housekeepers, says to me from the doorway, pulling me out of my fantasy.

I stifle a shriek and feel my cheeks heat. "Yes. Rinse them in the sink until they're not soapy anymore, then wash them the right way."

She points to a pile of white towels. "Those too." Her brow wrinkles. "I haven't known you long, but I thought you knew better."

Thank you. Of course I wouldn't do this.

Instead of saying it out loud, I give her a lopsided Margie Johnson grin. "What I get for listening to a podcast while I do laundry."

And putting myself in a position where I need saving from a man who's rapidly growing on me.

I'm finishing up a while after my shift should've ended, my brain already firmly back at the cabin, watching Rhys cook dinner, maybe with a glass of wine, most definitely while ogling his ass—I hope he wears jeans if he insists on cooking with clothes on—when my phone vibrates with a text message from Lucky.

> Dinner plans? Jack and Decker are coming for a cookout. You should join us. Bring Chex Mix.

Dammit.

Hang with Lucky or get lucky?

I wince to myself.

Never thinking that phrase again, because now I'm thinking about my half brother getting lucky, and despite only knowing he's my brother for a few months, and only seeing him in person for a week, he still already feels like my brother.

My phone buzzes again.

> Decker's dragging Rhys along too. Dude makes a killer apple cobbler. Like, you haven't lived until you've had it. So I know it's been awkward having him as a roommate, but for real, this apple cobbler will make you change your mind about him.

And now I'm smiling.

Because I still get to have dinner with Rhys without having to choose one over the other.

Even if there will definitely be more clothes involved.

Probably not a good sign, but while I've had the occasional fling here and there the past few years since my engagement ended, I haven't enjoyed the feeling of my body lighting up like I touched a live electrical wire around any of my choices in dates in—

Well.

Not since high school, when I had an irrepressible crush on a guy who was there on scholarship.

His father was a plumber, and his mother was an admin assistant somewhere.

His family wasn't the right kind of family.

So much so that my father made sure he didn't return for senior year.

It's one of those things I'm not supposed to know, but I do. Overheard the wrong things at the wrong times, and there was zero question.

My father knew I had a crush. My father didn't deem him worthy of me. My father eliminated the problem.

So at seventeen years old, I had to make the choice for the first time in my life.

A crush or my future?

I picked my future.

And I kept picking my future through college and beyond.

Oliver was the best choice, not because of passion or desperate love, but because he was smart and kind and agreeable, and if I was going to choose someone my family approved of, then I wanted someone who wouldn't make my life miserable.

And I did love him the only way I knew how to love someone.

Safely. Comfortably.

Daph's told us both we were boring together.

She was right.

He wouldn't have made me unhappy, but he wouldn't have made me happy either.

Set me on fire.

Been an obsession.

All with just a few touches and one soul-imprinting kiss.

Now I don't have to bend to whatever my family wants. I've made enough of a name for myself that if my current plans to destroy my father fail, I'll find another way.

And besides—this is, obviously, just a fling.

So rushing back to the cabin to see Rhys before dinner once I finally have the laundry room cleaned up?

Damn right.

Disappointed doesn't begin to cover how I feel when I get there and it's empty though.

I'd thought Rhys would be here.

That we'd get ready together. The long way. With equal parts assistance and interference from each other.

Apparently not.

I've fixed myself up in a fall dress, clearance rack cowboy boots, and a jean jacket, taking extra care with my makeup and picking simple hoop earrings—and I'm locking the front door so I can head to Lucky's house when Rhys pulls up in his truck.

"Want a ride?" he calls through the open passenger window.

Training tells me not to smile. Not to let them see when you want something. When something makes you happy.

Fuck training.

I'm not just smiling. I'm beaming. "Right now?"

"Already late, Skillet."

Dammit. "Then yes, thank you."

He jerks his head in a climb on up gesture. "Hop in."

"Did you come back here just to offer me a ride?"

"I can buy apples and the Chex Mix you'll claim you picked up and time it right to give you a lift."

There's a snort from the woods on the other side of the house.

We both look that way, him from the safety of the vehicle, me from the porch.

"Get in the truck," he murmurs. "Don't run. Just go quickly."

He's parked practically at the front door, so it's easy to do as he's asked.

I heft myself into the black leather passenger seat and shut my door just as the moose wanders into the yard.

"Has it followed us everywhere today?" I whisper, leaning closer to Rhys while I take in the immaculate interior. Freshly cleaned, or is it always neat?

I'm guessing always neat.

"Different moose at the center," he tells me.

"Seriously?"

He gestures to his head. "Antlers were smaller."

He doesn't start the truck, so we both sit, watching the moose wander through the yard, occasionally eyeballing us.

I have to lean closer into him to see the moose better, which means somehow, my hand ends up on his very solid thigh.

Gosh, whoops.

How did that ever happen?

Clearly he hates it because he covers my hand with his and brushes his thumb over my knuckles.

A subtle cologne tickles my nose. Something fresh, but also old. Like a grandpa's tobacco and the way the wood smelled like new pine last night when we were splitting it.

I glance at Rhys.

He's in dark jeans and a blue flannel that makes his eyes pop. The flannel's open over a tight white undershirt.

Most of the purple streaks have faded from his face, and he trimmed his beard down to scruff this morning, so the purple's gone from there too. He's sporting a plain black baseball cap that I want to push off his head so I can run my fingers through his hair.

And now I'm not just smelling his cologne.

I'm also smelling the scent of my own arousal as my panties get damp.

He shifts his gaze off the moose and turns it to me.

Then he smirks.

Like he knows he's tormenting me.

The moose glares at us.

"Oh, don't be so moody," I say to him, partially to distract myself, even if I'm still gripping Rhys's thigh. "We'll be back soon. You don't need to be so emo about being alone for a couple hours."

The moose stares at me for a beat, visibly snorts, and then moseys around to the back of the house.

"I've been honing my communication skills at work, but I didn't think they'd work on a moose," I murmur.

"Margot Merriweather-Brown, moose whisperer," Rhys says as he puts the truck in gear.

I laugh. "Hardly."

He lifts his brows and shrugs. "Looks like it from here."

The drive isn't long—maybe fifteen minutes—and I make Rhys stop twice for pictures of the view to send to Daphne.

Both times leaning over him in the car to point my phone out his window.

Both times getting the benefit of him dipping his nose into my hair and inhaling deeply while running a hand down my back.

We should not be going to dinner here tonight.

My brothers are going to figure out what's up in a hot millisecond.

"You stop and take pictures in Manhattan?" Rhys asks me after the second time I ask him to pull over for a photo.

"Sunrise and sunset from my place at least once a week, and regularly on the beach when I'm in the Hamptons or a few of my other favorite places."

His lips curve up in a soft smile as he pulls back onto the road. "Moose whisperer and hider of surprises."

"Now that you know my secret talents, what are yours?"

"Baking apple cobbler and knowing when creepy assholes are going to hit on the housekeeper."

I raise a brow at him.

And even though he's driving, with his attention on the curving roads as we enter a residential area, I'm positive he notices.

You can tell by the growing smirk.

Heaven help me, I love it when he smirks at me.

I may have been wrong about liking my men meek and mild.

I might like them better when they go toe-to-toe with me.

That might be what's been missing from my love life.

"Do you think Lucky has any firewood he needs split?" I ask. "So I can make myself useful while you're cooking?"

His smirk turns into a real smile. "His only fireplace is gas."

"Oh."

"Is that the face you make when you're disappointed at work too? Your normal job back home?"

I burst out laughing at the idea of letting anyone at work see when I'm honestly sad.

Support and build up my team? Yes.

Let them support and build me up?

Still working on that.

"Stop talking about who I really am," I tell Rhys. "I have to be Margie for the next few hours."

"Do you?"

"Yes."

"What's your trigger point? When do you know it's time to tell them beyond some made-up date you gave me to shut me up?"

I sink deeper into the soft leather passenger seat and sigh. "I'll know."

"That simple?"

"It'll be when I realize I've been hiding it longer than I should have because I like it when people like me for me instead of my titles and family and investments. Also, my sabbatical can only last so long before—before I need to go back."

He slides a glance at me as he pulls to a stop on the street behind a truck I recognize as Jack's. "Before all of the pieces are in place for whatever grand scheme you need them for?"

"I wish I could be offended by that," I murmur.

"Didn't mean it as offensive. I unfortunately think it's hot."

I smile at him. "How hot?"

"We're in front of your brother's place."

"That's a level of hot."

He pins me with another look, then smiles and shakes his head as he shuts the engine off.

But he doesn't immediately get out of the truck.

Oh, no.

The man gives me a slow once-over that has my nipples pebbling and my panties getting wetter.

Like he too would rather we'd been invited to this cookout another night, and like he too intends to tease and flirt with me all night long.

"Grab those apples and the Chex Mix, would you? Then I can tell your brothers you helped."

I'm laughing as I unbuckle and twist in my seat to look for the groceries in the back seat. As I'm twisted, another car pulls up behind us.

Two people are in front.

But neither is Decker.

And suddenly nothing's funny anymore.

"Oh, shit," I whisper.

Rhys glances behind us too, but I don't enjoy the way our shoulders are connecting the way I should.

Not when he's spotting the same thing I'm looking at.

His smile turns grim, and he grabs his phone.

"Tell me that's not the triplets' parents," I say.

"You seem like too big a fan of the truth for me to tell that lie."

I glance at him.

If he's amused, worried, or feeling anything other than calm, his poker face isn't giving it away.

While he checks his phone, I check mine too.

I have six messages from Lucky that have come in since Rhys pulled over for my last photos.

Shit. Jack invited Mom and Dad.

This will be fine. Right? Don't tell them.

I don't know how the fuck Jack missed that you were coming. Just be cool, okay?

If you got sick, I'd understand. Not that I want you to be sick. I'm just fucking nervous.

We do want to see you tonight. Awkward isn't our specialty though. Not when it's our awkward. We love it when it's someone else's awkward. Possibly we're dicks.

Let me know when you get this. Remember who you are—my friend who flunked out of nursing school and needed a job.

I text Lucky back that I won't mess this up, then glance at Rhys.

His gaze meets mine, and I swear there's a hint of amusement lingering with the recognition that tonight is going to be very, very awkward.

"Show time," he says. "Don't fuck up."

"I dislike that you're attractive when you're baiting me."

His whole face breaks into a heart-stopping grin that transforms grumpy bodyguard man into a mountain of a snack. "How terrible for you."

And then he's swinging himself out of the truck while I'm still grabbing the cloth bag of groceries.

Two breaths.

I give myself two breaths, and then I climb out of the truck too. He's right.

It's showtime.

18

Apples and anxiety

Rhys

The triplets are going to blow it.

Every last one of them is so tense that if I flicked them with a fingertip, they'd shatter.

Margie though—and yeah, I'm actively thinking of her as Margie tonight so that I'm not the one who spills the secret—is rocking it.

And not just with helping me peel apples at the island in the small kitchen, where she keeps accidentally brushing her arm against mine or angling her hip against the side of my thigh or grabbing the same apple I'm reaching for.

That part—the part where she keeps touching me—that part is driving me mad.

I want to toss her over my shoulder and take her out to the back seat of my truck and fuck her until we both get this out of our system.

If she's the firecracker in the sack that I think she is—then I'll need to work her out of my system several times.

Possibly several times a day. Every day for the next month.

Shit.

Down, boner. *Down.*

"Lucky was so helpful during my three months of nursing school," Margie's telling Mrs. Sullivan, who's sitting at the high countertop behind the sink on one end of the brightly lit kitchen. "You know how people are. If you say you think something isn't for you, they'll try to encourage you and say it gets better and you just need to stick it out a little while longer. But Lucky was the first one to tell me I'd be okay and I'd find my real purpose if nursing wasn't it. And I needed to hear that. I needed that kind of support."

Mrs. Sullivan beams at her. "That's my boy. He's always been so good at recognizing it's important to let people be who they are and to respect what they say they need."

While Margie's perfectly playing the role of nursing-school-dropout-turned-housekeeper, Decker and Lucky are quietly sniping at each other about potato salad.

Jack's noped out of the whole thing and is out on the back deck, supposedly manning the corn cobs on the grill and talking to Mr. Sullivan.

No one's touched the Chex Mix. Not even to open the bag. It's just sitting there on the counter beside the fridge.

"Are you seeing anyone, Margie?" Mrs. Sullivan asks, her gaze flitting to me and making me very glad the counter is high enough to hide the problem in my pants.

Just barely, but it is.

"I'm working on me solo for a while instead of working on me in relationships," Margie replies.

Mrs. Sullivan's gaze slides to her two boys.

Specifically lingering on Lucky, if I'm reading this right.

Then she looks back at Margie with a knowing smile. "No better place than Snaggletooth Creek to work on yourself."

"It's been good so far."

"With friends like my boys? I'm sure it has."

Mrs. Sullivan doesn't mean *friends*, and she doesn't mean *all* of her boys.

Not with the look she slides between Lucky and Margie again.

I glance at Margie.

Now that I know her a little better, it's easier to tell when she's been thrown for a loop.

This—Mrs. Sullivan implying Margie's here for a hookup—is loop territory.

While her face is mostly placid, her right eye has pinched the barest amount behind her glasses, and her lips have gone flat.

I bump her from the side with my hip. "Leave some apple for me to make magic, Skillet. Don't take it all off with the peel."

Her face smooths out, and she gives me a playful smile. "Have you looked at how much apple you're taking off with *your* peel?"

I grab one of hers and one of mine and lift them to the light to inspect them. "You're worse. Look. There's at least three extra millimeters of apple width on your peel."

"You can see *three millimeters* with your eyeballs?"

Lucky and Decker quit arguing about the mayo measurement for the potato salad and look at us.

"You can't?" I reply to Margie. "Time to get your prescription checked."

"Quit flirting with my—friend," Lucky says.

His mom turns a startled look at him, then peers closer at Margie, who deftly gathers up a load of peels, head down like it was when she was facing Jonas Rutherford the other day. She turns away and dumps them in Lucky's compost bin.

"There. *Now* we can't argue about who left more apple on their peel," she says.

"Still you," I mutter.

"Just for that, you're cutting them yourself."

"Have to. They need to be uniform. You'd probably do some chunks and some slices, and it'd be ruined."

She's pursing her lips together, but you can still tell she's smiling. "I'm going to see if Jack needs anything. He was so nice too, Mrs. Sullivan. He changed the timing belt on my van when it broke after I got here."

"Just Jack?" I tease.

She grins at me. "Only people who don't give me shit about how I peel apples get credit for fixing my car."

Lucky's glaring at me.

Decker's not too happy either, but in Decker's case, it's definitely not the *don't hit on my sister* problem that Lucky's having.

Decker, I'm nearly certain, is glad that no one's implying Margie should date Lucky anymore. And also pissed at me because he can't tell if I'm playing a part or really falling for the sister I'm supposed to be investigating.

"Lucky, do you—" his mom starts as the door closes behind Margie, but he interrupts her.

"Mom, tell Decker that Grandma's potato salad recipe is wrong with how it's written, and we need to double the mayo and add dill."

She shoots one more look at me, but this one holds an exasperated smile. "Do you have family members who intentionally wrote down recipes wrong so that no one else could make them correctly, Rhys?"

"No, ma'am. I cooked with my mom until she died, so I would've known if she was hiding anything."

"Maybe you should make the potato salad if you know her recipe."

"Prefer coleslaw myself. The vinegar kind."

Margie breezes back into the kitchen. "Jack says yes to dill, no to doubling the mayo," she reports. "And is the chicken ready for the grill? I can take it out if it is."

"No chicken," Lucky says at the same time Decker says, "We're doing kabobs."

Margie makes an *oops* face that I'm completely positive is an act. "Oh, right. I knew that."

"You ever have kabobs?" I ask her.

"No, Rhys, I've never been to a cookout where someone made kabobs." She shakes her head at Mrs. Sullivan. "Men. Am I right?"

Mrs. Sullivan laughs. "And now you know what my entire life has been like. I've spent the past thirty-odd years surrounded by only men."

"You've had Sabrina and Aunt Traci, and they were over all the time," Decker reminds her.

"Still outnumbered."

"Not with the size of Sabrina's personality," Jack calls from the deck.

"That all three of you tried to keep up with," Mrs. Sullivan says.

I know the triplets have another cousin, but there was some drama with him a couple years ago, involving when he almost married Emma, Jonas's wife, plus some other things, and they don't talk about him anymore.

Apparently they don't talk about his parents either.

"Son, best to quit when you're not so far behind that you can't see where you started anymore," Mr. Sullivan says. His voice is softer but still carries through the screen door.

I grab a knife and start cutting apples.

Margie digs into the fridge and comes up with the kabobs. "Okay to take these out?" she asks Decker and Lucky.

"Yeah, get 'em going," Decker says.

While Decker's distracted with answering her, Lucky adds an extra scoop of mayo to the potato salad, then screws the lid on and moves around me to put it away.

"Are you serious?" Decker mutters as he looks down at the potato salad.

"You're not letting the flavors blend long enough anyway," I tell him. "Won't actually matter in the end."

Mrs. Sullivan giggles.

I eye her. "You know the real recipe, don't you?"

"Who, me? I'm only an in-law. I don't get the real Sullivan family recipes for anything."

Her smile says she's lying.

For a moment, I wonder how things worked out that Mr. Sullivan isn't the triplets' biological father.

And then I remind myself it's none of my business.

My business is telling Decker if he can trust Margie.

And honestly?

I think the answer's yes.

She's going to want something from him and his brothers that they might not want to give, but I believe her when she says she doesn't want collateral damage.

I believe she wants to fit into a family.

And if I'm wrong—

If I'm wrong, I'm wrong. There's enough to be suspicious of in life.

I want to keep my rose-colored glasses on when it comes to Margie-Margot.

To be brave again.

To not be afraid to live.

The apple cobbler goes in the oven as the kabobs come off the grill, and we all head outside to eat in the cool evening. Jack and Lucky flank Margie, with Decker and me across the table and Mr. and Mrs. Sullivan at either end.

Mrs. Sullivan grills Margie on where she's from and how she's liking Snaggletooth Creek and if she thinks she'll settle here long-term, and before long, even the triplets have calmed down.

They have no idea they're dealing with a world-class achiever.

They think she's just a nice person who's putting effort into not messing up in front of their parents.

Not that the favor is being returned.

Their mom is dishing out a lot of, "Lucky, did you hear that? Margie loves cooking shows. You two should compare notes and cook together sometime," and "Lucky, you should take Margie to Sir Pretzelot if she loves this bread that much," and "Lucky, Margie's never been white water rafting! What are you doing tomorrow? You should take her."

"Rafting season is long over," Decker says.

Jack takes a more direct approach. "Mom, leave him alone."

"What? I'm just trying to be helpful. You boys so rarely have friends in town like this where you can really show them around."

"He's not into Margie like that," Decker says.

Mrs. Sullivan rolls her eyes. "Because of the curse?"

"*Shh*," Decker hisses.

"It's not because of the curse," Lucky says.

"Curses aren't real," Mrs. Sullivan adds.

"Don't curse it worse by saying curses aren't real," Jack says.

"Don't mind them," Mr. Sullivan says to Margie. "They do this every time a new female-presenting person moves to town and so much as looks at one of the boys."

"They've never let a friend stay in Grandma's cabin," Mrs. Sullivan points out.

He smiles at her. "They have *two* people staying in Grandma's cabin. Possibly they're playing matchmaker."

"We are *not*," Decker says.

"Unless you're just pretending you can't read a calendar right," Jack says.

Margie's nostrils wobble.

So do her lips.

"Is that the apple cobbler?" she says. "Do you all smell that too? Oh! Lucky. I almost forgot. We saw the moose again as we were leaving the cabin. And a different one at the retreat center today. Isn't that crazy?"

Lucky's all in on changing the subject. He leans into her. "Did you get a picture?"

She pulls out her phone and opens the photo app. "Just the one this morning."

"Holy shit. You really saw one."

"Was that before or after you two got yourselves stuck on the lift?" Decker asks.

That one's aimed at me.

And there's a little heat behind the question.

Guilt that I haven't filled him in on what I know makes my ears itch, but I keep a straight face while I answer him. "First thing this morning. Before the lift stopped."

"It was only down for like three minutes," Margie says. "And we were so close to the end that we didn't even get the good views. I'm still in awe of the mountains, and the view from the winery—just *wow*."

"Dude, you're getting reports about when the lift stops at the retreat center now?" Lucky says to Decker.

"Sabrina said Emma said Jonas thinks some of the staff are...*doing things*."

Margie's eyebrows bunch together. "Like playing pranks on the lift?"

The flat stare he aims her way is a clear *don't play stupid* look.

"*Ooooh*," she says. She looks at me and grins, then looks back at Decker. "So I did something really stupid at work today. Our boss sent Rhys to get me to clean it up."

She launches into a story about how she was listening to a podcast and lost track of what she was doing as she loaded the washing machine and didn't realize she'd grabbed the wrong soap until I tracked her down, selling it without selling it so hard that no one would believe her.

Which is fucking annoying.

She's good at spinning a story.

And the whole thing is true. Except for the part where it was her fault. That part isn't true.

So is she spinning other stories about what she wants?

Dammit, I hate this second-guessing.

The timer goes off on my phone, so I head inside to check the apple cobbler.

Decker joins me.

"You're messing around with her now?" The injured irritation in his voice says it all.

If I were to guess what the man's feeling right now, I'd say he's pissed, and he's pissed that he's pissed, because he doesn't want to play the brother card. He wants to play the suspicious card, but now he's playing both.

Fuck.

I make myself look my buddy straight in the eye, and I do the exact same thing Margie's still doing out on the deck with that story, and I tell him eighty percent of the truth. "I've been watching her all week, man. Digging into everything I can find. I don't think she's after anything except for wanting to get to know you."

"That's not your dick talking?"

"My dick is the most suspicious organ in my body. Be glad you know you're cursed. Would've saved me a lot of trouble if I hadn't had to learn the hard way not to trust the brain in my pants."

He cringes. "Sorry," he mutters.

"Also, you're welcome for being someone else she can have a crush on so your mom will drop it."

He cringes harder. "If she keeps suggesting Lucky hooks up with Margie—"

I grin. "Incest isn't on his bucket list? After you were discussing if she was hot last night?"

He shoves me. "Apple cobbler better be worth it."

Of course it is.

When I serve it up, everyone forgets about everything beyond the orgasms in their mouths.

And I forget about everything except how Margie looks when her eyes slide shut and her lips tip up in a blissful smile while her throat works as she swallows.

"You sure security's your thing?" Mr. Sullivan asks me. "When you can cook like this?"

"Let the man have a hobby, Dad," Decker says. "Not as much fun when your hobby becomes your job."

"*Wah, I get to do the thing I love most in the world for money,*" Lucky says.

"*It's so hard being me when I get to grump around pretending to have writer's block while my assistant does all the real hard work for my business,*" Jack adds.

Decker flips them both off.

They smirk.

Margie opens her mouth like she's about to say something, then shakes her head, her cheeks turning a little pink while she digs into another bite of the cobbler.

Her eyes lift to mine, and I swear hers are telegraphing *almost had a whoops there*.

Like she was about to say something about them reminding her of her and her sister.

Or about one of her employees. She has to have dozens of them.

A soft breeze blows in, carrying more of a chill than there was a minute ago before the sun dipped below the horizon.

Lucky rises and starts gathering dishes, but his mom stops him. "You hosted and cooked. I'll clean."

"I'll help," Margie says.

And she does.

Margie, the secret billionaire heiress in disguise, insists on staying until the dishwasher is running and the hand-washed dishes are all put away.

Then she hugs each of the triplets and thanks them for a fun evening.

And I don't feel bad anymore about the tiny little lies I've told Decker.

She *is* a good person.

Complicated, but good.

And I don't regret supporting the idea that she could belong here. That she could be one more member of their family.

You're such a sucker, my dick mutters.

I tell it to fuck off.

As much as I want it to, anyway.

Margot's right.

Felice hurt me. But no one wins if I keep hiding from living.

19

Secrets, secrets, secrets

Margot

We've just slid into Rhys's truck to head home, my hormones buzzing and my adrenaline crashing at the same time after having gotten through tonight without slipping in front of the triplets' parents, when my phone vibrates with an incoming call.

Rhys and I both glance down at it.

"My sister," I say to him.

"I thought your sister was Daphne."

I smile. "I changed her name to Jessica D in my phone just in case she called when I was with someone. Everyone knows seven million Jessicas. The D is for Daphne. Do you mind if I take this? She doesn't call often when I'm free and vice versa. Especially with us in different time zones right now."

"Might lose signal somewhere."

I slide my hand back to his thigh. "Yep. Exactly when we pull up to the cabin."

He starts the engine, then tucks his hand over mine while I answer the phone. "Hey. Everything okay?"

"Yes! It's great. Are you alone?"

"As good as alone."

"So you're with Cyril?"

"No, my roommate."

That gets a squeal that's loud enough that Rhys gives me the *so you've been talking about me to your sister* look.

"We just left Lucky's house," I tell her. "He had a cookout."

"I am almost insanely jealous right now."

It's so easy to smile at her voice. "Almost? Not all the way? You must've had a good day."

"Oh my god, Margot, I stopped by Bea's burger bus on my way home from work today, and people had launched a reverse protest to support her. It was so freaking beautiful. Simon's out in LA—he left for his movie shoot—so Oliver stepped in and did that thing Simon was doing with helping serve burgers shirtless, and Bea kept calling Ryker to run to the store for more ground beef, and I convinced her to make donuts for her secret menu item one day next week to celebrate having such a great day today."

I smile and sink deeper into the seat, idly stroking Rhys's thigh while I get the updates from Daphne on her best friend, Bea, and everything in Athena's Rest. "I thought Oliver already had a job and no plans to overachieve by doing something like getting two jobs."

She laughs.

"Today was charity work," he calls in the background. "Very different from a job."

"And do you remember the Camilles?" Daphne says.

"As in Bea's ex's family?" I ask. Bea had basically the worst breakup in history several months ago, so the fact that she's dating one of the world's current most popular actors now—her ex's favorite actor, in fact—is the kind of karmic justice that I'm here for.

Bonus that Simon's an incredibly nice guy and appreciates what he has in her.

"Yes," Daphne squeals. "Oliver ran into Damon Camille—he's the dad, Bea's almost father-in-law, the ambulance chaser attorney who's sued like half the town—and Damon was like *if you ever need legal rep-*

resentation and Oliver looked him dead in the eye and said I can afford every lawyer in Manhattan and then some, and I protect the people I love, and I hear you've been a dick to some of them, and I am so serious, the next day, Damon announced he's retiring. Retiring. Bea thinks Simon might've had a talk with him too, but there are two new big dogs in Athena's Rest, and the guard is changing, and it's beautiful."

"So Bea doesn't have to worry about him suing her for calling her bus Best Burger Bus anymore?"

"Margot, you're so far behind. She told the whole world about how Jake dumped her after stealing her restaurant, and that that's why she opened the burger bus. She rebranded it as Spite Burgers and started new socials and I think she's going to be the first billionaire burger bus owner in existence."

I crack up at that. "It's a long way from one burger bus to billionaire."

"She has a tip jar," Oliver says. "I can help her get there."

These two.

They're hilarious together.

"I've spent enough time with Bea that I suspect she'd be more than a little irritated if you did for her what you did on your road trip last month," I say to both of them.

"Huh. That's an idea," Oliver replies.

Daphne giggles. "Oh, she'd kill you."

"Good thing we're working on getting a dog so I'll know she's coming."

I sigh even as I'm smiling.

I miss my sister.

When I get back to New York, I need to make more time to see her. I don't want to be one of those CEOs who works sunrise to sunset. I want to be one who has the right team in place—a team who all have healthy work-life balances, which I personally believe is the key to maximum productivity.

I'm almost there too.

My staff is nearly large enough to support me when we move into the chief executive's suite.

And they're hella good too.

"If you do what you're inevitably going to do to Bea, leave my name out of it," I say to them.

"Tell me about the cookout," Daph replies.

My eyes nearly cross, and I blow out a breath of relief.

Running a hotel empire isn't as exhausting as lying to the triplets' parents. "Their parents showed up. It was so awkward, because they don't know who I really am—like the related part, because the triplets haven't told their parents that they know that their dad isn't their biological dad, and it's this whole big secret—and I kept thinking I was going to slip and blow it the whole time."

"Oh my god."

"Right? And then their mom started dropping hints that Lucky should try to date me."

Daphne cackles.

"That was fucked up," Rhys mutters.

"I think I'm going to have nightmares," I tell him.

He squeezes my hand.

"Are they going to tell their parents?" Daphne asks.

"I don't know. Secrets and families—they don't go together, you know? But this one isn't my call."

"Margot."

"Don't start. I'm not keeping secrets. I'm being strategic. And speaking of strategic, my roommate saved me from Jonas Rutherford today."

"No."

"Yes." I tell her the soap story, and she reacts even better than the Sullivans did.

"I got pictures," Rhys says to me.

"You didn't." I didn't think he was anywhere near the laundry room.

He grins, and my heart melts a little more. "Video too. I was stealthy. You never knew I was there."

"I'll send you proof," I tell Daphne. "But you can't share it. Not even with Bea."

"Ever or yet?"

"Yet."

"How much longer will you be?"

I cringe.

The right answer is I'll be home next week.

I shouldn't keep dragging this out with Lucky, Decker, and Jack.

I need to tell them who I am and what I want.

The timing's right, even if I'm lying to myself about wanting to see Oliver's family's company's shareholder meeting go the right way next week first.

My father's been buying shares of Miles2Go in a bid for a hostile takeover—he's always wanted to expand beyond hotels, therefore Oliver was an approved option of a boyfriend for me—and Oliver's about to distribute his quarter of the company's total shares to franchise owners after his choice of new CEO is approved by shareholders early next week.

There's no telling if the franchise owners will hold on to their new shares or sell them, which could put my father in a position to buy more, so I've convinced Oliver to wait a few weeks so that I can do what I need to do to ruin my father's reputation and make him undesirable for any other company he might want to take over too.

And make him not want to put himself in a public position about it either.

Which means next week is when I need to act.

Next week is when I need to tell the triplets who I am and what I want. Ask for their help and keep the ball rolling on my plans.

But I don't want to.

I want to have more time with them where they see me as a normal person with normal stresses and normal needs. When they don't think I'm pressuring them to tell their parents what they know.

I've been contemplating how I can accomplish my goal of showing my father and the board that the triplets exist while simultaneously keeping them out of the public eye if this works the way I want it to.

And I think I've figured out the best way to play this for everyone's advantage.

If they'll agree to it.

"Three weeks," I say to Daphne. "I'll be three more weeks."

"Because you need that long, or because you want that long?" she asks softly.

My eyes get hot. "Both."

I'm lying.

I don't need this long.

But between the fun with the triplets and getting to know Rhys—yeah.

I want longer.

I swallow hard. "Oliver?"

"Yep?" he answers.

"Still working on that thing I asked you about?"

"Yep."

"Thank you."

"You owe me the full story behind the request one day."

I smile. "Can't fully escape business life?"

"I can admire it from a distance."

"Wow. You two take background checks seriously," Daphne says.

We're not talking about the background check I asked Oliver to run on Rhys's old company, but Oliver doesn't correct her.

I don't either.

The fewer people who know what I'm planning, the better, and Oliver only knows I asked him to stall on distributing his shares to franchise owners, but not why.

He's probably making a few assumptions, but since he left the CEO life behind, he's taking the only tell me what I need to know tactic.

I appreciate that.

"They should be taken seriously," I say to Daphne, but my phone makes an odd noise, and a moment later, beeps with the dropped call notification.

I text her that I lost signal—it'll likely send when we round another corner or two—and sink even deeper into the truck seat.

We're almost to the cabin.

"You lied well tonight," Rhys says quietly.

"Do you think they'll appreciate why I lied to them about who I am when they've also asked me to lie to their parents about who I am?"

He blinks slowly. Then snorts and shakes his head. "No."

"Seriously?"

"It's always different when you want someone to lie for you than it is when they lie for themselves."

"Lies are lies."

"Agreed. But human beings in general have a but it's different for me mentality. It's different for them to ask you to lie so they don't have to tell their parents a secret than it is for you to lie to them to protect your own secrets."

"You have a fascinating understanding of humanity."

He lifts a shoulder. "Mom taught me to watch. So I watched."

And he's good at it.

The thing that's separated the people who stay on my security team from the people who don't make it through their probationary period is the exact thing Rhys has.

The clear, keen intellect required to both watch what's going on around him and then read between the lines and understand what's not said as much as what is.

Cyril's been with me as long as he has because he knows when to make up a situation requiring my attention to get me out of awkward moments with my family. He's as much personal assistant sometimes as he is protection agent, and I'm positive he has an idea of what I'm planning for my father.

Just like I strongly suspect Rhys has been connecting those dots since the other hints I dropped on the lift.

"Do you think they'll be mad?" I ask him. "When I tell them?"

"Decker will be mad because he's ready to be mad. Lucky will be hurt because he likes to see the best in people and he expects the same level of trust that he puts in them returned to him. Jack will be hurt too, but he'll also understand why you did it, so he'll logic his way into it hurting less."

I think he's spot-on. "Do you have any insights on if the triplets disagree about telling their parents they know about their dad?"

"Lucky's wanted to tell them from the beginning. Decker's wanted to keep it from them. Jack's been—well, he's been fucking Switzerland. But you heard what they said about the curse. They're all in together. On everything."

I stare out the window at the trees and brush illuminated by Rhys's headlights as he turns into the driveway. "Daphne doesn't know I've been on her side this whole time. Since she was disinherited."

"Doesn't she?"

"She might now. I hope she does now. But she definitely didn't at first. I thought—for a while, I thought she was replacing me with her best friend. And as much as I was grateful that she had Bea to lean on, it hurt to think I could be replaceable in her life when she could never be replaceable in mine. And that's when I knew I couldn't play the middle anymore. I couldn't be the CEO in training under my father and also be Daphne's big sister."

He doesn't say anything, but he's said enough that I can guess what he's thinking.

You have been though. You've been doing both.

"My life is about to change drastically," I whisper.

"And you're gonna fucking own it," he murmurs back.

Warmth spreads from my chest down to my arms.

The past four years, I've felt very, very alone.

And also like I deserved to be alone.

I didn't stand up enough for my sister, so I didn't deserve her. I stayed at Aurora Gardens instead of taking an immediate stand that I didn't work with people who were unnecessarily cruel, that I didn't want to be related to people who were unnecessarily cruel, therefore, I participated in the unnecessary cruelty.

And I questioned myself—was I playing the long game, or was I staying where it was safe out of fear of how it would look or how it would feel to do the same thing Daph did and walk away entirely with her head held high?

She bloomed and thrived in her new life, and she started it with nothing.

They even turned off her phone without giving her a chance to salvage her number.

She owned it.

She owned her new life while I set myself on a course of action that I knew would take a long time, that I couldn't tell anyone about, and that I've been fucking determined to succeed at, but where I've been the only person who could tell me that I was doing a good job and that my plans would work.

So having Rhys believe in me?

Having him tell me I'll rock the next chapter of my life?

It's an unexpected boost that I didn't realize I wanted—needed—and it's doing funny things to my insides.

He pulls the truck to a stop in front of the cabin, shifts into park, kills the engine, and unbuckles his seatbelt.

I unbuckle too, but when he reaches for his door, I reach for him.

Because this man?

This giant of a man with a steady heart and a sharp mind and a steely determination to embrace justice for his own reasons?

I need to kiss him.

I need to kiss him until I can't breathe.

And I need it right now.

20

The best ideas are bad ideas

Rhys

Kissing Margot is a bad idea.

But it's the only idea—it's been the only idea—and every part of me is on board.

My hands. My mouth. My dick. What's left of my brain after her lips touch mine.

And she's not a start-softly kisser.

Not tonight.

Tonight, she's an if we're doing this, we're doing this kisser.

She knocks my hat off and plunges her hands into my hair while she devours my mouth with hers, and I can't stop the feral, possessive growl that rumbles low in my throat as I reach across the console to pull her closer to me.

I haven't made out with a woman in my truck since I was a teenager, and having Margot crawl into my lap in the driver's seat is turning me on in a way I haven't been aroused in what feels like just as long.

Her ass lands on the steering wheel, and the horn honks, which sends us both into a fit of laughter.

I hit the button to recline the seat while peppers kisses over my lips, but the motor is so fucking slow that her ass honks the horn three more times before my seat's fully back.

"We should go inside," she gasps between kisses.

"No." I hook a hand around her neck and pull her tighter for a deeper kiss.

My cock is throbbing. My heart is racing. Her tongue glides against mine, and my brain forgets how to brain. I grip her bare thighs under her skirt, feel hot, smooth skin over her thick muscles, and my dick hardens to steel granite diamonds—if that's not a thing, it's what my cock is now—while my heart pounds even faster.

She pushes my shirt up, her hot little hands exploring my chest while she settles her hips over mine, cradling my hard-on with her pussy, and I get that warning sensation in my gut that tells me I'm two thrusts from blowing my load.

Inside.

She's right.

We should go inside.

"I've never done this in the front seat of a car," she says.

We should stay right here. "Truck's here all night."

She smiles and kisses me again.

Her hands are magic, skimming over my chest hair and finding my nipples, giving them a quick tweak before she glides her fingers down to the button on my jeans. "Stop me when I go too far," she says.

As if she could. "No too far. Kiss more."

She's giggling as her lips find mine. She pops the button on my jeans and dips her fingers beneath the waistband, the heady scent of her arousal tickling my nose.

And not for the first time tonight.

Remembering how she smelled on the drive to dinner—that's what's had me half-hard all night.

And now she's straddling my lap and I'm caressing her thighs and she's sticking her hands down my pants to—ahhh, yesssss, fuuuuuuuck.

Her warm fingers wrap around my cock, and it's all I can do to not come on the spot.

I squeeze her thighs.

"Oh, you're big," she whispers. "So soft too."

"I am not soft," I grit out, my breath coming in short, desperate pants.

I want inside this woman.

I want inside her now.

She chuckles and strokes me once more. "Your skin is."

I'm sweating with the effort of not coming in her hands, and I realize I'm clenching her thighs so tightly that she'll have bruises tomorrow. "Margot—"

She palms my cheeks as she scoots her pussy over my exposed dick, the thin fabric of her panties the only thing between us.

She licks my lips, her pelvis grinding against my aching cock, and I swat for the console between the seats.

Condoms.

Bought condoms.

At a store.

Tonight.

Her hands work their way into my hair again, fingers scratching my scalp while she explores my mouth with her tongue, and my eyes cross.

I don't know if they're open or shut, but they're crossing.

Has kissing and dry humping a woman ever felt this good?

My balls are wound tight. My cock's straining to be inside her.

God, the way her thigh feels—so strong, so thick, so perfect—and the way she still tastes like ice cream and apple and cinnamon—and now she's teasing the shell of my ear with one hand while the other strokes down my neck, over my shoulder—

Condoms.

There.

There.

My hand connects with the box.

Why didn't I open the fucking thing when I bought them?

Fuck on a crabcake, how do her hands feel so good on my chest?

"More," I gasp when I mean to ask for help opening the fucking box.

She scrapes her fingers down my chest while she lightly nips at my lower lip. "This?"

"Fuck, yes."

"Your body is magnificent."

"Less talk. Condoms."

Her eyes crinkle at the edges when she smiles at me, and I'm gone. I'm just gone.

My dick's still straining to be inside her, her hips still rocking against me and pushing me to the point of the good kind of pain, but she's smiling at me, her eyes dark and her lids half-lowered, mouth parted as she pants heavily too, and I don't need anything else.

Just for her to smile at me like that.

To make me feel valued.

Cherished.

Worthy.

Wanted.

She makes me feel wanted.

She takes the box from me, rips it open, and sends condoms flying everywhere.

I snag a strip off the passenger seat.

She takes it and tears the end condom open.

I shove her dress up, eye the skimpy pink panties covering her pussy, grab them by one of the strings over her hip, and rip the fucking thing apart.

"Why is that such a turn-on?" she says on a gasp while she rolls the condom down my length.

I rip the other side too, dipping my finger under the fabric as it falls away, through her curls and into the wet, slick heat between her thighs.

And she is turned on.

She's wet.

So wet.

"Oh, god," she pants as I slide a finger inside her.

"Kiss me while I fuck you," I growl.

She dives into another kiss, riding my hand while I fuck her with my fingers, my dick demanding to know when he gets a turn.

She gasps and whimpers, her tongue tangling with mine, her hips bucking erratically in my palm, all of her arousal coating my fingers and dripping lower.

I'm so turned on, my brain is cramping.

"So—good—harder," she gasps against my mouth.

I flick my thumb over the hard little nub of her clit, and her inner muscles clench around my fingers, squeezing them with a pulsing heat that once again tests the limits of how long I can go without blowing my load.

"Yes, yes," she pants.

She throws her head back, grinding down in my hand, and I lean up to lick her neck.

She shudders, goosebumps rising beneath my tongue.

The things I plan to do to this woman when I have her in that bed inside instead of the driver's seat of my truck.

"Oh my god, Rhys," she pants, her pussy still squeezing my fingers.

"Wait until I eat you," I growl against her jaw.

She shudders once more as I keep mercilessly thrusting my fingers into her clenched heat, the smell of sex thick around us.

"I'll fuck you with my tongue until you can't walk, and then I'll fuck you so hard with my dick that you'll see stars."

"Now," she gasps.

"You're not done yet."

"Oh my gaaaaahhhh," she pants.

I crook my fingers inside her and press hard on her clit, and she sings.

Swear to god, she hits a high note while her head rolls back again, her sweet pussy clenching even harder.

My hand is fully coated in her release, and I keep teasing that orgasm higher until she finally flops against me, panting and limp. "Holy shit."

"Not done yet, Skillet," I murmur.

She lifts her head, eyelids heavy, one eye a little crossed, her lips pink, the skin around them chafed.

And she gives me the sweetest, softest smile.

The kind that can crack a man in two.

Make him forget his own name.

Make him fall in love.

"We're not, are we?" she murmurs.

I lift my fingers and lick the salty, heady taste off of them.

She shudders. "Why is that so sexy?"

"Because you're fucking sexy, you gorgeous minx."

And then she's moving, shifting against my hips until she's sliding onto my dick.

Fucking heaven.

She shudders again. "How—so good—already?"

"More," I grunt.

She rocks on my dick, slowly lifting before sinking back down again with a soft gasp. "Talk dirty to me."

"You talk dirty to me."

She lifts herself again, almost all the way off of me, and hovers there. "You're so big."

"Not—dirty."

Her hips flex, and she rides down on my hard-on again. "Brain scrambled."

I push her dress higher. "So good."

"So perfect."

She rides me in the front seat, her slow, easy pace becoming frantic as I find her breasts and stroke the underside, then over the top, making circles without reaching her nipples.

"Rhys—"

"Only dirty-talkers get their nipples pinched."

Why am I doing this?

Why am I torturing myself too?

I want to come.

I want to come inside her, hard and furious, until there's nothing left of me.

But I want her to come again first.

"You should've fucked me from behind while I was cleaning up your mess," she gasps while she rides me faster. "Snuck into the laundry room and pulled my pants down and fucked me with your long, thick, hard cock. There. In the bubbles."

"Close enough." I thumb her nipples, then pinch them both.

She cries out and grinds harder against me. "More."

"You like?" I like.

I like the feel of her tight little nubs between my thumbs and fingers.

"Yes."

One little word, and she has me at my breaking point. "Margot—"

"How—so good?" she gasps. "Again?"

"Baby, I can't—" I start, and then I feel it.

Those walls clenching around my dick.

"Oh god, oh god, I'm coming." She grips my shoulders while she strains down against my cock, and I let go too, coming fast and thick and hot while she milks me with her sweet, hot, wet pussy.

"Fuck, yes," I groan, my head dropping back while I let everything go.

Everything I have.

More.

Bursting out of me in an orgasm not just in my dick, but in my brain, in my heart, in my gut, in my soul.

I think this woman owns me now.

21

Can't get enough

Margot

I've never been a prude about sex.

But I've also never had my entire world blown like that before.

We stay in the truck, me splayed across Rhys, him with his arms spread as far as they can go in the confines of his truck, both of us panting until we catch our breath a while later.

"Again?" I finally whisper as I realize how dark it is outside.

Rhys chuckles beneath me.

I'd give myself a high five for prompting a laugh from this grumpy mountain of a man if I had the energy.

"Good thing I'm trained to push my body past its limits," he murmurs.

"Was that past its limits?"

"No."

"Liar."

"Still breathing, aren't I?"

He is.

He's breathing deep and steady, with his heart thumping solidly beneath my ear.

He's still in his flannel, with his undershirt pushed as far up as it'll stay, courtesy of me.

I smile and press a kiss to his chest, getting mostly white T-shirt under my lips.

"Two more minutes," he murmurs, kissing the top of my head.

"And then?"

"And then I'll carry you into the house and show you what I can still do."

The truck smells like sex and leather, and I'm realizing how quickly the temperature is dropping.

Not that I mind.

It's comfortable here.

As comfortable as it can be with both of us squished into the driver's seat.

I start to giggle.

Yeah.

Giggle.

I laugh regularly.

Cackle sometimes too.

But I've never been a giggler.

"You doubt me?" Rhys asks through a yawn.

"Never. Just—just happy."

I don't elaborate on the realization that I haven't been as happy as I want to be.

Don't think I need to.

Rhys—he seems to be in the same spot.

Or worse.

He heaves a thick, heavy sigh, and then he shifts beneath me. "I'm keeping your panties."

I smile until my eyes sting with it. "You break 'em, you buy 'em."

He laughs.

And then he's in motion, tucking my dress down, disposing of the condom in a tissue from a pack neatly stored in the console between the seats, and somehow buttoning his pants back up despite the lack of help I give him.

I kinda want to stay splayed here forever.

But he's opening the truck door, illuminating us with the cab light. "Grab more condoms."

A delicious shiver slinks through me. "Bossy."

"As if you can talk."

We unpretzel ourselves, and I drop the three condom strips I can see into the box while he slides out of the truck.

When I turn to get out too, he's blocking my way.

"What—" I start, and then I understand as he tugs my legs around his waist and lifts me.

"Oh," I murmur, looping my arms around him and hooking my ankles behind his back.

He shuts the truck door, and I make myself useful by pressing kisses to his neck.

"Fuck, Margot," he whispers.

"Does your dick taste as good as your neck?"

His rough grunt is the only acknowledgment I get.

He's parked next to the door again, so it's a short walk in, though it takes him three tries to get the door code entered right.

I'm sure that has nothing to do with me licking him just beneath his ear or with me playing with his hair.

But then we're inside, and he's palming my ass with both hands, carrying me through the dimly lit house while kissing me hard and deep, his tongue tangling with mine, until he's striding into the bedroom, laying me on the bed and following me down.

I left a single lamp on, and it's causing shadows to fall across his face as he looks at me.

"Clothes off," I order.

He pushes up long enough to shake off his flannel and strip out of his undershirt, and holy god.

I can't keep my hands to myself.

Not when there's that broad expanse of chest sprinkled with dark hair that swirls around his two perfect copper nipples to explore.

With my tongue.

"Margot," he says again, that same warning tone he used in the truck when I know he was close to coming.

"What?"

"You're still dressed."

"I'm not wearing any panties. Or a bra."

His pants tent like he didn't just come in the truck, and I grin as I reach for the button on his jeans again.

He shucks his shoes as I push his pants and boxers out of the way, and I get a full view of the beauty that is Rhys O'Malley's penis.

He really is large.

Thick, slightly curved, with a jagged purple vein looping just beneath the blunt tip of his head and heavy balls nestled in a bed of dark curls.

He catches my wrist as I reach for him. "You. Naked."

I bat my lashes at him. "I forgot how to take my clothes off."

He stares at me for a beat, and then that smile pops out again. "Did you now?" he asks as he crawls onto the bed.

I nod. "Brain go poof."

He peels my jean jacket back off my shoulders, pausing to press kisses to each of my shoulders, then trailing his tongue down each of my arms as he exposes them too. "You're leaving these boots on."

My vagina squeezes, pleasure pooling already between my legs again. "You like a woman to wear shoes to bed?"

"That's a lot of words for someone who forgot how to take her own clothes off."

I like this man.

I really, really do.

He's funny and quick and everything about him screams I just want someone to love me as much as I'm capable of loving them.

Once he has my jacket off, pausing to linger with my hands, pressing kisses to my palms and my wrists in a way that makes me shiver from a place deep in my soul, the part of me that's always taking care of things and never asking to be taken care of—not emotionally, anyway—he makes quick work of pulling my dress over my head.

He looks at me, hungry eyes scanning me from head to toe and back again while I lean on the bed in nothing but my cowboy boots.

But again—he makes slow work of sliding his hands down my body, kissing and licking and nipping at my neck, then my shoulder, my breasts, down to my belly, while we whisper nonsense mixed with arguments about me getting a turn to touch him and him reminding me that I'm a terrible apple slicer, which is so unrelated to everything that I laugh until he dips his tongue over my belly button.

And then nothing's funny and everything's hot and heavy and hurried.

The man settles between my thighs, hooks one of my legs over his shoulder, and eats my pussy like he's been denied food for a month.

He's rough and not shy about using his teeth on my inner thigh and my clit and knows when to tease me and when to finally let me come.

And after he's made me scream his name with his tongue, he grabs a condom, rolls me onto my stomach, and grips my hips while he takes me from behind.

I have never—ever—in my entire life—been so thoroughly fucked.

"You're going to break me," he murmurs after he's collapsed beside me on the bed, both of us spent from coming again.

Again.

The man's given me four orgasms in an hour.

Good thing I'm off tomorrow.

I might not be able to walk.

"Who's breaking who?" I murmur back.

He shifts, grunting as he moves. The room plunges into darkness, and then he's pulling me against him.

"Rhys?" I whisper.

"Mm?"

"I'm still in my cowboy boots."

"Are you trying to make me hard again?"

There I go, giggling once more. "And it'll get cold in here."

"You've been cold?"

"No. Not under the covers."

More grunting.

Some swearing.

I start to move, but he sits up faster than I can, probably because he's cheating.

It's hard to want to move when he's trailing his blunt, rough fingertips down my bare legs.

One of my feet comes out of a boot, which thumps to the floor, followed by the other.

"Socks?" he says.

I can take my own socks off. But I murmur a soft, "Off, please."

He peels them off, kisses each of my big toes, grunts and grumbles a little more, and then he's rolling me under the quilt. "Better?"

"Almost."

The floorboards squeak under him as he leaves the room.

I sit up. "Rhys?"

"Condom."

"Again?"

"Getting rid of it."

He returns to the bedroom a minute later and pulls the quilt off me. "What—oh."

He brought me a warm washcloth.

And he's using it to clean me between my legs.

I grab his arm. "Rhys."

"Yeah?"

Thank you isn't enough, so I hook my arm around his neck and pull him close, kissing him softly.

He sighs against my lips, finishes wiping me, then tosses the washcloth on the floor and finally—finally—climbs into bed with me.

"You're softer than I thought," he murmurs between kisses while he strokes my back.

"Wasn't always."

"How do you balance it?"

"Therapy, meditation, and channeling my stubborn nature."

He huffs out a soft laugh. "The way I could've guessed that…"

"I got oldest daughter syndrome in spades."

Our legs are tangled, each with one arm wrapped around the other, and peace is creeping over me.

"Tell me about being in the Marines," I murmur.

"Which part?"

"Where you lived. Did you ever spend time overseas? How long were you in? What was your favorite part? What do you miss?"

"Are you tired at all? Or do you ask this many questions in your sleep?"

"I'm tired."

"You sure?"

I stifle a yawn. "Mm-hmm. Tell me your favorite part."

"The people," he says softly. "Always the people. Then the mission. Being part of something bigger than myself. With other people who believed in the same thing."

"Mm."

He cups his hand behind my head and kisses my forehead. "Go to sleep, Margot. Need your rest so I can fuck you senseless again tomorrow."

I think I giggle.

Not entirely sure.

Because all of this peace—it's taking over.

And I think I'm falling asleep.

22

And she can cook

Rhys

I sleep so hard that when I wake up, I don't know where I am.
Or who I am.
Or even what I am.

I just know my bones—if I have bones—feel rested in a way that they haven't in months.

Probably years.

The room slowly swims into focus—brightly lit by the morning sun streaming through the window—at the same time something savory tickles my nose.

Margot.

I roll over in the bed, looking for her, but she's not there.

The scent of—is that roasted vegetables? Bacon? Both?

Something.

She's in the kitchen.

My smile pops out all on its own. Didn't prompt it myself, couldn't stop it if I wanted to.

I don't want to know how much of a lovesick puppy I look like, so when I use the bathroom after grabbing my pants off the bedroom floor, I avoid glancing at the mirror.

There's a fire going in the living room, and Margot's in the kitchen, sautéing vegetables in the same cast-iron skillet she used to attempt to maim me a week ago.

She smiles at me when I amble in.

Is that her lovesick puppy smile or just her normal smile?

Dammit.

Welcome to the overthinking show, starring me.

"Morning," she says, her voice brighter and cheerier than the sunshine. Her hair's clipped in a messy something on top of her head, and she's in polka-dotted pajama pants that hang low on her hips, showing off a slice of her belly that her lavender tank top doesn't cover. And—my favorite part—clearly no bra. "Do you like omelets?"

Don't overthink it, I order myself.

As if that's possible. On the one hand, I'm overthinking everything.

On the other, seeing her nipples poking against her tank top has my brain short-circuiting again.

I cross the kitchen to loop my arms around her from behind and press a kiss to her hair, my cock slowly waking up to the realization that there's a pretty woman with hard nipples right here. "Mm-hmm."

"Allergies?"

"No."

"Aversions?"

"Being hungry."

She laughs and wiggles her butt into me. "Better do something about that then, shouldn't we?"

My stomach rumbles an agreement. "You made a fire?"

"Chilly mornings call for using the fireplace."

I slide my hands up her sides. Is there nothing she can't do? "Mm."

"Sleep well?"

"Mm-hmm. You?"

"Like a log. Was I snoring?"

I breathe in the scent of her hair again. Me, down bad?

Clearly.

There's no other way for me. "Wasn't awake enough to notice."

A timer sounds on her phone, and she hip-checks me with her whole ass, which takes my cock from half-mast to raging boner.

"Two steps back, Mr. Happy," she says with a grin. "The biscuits are done."

"Biscuits? Homemade biscuits?"

"My first culinary masterpiece."

I release her so she can check the oven, and that's when I realize her phone has gone back to playing soft music. Jazz or blues.

Something instrumental and melodic and gentle.

It fits the morning.

She pops a half dozen thick, fluffy, perfectly browned biscuits out of the oven, then gestures to the coffee pot. "Help yourself."

Ah.

Right.

Her one failure in life. Making coffee.

I should've been up earlier to fix this myself.

"I've had your coffee," I remind her.

She smiles and rolls her eyes as she grabs another skillet. "How many eggs would you like in your omelet?"

"Three, please."

I help myself to the coffee despite giving her crap, and it's night and day different from what she made on Monday.

"You make this?"

"Lucky told me they stocked coffee here. He didn't tell me it expired before they all inherited the cabin and they each think the others drink it, so they all bring their own when they stay here. I got some beans at Bee & Nugget the other day too."

"Walking a fine line there, taking free housing but spending money for nonessentials at the coffee shop."

"Someone left a big tip, so I decided to splurge and support a local shop." She gestures to the eggs and cheeses on the counter beside the oven. "And Cyril delivered groceries this morning, so no one knows it was me. He has the rest of today off, by the way. I told him I wouldn't be leaving the cabin."

"That mean I'm hired?"

"It means you're trustworthy and knowledgeable about my particular situation and he can take the weekend off."

I smirk at her. "Don't hire people you sleep with?"

She smirks back. "Don't usually hire people who blackmail me. But you're kinda cute, so I guess I can overlook a few bad decisions."

"Kinda cute?"

"In a grumpy lumberjack kind of way."

"I am good with…wood."

She visibly shivers, and her cheeks take on a pink hue.

But I don't think she's embarrassed.

I think she's getting warm.

"Yes, you are," she murmurs.

"Maybe if you're a good girl, you can play with my wood again."

She slides me a look. "Splitting and riding?"

If I wasn't hard as steel before, I am now.

Sweating a little myself too. "Not at the same time."

Her carefree laugh settles in my soul, and I lock it away to remember it later.

Because there will be a later.

When she goes back to her normal life and I go back to—fuck if I know right now.

Something.

But that's a tomorrow problem.

Not something I'll let ruin today.

She was right yesterday.

I deserve to live, and I shouldn't hide the rest of my life out of fear of pain.

I lean against the counter and watch her while I sip my coffee, the music the perfect touch to finish off this cozy morning.

Margot's art in motion.

Far more proficient in a kitchen than she lets on, if the way she's cracking eggs one-handed is any indication.

"My mom was my hero," I say quietly as she shreds cheese over the first omelet in the pan.

She slides me a look. "Yeah?"

"Didn't do it on purpose, I don't think, but she taught me badass women are the best women."

Margot's smile softens. "She was a badass?"

"Ran a tight ship in a male-dominated field, and also made me pancakes on Saturday mornings and put notes in my lunchbox every day."

"My parents taught me my worth was dependent on my success, and they didn't like that I wanted to hang out in the kitchen to watch our chef cook."

"I'll still like you if these taste like shit."

She doesn't laugh. "You're a testament to what an amazing person your mother must've been."

I absently rub my chest, right over my heart. "Past year hasn't felt like it."

"Something I learned watching Daphne—everything's temporary. Good times, bad times, happiness, sadness. We're never one thing. We're all complicated messes doing our best in whatever situations we find ourselves in, and most of us are good at our cores. I don't need to have known your mom to know she would've understood that too. Here. How's this look?"

She slides the first omelet onto a plate, and my mouth waters so hard I almost drool. "Like a fairy princess cooked me a magic breakfast."

Her smile hits me in the heart.

The way she goes up on tiptoe and hooks a hand behind my neck to kiss me softly does far more damage than a simple hit though.

She tastes like everything that's been missing in my life.

And I need to keep perspective.

Appreciate this for what it is, not what it can't be.

"You're just as good at that in the morning," she whispers as she pulls out of the kiss.

"I can do it all day long."

My stupid stomach grumbles again.

She flashes a grin. "Maybe after food? There's jam in the fridge." She sets two biscuits and two slices of bacon from another pan on the plate with the omelet. "I'll be just a minute for my omelet."

By the time I have both of our coffees, the jam, butter, and my plate at the table in the front room, she's serving up her own omelet too.

Instead of across from each other, like we were last Sunday night when I shared my beef and barley stew with her, we sit huddled together on one end, her at the head of the table, me on the side next to her.

Her feet tease mine under the table while we eat and trade stories about the craziest things we've ever seen in life.

Mine includes discovering I'm accidental temporary roommates with a billionaire heiress pretending to be a housekeeper who can cook a killer breakfast.

Hers includes taking down an intruder in a cabin with hair dye, flour, and a cast-iron skillet.

After breakfast, when I tell her I'll clean, she insists on helping.

Though by helping, I really mean seducing me in the kitchen until I'm banging her against the fridge.

I repay the favor by helping her shower.

There are a few more orgasms involved.

Enough that when we make it back to the living room and I get the fire rekindled, we both pass out on the couch for a long nap.

And thank fuck we're dressed, because when we wake up, the triplets are staring at us.

"We knocked," Decker says dryly as Margot—Margie Margie Margie, I remind myself—yeah, as Margie lunges off of me.

Leaving a little bit of drool on my arm where she was sleeping.

"Three times," Lucky adds. He's smirking.

Jack's staring at the ceiling. "I told them we should come back later. Or, you know, call first."

Margie smooths her hair down, her hand freezing just below her ear. She's not wearing her glasses.

"Bathroom," she stutters. "Back in a minute. Bathroom."

After she disappears down the hallway, all three of the triplets assume matching stances.

Legs wide, arms crossed, and some form of *what the fuck are you doing with my sister?* etched on their faces.

"What?" I say. "You know how hard it was to keep our stories straight last night? Wore us both the fuck out."

Decker pulls a strip of condoms out of his back pocket.

Look exactly like the kind I bought yesterday.

"Found these on the ground by your truck," he says.

"I told you to leave them alone," Jack mutters.

"I'm just glad you're practicing safe sex with whoever you're old enough to practice it with," Lucky says. "Can't be too careful. You wouldn't believe the STIs I get to treat at the retirement home. Those people are frisky, and they think vasectomies and menopause mean the danger's all gone."

All three of us stare at him.

He winks at me. "You're welcome."

Now Jack and Decker are glaring at me again too.

"Would've said thanks before you said I was welcome," I tell Lucky.

"Hey," Margie says behind them. "Do you know I haven't gone hiking at all since I got here? And I have to work tomorrow. Do you all hike, or just you, Jack?"

"We came to invite you to a party at Sabrina and Grey's place," Jack says. "Unless you're...busy?"

"Don't you ever get tired of people?" I ask him.

"Yes," Decker answers first.

"Not really," Lucky says.

Jack shrugs. "Sometimes, but not today."

"You want to come?" Lucky says to Margot—Margie. "Only nice people. No parents. And Sabrina knows."

"Grey—is he one of my bosses?" Margie asks. "Would that be weird?"

"He'll be chasing Henry and trying to keep him from eating dog fur," Jack says.

"Henry's their kid. He's almost two," Lucky supplies.

"Also, we'll give you a hundred bucks to say you're the one who brought the cheese puffs to share," Jack adds.

"Okay, that part's funny," Decker mutters.

Margie looks at me.

I shrug. "No idea. I'm missing something too."

"When Sabrina and Grey were dating—" Lucky starts.

"Pretending they weren't dating," Jack interrupts.

"Yeah," Lucky says. "When Sabrina and Grey were pretending they weren't dating, they had this…incident…with powdered cheese."

Even Decker's grinning now. "So we bring cheese puffs or cheese popcorn every time we see them."

"They were orange for days," Lucky says.

"They weren't, but that's the story we tell everyone," Jack corrects.

Margie smiles at all of them. "And you had nothing to do with it?"

"No, that was all—" Lucky stops himself and clears his throat. "That was someone who's no longer with us."

"Oh. I'm sorry."

"We're not." Jack grimaces. "He was a fuckmuffin. And he's not dead. Just basically banned from town."

"I see." Margie clearly doesn't see.

I don't see fully either, but I'm going to assume it has something to do with the cousin they don't talk about anymore.

"Will they be the only other people there? Sabrina and Grey?" Margie asks.

"And Zen. They're cool. You'll like them. Plus Theo and Laney will be there with their kids," Jack says.

Lucky nods. "And Emma and Jonas too."

Margie flinches.

"Don't let the movie star thing intimidate you," Jack says, completely reading the flinch wrong. "He's a nice guy. Mostly normal. Especially when Theo and Grey trick him into drinking the alcoholic kombucha. Then he's just funny. Dude's a lightweight and always gets three in before he realizes he didn't look at the can."

"We told him he has to be nice to you and not talk to you unless you approach him," Lucky adds.

"And no pictures so no one can say you're getting special treatment at work," Jack adds.

Margie looks at me.

I shake my head no as subtly as I can.

The slight lift of her brows clearly replies no shit.

"C'mon, Margie, it'll be fun," Decker says.

Decker.

Mr. Grumpy wants his sister to come have fun now.

The fucker.

"Plus, if you come, we win a bet with Theo," Jack adds.

"A normal kind of bet?" Margie asks.

The three of them grin at each other, then at her.

"Only way to see is if you come," Lucky says.

Jack gets in on it too. "Once-in-a-lifetime opportunity here. Sabrina and Grey almost never host anything since they're always running everything at Bee & Nugget."

"And that means it's a once-in-a-lifetime opportunity to peek inside Grey's kombucha cellar," Decker adds.

"Dude. You've been in the kombucha cellar way more than once in your lifetime," Jack says to him.

"You can never spend too much time in the kombucha cellar," Decker retorts.

"It's a special kombucha cellar," Lucky side-whispers—loudly—to Margie.

"Clearly," she murmurs.

"Glad you're in," Lucky says. "Because they're actually having a party just for you, which we weren't going to tell you so you wouldn't feel obligated to come."

"Absolutely," Jack agrees. "We don't manipulate people."

Decker shakes his head. "Nice going, dumbasses. Way to be subtle."

"Subtle's your thing," Jack replies.

Lucky nods. "So much so that sometimes people don't understand your books at all."

"Plus, if we wanted to manipulate anyone, we'd mention the Hatch green chile bison burgers," Jack adds.

Lucky nods emphatically. "No one can resist the Hatch green chile bison burgers."

I look at Margie again.

Total poker face. "The fact remains that you're asking me to go to dinner with my bosses."

"Who aren't involved in operations at all," Jack responds instantly.

"They'll be offended if you don't come," Lucky adds.

"They're our best friends," Decker says. "They want to meet our sister."

Fuck.

She can't say no to that.

Not when Decker's owning her as a sister.

Sure enough, she's now smiling brightly at the triplets with a smile that I'm positive is forced and fake. "Then I guess it's settled. We're going."

Bad idea.

But if it's a bad idea, it's a good bad idea.

She gets to hang with her brothers.

I get a green chile bison burger.

And to watch her hang with her brothers.

And hopefully another opportunity or two to be her hero.

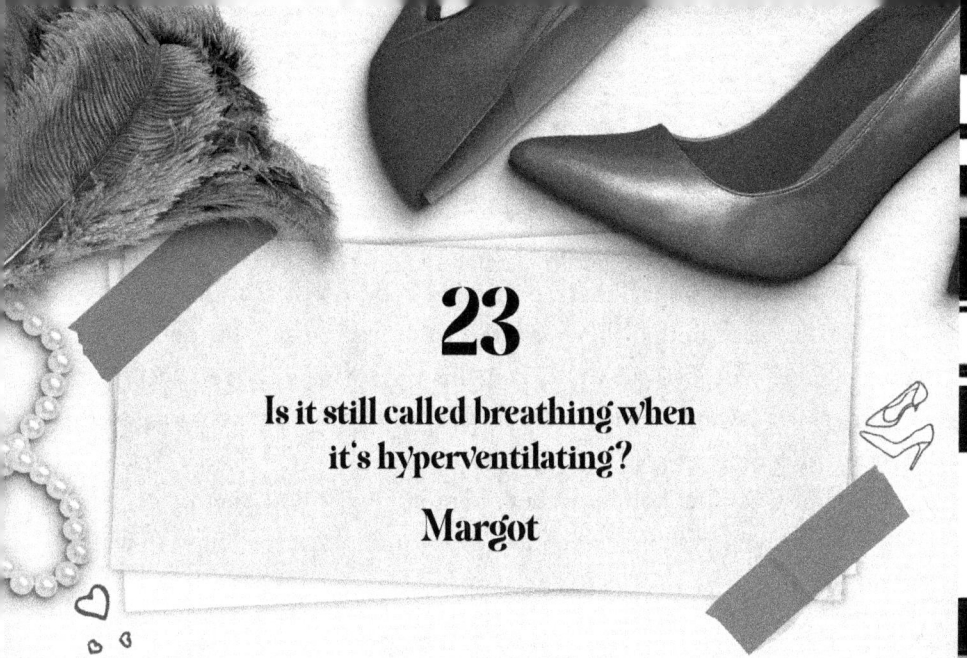

23

Is it still called breathing when it's hyperventilating?

Margot

Sabrina and Grey have a beautiful home nestled into the forest on a mountainside. It's newly renovated, with wood and stone touches everywhere, inside and out. Flagstone patios and rock gardens ring the immediate perimeter, with wildflower gardens scattered beyond. Inside is classy but cozy, with high-beam ceilings and oversized furniture and local artwork scattered among pictures of the couple, their dogs, and their baby, along with several of Sabrina and her two best friends—sometimes just the women, sometimes the women with their husbands too.

And as the triplets promised, it has an epic kombucha cellar that takes up half the lower level, which is where I am now.

Unlike my father's wine cellar, which is absurdly large and stores more bottles of wine that he keeps for investment purposes than bottles he intends to drink, the kombucha cellar is a working cellar, where kombucha is actively brewing in five large glass tanks on one wall that has a painting of the mountains behind it.

"Different flavors," Zen, who was introduced to me as Grey's close relative and best friend, explains to me when I ask why they're different colors.

Zen's tall and lanky with short blond hair and a way of looking at you that promises the sassitude is hanging out just beneath the surface, waiting for an excuse to emerge.

"From different honeys, or different additions?" I ask.

"Some of both." They gesture to the first tank. "This one's honey only. Same with this next one. But this one—this one, we added raspberries and lavender. Then mint here. And my personal favorite of the moment, lemon ginger."

"You run the kombrewchery here in town?" I ask them.

"I run everything here. Some people aren't smart enough to realize it though."

I smile.

They smile back, but then narrow their eyes. "You have secrets, don't you?"

Once again, I find myself liking someone for their suspicion of me.

Probably a sign I need to come clean. And soon. "Everyone has secrets."

"Don't let yours be the bad kind." They bend over, catching a runaway toddler with short dark curls all over his head. "And you—you're supposed to be upstairs. Margie, meet Henry. Henry, say hello to Margie."

The little boy sticks a finger in his mouth and looks at me with big green eyes, not saying a word.

"Hello, Henry," I say.

"Got boogie?" he replies, sticking a finger from his other hand up his nose.

"Uncle Theo's in trouble," Zen mutters. "I told him to quit teaching all of you that." They jerk their head toward the door. "If this one's here, the others and the dogs will follow. But help yourself to anything you want."

"I won't be grabbing the last of anything special?"

"It's all special, and we'll keep making more special, so it's the kind of special meant to be consumed and enjoyed and remembered."

It's impossible to not smile at that sentiment.

"This one's okay?" I snag a beer-size bottle in one of the rows on the wall.

Zen smiles. "Best one. Take it."

"Would you say that about all of them?"

"Da boogie in da nose," Henry says.

"Got that right, kid," Zen says.

"Alcoholic or not?" I ask with a nod toward my bottle.

"If I answer that, I'm breaking the rules of kombucha roulette."

I laugh. "Got it." I take a second bottle and trail Zen upstairs.

Rhys is making himself useful at a large island in the kitchen, which opens into the living room, where Decker and Jack are deep in discussion with Theo, who's once again holding a sleeping baby in his tattooed arms.

I set the bottle beside Rhys's cutting board. "Workaholic much?" I murmur.

"Best view."

"You like kombucha?"

"Guess we'll find out. You?"

"We don't have kombucha in Iowa."

He grunts.

I suck in a smile.

Not like I'm going to tell him I drink it when I'm at my beach house, much like he's probably not going to smile at me like he did last night when we were alone. "But apparently it's a secret if it's hard or soft. So consider yourself warned."

A woman breezes through the back door, freezes when she spots me, and lights up. Her brown hair is tied back at the base of her neck, and her blue eyes are sparkling. "You must be Margie." She walks closer and extends a hand. "Hi. I'm Laney."

I shake and smile back at her, feeling suddenly on edge. Well, more on edge. "Nice to meet you. Have you met Rhys? He's Decker's friend."

Rhys nods to her, still slicing tomatoes.

"I think we ran into each other the last time he was in town," Laney says to me. She tilts her head, studying me.

Rhys takes a subtle half step closer to me.

"Crazy," she murmurs.

"What?" My heart is starting to pound too hard.

I know who Laney is.

I know people at home who know who Laney is too.

She's a badass businesswoman in her own right, working for her family's custom online photo gift company that they founded here. They entered the internet business era at exactly the right time to hit it big.

My father's talked about them.

And did the triplets—I scan through my memory banks, and yes. Yes, Lucky definitely described Laney in terms of Kingston Photo Gifts when he was telling me about his friends. I can confidently know who she is as Margie Johnson without tipping my hand that I researched her.

"I half thought the triplets were making you up to prank us all, but you have the same nose," she says. "And your eyes are shaped the same. Oh my god. You have their ears too."

"They are related," Rhys murmurs.

"Hearing it from them and seeing it are two different things."

I keep my smile plastered on while two other women—Sabrina, the shorter redhead from Bee & Nugget, and Emma, the taller blonde who's married to Jonas Rutherford, both of whom are in pictures all over the house as well—come in through the back door too.

"Oh, she's here," Emma squeals.

"I told you she's real," Sabrina replies. She greets me with a quick hug. "I'm so glad you could make it. How was your first week of work?"

"Look at her nose," Laney says to Emma.

Emma stares at my nose. "Oh. That must be why Jonas thought she looked familiar. Because it's like staring at half of another one of the triplets."

"Right?"

"It's so weird how people can be related and not know it."

Sabrina and Laney both look at her.

"Really?" Laney says the same time Sabrina says, "You can't imagine how that could happen at all?"

Understandable.

Emma had five minutes of fame as a runaway bride several years back. She and Jonas ended up at the same resort where she was honeymooning solo and he was hiding after a rough divorce.

And Bash, their son, was the result.

But Jonas didn't know it until about two years ago.

He left the nonprofit I know him from when he finally got the messages Emma had sent him when she found out she was pregnant.

But the triplets didn't tell me that. I'm positive they haven't mentioned much about Emma beyond who she's married to. So I need to pretend I don't know that either.

Emma grins at her friends. "I mean, yes, that might've been Bash one day, but Jonas found us again, so there are officially no more secrets in our group about who's related to who."

Rhys coughs.

The three best friends look at him.

I contemplate stepping on his foot. Hard.

"Inhaled dust," he mutters.

"Don't do that while you're handling a knife," I advise.

"So you two are still sharing the triplets' cabin?" Sabrina asks us.

"Knock it off, Sabrina," Jack calls.

"Don't yell next to the baby," Theo says.

And then he sneezes so loudly that Rhys and I both jump.

"What—" Rhys starts as the baby shouts, then settles right back against Theo's shoulder.

"Speaking of the baby, where are the rest of the kids?" Laney asks, like the sneeze was no big deal.

"Uncle Lucky has them," Rhys tells her while Emma murmurs to me, "He always sneezes that loud. Sorry. Should've warned you."

"Zen's with the kids too," Sabrina says. "I got a text. They're in the playroom."

"If the triplets ask you to play rock paper scissors to change diapers, don't do it," Emma tells me.

"She can hold her own with rock paper scissors," Rhys says.

I nod. "It's apparently genetic to beat Jack."

"That was funny as sh—shitake mushrooms," Decker says as he ambles in.

"Did you know you have the same nose and eyes and ears?" Emma asks him.

"It makes me feel like I know Margie from somewhere," Laney adds.

I pop the top on my kombucha bottle and take a sip that I hope would be a normal Margie Johnson-type sip to try something new.

Lemon blueberry.

"This is delicious," I announce. I shift the other bottle closer to Rhys. "Here. I brought you one to try too."

He nods, clearly his version of thanks, even though I already told him I gave him a bottle, and he gives me another look.

The same one he's been giving me since I said I'd come here today.

The one that says *you picked playing with fire, you get to deal with the consequences* with a side of *but I'm here if you need me*.

It's comforting.

At least, until the back door swings open and the last two men at the party walk in the door.

I grab my bottle and take another gulp. Why didn't I add bangs to my look yet? And colored contacts. I could've gone brown-eyed, and then I wouldn't be avoiding looking at Jonas.

Also—I suddenly understand the large furniture.

Grey Cartwright is as tall as Rhys. Easily.

He's not as broad—honestly, who is?—but he's still a very big dude. He has to bend to drop a kiss to Sabrina's head. "Making our guests do all of the work?"

"I'm an excellent delegator," she replies.

Grey introduces himself to Rhys and me and tells us both to quit working.

Jonas gives a friendly wave and heads through the kitchen toward the stairs at the far end of the room, between the living room and kitchen. I haven't been to the upper level, but that's where Zen headed with Henry, so I assume that's where all of the kids are.

"Grey's right," Jack says as he and Theo join the rest of us in the kitchen. "You two—quit working. Margie, you see the back patio yet?"

"Yeah, go out to the patio," Lucky agrees as he trots down the stairs. "See if you can draw a moose in. I still want to see a moose."

"You've seen a moose," Jack says.

"Have not."

"You have to have seen a moose," Decker insists.

"Nope," Lucky repeats.

And that's how I end up on the back patio, under a wide porch umbrella on a cushioned outdoor couch between Laney and Sabrina, with Emma in a matching chair beside us and chips and guacamole before us, and my half brothers in the loveseat and other chair rounding out the sitting area.

A massive Saint Bernard is lying on the ground behind us with a chocolate lab beside him, and Jack's dog is resting by his feet too.

Rhys is with Zen and the husbands at the grill on the other side of the patio, their voices low and indistinct as they tackle grilling the meat while two of them now hold babies and keep an eye on the two toddlers and one preschooler playing on a very small playset just beyond the patio.

"Want all of the tea on the triplets?" Sabrina asks me.

"You spill our tea, we spill yours," Decker says.

She dips a chip in guac and laughs. "Ooh, I'm so scared now."

Henry runs up to her. "Mama dip?"

She pulls him into her lap and shares her chip, and soon Laney and Emma also have kids in their laps sharing food while the six of them—the triplets and the three women—tell me stories about their childhood together, with the occasional interruption from Theo at the grill anytime he's made out to be the bad guy.

It's easy to convince myself I belong here.

That I'm soaking up stories about family I didn't know I had, getting caught up on their lives.

But the lie about my identity is eating at me.

Especially anytime Laney squints at me, or when Jonas shoots looks at me down the table while we're eating the famous Hatch green chile burgers, or when I tell a lie about growing up in Iowa.

It's honestly giving me a headache.

Even with Rhys speaking up at the other end of the table every time—every time—I have to lie or feel on display, asking questions about the retreat center or Snaggletooth Creek or about how soon ski season starts to draw attention away from me.

Finally—finally—dinner's over, we've all had dessert, and the under-five crowd is uniformly melting down.

Rhys rises and stretches, then looks at me. "We should get out of their hair, Marg—"

I blink at him.

He put the hard g on the end of that.

And now everyone's looking at him.

My face gets hot.

His is going pink.

"Margs," he finishes.

Lucky growls. "You have a nickname?"

"I'm trying to stay neutral here, but seriously?" Jack adds.

Decker just glares at Rhys.

"Oh, grow up, all of you," Sabrina says as she hands Henry off to Grey. "Grown-ups get to do grown-up things."

"I love it when my friends find people who make them happy," Emma says. "Family too, I guess."

"Thanks, Em," Theo says. "Appreciate being an afterthought."

She grins at him.

And the baby in her lap makes a noise that's followed by another noise that I don't know well, but I can assume what just happened in that kid's diaper.

Theo grins back at Emma. "See? That's what happens when you make your brother feel second-rate."

"I'll get her, Em," Jonas says, rising too. I've managed to avoid him, but he smiles at me. "If you leave before I'm back, nice to see you again. You too," he adds to Rhys.

Rhys nods.

I murmur something that I hope sounds like nice to see you too, but my head is pounding and I want to go home.

"Won't be saying that after next week," Grey mutters to Theo, who gives him a death glare that makes Grey giggle.

"Stop, all of you," Laney says. "It's like having three extra toddlers."

"You knew what you were marrying," Zen replies, which has everyone else at the table laughing.

Laney rolls her eyes, then smiles at me. "Sorry for all of the inside jokes."

"I have friends like that back home too," I say.

It's true, though I'm not as tight anymore with a lot of them as I used to be, and now Daphne has more inside jokes with Bea than with me.

Or so it feels sometimes.

"Don't let these guys talk you into anything else tomorrow," Emma says to me.

"I'm working tomorrow."

"Ooh. Right. Getting ready for the…big event."

I squint at her.

She shifts away to answer Bash, the almost four-year-old.

Laney's suddenly grabbing things off the table to take inside.

Sabrina's checking on the dogs.

Everyone except Rhys and Zen is suddenly very busy.

I lock eyes with Rhys.

What the hell is the big event?

One corner of his mouth crooks up.

He knows.

"Hope you read your contract thoroughly," Zen mutters to me.

"C'mon, Margs," Rhys says. "These people have kids to wrangle."

"We don't," Decker says.

"Game night," Jack says.

"At the cabin," Lucky agrees.

"Margie has to work in the morning," Rhys reminds them.

"What is she, fifty?" Jack says.

"Can't stay up past eight anymore?" Lucky adds.

I rise out of my chair and reach for my plate, but Laney grabs it before I can. "I've got this. It was so nice to meet you. I hope the triplets are everything you ever wanted in half brothers. We kinda like them around here."

"I can see why. Most of the time."

Everyone around me cracks up.

Rhys loops an arm around my shoulders and steers me around toward the walkway nestled in the stone gardens that'll take us to the front of the house and his truck.

"We're coming for game night," Lucky calls.

I say goodbye to Bandit and tell the triplets I'll see them soon.

And as soon as I'm in Rhys's truck, I slouch so deep in the seat that I almost can't see over the dash.

Or maybe that's my eyes closing that keeps me from seeing.

The truck shifts as Rhys climbs in too.

The console between us pops open, and then I hear a bottle rattling.

I peek one eye open.

Rhys holds out two over-the-counter painkillers. "Headache?"

"You're really good."

He winces. "If you want me calling you Margs for the next week."

I swallow both pills with the water bottle he also offers me. "The nickname was a good cover."

"I don't usually slip."

"I can hardly remember my own name right now." I glance at him again. "What's the big event next week?"

He winces again, but then he starts to grin as he puts his truck in gear. "It's technically top secret. Need to know and all that. Not sure a housekeeper needs to know."

"Do you have any idea how badly I'm about to kick your ass in any game we decide to play at the cabin? Headache or not?"

He settles his hand on my thigh as he steers us down the driveway. "I like your ruthless side."

"Do you?"

"I do. No pretenses. No fear. No trying to be agreeable for agreeable's sake. Means I know where I stand."

"You're standing on the edge of pissing me off for not telling me what you know."

My head still hurts, but I'm smiling at him as I say it, and he's actually laughing.

"What in the—oh my god. Are they hosting GrippaPeen people?" I whisper.

Because that's suddenly the thing that makes the most sense.

Why everyone thinks it's hilarious and Theo didn't think they'd come and no one wants to talk about it.

He made his money doing nude videos for the site, and he's one of their most famous success stories. The last video he posted, though, he told the world his penis was now for one woman and one woman only, and that statement made him into a complete legend.

Rhys is smiling so wide it might break his face. "Guess you'll have to wait and see."

24

Keeping my secrets straight

Rhys

The triplets crash the cabin for Monopoly and stay until almost midnight.

Margot lets herself go and wipes the table with them because of course she does.

Their mistake in suggesting Monopoly.

But it's fun to watch the four of them interacting, especially knowing Margot's not hiding much of who she is tonight.

"Worst game ever invented," Jack mutters as they leave.

"Worse than worst," Decker agrees.

"What's that word, Mr. Writer Dude?" Lucky says. "You know all of the words, so you must know that one too."

He's the only one of the three of them who was completely amused by Margot's tactics.

Thought it was cute that a housekeeper from Des Moines could be a shark at Monopoly.

But all three of them hug her, clearly easily forgiving her for what she's done to their pride tonight.

"Lucky's going to hate me most," Margot says after they're fully gone.

I distract her from worrying about it by tossing her over my shoulder and taking her to the bedroom.

I'm barely conscious when she leaves for work Sunday morning, though I'm not far behind her when I arrive at the retreat center.

I'm not scheduled to work, so I claim I wanted to soak up the vibes of the place while off duty as my excuse to keep an eye on her.

Not that it's necessary.

Only three guests are left to check out, and no one else is coming until Tuesday.

Completely clearing the place out before a bunch of people who make money by being naked on the internet show up.

She gets off work early, and I treat her to a steak dinner at the cabin.

The way she moans over it has me hard so fast it feels like I got punched in the gut, and I decide I like eating her for dessert better than I like any sugary confection I might whip up.

She doesn't object.

And I'm gonna need another box of condoms.

Monday's slow at the retreat center, so we're both off early again.

She makes me dinner and eats me for dessert.

My life is a revolving door of work and sex and food, and I don't hate it.

Margot isn't scheduled on Tuesday to make up for working Sunday, and she swears she has real-life work to catch up on, won't leave the cabin, and her head of security is on the clock anyway, so I have a Margot-less day, for the most part.

I hit Bee & Nugget for coffee with Decker before heading in for my shift.

"I think I like her," Decker tells me over lemon scones and coffee.

"She's likable," I agree.

He scowls at me. "Fucker."

"Glad you're finally moving on after the shit show of your past year, Rhys. I like seeing my friends happy."

Sabrina snickers as she refills our coffees. "He's got you there, bud."

"Thanks for dinner Saturday. It was fun," I tell her.

"Margie's great." She stares me straight in the eye without blinking for too long. "Laney and Emma and I really like her."

Decker looks between us, clearly noticing something in her tone too.

A creeping sensation hits my neck. "Must be something to that genetic lottery," I say.

Sabrina smirks. "Margs. What a great nickname."

Fuuuuuck.

I don't like her tone.

"Call her Skillet sometimes too," I say though.

"Think she'll stay here long-term?"

"We haven't talked about that."

"You going to?"

"Like it here," I reply.

"That wasn't a yes or no."

I shrug. "Been working through some shit."

She smirks again. "I'll bet you have."

"Stop implying crap about my sister," Decker mutters to her.

Sabrina's gaze settles on me too long again.

"Have a feeling this will be a make-or-break week," I say, like I'm not starting to break out in a sweat.

And it's not even my secret.

I'm sweating because I think Sabrina knows Margot's secret.

She purses her lips together, still smiling.

"Margie know yet?" Decker asks me.

For a second, I think he's asking me if Margie knows who she actually is—like she'd have doubt about her own identity—but then my brain catches up.

He's asking if Margie knows who's coming to the retreat center this week. "Director informed the staff last night. Reminded them about that…one clause…in the contracts."

The nudity clause.

All staff was told they might encounter nude guests from time to time because of the artistic nature of the retreat's purpose. Apparently one of the housekeepers—Louisa—opted to take this next week off work, which wasn't unexpected.

It's part of why Margot was able to get a job so easily here.

They knew they'd be down a housekeeper.

How long she'd be able to stay after this if she were really Margie Johnson is another question.

Decker stares at me a beat, then he starts grinning too. "Gonna bother you for her to see that much dick?"

Semi-legit question.

Only male creators this week.

Have a feeling they'll be letting everything hang out as often as possible.

"Stop talking, Decker," Sabrina says.

Someone calls her name, and she gives him one last warning finger waggle before heading over to check on the other customers.

I glance around the café.

Not too crowded today.

Decker's doing the same. "Crazy how well this town can keep a secret when it matters," he says.

I angle another look at him. "Like that you know about your dad?"

He grimaces.

"Should tell him," I add. "He's still your dad. Always will be."

"What if—" He visibly swallows and looks down at his mug. "What if he doesn't know?"

"He knows."

"How the fuck do you know that?"

I shrug. "Just a gut feeling that he's probably always had a gut feeling."

"My mom—"

"Yeah. I know."

None of them want to find out their mom cheated on their dad.

None of them want to find out someone hurt her either.

And it's hard to imagine another scenario.

Decker might still be telling himself they were sperm donor babies, but the odds of that are slim to none.

People in Margot's zip code don't donate their swimmers to sperm banks.

"I would've wanted to know Felice was cheating on me much sooner than I found out," I tell Decker. "Not your fault your parents made the decisions they made. Individually or together. But you know they each made decisions, and you know it's stressing you and your brothers the fuck out not knowing who knows what. Tell them. Get rid of the secrets. Might be shitty for a while, but you're all tight. You'll come out stronger on the other side."

He keeps staring at his coffee cup.

And then he sighs long and deep. "I'm glad she's been good for you."

I don't blink at the shift in the conversation, and I follow where he's coming from.

Two weeks ago, I wouldn't have given him this advice.

But now—yeah.

Now, I'm on the other side of some shit myself.

I smirk at my own coffee. "Figure it's easier to tell you than it is to hit you with a frying pan."

"If I knew that's what you were looking for in a woman, I could've asked my assistant to find someone for you."

I snort.

He chuckles too.

"Don't do your own dirty work?" I ask

"Fuck, no. Not when I have a Nell. She's damn good at it too. Not kidding when I say my world would fall apart without her."

"Make sure you pay her enough."

He winces. "Yeah. As soon as she got the photoshoot proofs, she knew it was Lucky and not me. She's fucking good."

"She blackmailed you?"

"No, she gave me a lecture on being authentic."

"She really knew it was Lucky?"

"Yeah. And he swears he didn't tell. She just—she just knows things."

"Huh."

"What?"

"If she's that good at everything…maybe have her tell your parents you know."

We stare at each other a second, and then we both crack up again. And it feels good.

I'm still hiding something from my buddy, but fuck, he's hiding shit too.

We're all hiding shit.

For just a little longer.

25

Dick is the worst

Margot

"If the dick gets to be too much, text me," Rhys says as we climb out of his truck at the retreat center Wednesday morning.

"I can handle a little dick," I reply, then glance at his crotch. "God knows I've been getting more than a little."

"Ready and available anytime you want to pull me into a closet again."

We had sex in the shower not thirty minutes ago, and my hair's still wet, but a bulge is already growing behind his fly.

And now I'm also turned on as I shut the door.

Word is, Theo might stop by, but Jonas and Grey are steering clear of the retreat center this week, which has me relaxed enough that I'm good with the distraction of being turned on by Rhys at work.

"Talked to Decker yesterday," he says to me while we head toward the main building, our arms brushing. "Told him I thought they should tell their parents."

I glance up at him. "What did he say?"

"Nothing much. Think he's still on the no drama is good drama train." He glances down at me as we reach the door. "It's gonna come out, Margs."

"I know," I say on a sigh.

It's inconceivable to me that the triplets' mom wouldn't know who my father is.

Which means if the triplets tell their parents they know, they'll also likely tell their parents that I'm their half sister, which would mean I'd need to come clean.

Pretending I'm another of Tobias Merriweather-Brown's illegitimate children won't last long once the triplets start googling.

My disguise is good, but not that good.

"Not trying to make trouble," Rhys adds while we make our way into the staff room.

"I know. I respect where you're coming from."

"Figured you would."

Warmth glows in my chest as I pin on my name tag.

He sees me.

He sees me enough to trust me when I tell him I don't mean any harm by hiding my identity, and he trusts me enough to tell me the hard things too.

"I'll tell them this weekend," I say quietly. "After I help here, since they're down a housekeeper already."

The Miles2Go shareholder meeting was Monday. They approved Oliver's choice for a new CEO, which means Oliver's following through with his plan to give away all of his shares to the franchise owners as soon as I tell him I'm ready for him to proceed.

It's time.

It's time to ruin my father's reputation and drive him into retirement.

And hope this works.

"I like them," I confess in a whisper.

Rhys squeezes my arm. "I know."

He puts his things in his locker. I put my things in my locker. Zelda, the other housekeeper, joins us, and we trade pleasant good mornings before I head out to start on my list for the day with Rhys behind me.

We climb the staff stairs, then slip out the door onto the main floor between the dining room and the reception area.

Three men are in the lobby, all of them buck naked, taking videos, phones held over their heads, I assume for maximum video coverage of their visible hard-ons.

"Promised you a treat, my pets," one of them says, "and you're getting triple-dicked!"

"If you're not following my buddies, you're missing out on triple the fun," another says.

"Link in bio to my besties' channels so you can subscribe there too," the third says.

All three of them thrust their pelvises and stick their tongues out.

Rhys sighs quietly next to me.

I tuck in a smile.

It's going to be quite the week.

"Wrap the video and cover your junk, gentlemen," Rhys says to them. "No signs, no nudity."

That's the rule this week.

The creators are free to make content here in whatever level of undress they prefer, so long as they mark the area with signs for general awareness so that the staff doesn't unexpectedly encounter—well, exactly what Rhys and I have just encountered.

Drawing a line between creativity and full nudist colony, I suspect.

Once a place gets a reputation, it's hard to change it back.

I've seen a workshop schedule too, with business topics taking as much space on the agenda as creative topics, plus lots of free time for developing content.

The three naked men look Rhys up and down.

"You real security, or is that your bit?" the tallest of the group asks him.

He taps his name tag and gives them his growliest stare.

"Are you hairy?" the shortest asks. "My followers love hairy."

"Mine are into muscles," the third and most built of the three says.

"You look like you have both. We could make you a star."

"Seriously, you wouldn't believe how much people will pay for five minutes of video a day. And you can do it without showing your full dick too."

"Big feet are mad popular."

All three of them look at Rhys's feet.

"Get to work, Margie," Rhys mutters. "I need to handle this."

I stifle a snort at his wording. "See you at lunch. Good luck."

My morning is relatively uneventful, if uneventful is only running into three or four more naked people.

But as I'm headed back to the lodge for lunch, the hairs on the back of my neck stand up.

I glance around and spot a dark-haired guy with thick chest hair taking nude selfies in a wildflower garden.

Déjà vu hits me, like I've seen this guy in this wildflower garden before.

I haven't—I'm positive I haven't—but there's something familiar about him.

Still, I duck my head and continue down the path to the lodge, trying to place him.

Any subscriptions I ever had to GrippaPeen channels were mild curiosity that petered out—yes, yes, pun intended—after a few months, and he definitely wasn't one of the creators I followed.

When I scroll socials on my phone, I generally get cute dogs and home improvement videos with the occasional cooking content added in, so he wouldn't be familiar from there.

Maybe he also does a cooking channel?

The most successful creators, as I understand it after overhearing things this morning, do something other than simply dance around naked.

Apparently Theo knitted while expressing words of encouragement.

There's a creator here this week who mows grass naked.

I know this because Rhys texted that information to me with a facepalm emoji, along with the tidbit that the dude brought his lawnmower, and I didn't need him to say anything else to hear him grumbling that we'll probably need emergency services more than once whenever that guy starts recording.

Especially since there's more rocky dirt than grass here.

It's been dry for too long.

I'm honestly in awe that the wildflower gardens are still as healthy as they are. Desert flowers are amazing.

Rhys isn't in the staff room for lunch—apparently all of the security guys and grounds crew got roped into moving tables in the dining room to set up for some special event this afternoon, and all of the creators are taking their lunches outside or to their rooms.

He arrives to eat his lunch as Cynthia walks into the staff room, pins me with a look, and says, "You're on bubble patrol again, and if they ever let these people back, I'm quitting."

I look at Rhys.

He gives me the subtle headshake of I didn't do it this time.

We all head down the hallway to the laundry room.

Five naked men are flinging bubbles at each other as they pour out of three separate washing machines, while five other people take video from all angles around the room.

Rhys sucks the deepest breath in through his nose that a person can possibly suck in through their nose.

I slip out of sight, pursing my lips together.

"That would be hilarious if it didn't have to be cleaned up," Zelda whispers to me.

Rhys shoots us both a look, then steps into the laundry room.

"Oh, it's the thick bear," someone says.

"Dude, seriously, take your shirt off and we'll make you twenty grand by dinnertime."

"If cleaning this up isn't part of your videos, you're being ejected," Rhys says.

Ejected.
Umpire.
Baseball.
Naked guy in the flower garden.
Summer fling.
Oh, fuuuuuuuuck.
No.
No way.
I slip back to the staff room.
What was his name?
I can't remember, so I open a browser and search for baseball umpire grippapeen, and oh, shiiiiiiiiit.
"What?" Rhys says to me from the doorway.
I open my mouth.
Shut it again.
He steps in the door as a dark-haired guy pauses behind him and squints at me. "Margot?"
I make eye contact with Rhys, who instantly turns around. "No visitors in the staff areas," he growls.
As if a dozen or more other people at this point haven't broken that rule.
"Margot?" the guy repeats. "Is that you?"
"Leave my housekeeper alone. No signs, no nudity."
I busy myself with cleaning up everyone else's lunch trash.
"No, I know her," the guy insists.
"Johnson, you know this guy?" Rhys says.
I shake my head.
"Must be mistaken," Rhys says. Orders, really.
I like when he uses that tone when we're in bed.
It's such a fucking turn-on to be ordered around by a massive guy who couldn't honestly hurt anyone without solid cause.
"Sorry," my old fling mutters. "I really thought that was her."

"Even if it was, you don't get to talk to her," Rhys growls. "Understand?"

"Yeah, boss."

"You might like walking around with your junk out, but our staff gets all of the privacy they deserve."

"Got it. Fuck, I got it already. I'm mistaken." He snorts. "Like she'd be here cleaning up after other people. I'm such a dumbass."

Rhys glares at him until he retreats up the staff stairs, white ass cheeks gleaming beneath his tan.

When he's gone, Rhys glances back at me.

I wince. "A rebound has never been a bigger mistake."

Thunderclouds move through his expression.

My vagina tingles.

More creators flow past him, checking out the laundry room.

I bite my lip.

Half the conference is here.

And big, broody, protective, possessive Rhys?

He blinks, and his eyes go dark.

"I need to get back to work," I say, my voice barely working.

He steps sideways.

I slip past him.

He follows me down the hall to the back door.

Around the corner to the garden shed.

Inside, where he locks the door.

I climb him and press my mouth to his as he presses my back against the wall, working his hands between us until his fingers are slipping under my pants and teasing my clit.

"The only dick you get to think about is mine," he growls.

"It's a good dick."

"You're wet."

"For you."

"Better fucking be for me and no one else."

He presses my clit hard while thrusting his fingers into me, and I bite his shoulder to keep from screaming as the fastest orgasm of my life overtakes me.

I'm still coming when he pulls his fingers out, sets me on the ground, and bends me over the seat of a riding lawnmower. "I'm taking your pants off," he tells me.

"Yes," I gasp through the tingles still spreading through my body.

"And I'm going to fuck you until you can't see straight."

"Please," I say on a puff of air.

He strips my pants to my knees, then strokes a rough hand over one of my butt cheeks.

I hear foil tearing, then Rhys grunting, and then his cock pokes between my thighs. "Why is it never enough?" he says as he thrusts into me.

I stifle a moan and tilt my hips to take him deeper. "Good—this."

"You like this?" He pumps harder, the angle hitting me in all the right spots.

"Feels—magic."

He grips my hips in his large hands, slamming into me while I grasp the seat beneath me.

"Cannot—get—enough," he says again.

He's on the verge too.

I can hear it in the way his voice is straining.

Knowing that he wants me, that he wants me this badly—god, it's addictive.

Heady.

Being wanted—being wanted beyond rational control—no one wants me that badly.

Except Rhys.

When he knows who I am. The lies I've been telling. The potential I have to hurt his friend.

But he still wants me.

He grips my hips tighter, his fingers digging into my skin, his cock hitting that sweet spot exactly right to—

"Oh god, Rhys, I'm coming." I gasp as the shock ripples through my body hard and fast, even harder and faster than my first orgasm.

He groans and stills behind me, buried deep, the spasms in his cock as he comes beating in time with my own release.

"You—so—everything," he grunts.

I love you.

Oh, god.

Oh, god.

Surely not.

No, no, no.

I can't.

I don't know how.

This is—it's infatuation.

Sexual satisfaction.

And I'm the asshole who's mistaking it for love.

He sags behind me. "Fuck, Margot," he whispers.

I gasp for breath, my eyes stinging, realizing how uncomfortable this stupid riding lawnmower seat is on my boobs.

And then I start laughing because I don't know what else to do.

He sucks in a breath. "Jesus, not while I'm still inside you, please, for the love of my balls."

"Why does this place even have a riding lawnmower?" I ask.

His cock slides out of me, leaving me feeling empty and exposed.

But only for a moment before he's using a tissue to wipe me between my thighs, then pulling my pants up.

Touching me.

Caring for me.

Goddammit, I'm already on the verge of crying. He needs to stop being—well, everything.

Everything good in the world.

Everything I don't deserve yet.

"For convenience when I want a good place to bend you over in private," Rhys murmurs.

He pulls me upright, twists me around, and wraps me in a hug.

It's one of those tight, full-body hugs that makes me feel like the rest of the world doesn't exist.

Like I'm safe.

Protected.

Shielded from the outside world and all of the bad it can bring.

"I want to ask the triplets to be the scandal that will take my father down and destroy him," I whisper, the words tumbling out without filter because I need to do something to be real, to pull myself back to who I am, to what I can and can't offer a man.

"I know."

"He tried to destroy my sister. He deserves—he deserves to pay."

He squeezes me tighter. "Money can't buy a soul. Even if you never destroy him—he's not happy. He's never been happy. But you can be."

I shudder as my breath leaves me. "Why are you so wise?"

"Grief, life, trauma, and good genes. Plus my brain works better after lots of sex."

I know he's joking, but I don't laugh.

Instead, I squeeze him tighter.

"O'Malley, where are you?" his radio squawks. "Got a situation in the spa."

He sighs and releases me, unclipping his radio. "On my way," he says.

He looks down at me in the dim light, and I swear he wants to say it too.

I love you.

Jesus.

I need to put a stop to this.

Otherwise—otherwise, I'm going to hurt him, because I can't—I can't be everything he deserves.

He hooks a hand behind my neck, kisses me hard on the forehead, and sighs. "Be careful. Consider quitting."

"You too," I say.

He double-checks his pants, which is good, because his fly's down, and then he slips out the door.

I wait a minute, then I follow.

No one notices me.

Which is so strange.

Because I feel like I'm a giant neon sign flashing Hot Mess in Distress.

I suck in a big breath, blink back all of my emotions, and get to work.

I'm mistaken. Rhys isn't falling for me. He knows what this is.

And I need to remember it too.

26

Down badder and badder

Rhys

We make it through Thursday, and then Friday morning, with much of the same as there was Wednesday.

With one notable exception.

Every last one of the GrippaPeen creators has been leaving massive tips for the housekeepers on a daily basis.

They clearly know they're wreaking havoc, and they're paying the staff well to compensate for their troubles.

"The money so totally makes up for having to see so many penises," Zelda's saying to Margie over lunch on Friday. They're at the table. I'm leaning against the counter, pretending I'm scrolling my phone while I eat a peanut butter and jelly sandwich, which is honestly one of life's underappreciated culinary delights.

"I'm still in shock that they're this generous," is Margot's very measured answer.

Zelda's face scrunches. "Hey, how bad are you hurting for money?"

Margot looks up from the sandwich I packed her this morning. "I always get by. Why?"

Zelda nods toward me. "I was just thinking we should share with all of the staff."

Margot smiles. "I wasn't going to suggest it in case you needed the money, but yes. I'm in. Here. Take mine and figure out the best way to split it all." She reaches into her pocket and pulls out several hundred-dollar bills, then a few more, and then a few more.

She reaches deeper into her pocket, and— "Oops. One more. I think that's it now."

Zelda looks at me again. "I don't know what your situation is either, but those guys might have a point about you trying this for a few months."

"I'm good," I say.

Margot's smile turns me inside out.

Every fucking time.

Something shifted in the garden shed, and if I thought I was down bad before, that's nothing compared to now.

I open my eyes, I think about her.

I brush my teeth, I think about her.

I see a flower, I think of her.

I see the wind blow through the yellow aspens, I think about her.

A pinecone drops on my head, I think about her.

I eat a sandwich—you get the idea.

I'm obsessed.

And I don't care.

I probably should—she's telling the triplets tomorrow, and that's when everything changes one way or another—but right now, I don't give a shit if she hurts me.

My rose-colored glasses are firmly in place, and I'm convinced we're going to have some kind of happily ever after no matter what.

"I'm almost going to miss them when they're gone," Zelda murmurs.

"Didn't know we'd be getting paid for this much…entertainment," Margot replies.

"I'm not quite ready to go back to boring."

"We'll always have the memories."

The GrippaPeen conference technically ends this afternoon, with the creators mostly checking out tomorrow and no other guests arriving until Monday, so because Margot came in last Sunday, and since Louisa is back on the schedule with the nudity being over, Margot's off the next three days.

Likely technically forever after her talk with the triplets.

Which I'm starting to hope she delays.

I like things the way they are now.

Work hard here during the day. Then when we get home, it's dinner, sex, dessert, sex, sleep a little, sex, sleep a little more, sex, shower, sex, breakfast, sex, and then work again.

With talking in between too.

Though I might've missed some sex on that list.

Dammit.

I'm about to pop a boner again.

You'd think my dick would be exhausted, but no. He's raring to go like he hibernated, and now it's sex marathon time for as long as we can get it.

Cynthia sticks her head in and looks at all three of us. "Incident with a merlot, a white couch, and a taxidermy pig. Who wants to handle cleanup at the winery?"

Margot smiles at her. "I'll get it."

"Why do you keep volunteering for the worst jobs?" Zelda asks.

"Just in case they do something even worse next," Margot replies with a cheeky grin.

"There's nothing worse than red wine," Cynthia says.

Margot shrugs. "I like putting things back the way they're supposed to be."

That's what sticks in my head all afternoon.

Putting things back in place the way they're supposed to be.

She can't fix her family.

Can't put Daphne back in the way it was before.

So she's putting her father where he's supposed to be.

Putting things as right as she can make them.

For me too.

Sometime this week when she wasn't working and we weren't having sex, she read through the court filings in the lawsuit war I had with Xavier those first few months after I departed Technique Group. With my permission, she passed it on to her friend back in New York, who's going to make sure people in New York start talking about it.

The whole thing flew under the radar. Xavier had blacklisted me so thoroughly that I didn't have any local friends in the industry that I trusted to talk to about it, or to ask to talk to other people about it, and it wasn't hard to see that if I'd started yelling about suing him, I'd look like the pathetic loser who couldn't accept that I was bad at my job.

The accusations of financial mismanagement that I had based on what little evidence I could gather before going to court are still enough that he'll take a reputation hit, which will help me look less like a fool grasping for straws too.

But the idea of vengeance isn't what's making me happy.

That's all Margot.

I find her with Zelda near what's supposed to be the end of her shift.

They're huddled in the doorway to the dining room, which has been cleared of all tables again, with chairs set up for the sixty or seventy creators who've been here this week.

A familiar face is at the front of the room, on a makeshift stage, microphone in hand, about to start speaking.

"Oh, good, I'm not too late," a feminine voice murmurs beside us.

I glance down and spot Laney Monroe.

She's beaming at Theo on the stage.

He pulls a face at her, then smiles softly, and then he lifts his microphone. "Afternoon, naked people."

Cheers and shouts erupt in the room. Someone yells take it off. Someone else throws a ball of red yarn at the stage.

"Is this awkward?" Margot murmurs to Laney.

Laney shakes her head, still smiling. "We all have our stories about how we got to where we are. This is his."

"Settle down, settle down," Theo says. "I'm only here for five minutes, so if you want to hear what I have to say, you have to listen now."

The room falls into immediate silence.

Clearly, they believe him.

"Wish that worked on toddlers," Laney says.

Margot—shit, Margie—smiles and doesn't answer.

Theo glances back at Laney again.

She nods to him.

I slip behind Margie and settle a hand on her waist.

She leans back into me.

And Theo starts talking again. "When I started my channel, I was talking to myself," he says. "Telling myself the things I needed to hear. Teaching me to believe in myself, that I was good enough, that I deserved room and space to grow and learn. I did it naked because emotions are—they're hard, my dudes. Being emotionally exposed is harder than being buck naked in a crowded room. And I'd know. That's how I got my first detention."

Snickers go up around the room, and Laney laughs too. "I remember that."

"Thing is, anyone can get naked," Theo continues. "I hear you've all been naked half the week here. But the thing that'll bring you success—and I don't mean on a subscription channel, I mean in life—is embracing who you are and what makes you unique. Not if your dick's tattooed or has a weird curve. But the part of this that's unique." He taps his heart.

Margie glances at Laney, smiling softly at the woman who's beaming at her husband on stage.

I want that.

I want a life with someone who'll watch me do what I'm best at and beam with pride over it.

Someone who's as much my partner as I want to be hers.

That was lacking with Felice.

I was behind her one hundred percent. But I don't think she was behind me.

Ever.

"Success is half luck," Theo says. "I wasn't the first dude to try naked knitting for subscribers. Wasn't the first dude to give life advice and tell my people they were all good enough exactly as they are. But I was the first dude who got popular for doing it. Still don't know why it was me, but it was. And so that's why I'm here. To talk about how I'm better than all of you."

The crowd roars with laughter as Theo cracks a grin.

"So Theo," Laney murmurs with a smile.

"Kidding, kidding," he says. "Only way I'm better is that I found the best wife in the world and she gave me two babies who are just like her. Sorry to disappoint if any of you were hoping to get someone better."

"Dammit, Theo." Now Laney's swiping her eyes.

Margie leans back into me.

I press a kiss into her hair.

Laney's great.

But she's no Margie-Margs-Skillet-Margot.

"I can't tell you how to make your channels more popular," Theo says. He shrugs at someone I recognize as an executive from the GrippaPeen website. "It's the truth, dude. I can't tell you what content style will take off next. But I can tell you it doesn't mean shit if the rest of your life isn't full. Laney makes my life full. And not just because she accepts me for who I am, but because she supports me when I say crazy shit like I want to buy that ski resort with our friends and give creative people a place to get away and focus on art."

He grins back at Laney over the crowd. "Yeah, I know, princess. It's not crazy to give back to the world. Not crazy to support a community. Not crazy to do good things with the gifts we've been given."

He sweeps his gaze over the room. "And that is what I want you to take away from my five minutes here. No one—none of us—succeeds all on our own. We're part of something bigger than ourselves, no matter how we express our art. And we owe it to the world to give back what it's given us. Without that, it doesn't mean shit. I'm outta here, motherfuckers."

He steps back, sneezes so loud several people jump, takes a bow, and then ducks out a side door.

The room bursts into a standing ovation.

"What just happened?" I murmur to Margie.

"Apparently Theo Monroe?" she replies.

Laney's laughing, still wiping her eyes. "That is absolutely what happens when Theo's around. Are you off soon? We're having an after-party to celebrate him being brave enough to talk to a room full of people. The triplets are coming. Some other family too."

"Oh, we wouldn't want—" Margie starts, but Laney makes a face, cutting her off.

"You're not intruding. You're invited and welcome." She winks at me. "Unless you have something better to do?"

I shouldn't be getting hot in the cheeks.

But I am.

Margie looks up at me.

I look down at her.

"It's an old-people party," Laney adds. "You'll be home before nine because we pass out about as soon as we get the kids in bed."

"We'll consult our calendar," I say.

"You two are adorable," Laney murmurs. She glances at her phone, then smiles at us again. "Gotta go play bodyguard for my husband and get him out of here before his fans find him."

I let Margie go. "I'll help."

Laney sighs. "I'd say I can handle this myself, but…"

"I've been here all week. No need to explain."

Margie smiles at me. "See you at the truck after we get this cleaned up."

That—that's what has me smiling too.

I don't want to go to a party.

I want to go back to the cabin with Margot and enjoy the fuck out of the time we have left here before any potential shit starts hitting the fan.

Who knows?

Maybe there won't be any shit at all.

The triplets are friends with rich and famous people already. Margot has lawyers at the ready to defend against anything her father might try if he finds out about the triplets. And I'll vouch for her character.

Maybe we've been worried for nothing.

Maybe they'll understand.

And maybe life will stay rosy.

I can hope, anyway.

27

The fan will now spray the shit

Margot

Much like I can't say no to my sister, I can't say no to my half brothers either.

And that's why Rhys and I are hanging out at Laney and Theo's house with far more people than there were at Sabrina and Grey's house last weekend.

We're here because my brothers badgered me to come.

I want one last night of fun with them before I drop a few surprises on them tomorrow.

"Is this everyone who's ever lived in Snaggletooth Creek?" I ask Lucky over the noise of the rest of the crowd gathered inside, out of the rain that blew in just after we got here.

The good news? With this many people, it's easier to duck Jonas, whom I spotted with Emma and their kids not long ago.

The bad news? I'm not a huge fan of being in crowded spaces with people I don't know and limited escape routes.

Even here in Snaggletooth Creek, where everyone I've met so far has been kind and has no reason to make me uncomfortable or put me in a precarious situation.

"Only about half," Lucky replies with a grin.

"This would get shut down by a fire marshal," Rhys says.

He's at my side, not even playing that we're not hooking up. His hand's gripping mine, and he has his body angled so that he's half shielding me from the room, and so that he can see both of the entrances to the living room where we're standing near the front door.

Lucky laughs. "Security-minded to the end. Don't worry. We know everyone here."

"Is Decker's neighbor here?" I ask.

Lucky cringes. "Hope not. That'd get awkward."

The party isn't limited to adults, and based on the number and ages of the kids, I'm guessing daycare and preschool friends are among those here. Most of the kids have disappeared into a large playroom off the kitchen, and I heard a rumor that Laney and Theo rounded up their seven cats—yes, *seven* cats—and took them to a different house rather than risking the cats freaking out at this many people.

"Was Theo's speech everything we all imagined it would be?" Jack asks as he joins us.

"It was inspiring," Rhys replies.

Jack and Lucky both snicker. "He...rose to the challenge?"

"Knock it off," Sabrina says as she slides into the group with us. "Laney showed me the video. It was really sweet, actually."

"I didn't realize she was recording it," I say.

"She asked the operations manager to do it."

"Oh."

"Cynthia got Laney in the video some too. It was adorable to see her get teary-eyed over him talking about his former profession. If you'd told me in high school that they'd settle down together after Theo gave up his job as an adult entertainer for her... Just no way. I never would've believed it."

"She's not posting that video, is she?" Rhys asks, taking the words right out of the frozen part my brain that's having an instinctive fear response to the idea of a video like that going viral.

I was standing right next to Laney.

I might be in that video too.

Someone could recognize me, and then my father would see it, and then—

Stop thinking, Margot. Everything's fine.

"Nope. Friends and family only." Sabrina gives my brothers a cheeky grin. "Clearly, *favorite* friends and family only. You must not be it. Have you seen Zen? They're not a big fan of crowds like this."

"Saw them leaving," Decker says as he rounds out the family group. "Said they'd call later."

"Hey, Grandpa's here," Lucky says. "Catch you later. Margie—ah, yeah. Have fun with Rhys."

Decker snakes through the crowd with Lucky on their way to talk to a tall older gentleman who's just inside the kitchen with his arm tucked around a shorter older woman.

"You any good at darts?" Jack asks me.

I shake my head. "One talent I don't possess."

"Excellent. Lucky and Decker always kick my ass. Be nice to win for a change."

He grins, and I laugh at his honesty. "Great. Lead on. I can't wait to lose."

He leads me and Rhys downstairs to a walk-out basement where he waves at his dad, who's playing pool with someone I don't recognize.

"Your parents are here?" I murmur as he hands me a set of darts.

"Yeah. Sabrina's mom and Theo and Emma's dad too."

"Big party. They all know about what was at the retreat center this week?"

Jack snickers. "No. They think we're celebrating a random anniversary related to Theo not getting detention for something when we were kids."

"Seriously?"

"He set a new standard for troublemaking. Decker and Lucky and I have bets on how much heartburn his kids give him before they're eighteen. My money's on the oldest. You never suspect the oldest."

"Are you the oldest?" I haven't asked that yet.

"Middle."

The way that makes so much sense...

"Now, here's how you throw a dart," he says to me as he turns to demonstrate.

"Don't listen to him," Rhys says. "He wants you to lose. And it's about that Monopoly game last weekend, not about who beats him in darts."

Now that cracks me up.

And even I can tell Jack's completely lying as he explains the best way to hold a dart. He's emulating throwing it with the pointy side aimed away from the board.

We get three games in, with me performing better than expected, before I realize just how crowded it's getting here in the basement too.

I reach for my phone—I know Rhys has me, but when there are this many people, I like to know Cyril's nearby too.

But my phone isn't in my pocket.

I pause.

"You okay?" Rhys murmurs.

My own security training kicks in, and I blurt an answer I know he'll understand. "I was going to take a picture, but I don't have my phone."

Jack glances at me. "You lost your phone?"

I pat my pockets, front and back, and a sliver of panic starts to work its way into my chest.

When did I have it last?

Surely someone couldn't have taken it out of my pocket without me noticing.

And even if I hadn't felt it, Rhys has been watching.

"Where've you been?" Jack whips out his own phone. "We'll look for it. Case? Color? Homescreen?"

"No case. It's black. Black home screen. White clock. I was upstairs and then down here."

He squints at me. "You know you have a boring phone?"

"Did you bring it inside?" Rhys asks me.

"I thought so."

He's wearing a straight face, but I can feel him tensing. "Let's go check the truck."

"I told Decker and Lucky to look for it too," Jack says. "We'll find it."

We split up, and Rhys and I head outside.

"I was having such a nice time, I wasn't paying attention," I whisper to him.

He squeezes my hand. "Good."

His truck is many cars back on the long driveway up to the house, and we're completely alone by the time we reach it. He swings open his door, then quirks a look at me.

"Is that good or bad?" I'm holding my breath.

If I lost my phone and the wrong person sees the wrong person calling me—

It's one thing to tell my brothers who I really am tomorrow.

It's entirely different for a potential enemy to have that knowledge first.

"It's good." He reaches in, and when he turns back around, he has my phone in his hand.

"*Oh my god*, thank fuck," I breathe.

I reach for it, but his entire demeanor has shifted, and he's suddenly shoving me behind him, between the truck and the world, his back to me.

And just as quickly, he relaxes. "Evening, Mrs. Sullivan," he says.

I peek out from behind him and give her a small finger wave, but the look on her face makes the hairs on the back of my neck stand up.

A shiver slinks down my skin.

She doesn't answer Rhys.

Instead, she keeps staring at me. "What are you doing here?"

I make myself smile. "Looking for my phone. I lost it."

In the dim light from inside the truck and the garden lamps lining the drive, she's barely illuminated, but it's enough to see that she's bouncing on her toes and that her hands are curled into fists. Her whole body vibrates with an uneven energy that I don't like, but the shine in her eyes and the wobble in her lips has me putting a *slow down, this is okay* hand to Rhys's back as she speaks again. "You need to *leave*."

"Mrs. Sullivan—" I start.

"I have protected them for *years*," she whispers. "Do *not* hurt them."

Fuck.

Fuck, fuck, *fuck*.

She knows.

She knows.

But she's not angry.

She's scared.

"I know," I whisper back, trying to keep a wobble out of my voice at the instant understanding of the lengths she'd go to in order to protect her sons.

The lengths my father wouldn't go to in order to protect me or Daphne.

But the bigger problem—this is happening.

It's happening, and it's happening *now*.

I hold my hands at my side, nonthreatening, as I fully scoot out from behind Rhys. "You've done an amazing job. I don't want to hurt them."

"Then *go*."

"It's not that simple—" I start, but movement behind her catches my eye, and I freeze.

Laney's here too.

Mrs. Sullivan didn't come alone.

"It's true," Laney says as we lock eyes. "You're not *Margie Johnson*. I thought it was weird that you looked like *you* last week, but that you couldn't possibly be—but you are. Aren't you?"

I swallow.

Laney's parents grew their fortune on their own. They're what my father would scoff at as *new money* even as he admires their business model.

She wouldn't have had the same kind of childhood I did.

The same kind of training I did.

The same kind of expectations I did.

But she has every bit of the poise and confidence and outrage I'd have if I were in her shoes right now.

And she's pissed.

Pissed in ways I never understood until Daphne was disinherited.

"There are reasons—" I start.

She snorts softly. "There always are, aren't there?"

"Mar—Margie's not hurting anyone," Rhys says to the other two women.

I grip his shirt tighter. "I simply wanted to get to know them."

"By lying about who you are," Laney says.

"Do you understand how much damage you've already done?" Mrs. Sullivan's voice cracks, and she swipes at her eyes. "They were never supposed to know."

"I didn't—" I cut myself off, shaking my head. She won't care that they found out on their own because of the DNA tests. "You're right. It would've been better if they'd never found out. But they did, and we can't hide it anymore."

She jerks like I've punched her. "The hell we can't. You—you need to *leave*."

"Does your husband know?" Rhys asks.

"Don't answer that," Laney says to Mrs. Sullivan.

"I won't tell him," I say. "It's not my place. But I *am* telling your sons. They deserve to know the truth. They *need* to know the truth. For their own protection."

"You will *not*—" Mrs. Sullivan starts, but she freezes at the sound of heavy footsteps approaching.

"Hey, found your phone," Lucky says as Rhys tries to shield me again.

I make eye contact with my half brother.

The one who's trusted me the most from the beginning.

His easygoing smile freezes on his lips, even as it fades from his eyes as he studies the group of us.

He stops before he fully reaches the little circle we've made, like he doesn't want to come inside our group where it's tense. "What's going on?"

His mother points at me while she huddles close to Laney. "She's not who she says she is. You can't believe anything—*anything*—she's told you."

Lucky looks at me again, and the bottom of my stomach drops out.

He's kept this secret—that he's known his dad isn't his biological dad—for years.

He's also shielded his parents from the truth at his brother's request for years.

And now it's coming out.

Has to be something of a relief.

But also scary as hell.

"Let's all take a deep breath—" Rhys starts, but Laney shakes her head at him.

"You're not *deep breath*-ing your way out of this. You knew, didn't you?"

"He's not wrong," Lucky says, more cautious than I've heard him at any point the past two weeks. "Deep breaths never hurt anyone. Let's back up, and—"

"Found your phone," Jack says as he and Decker both approach too.

My gaze flies to Rhys's.

"We found her phone," he says, still looking back at me.

"No, I found her phone." Lucky lifts a black phone with a white clock that's similar to mine, but not the same.

Jack holds up something similar. "You found someone else's. This one's—wait. Something's going on here. What's this? What's happening?"

"You need to *leave*," Mrs. Sullivan hisses at me again.

I hold up a hand. "I'm not him," I say quietly. "I am *nothing* like him. I don't want to—"

"I don't want you to say another word," she interrupts.

"Mom? What's going on?" Decker's the first of the three to slip to her side and wrap an arm around her.

"She's lying," Mrs. Sullivan says. "Whatever she's told you, she's lying. You can't trust her."

My eyes are getting hot, and my nose feels swollen. I've never wanted to hug another woman as badly as I also want to yell at her in my life.

She's hurting.

We're all hurting.

I don't know the circumstances around whatever relationship she had with my father, but she clearly knows who he is and what he's capable of.

But her kids are grown adults.

They deserve to know the truth.

They *want* to know the truth, or they wouldn't have invited me here.

And I meant it when I said they need to know the truth.

They need to know it so that when my father finds out, he can't blindside and destroy them.

"Hear her out," Rhys says.

Much as it's comforting to know he's on my side, I don't think hearing me out is happening tonight.

No one here wants to hear me out.

I'm the enemy.

I'm the enemy that I've tried desperately not to be.

I swallow again as three identical sets of eyeballs aim in my direction.

"You've been lying?" Decker says.

"Only about my name and a few small inconsequential details." I can't make my voice any louder than a whisper. "I'm not Margie Johnson—"

"You're not Margie?" Jack's brow furrows.

"No. That's not my real name. But I honestly am your half sister."

"Make her leave," Mrs. Sullivan says.

Laney sighs. "She can leave, but it won't fix what's broken."

"They'll hurt my boys." Mrs. Sullivan's voice cracks again.

"No one will hurt—" I start, but Jack interrupts me again.

"Who are you?"

"I'd like to know that too," Lucky says.

The confusion and hurt in his face—*dammit*.

This isn't how I wanted to tell them.

But if there's one thing that life's taught me, it's that you're never really in control.

You just think you are.

"My name is Margot," I say, looking at each of my half brothers in turn. I pull my glasses off, grateful when Rhys easily slips them from me and puts them in his pocket. He's *here*. Quiet, but I can feel his support. And that means he's risking a friend.

For me.

Do I deserve that?

Do I?

"I didn't tell you my real name because—because it's not—because we're related to—" I huff out a frustrated breath.

Why won't the right words come?

Because there are no right words.

"Because she was protecting you," Rhys says for me.

I cringe.

If I were truly protecting them, I wouldn't be here.

I would've sent a team of attorneys to handle this on their behalf in a way that would make damn sure my father could never hurt them.

So yes.

Yes, I could've done this better.

But I wanted revenge.

And I wanted to get to know them.

Two birds, one stone.

Decker glares at Rhys. "Protecting us from fucking *what*?"

Those words—those words, I have. "Threats and intimidation and everything my father would throw at you to keep you silent."

Lucky rears back. "*You know him?* Our—our biological—you know him?"

"He raised me. He's not a nice person. And he wouldn't like knowing that you exist."

Mrs. Sullivan is leaning so heavily on Decker that if he moves, she'll fall over. "Make her leave," she whispers. "Please make her leave."

Crying is weakness.

That's what my father always told me.

Fuck my father.

Crying is real. It's human. And too many of us are in pain for me to not want to cry right along with this woman who's been doing her best for her sons for decades.

Has she made mistakes?

Who hasn't?

Not my place to judge, and there are more important things to hash out than how we all got here.

"He will hurt them over my dead body." My voice cracks while a tear slips down my cheek. "There is nothing—*nothing*—that I won't do to make sure he never has the chance to hurt any of you."

"Who is *he?*" Decker demands.

"Tobias Merriweather-Brown," Laney answers for me. "CEO of the Aurora Gardens empire."

Mrs. Sullivan flinches like she's been punched. Lucky joins Decker in flanking her. "It's okay, Mom. We've got you," he murmurs.

"Some big corporate dude?" Jack says.

"Second-generation billionaire hotel king," Laney says. She nods toward me. "With Margot being next in line."

Jack sways like he'd like to sit down.

Lucky and Decker huddle tighter around their mom, and my heart squeezes again.

I don't think they care how or why she slept with someone who wasn't their dad.

They're with her to the end too.

And that's family.

That's the kind of family I want.

The family that forgives when you fuck up. The family that stands by you in the storms. The family that embraces you for your humanity instead of your perfection and productivity.

I want it so badly while realizing it's slipping out of reach that I can't suck in an even breath while I swipe at my cheeks.

Rhys tightens his grip on me. "It's okay," he murmurs.

Trying to be that family for me while Decker turns the darkest, most outraged glare I've ever seen on the man who was his good friend five minutes ago.

I'm breaking them apart.

I'm causing collateral damage.

I'm doing all of the things I never wanted to do.

"So you lied because, what? You thought we'd want money?" Decker says.

Rhys growls softly.

"No, because—" I start.

"Because you're spying on the retreat center so you can build your own?" Jack says.

"*No.*"

"Because it's fun to dick around with nobodies?" Lucky says.

That one hurts. "You aren't a nobody. You're—you're more *somebodies* than my parents will ever be."

"Hey, guys, I found Margie's phone," Mr. Sullivan says. "Whoa. This feels heavy. Everything okay?"

Fuuuuuuuck.

My eyes burn more, and the tears come faster.

He's going to hurt.

He's going to hurt hard when he deserves nothing but happiness for the man he's been.

"Good fucking thing you're already at your car," Decker mutters.

Mr. Sullivan's brow furrows as he looks at his wife. "Sweetie? What's wrong? Did someone—did someone die?"

The triplets share one of their classic silent communication looks.

"We need to go home and have a talk," Decker finally says.

"Probably need to return a few phones first," Rhys mutters.

Decker flips him off, then looks at me. "And you—you need to fucking go home too. And I don't mean to my cabin. You can get the fuck out of there, or we'll have the sheriff remove you."

"I don't—I'm not—I won't—" I can't find the right words.

I've been rehearsing what I'll say in my head all week, and now, under the glare of three men who've come to represent family to me, none of it is adequate.

I can't say *I'm sorry*.

It's not enough. It will never be enough.

Because I'm sorry for so much more than lying to them.

I'm sorry we share genes because of a terrible human being. I'm sorry that they found out because they jokingly took a DNA test to make sure they were related to each other, which is so classically funny and perfectly *them*. I'm sorry that their family—their *real* family, the family that's been there for them from birth through childhood and young adulthood and through their lives until now—will hurt because of the lies.

Possibly for years to come.

"Let's get out of here," Jack says to all of them. "Laney—take the phones?"

"Of course," she murmurs.

He ignores me while he hands over the phone he found to Laney. "Let's go. Mom. Dad. I'll drive."

Mr. Sullivan looks at me.

Really looks at me.

"I'm sorry," I whisper.

It's so fucking inadequate.

I'm so fucking inadequate.

Arrogant enough to think I could do this without hurting anyone.

Still so much like my father no matter how hard I've tried not to be.

Mr. Sullivan looks back at his family, then dips his head and heaves a sigh that I feel deep in my own toes.

Like he knows.

Like he knows this day that he'd been dreading would eventually come, but he didn't want to face it, and now he has to, and there's no telling where his life will go from here.

Maybe I'm wrong.

I *hope* I'm wrong.

I hope he's always known.

But there's a difference between *known* and *suspected*.

There's a difference between *my wife and I have already had this conversation* and the slouch of his shoulders and the ragged way he's sucking in breaths now.

And it's my fault.

If I'd stayed away—if I'd stayed away, if I'd never thought of using the triplets in my revenge scheme, they could've kept this secret forever.

Or at least discussed it with their family on their own terms.

I'm a goddamn monster.

It's in my blood.

And you can't fight what's in your blood.

"You shouldn't have come here," Decker says to me. "And you—" He looks at Rhys, disgust coloring his expression. "I thought I could trust you. I thought we were friends. But you'd give it up all for a woman you barely know?"

Rhys flinches. "It's not—"

"It's what? You're in *looove*?"

Rhys flinches again, harder this time, and I don't know what that means either.

That he loves me?

That he doesn't?

That he's on my side?

He shouldn't be on my side.

I don't deserve people on my side.

I hurt them. I will always hurt them. It's too ingrained in me to win at all costs to not hurt everyone I love and everyone I want to love.

I can't see the line where I don't cause collateral damage.

"Shut up," Lucky says to Decker. "Not helping."

"Nothing's fucking helping," Decker replies. "You know what would've helped? If *someone* hadn't decided his dick was more important than blindsiding a friend."

"That was my fault," I say quickly, because Rhys doesn't deserve this. He doesn't deserve to hurt more because of me and my mistakes. "I—I blackmailed him."

"She did not," Rhys says.

"I did—"

He cuts me off again, looking at Decker. "You knew the risk that it would all come out when you invited her."

Decker snorts. "Not the full risks." He nods toward me. "Only *she* knew how bad it could be."

"That's fair. Blame the child for the father's actions. Way of the world, isn't it?"

"Stop it," Lucky says. "Mom, Dad, we're leaving. Margie—Margot—whoever you are—I can't talk to you right now. We have bigger things to handle."

It's not just a punch to the gut.

It's a thousand little splinters to my heart.

I have a family that I need to take care of and you, Margot, are not it. You're not family. You don't count. You don't belong.

He's not wrong.

I don't belong.

Not here.

Not in my job.

Not in my family.

I don't even deserve Daphne.

And Rhys—*Rhys*.

Rhys and that massive, massive wounded heart—my god, he deserves so much better.

I suck in another shaky breath. "I didn't—I didn't want to hurt anyone."

All of them ignore me as they hand over the phones they found to Laney, then turn and head back toward the party or their own vehicles or wherever they're going.

To anywhere but here.

All of them except Mr. Sullivan.

He looks at me one last time, his eyes pinched and watery, mouth turned down, a sad hollowness lingering around him.

And then he notices Lucky pausing for him, and he's leaving too, with Lucky's arm slung around him.

Rhys grips my hand tight while Laney lingers, watching us.

"Go on," I tell her. "Yell at me. Tell me how awful I am."

Her gaze dips briefly to the ground, then lifts back up to meet mine. "Your article in *Business Women Weekly* about increased productivity through staff care and support last year changed my work life. I quote it all the time, and you're right. It works. Thank you."

I brace myself, waiting for the *but*.

All I see, though, is sadness and sympathy. "And as the daughter of a suspected cheater with an ungodly amount of money and resources at his disposal to cover it all up," Laney says, "I'm sorry for what yours has undoubtedly put you through. We all deserve better."

She gives my shoulder a slight squeeze, and then she, too, turns to leave.

"Do you think they'll forgive me?" I ask her.

I know the answer.

The right answer.

The right answer is *no*.

I broke them. I broke their family.

I don't deserve their forgiveness.

Much like I don't deserve Rhys's either for what I need to do next.

Laney meets my eyes again. "I think they have a bumpy road ahead of them with family in general. Take all the time you need, but it's probably best if you don't come back inside."

You're not welcome here anymore, Margot. You were never welcome as you.

That's what I hear echoing in my head as the woman most like me here, the woman who could've been a tight friend who would've understood things that sometimes even Daphne doesn't, walks away.

Rhys pulls me into a hug that I shouldn't take and that I don't deserve.

I squeeze him back while my brain does what my brain does and asks me how to salvage the situation so that I can still destroy my father.

Fucking brain.

No matter how much I try, I still haven't trained it to take a back seat to my heart.

I don't deserve my half brothers.

Or anyone.

28

Is it heroic or is it chickenshit?

Rhys

Margot hasn't said a single word in the hour since we left the party.

Not on the drive back to the cabin.

Not while she's packed her bags.

Not when Cyril shows up on the doorstep and starts rearranging the bags she'd already put in the van to make them fit better.

She even ignores a call from her sister.

And my heart is about to flee my chest.

"Margot," I finally say as she stands in the doorway of the empty bedroom, staring into it at the rumpled sheets on the bed and the throw pillows tossed in a corner.

She looks up at me, eyes hollow.

"Are you—" I start, then have to stop to clear my throat. "Are you okay?"

Of fucking course she's not, dumbass.

Not like I'm going to ask her if we're okay though.

The tightening in my gut and the tinny taste in my mouth tells me I don't want to ask that question.

"I'm a terrible person," she whispers.

"You're not."

"No, I am. I'm fighting nature and nurture and I'm tired and I don't want to be a better person anymore. I want—I want to go home to my sister because she'll love me no matter what, even when I don't deserve it, while I learn to live with the knowledge that I will never be able to learn how to love people."

I try to swallow and feel like I'm choking on my own tongue.

She can't leave.

Not like this.

"You—you do," I force out. "You know how to love people." Please love me. Love me the way I love you. "What they said—what they did—it's always been building to a shitty end, and they know it. They'll come around. They know it wasn't your fault."

She shakes her head. "They shouldn't. I—I'm not a nice person. If you knew the things I think—"

"I know the things you do. What you do matters more."

"Maybe to you. But I—I'm not ready for this, Rhys. I shouldn't have come here the way I did. I shouldn't have thought I could pull off asking complete strangers to help me avenge someone whose actions thirty-some years ago are now pulling their families apart. But I did, because I'm selfish and cold and calculating and—"

"No, you're not."

"Yes, I am. I'm trying not to be, but I still am. And I won't—I can't—I won't walk into a relationship as anything less than the very best version of me, and I'm not there yet. I might never be there. And that's—that has to be okay."

"The people who love you want—they want to help you on your journey. They want to support you." I love you. I want to support you.

But I can't say it.

I can't force the words out.

Who the fuck am I to think I know her better than she knows herself?

Who the fuck am I to think I can be the person she'd want to trust and lean on?

Her eyes get shiny, but she visibly swallows and blinks hard, and I'm suddenly looking at a confident, strong, take-no-prisoners warrior who has her shoulders back and her head held high and her chin set in steely determination despite the glassy sheen in her eyes.

"You have been so much more than what I deserve," she says quietly, "and one day, you'll find—"

"Stop," I whisper, my heart already bleeding. "Don't say it."

"One day, you'll find happiness beyond your wildest imagination, and you'll deserve every ounce of it."

You're my happiness.

But again, I can't force the words out of my mouth.

Because I had that happiness once—and she left too.

"I have to go." Despite her physical poise, she's speaking so softly I can barely hear her.

Or maybe that's the roar of protest raging in my ears making it hard to hear anything else.

"I've realized what I need to do at home," she continues. "So I'm going to go do that. And I will forever be grateful for your support and belief in me these past two weeks."

"Don't—" My voice cracks, and I can't continue.

"I'll have a personal recommendation sent over by tomorrow night, and I'll pass word to Jonas that he should do the same. Through someone he'll still trust. Not me directly."

"Margot."

"Thank you, Rhys. I knew this trip would change my life. I hope someday you'll look back and find some good in it too."

My fingers tingle. My thighs quake. My stomach is churning straight acid, and my heart—it's retreating into itself.

Into safety.

Into that place where it doesn't care because if it doesn't care, then it can't hurt.

faking cinderella

Fight for her, dumbass, some small, hazy voice whispers in the back of my brain. Fucking fight for her.

But I don't listen to it.

It's safer to not listen to it.

Everything about the past year tells me I need to be safe.

Especially when she clearly doesn't want me.

And then she's gone, slipping out of the cabin and into the night.

Leaving me alone.

Alone, and lonely, and once more unable to trust my own heart.

29

And I can never love anyone

Margot

I cry the entire flight back to New York.

We land sometime after two a.m., and Cyril escorts me into my Manhattan penthouse shortly before three, just as he has thousands of times before in my normal life.

The city lights sparkle below me, and the half moon hangs low in the sky, on its way to bed shortly, with the sun chasing it by a few hours.

I live on top of the world, a thousand feet in the air here in Manhattan, where I've furnished my space with plush, comfortable furniture, decorated in warm pastels that might not be the current style but make me happy.

And today, I don't feel like I deserve to be happy.

I hurt people.

I went to Snaggletooth Creek, saying I didn't want to hurt anyone—that I wanted to avoid collateral damage—and instead, the brothers I desperately want to have in my life are dealing with a family crisis because of me.

Because of my arrogance in thinking that I could pretend to be someone I'm not, that I could lie to them without consequences.

And Rhys—

My god, Rhys.

I'm not whole enough on my own to be the partner he deserves.

I'm not good enough for him.

I probably never will be.

For a while, I convinced myself that we were just having a fling, but every time I looked at him—I knew.

I knew he was catching feelings.

I knew I should've called a stop to it after the first time, because I was also catching feelings.

Feelings that I can't indulge in.

Knowing that I hurt him too, that I hurt the kindest, most understanding, most patient, biggest-hearted man on the planet—that wounded look in his eyes will haunt me for the rest of time.

That's the worst part.

The part where the best man I've ever known—the man who will likely haunt every waking moment of my life and my dreams too—is collateral damage to my innate personality.

"You need to sleep," Cyril says behind me as I stare at my dimly lit living room and into the city lights sparkling in the night beyond.

"I need to make this right. As—as right as I can."

"After you sleep."

"You're off duty. Go home and sleep yourself. The rest of the team will cover me this week."

"You ask them to help with your plans here?"

I flinch. "No."

"Would you?"

"My plans have changed."

"Hmm."

I eye his reflection in my windows. "I said, you're dismissed."

"You didn't cheat. You didn't spend thirty years lying to your kids about their genes. You're not the bad guy here."

"I lied to them."

"Having insecurities that they wouldn't like you because you don't like yourself isn't the same as having malicious intentions."

I flinch again.

"You're a good person, Margot. I'll see myself out."

The door shuts before I can formulate an answer.

I slip into my office and power up my computer.

There's work to be done.

But I fall asleep at my keyboard before I've made enough progress, and I wake up a few hours later to hundreds of pages of nonsense, courtesy of my face on the keyboard.

I make myself a cup of tea to calm my stomach and try again.

But it doesn't work.

No matter what I type as I'm trying to decide what I want to say to my father, none of it feels right.

I check my phone.

No texts from Rhys.

No texts from Lucky.

No missed calls.

No one checking on me.

No one yelling at me either.

I wouldn't mind being yelled at. Pretty sure I deserve it.

No, you don't, I hear Rhys saying in my head.

Even in my imagination, he's too good for me.

My nose tingles and my eyes get hot again as I call Daphne.

She picks up on the third ring. "Hey, you. How's Colorado?"

"I'm back in Manhattan."

There's a pause, then, "Are you okay?" whispered so softly, with so much more care and concern and love than I deserve, that my only answer is to sob.

"Margot," Daph whispers. Then, louder— "Oliver, we're going to Manhattan."

"No," I protest.

Daphne hates the city.

Bad things happen to her when she's here.

I don't want to be another bad thing.

She's had enough bad.

"Stop me," she says.

"You—you hate—the city," I cry.

"But I love you, and you need me, and I'll be right there."

I try to argue, but instead, three hours later, she's barging through my door. "Margot?"

"In here." My face hurts from how much I've cried, and my voice is thick and froggy. I'm buried under a fluffy peach blanket on my couch while I watch that ghost show that Rhys and I watched together the night that I made him popcorn.

Daph throws herself on me and hugs me so tight, I almost can't breathe.

I hug her back even tighter.

I don't want to breathe.

I just want—to not be alone.

"Will you always love me even when I don't deserve it?" I ask her as the tears start all over again.

"You always deserve it." She kisses my head. "All of us always deserve it."

It was just a month ago that she was crying in my arms and pouring her heart out while I brought her home from the road trip where she fell in love with Oliver, and now here we are, with me crying in her arms.

The last time I cried like this?

Never.

Merriweather-Browns are business people. We keep our emotions locked up tight. The world is watching at all times.

But the world wasn't watching me the past two weeks.

The world hasn't seen my secrets the past four years.

And here—here, I know I'm safe to let it all go.

Because even though she shouldn't, my sister loves me.

She hugs me tight while I cry myself out, and once I'm almost under control, the scent of bacon tickles my nose.

"I brought help," Daph says. "Bea and Oliver are cooking breakfast."

And I break into sobs all over again.

"Hey, Margot," Bea calls from the general direction of the kitchen. "I love your stove. This griddle is perfect for pancakes."

"We didn't want Daphne coming to the city unchaperoned," Oliver adds. "We're not listening to a thing though."

"Unless you want us to," Bea agrees.

"We all love you and won't judge," Daph says. "But they'll leave if you want them to. They won't go far because they don't trust me—"

"She might stow away in some random person's car again," Oliver says.

"Or lead the wrong kind of protest," Bea says.

"Or try to rescue the polar bears from the zoo," Oliver continues.

Bea makes a thoughtful noise. "Does the zoo here have polar bears?"

"You're Daphne's best friend, and you don't know if the zoo has polar bears?"

"She forbade me from acknowledging the city exists. Being here with her is new territory, and I forget what I'm supposed to know and not know."

Listening to them is oddly normal, like they've been doing this for years instead of only getting to know each other for the past few weeks.

And it's comforting.

Like life will go on after my broken heart stitches itself back together.

As much as I'll let it, anyway.

"The triplets hate me, and I fell in love with one of their best friends," I tell Daph.

"Your roommate?"

"Yes."

She watches me carefully. "Does he hate you too?"

"He should."

"No one should hate you."

I grimace. "I—I broke up with him last night. I mean, we weren't technically dating, but we're definitely not now, because I told him it's over."

"Why?"

"Because I—because he—he deserves so much better, Daphne."

"Margot Francesca Merriweather-Brown, how fucking dare you."

"Francesca? That's what the F stands for?" Oliver says as he sets a plate of pancakes, scrambled eggs, fruit, and bacon on my coffee table, complete with napkin and silverware.

"You didn't know Margot's middle name?" Bea calls from the kitchen.

"I always thought the F was for fucking. Because she's Margot Fucking Merriweather-Brown," Oliver replies.

Daphne giggles, tries to stifle it, and then giggles again. "You did not."

"He's really obnoxious now," I tell her. "Annoyingly obnoxious."

"Oh, no, not annoyingly." She grins. "Just the right amount. I freaking love it."

"Want me to kick them out?" Bea asks me.

I shake my head, then wince.

Head hurts.

Rhys would—fuck.

Rhys would've already handed me painkillers. He would've seen it before I did.

Because he's a million times better of a person than I am.

And now my eyes are watering again.

Bea appears with a mug. "Fresh tea," she says as she hands it to me. "Peppermint."

"Thank you," I whisper.

Daph grabs the plate and forks up a bite of eggs, but she doesn't eat them.

She waits until after I've taken a sip of tea, and then she tries to feed me. "Eat. And then we're talking more."

"I don't deserve you either," I whisper.

"You have ten seconds to tell me what the ever-loving hell you did to make you think you're a terrible person before I'm stealing your phone and finding another way to get answers."

I don't think she could crack the passcode on my phone, but it's Daphne.

You never know.

So between sips of tea and small bites of breakfast, I talk.

I start at the beginning, all the way back to my first communication with Lucky through the MatchDNA site, through arriving in Snaggletooth Creek, meeting Rhys in the middle of the night, him figuring out who I was, our negotiations for his silence, him teaching me to split firewood, getting to know the triplets, the GrippaPeen convention and almost getting made by a former fling and Jonas Rutherford, up to last night, when Mrs. Sullivan made it clear that she knew who I really was.

"And I—I left before I could tell them that you're innocent and they'd love you," I finish.

Which isn't finishing.

Because I haven't told her—them, actually, since Bea and Oliver are both in the living room with us now—that I broke up with Rhys because he deserves someone who's already whole enough to be in a real relationship.

Someone who doesn't fuck up when she tries to start any kind of new relationship.

Not the way I fucked up with my brothers.

"Margot, you don't need to tell them I'm awesome. I'll prove it to them soon enough."

"They were so mad. I—I might've fucked it up for both of us."

"Then they don't deserve me or you. Family forgives."

I cringe. "Daph—you know our father would make their lives hell if he knew about them, right? It's—it's not entirely safe for them to know who he is."

"Do you think they'll want something from him?"

I shake my head. "No. They have everything they want and need already. I shouldn't—I shouldn't have gone."

I hurt them.

I hurt Rhys.

I hurt myself.

I hurt Rhys.

She points a piece of bacon at me. "Just because our father's a dick of the highest order doesn't mean we don't deserve to get to know our siblings."

"I should've told them the truth from the start."

"Hard disagree," Oliver says, weighing in for the first time.

Daph nods as she munches on her bacon. "Same."

"Speaking as somewhat of an outsider to this, I'm also on page you weren't wrong," Bea says.

"That's not you were right," I point out.

She lifts a shoulder. "Life's complicated. If like, some famous boy-bander-turned-fashion-mogul or, say, one of the Rutherford brothers showed up at my doorstep like, guess what, we're related!, I think I'd freak out and start looking for paparazzi everywhere and worry I couldn't trust anyone anymore because I didn't know who wanted to make new friends with me for me or because of who I was suddenly related to."

Daph blinks at her. "That's basically exactly your life now with you dating Hollywood's hottest leading man."

"Exactly. I more or less do know what they're going through."

"They're friends with the Rutherford brothers already," I tell her.

"Friend-friends? Not just acquaintance friends?"

"Friend-friends," I confirm.

"I never knew Beck Ryder was your favorite Bro Code band member," Daphne says to Bea. "I always pegged you for a Davis Remington stan."

"I'm a sucker for a golden retriever type. What can I say?" Bea grins. "But Davis Remington definitely would've shown up in disguise if he was coming to tell any of us he was secretly our half brother."

"You would've always wondered if they liked you for you or if they liked being related to... well, this," Oliver says, gesturing to the view and my penthouse in general.

"They're friends with people who have this," I reply.

"Not the same as being related."

"You know, don't you?" I say to him. "The bigger reason I didn't tell them."

"Know? No. That's too much thinking. Take an educated guess when my brain insists on being an asshole that wants to think about it anyway? Yeah. Yeah, I have a guess."

Daphne grins. "Your brain likes thinking."

"Stupid brain."

Stupid brain.

My eyes start to water again.

My stupid brain is broken too.

Daph leans closer to me. "Are you really trying to destroy our father?" she murmurs.

"Yes. I mean—that was the plan."

"Margot." She squeezes my arm. "If that'll make you happy, I'm here for it, but don't do it if you're doing it just for me."

I glance past her at Oliver again.

He pretends he doesn't know I'm looking at him.

Bea's concentrating hard on her breakfast plate too.

"I dislike injustice," I tell Daphne. "I don't like that no one has ever held him accountable for any of the shitty things he's done. So yes, I'm partially doing it for you. I'm partially doing it for me. And I'm partially doing it for the world at large."

"Is that why the triplets are mad? Because you asked for their help?"

I shake my head. "They were mad that I lied about who I really am. I think they realize how much it might complicate their lives to be related to us. If I'd never taken that test, if we'd never found out we were related, if I hadn't gone to Colorado—then they wouldn't have to worry about what their sperm donor might do."

"Margot. Their mother knew who he was."

"You can't blame her for keeping that from them though. She—" I rub my eyes.

The pain and fear etched in her face last night—

I did that to her.

I'm not my father. I bear no responsibility for whatever happened between the triplets' mom and my father.

But it is my fault they had to face it as a family.

"She was protecting them," I finish softly.

Daphne sighs heavily, which is one more thing weighing on my conscience.

I don't want to be the reason she worries.

"If you ask me," she says, "they should be thanking you. What if our father had taken a DNA test to squirrel out any kids he didn't know about? What if he'd gotten to them first?"

"And that's why I have to finish what I've started. I need him to know in no uncertain terms that it's time to pay for his sins and disappear from the public eye. Forever."

She tilts her head at me. "Justice will always find a way, even if you don't help it along."

"I need to help it along."

"You taking over Aurora Gardens?" Oliver asks me.

"That was the plan."

"Was?"

"I've been planning this for four years. Since—since our parents demonstrated in no uncertain terms that they don't know the real meaning of family."

"Margot," Daph whispers, her eyes going shiny.

I sling an arm around her shoulders and give her a side hug. "I was always Team Daphne. I'm sorry I didn't tell you sooner."

"Stop making me cry and finish your breakfast."

"Whatever you're still planning, I'm in," Oliver tells me. "I'm Team Daphne too."

"Don't really expect I can do much, but same," Bea says.

I stare down at my half-eaten breakfast. "I don't know what I'm planning anymore."

Oliver heaves another gigantic, exaggerated sigh. "Fine. Fine. You can use my brain to help figure this out."

Daphne's wiping her eyes. "My brain is hardly useless, you two jackasses," she mutters. "And I can't even tell you the number of times I've fantasized about how fucked our father would be if you just quit. You could buy a few smaller hotel chains and build them bigger and better than Aurora Gardens, and you could do it in your sleep. He thinks he's so smart, and he thinks he's so in control, but he never made you sign a noncompete, did he? And any nondisclosures only mean you can't share company secrets, right? There's absolutely nothing stopping you from using everything he ever taught you to beat him at his own game."

I swallow and tilt my head at my sister. "You know about the lack of a noncompete?"

"Being uninterested in business doesn't mean I'm stupid."

"Daphne. I don't think you're stupid."

"Smarter than half the rest of us put together," Oliver murmurs.

She grins. "It's nice to finally be recognized."

"I get why she's not allowed to come to the city now," Bea murmurs.

"Same, but I don't dislike it as much as I probably should," Oliver says.

"So. First we destroy our father, and then we get you your man back," Daphne declares. "Easy-peasy. When do we start? Or do you want to get your man back first, and then destroy our father?"

Now my eyes are stinging again. "I'm not getting my man back."

"Margot."

"I'm broken, Daph. My heart—it doesn't work right."

"Clearly, Ms. Spent Four Years Planning to Avenge Your Sister," Bea murmurs.

"Revenge isn't—it's not—revenge isn't good. It's not—"

"Justice is always good," Bea says. "Is it justice to let powerful people who hurt others for sport stay in their positions when you can take them down? Calling it revenge instead of righteousness doesn't make it any less honorable and admirable."

"Doesn't it?" I ask.

"There's no one else to hold your father accountable, Margot," Oliver says. "There's no one else in a position to make him pay. You can't wait for karma when karma's been waiting for you." He cocks a brow. "Just like trickle-down economics. It starts with us, because there's no one else."

"How many more people will he hurt if you don't stop him?" Daphne says.

God.

How many people has he hurt in the past four years when I've been planning revenge instead of seeking it?

The staff that he yells at.

The women he hits on.

The people who clean up his messes when he's plenty old enough to quit making fucking messes?

"That?" Daph says. "That feeling in your gut right now? That question you're asking yourself? That is all the proof you need that your heart works right."

"I should've ended this years ago," I whisper.

Daph hugs me. "Can't change the past. Only the future. Neither of us asked to be born into a family of fucknuggets or to be raised by people who didn't know how to love us. But how we handle it—that defines who we are. Always trying to do better—that does too. So. What do you need help with to do this job you never asked for but are the only person who can do it anyway?"

Oh my god.

Oh my god.

I have the words now.

I know exactly what I need to say.

"You've already done it all," I tell them. "Thank you."

Daph grins. "Our pleasure. Think we can get in some trouble in the city now since our job here is done?"

"No," Oliver and Bea say together.

She gives an exaggerated eye roll. "Jeez, who invited them? They're no fun. Also, Margot, when are we calling your roommate to tell him you love him?"

My heart skips a beat.

Call Rhys.

Tell him I love him.

Risk—risk being happy. With him.

Or hurting him.

I'm not low-maintenance. My life moves fast. I'm in charge, and I'm about to embark on a brand-new adventure that will require so much of my time and energy and—

I shiver.

"Rocking chair test," Daphne declares.

"Rocking—what?"

"Rocking chair test," Bea says. "It's how we decide if we're going to do something scary so that one day we can tell all of our great-nieces and nephews and Simon's grandkids about how much fun we had living."

"Scary like falling in love so that maybe it's our own grandkids we're telling all of our stories to one day," Daph says.

I ignore the sliver in my heart reminding me that Daphne and Bea have a connection that I don't because they're letting me in.

They're letting me into this connection.

Daph nudges me. "So do you want to sit on the porch with us one day and tell whoever's grandkids about how you bossed up and took a chance at falling in love with a man who turned your insides to goo and made your world bright and amazing and beautiful, or do you want to sit quietly by and know you weren't brave?"

"One, rude. And two—" I suck in a shaky breath, because two matters more. "Two, I don't want to hurt him."

She shrugs. "Hurting the people you love is inevitable because we're all fucked up in our own ways, and it's impossible to love someone without showing them all of your sides. But when it's real love—not manipulative love, not controlling love, but real love—then you take the bad with the good. Love's not perfect. And that's why it's beautiful."

"How did you get so smart?"

"I had a good teacher." She grins at Bea. "The best, in fact."

"I didn't—" Bea starts.

"Yes, you did," I say.

"It was definitely all you," Oliver agrees.

"Thank you," I add to Bea.

"Sincerely, thank you," Oliver agrees.

"Dammit, you're making both of us cry now," Daphne says as she and Bea swipe at their eyes. "Margot. Call him."

"I will." I swallow. Probably. Maybe.

He truly does deserve so much better than me. "But can I handle one crisis at a time? I don't—I don't want to wait any longer for what I need to do here. If someone in Snaggletooth Creek slips now that the secret's out—I can't risk our parents hurting our brothers. Where's my phone? I need to call in a few other people for support. I have some work to do, and I need it all done yesterday."

I flinch at my own words.

"You need it done yesterday to protect people," Daph says gently. "Margot—this is when it counts. Don't feel bad for asking for help to do the right thing."

I throw my arms around my sister and hug her tight.

She's right. And I have work to do.

30

Nothing is right

Rhys

I feel so naked with Margot gone that I keep checking to make sure I'm wearing clothes. Can't sit still. Can't sleep. Can't eat.

Decker's not returning my texts, including the one where I told him I'm not leaving his cabin until he talks to me face-to-face and hears my side of this story.

And my heart—I don't even know if it exists anymore.

I know I want it to.

I know I don't want to live through another year of hell like this past one.

But I don't know what the actual fuck to do to keep my life from feeling like it's spinning out of control and my heart from giving up and going back into hiding.

So early Saturday morning, as soon as the sun's up, I'm out back behind the cabin, tackling the last of the logs that need to be split.

Not for Decker.

But because I need to picture the faces of all of the people who've pissed me off.

For once, Xavier's or Colt's or Felice's isn't the first face I see.

The first face I see is a man I've only seen once in my life.

Margot's father.

The triplets' biological sperm donor.

The man who's upended too many fucking lives to count.

That's who I see when I'm swinging the maul with everything inside me, to the point that I split the chopping block too.

I growl with frustration and turn to throw the maul, and that's when I spot Decker.

No, not Decker.

That's Lucky leaning against the side of the cabin, wearing clothes just similar enough to Decker's usual outfit that he threw me off, watching me.

"Knocked," he says. "No one answered."

He doesn't look mad.

Just tired.

"She's gone," I grunt.

He swallows and looks down. "Yeah. Got that text."

I want to demand to know what it said. Exactly what it said. Every letter. The spacing. The punctuation.

Instead, I eye him. "Your dad okay?"

He sighs. "Okay as he can be."

I don't ask for more details.

Not my fucking business.

"They almost split up," he says. "Before we were born. They'd been trying to get pregnant for a few years, nothing was working, fertility treatments and all of it—just so much stress. So they decided they were going to split. Just couldn't—couldn't keep doing it. Mom had a fling with some guy who charmed her in a hotel bar while she was staying there, deciding what she wanted to do next, and a few weeks later, bam. Positive pregnancy test. She didn't know if we were Dad's or the other guy's—more details than I wanted there—but when she started thinking about raising us alone, even before she knew there were three of us, and then thought about all the work they'd put into getting pregnant and depriving Dad of that—"

He cuts himself off and shakes his head.

"She loves you," I say.

"Yeah. She does. Loves him too. Can't not. He's—he's the best."

"Fucking lucky you have both of them."

"I know."

He toes the ground, hands in his pockets, still looking down.

I curl my fingers into fists.

Not because I want to hit him, but because I want to hit something.

Anything to keep the raging fury in my wounded soul from consuming me and destroying my battered heart forever.

This is why I didn't want revenge on Xavier.

Because anger and rage and vengeance—I knew they'd consume me.

And now I'm feeling torn in every direction because of what I want for myself and what I want for my friends and what I want for Margot, and I can't—fuck on a rice cake, why can't I just feel less? About anything?

"Tobias Merriweather-Brown is a fucking bastard," I say. "She wanted—she wanted your help taking him down. But not if it would make you collateral damage."

"Taking him down how?"

"Forcing him into retirement. Exposing him as a cheater."

He shakes his head.

"To avenge her sister," I add. "You have another sister. Daphne. Margot—Margot talks about her like she's a unicorn princess made of fairy dust and mischief and heart."

Lucky eyes me. "The sister who stole Mar—Margot's fiancé?"

Figured they would've looked her up and found the articles.

I want to read them over again from the start, just to feel close to her again.

"Didn't steal," I say. "Margot and Oliver broke up years ago. They're tight. The news articles—it was a cover story so no one would suspect she was here. Getting to know you."

Talking about Margot—defending Margot—it makes me feel like I'm eating ash.

But it's also making my heart beat again.

Softly.

Tentatively.

But still beating.

"Why didn't she tell us who she was?" I know that pain in Lucky's voice. The sound of betrayal. The sound of heartbreak. "We—fuck, she has to know we wouldn't have cared how rich she was. Look who our friends are."

"You know what her parents did to her sister?"

Lucky nods.

"You try growing up with that and tell me—"

Fuck.

Fuck.

Just thinking about it has my throat getting choked up and my sinuses getting hot and that rage billowing all over again.

Lucky lifts his brows. "Tell you what?"

"Tell me you wouldn't be insecure as shit and terrified to let someone actually love you for who you really are," I finish thickly.

Goddammit.

That's why she left.

She meant every fucking word.

It wasn't an excuse. Not a story because she's not who she showed me she was the past two weeks.

It's because that woman—my woman—the woman who seemingly has everything, has never fully had the things that matters most.

Unconditional love.

Unconditional forgiveness.

Unconditional support.

Lucky's watching me. "You okay?"

I press my fists into my eyes. "I'm going to New York. To help her. To be by her side for whatever the fuck she needs. And if you and your brothers aren't coming with me to have her back, fuck you all. She's a good—no, she's the best person. She has all of the fucking money in the world. She has every resource, every advantage, every avenue open to her, every way she could've swooped in here and made your lives hell if you didn't cooperate with whatever her plan was to take her father down, and the one thing she kept talking about was being a better person and not asking you for anything if it would hurt you. If you—if you're not willing to give her another chance, then you don't fucking deserve her."

If I don't give her another chance—if I don't fight for her, if I don't show her that I don't want perfect, that I want her—then I don't deserve her.

Sweat's not just beading at my hairline. It's streaking down my face.

My heart's beating in absolute terror.

What if—what if I fly across the country, track her down, tell her I love her, tell her all of this—that I want to be by her side while she keeps growing and healing and finding her whole self, that I want to love her and laugh with her and cook with her and watch TV with her and make a life with her, flaws and insecurities and fears and all—and she still doesn't want me?

What then?

But what if she does want me?

What if she does want me, and I'm too fucking scared to be her hero?

"You love her," Lucky says.

"She brought me back to life."

"How long—how long did you know who she was?"

"Almost from day one."

"And she knew you knew?"

"From day five."

He stares out into the woods surrounding the cabin. "You watched her when you knew who she was and she didn't know you knew?"

"Wanted to—wanted to figure out if I could trust her. Like Decker asked me to. And she—she's a good person, Lucky. The best person. You can't—you can't fake what she did. Who she is. She's like your friends—doesn't think she's any better than anyone else. She'll get down on the floor and help clean up a spilled tray of coffee because it fucking matters. And she didn't have the advantage of growing up here, with people who loved her the way your parents and family and friends love you, teaching her that helping others, that being part of a community, matters. She had to teach herself."

Lucky suddenly gasps as he looks behind me.

"What?" I spin and spot it.

The moose.

Margot's moose.

"Holy shit," Lucky whispers. "I've never seen one before."

"It likes your sister."

Thing's too close.

Way too close.

It eyes me, then Lucky.

And then it snorts and turns around and walks back into the woods.

"Okay," Lucky says. "Okay. I'll talk to my brothers. I—yeah. Wow. Give me an hour, okay? Maybe two." His brow furrows. "Maybe she did get hit with the curse too."

"The fuck?"

He shrugs at me. "She fell in love, and our family—"

She fell in love.

He thinks she loves me back.

I fumble for my phone, get it out of my pocket, and drop it on the wood pile.

When I lift it—are you fucking kidding me?

I gape at Lucky. "It fucking broke."

He stares at me a beat, and then the bastard starts laughing.

I growl.

He laughs harder, holding up a hand. "Just let me have this," he wheezes. "Let me have this. And then—yeah. Then we're gonna go make a bunch of shit right."

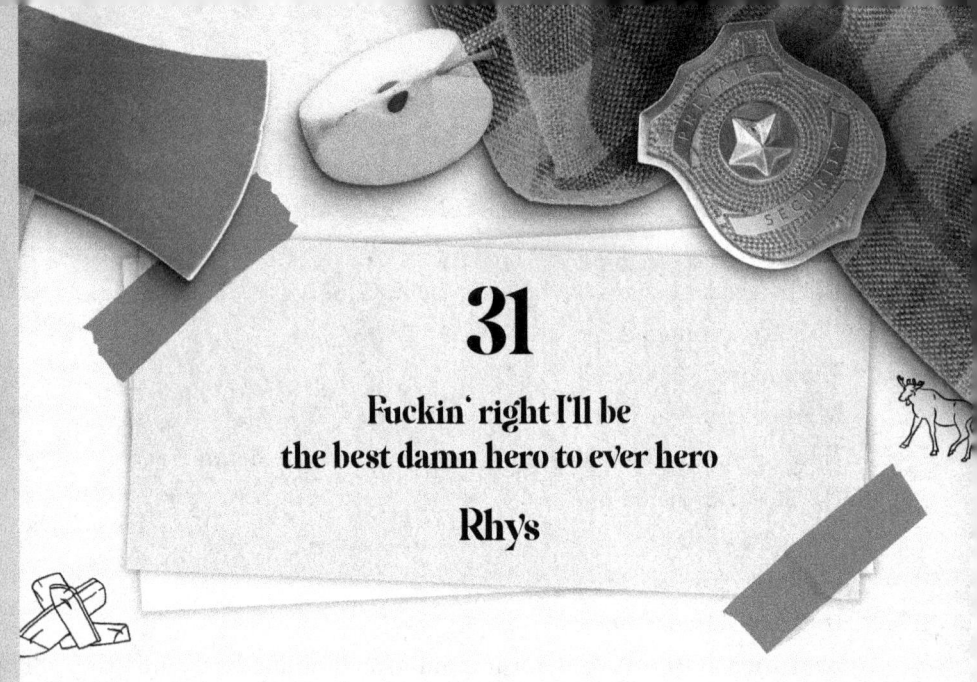

31

Fuckin' right I'll be the best damn hero to ever hero

Rhys

Between having to get a new goddamn phone and the time it takes Lucky to convince Decker and Jack that they all have to leave their parents right now to fly across the country, then the time with us arguing over the best way to get across the country, it's Sunday morning before we land at a private airstrip near Albany, New York, in a plane that Theo chartered for us.

I texted Margot last night, a simple I believe in you and I'm not giving up on you, after I got my new phone, but it's still showing as unread.

And now I'm wondering if I have her real number or her burner number.

Lucky didn't text her. Element of surprise, my dude, was all he said.

Even Decker smirked at that.

"You're not still pissed?" I ask him as we load into a private car, also booked courtesy of Theo.

They went to him first once they agreed to ask their friends for help because they knew he'd say yes the fastest.

Laney likes Margot. Laney and Margot have a lot in common. And Theo still wants to punch his father-in-law some days, so he appreciates falling in love with a woman who has shitty parents.

Decker heaves a sigh. "You pulled a fucking technicality on me. I respect that."

"He was also protecting us," Jack says.

"He's seen things," Lucky agrees. "He knows better than we do how badly this could go."

"It's not gonna go badly," I say with a confidence I don't feel.

What if—what if the past two weeks really were a dream?

What if she's not in New York?

What if I never see her again? Never get to talk to her again?

Never get to ask her to love me?

"No hyperventilating in the car," Lucky says to me.

"Not hyperventilating," I grit out.

"Do you think Daphne's our kind of mischief, or is she some kind of mischief that we won't understand?" Jack says.

Because that's the best plan I have with Margot not answering her texts and her security guy not replying either.

Track Daphne down.

Ask for her help.

And see where we go from there.

Athena's Rest isn't far from Albany, but when no one answers at the apartment that I've been told is Daphne's, and no one answers when we ring the gate at the house where her best friend's boyfriend lives, we do the only thing we know to do.

And we try to track down the burger bus.

I overheard Daphne telling Margot about it while we were driving home from the cookout at Lucky's place.

It's our best lead.

And finally, close to eleven, we spot it in a parking lot near a lake where some kind of carnival seems to be going on.

Takes forever to find parking, and then another forever to walk through the crowds to the food trucks, and then another forever to wait in line.

"Better not run out of burgers," Decker says. "I'm hungry."

"Smell amazing," Lucky agrees.

"Should one of us hop in line for tacos instead, just in case?" Jack says.

"Could you three focus?" I grunt.

"Not when we're this hungry," Jack replies.

"We're unbearable when we're hungry," Lucky replies.

"Is that Daphne?" Decker says.

We all look where he's pointing, then all of us shake our heads at the same time.

"Too old," Jack says as Lucky replies, "Her latest socials have her with pink-and-white striped hair, not purple, and there aren't any tattoos."

"I can't decide if I want to threaten to punch this Oliver guy or hug him," Decker says.

"Hug," Lucky says. "He's a good dude."

"We haven't met him yet," Jack says. "It might be all an act."

"You saw the news articles about him and Daphne giving away all of that money on their road trip last month," Lucky replies. "And the video of him taking down his own father for the good of Miles2Go?"

"Their Landslide Slushy is the best," Decker says.

We all pause and look at him.

"What?" he says. "A guy can't like a slushy?"

"You don't strike me as the slushy type," I say.

Lucky pokes me. "Dude. Move. It's our turn."

Shit.

He's right.

I step up to the window, where a woman with curly brown hair tied back behind a rainbow bandanna is waiting at the window while a shirtless dude who looks like the videos I've seen of Oliver stands next to her and flexes his biceps. "Burger and a show," he says to me.

I ignore him and focus on the woman. "Are you Bea?"

"Hi, yes. Can I get you a burger?"

"Where's Daphne?"

Her eyes get round, and she shoots a look at Oliver.

"Déjà vu," she murmurs.

He growls and leans into the window, glaring at me. "Who the fuck are you, and what do you want with my girlfriend?"

"Oh my god, that will never not be hot," a voice says inside the bus.

Bea presses her lips together like she's trying not to smile, but then her eyes go even rounder than they were before.

She's spotted the triplets behind me.

"Well?" the guy I'm assuming is Oliver says. "What do you—"

Bea grabs his arm, cutting him off.

"Daph? You need to come here," she says.

Oliver looks past me, and his eyes go round too.

"Keep threatening him," Decker says. "I might still be a little pissed, and this might be fun."

"Don't be an asshole," Jack mutters.

"We're actively working against the curse, remember?" Lucky adds.

A woman with flaming pink-and-white striped hair and fairy tattoos on her arms steps into view, a small smirk on her face that fades into yet one more person gaping at the three men behind me.

"Oh my god," she whispers as she blinks quickly.

It's crowded as fuck here. "Can we talk somewhere in private?"

She keeps gaping at the triplets.

"Back of the bus," Bea says. "Go on. That's where—well, that's apparently where we do this."

"Can I get a hamburger?" Jack says to her. "I can't remember the last time I ate."

"We're starving," Lucky agrees. "And we'll pay."

"I got theirs," Oliver says to Bea. He, too, gestures to the back of the bus.

I grab two of the triplets by their collars and drag them around to the back, and the third follows.

Daphne meets us at the back, still gaping.

"Your sister's not answering my texts," I say as I climb inside. "We're here to do whatever she needs us to."

"Not coerced at all," Jack says.

"No emotional manipulation," Lucky adds.

"I'm trying to be pissed, but you really do look like the kind of fun we could spring on the Tooth," Decker says.

I twist my neck to look at him as he's the final one of our bunch to climb into the little seating area at the back of the bus. "Are you for fucking real right now?"

"And I thought my vibe sparkled," Lucky says, squinting at Daphne like he's getting a better look now.

"You have my brother's eyes," Jack says.

"Can we do this family reunion in the car on the way to wherever it is that Margot's hiding?" I ask. "Whatever she's planning, she's not doing it alone. We want to help."

"The city again?" Oliver says dramatically from just beside the window, where he's not trying to sell burgers anymore.

Bea's brows go up. She's also abandoned her customers.

We get a look from a grumpy guy who's manning the kitchen setup, but he just rolls his eyes and goes back to his work.

"Two days in a row?" Bea says. "When we barely got out yesterday without an international incident? This doesn't seem like a good idea."

"Are you Rhys?" Daphne says to me.

I nod, glancing past her at the kitchen guy again.

"He's family," she says, clearly understanding my hesitation to speak in front of strangers. "Steel vault with secrets, mostly because he doesn't want to know them in the first place. Show me your hair."

I pull the cap off and dip my head so she can see the purple at the top.

She squeals and claps her hands. "It is you! And you're here to help Margot?"

"Yes."

Her smile is the first thing that's reassured me since Mrs. Sullivan pulled Margot into that office Friday night.

The first thing that's given me the ability to draw a full breath.

"She's been tied up with admin work all weekend, but I think you can probably get to the city in time to catch her having dinner with our parents tonight," Daphne says.

"Oh, shit," Lucky mutters.

"Dinner with your parents?" Jack says.

"Is it gonna be as ugly as I hope it is?" Decker asks.

Daphne grins even bigger. "I have a feeling it might be." She waves her hands at her face like she's trying to cool it down as she looks at me. "I can't believe you're real. And them too."

"Them too?" Jack echoes. "We're just them too?"

"My dudes," Daphne says, "if you had any idea how much Margot has needed someone who would turn her insides to jelly and then come storming in here like an avenging angel ready to stand by her side while she does the scariest thing she's ever—yeah, sorry, right now, you're them too. Tomorrow and probably the next year or two, you take top billing. I mean, after this guy." She hooks a thumb toward Oliver. "But today, I'm gonna do a little swooning for my sister, okay?"

I swallow. "You think—you think she'll be happy to see me?"

Daphne and Bea share a look, then they both look at Oliver.

He holds both hands up. "Don't look at me. I'm boring. I don't turn anyone's insides to jelly."

"Not according to what I accidentally walked in on a few days ago," Bea murmurs.

He grins at her.

"Shit, are we supposed to threaten to beat this guy or be happy for them?" Jack says behind me. "What did we decide?"

"Bea, can we use Simon's car again?" Daphne says.

"Again? You've seen her?" I ask.

She grins at me. "Have we ever. Ryker. The burgers. These guys are hungry."

"Sorry, Bea," Oliver says. "I'm going with them."

"As you should," Bea says. "Go on. Remember everything. I want the full story. All of the details."

"Wait." Daphne looks at me. "You have video of Margot cleaning a room full of bubbles?"

"I'll show you in the car."

"Good enough. I probably have to make some phone calls and pretend I'm smart enough to talk about lawyers and shit like that while we're in the car too." She looks past me at the triplets again, squeals, then throws herself at Lucky. "Oh my god, I have brothers."

"We're the best brothers," Jack tells her.

"Lifetime of experience," Lucky agrees.

"Hope the curse didn't bounce on to you too," Decker mutters.

"Hug in the car," I order.

Oliver grins at me while he pulls his shirt on. "Are you always bossy?"

"Yes."

His grin grows. "This is gonna be fun to watch."

"Make her uncomfortable and die."

"Margot or Daphne?"

"Yes."

Bastard grins even bigger. "I like you. Looking forward to being brothers."

Fucking twatwaffle's making my eyes burn now.

Brothers.

I've never had brothers.

Not real brothers.

But in five minutes—in five minutes, I think I could be brothers with Margot's ex-fiancé. The guy who's now dating her sister.

How the fuck could she possibly think she's not good enough to be loved?

"Let's go," I grump.

"Daph?" Oliver says. "You sure about this?"

She pulls back from hugging Decker—she's been making her way down the line—and gives him a feral grin that's also in Margot's arsenal. "For any other reason? No. For this one? Oh, fuck yes."

Same, Daphne.

Same.

32

This ends now

Margot

I've never loved my parents' home, but pulling up to it today, there's a new level of distaste in my mouth.

I look down at my phone again, at the message from Rhys, short enough to see in the preview without opening the full text.

> I believe in you and I'm not giving up on you.

My heart thumps with equal parts pain and hope.

I'm not okay.

I do have a lot of work to do.

But maybe I don't have to do it alone.

Even if I'm still terrified I'll hurt him.

My driver opens my door, and I step out into the sunshine, then just as quickly into the shadows as I make my way up the steps of the Upper East Side brownstone that my grandfather bought and then passed down to my father.

The house I grew up in.

The house that will never be home in any sense of the word again.

I ring the doorbell, and the housekeeper lets me in.

She and I catch up as she shows me to the dining room.

How did I do it?

How did I come to Sunday afternoon dinner here with my parents once a month for the past four years?

How did I sit under the paintings of our family that were swapped out after Daph was disinherited and didn't come running back home begging for forgiveness the way my parents thought she would?

How did I stare at the moose head on the wall?

It makes me ill now, the thought of my grandfather hunting the ancestor of that majestic creature who scared the shit out of me over the wood pile at the triplets' cabin.

If he'd done it for food—but no.

It was for sport.

Maybe I do know how to love.

Maybe I do have it in me.

My father strides into the room, dressed down for the weekend in casual slacks and a polo.

Probably spent the morning golfing and networking.

His hair is more gray than brown, but it's slicked back in his usual style, and I can't look at him without seeing Lucky, Decker, and Jack now.

The eyes.

The nose.

The ears.

For a hot minute, I wondered if maybe my father wasn't my father. If maybe my mother had cheated.

But no—there's so much familiarity that it would be impossible for him to not be the biological father to all of us.

"Margot," he says as he takes his place at the head of the long dining room table. "I trust your little vacation was fruitful."

Barely a month ago, he tracked Daphne and Oliver down on their accidental road trip—intentional road trip on Oliver's part, accidental where Daphne ended up with him on it—and essentially told Oliver that Daphne wasn't his first pick of daughters to marry to merge our family's companies, but she'd do.

She'd do.

His own daughter.

Good enough for a business deal even if she wasn't good enough to be a part of the family anymore.

"It was what I needed," I reply in the measured tone he expects.

"Good. You should be back in the office. Long vacations aren't acceptable when you're at the top. Too many people watching you to set the example."

"I don't expect anyone else will make it necessary by stabbing me in the back the same way again," I murmur.

The words taste like vomit.

Daph didn't stab me in the back.

She hid away and fell asleep in the back seat of Oliver's car while waiting for him to get in so she could tell him he wasn't good enough for me.

The irony that they'd grown into being what each other needed isn't lost on me, but mostly, I'm happy for them.

He adores her, and she deserves that.

She's head over heels for him, happier than I've seen her possibly ever, and she deserves that too.

"Margot, my darling, you poor thing." My mother sails into the room, pausing to kiss my cheeks and giving me a hug that I wouldn't have considered limp until Rhys hugged me.

The man knows how to give a hug.

I miss it.

I miss him.

But I keep my eyeballs under control while my mother hustles me into a seat and then walks around the table to her own seat, more or less ignoring my father.

I wouldn't ignore Rhys if he were at the table with me.

Ever.

He's too fascinating.

Too kind.

Too easy to love.

Daph—she was right.

I do know how to love. I still have so much to learn, and I'll still make mistakes, but it's in me. There's love in me.

The housekeeper and chef both slip into the room with plates for us, moving silently. My father's pouring wine. My mother's fussing with her napkin, like it wasn't folded properly before deigning to take a spot in her lap.

Now, I tell myself. Do it now.

"Wine?" my father says to me.

"No, thank you. I'm not staying."

My father nods. "Good, good. Get back to the office. Catch up on the weekend."

"Or maybe you're seeing friends?" my mother says. "Friends are so important during major life crises."

My heart is pounding hard and steady, but there's no panic.

Only relief at what's finally about to be over. "I'm not seeing friends. And I'm not going to the office."

My father grunts. "Think of the example, Margot."

"I'm quitting."

He snorts.

My mother looks at me, and for a split second, I think she's seeing me, but then she laughs her tinkling fake laugh. "Quitting. Oh, Margot, you must have had quite the adventure if you're making jokes."

"I submitted my resignation to human resources ten minutes ago," I say. "My last day with Aurora Gardens was three weeks ago."

My father finally looks at me too. "You're not quitting."

"I am."

"I don't know what the hell kind of vacation you went on that you'd come home thinking you can—"

"I wasn't on vacation. I was meeting my half siblings. The half siblings you all pretend we don't have. Fascinating people. Surprisingly powerful friends." I lift a shoulder. "Must be something about nature there."

My mother's going pale.

My father's going red. "You will stop telling stories right now."

I look him square in the eye. "Make me."

His jaw flaps.

"You are an adulterer and a terrible human being," I say to him. "I want absolutely nothing to do with you for the rest of your natural life. I'm only here for the satisfaction of telling you that no matter what you do, no matter where you go, no matter who you pretend to be, I will always know that you're a wretched human being who has failed to take me down that miserable path with you."

I rise. "And you," I say to my mother, "I'd feel sorry for you if you'd ever, ever, just once in the past four years, reached out to Daphne. Your daughter. Your daughter that you abandoned in the very worst possible way. I don't care that you're married to a serial cheater. I don't care what stories you tell yourself to justify what you've done to Daphne. I don't care that you're my mother. You don't deserve the title."

Saying it doesn't make me happy.

Only sad.

But saying it—I have to.

For Daphne.

For me.

For the two little girls we were who thought that our mother would love us and protect us and cherish us.

"Where do you think you're going?" my father roars as I head toward the door.

"To a happier life," I reply.

"Stop her," he orders the housekeeper.

I lift a brow at her. "If you're looking for alternate employment, I'd be happy to write you a glowing letter of recommendation and pass your name around a few circles."

"You cannot—" my father sputters, but I cut him off.

"I can, in fact. I have no noncompete. I have plenty of ideas that have nothing to do with Aurora Gardens. My attorneys assure me that

I can do more or less whatever I wish, with whomever I wish, whenever and wherever I wish. And what I wish—"

Something clatters outside the room, interrupting me.

The housekeeper purses her lips and lifts an innocent gaze toward the ceiling, then quietly slips out of the room.

And then someone walks into the dining room.

Someone tall.

With brown hair.

Brown eyes shaped like mine.

Ears like mine too.

I suck in a wobbly breath as Lucky grins at me. "Hey, sis. Did we miss the show?"

"Who the fuck are you?" My father's angry shout behind me is almost enough to make me flinch, but my brother's pulling me into a tight hug, and nothing—nothing—could make me afraid now.

"Where's my security?"

That's an excellent question that I suspect my brother can answer, and I cannot wait to hear it.

"He really is an ass, isn't he?" Jack says behind Lucky.

"You're here," I whisper as I spot Decker too.

"Family sticks together, good times and bad," Decker says.

I shudder and jerk my head toward my parents. "This is not family."

"They know," Daph says cheerfully.

"Daphne?" I gasp.

Lucky lets me go and steps around me.

Jack and Decker follow him.

Daphne grins at me.

"So you're our sperm donor," Decker says.

Jack glances at Lucky. "I thought he'd be prettier."

"My medical training says he's on the verge of a stroke," Lucky replies. "I should probably leave while I still have plausible deniability about walking away from a medical situation."

"Who the actual fuck are you?" my father demands. "And what the actual fuck do you think you're doing here?"

Lucky's hand shoots in the air. "I know! I know this answer. We're Karla Sullivan's sons."

"Remember her?" Jack says.

My father sneers at them. "I have no idea who that is."

"You fucked her in a hotel room in Denver while your wife was pregnant with Margot," Decker supplies.

My mother gasps.

"And a DNA test says we're Margot's half-brothers, so either you're our father, or you're not hers," Lucky adds.

That finally lands.

"Get out of my house," my father roars.

Daphne, who hasn't flinched at all, tucks her arm into mine. "I like them," she whispers.

"How—" I start.

Her grin keeps growing. "They came looking for you at the burger bus."

"So here's how this is gonna go," Decker says. He and Lucky and Jack are a wall between our parents and Daph and me. "You're gonna quit your job and retire somewhere that none of us ever have to think about you."

"You're also going to give us each fifty million dollars to pay for college, the emotional damage done to our family by your actions toward our mother, and for the horrible way that we had to find out we're related to such a piece of shit," Jack adds.

"Oliver made him say that," Daphne whispers to me. "They don't actually want money."

"And if you don't, we're going to the press," Lucky says.

"That too," Daph murmurs. "But I think they'll actually do that one."

"I still love Oliver," I murmur back. "But not the way you do."

"Best kind of family. A little dysfunctional, a lot of love."

I can't believe she just made me giggle here.

"Also, lose the moose head. That's gross," Decker says.

"Why the fuck isn't Daphne in the family paintings? She's the best of all of you." Jack glances back at me. "No offense, Margot."

"No, no, I fully agree," I reply.

"You're going to donate another hundred million to a fund to save the polar bears," Decker says.

Daph sucks in a breath.

Apparently Oliver didn't tell them to say that.

Which means—

I suck in a breath.

Does it mean what I think it means?

That someone else—someone I miss terribly—told them to say that?

But no—when I look back at the door, it's empty.

"And again, going to the press if you don't," Jack says.

"Fun thing about the press these days is that they'll print anything halfway believable," Lucky says.

"And I make shit up for a living, so I know how to make this story fucking sparkle," Decker says.

Jack nods. "We help from time to time."

"We don't need money to make your life hell," Lucky chimes in.

"We'll do it for fun," Decker says. "And we'll be good at it."

"Because you're a dick," Jack adds.

"A dick who's never going to bother us or our sisters or family ever again."

A tear slides down my cheek.

Daph leans her head on my shoulder. "Honestly, best brothers I could've ever asked for. And Bea has some pretty awesome brothers."

"Where is my goddamn security?" my father bellows. "You'll do nothing—"

"DNA doesn't lie," Lucky says.

"We're your sons," Jack agrees. "Not happy about it, but dude, we have the same eyes and the same noses too. Unfortunately for us."

"And if you want to accuse us of lying about it, we'll take you to court and make you prove you're not," Decker finishes.

My god, the way I love these men.

It's like having Daphne and me all rolled into one.

"Anything you want to add, Margot? Daphne?" Decker looks back at us.

I shake my head and swipe my cheeks.

"Margot said it all already," Daph says. "They're not our problem anymore. We just want to live our own happy lives."

"Great," Decker says.

"Have fun being miserable." Jack waves.

Lucky steers them toward the door, hustling Daph and me too. "Our lawyers will be in touch," he calls back over his shoulder.

I look left and right as we leave the dining room, the five of us hustling down the steps to the door, but I don't see—

I don't see what I want to see.

My heart.

I don't see my heart.

"The polar bears?" Daphne whispers. "You didn't tell me you were going to make demands for the polar bears."

"We, ah, had some time for research on the plane," Lucky says.

We tumble out the front door, where the security agents who weren't inside to help my father are all reconverging after clearly getting their attention split.

They look at me, concern fading to worry as they spot Daphne too.

She finger-waves at them.

The door to a black SUV opens at the curb, and our brothers hustle me inside.

I freeze halfway up.

"Rhys," I breathe.

"God, you're fucking beautiful," he breathes back.

I tumble the rest of the way into the seat, and the door closes behind me, leaving Daph and our brothers on the street.

"They're taking the other car," my driver says as we pull away from the curb.

I blink at Rhys.

Open my mouth.

Try to talk, but I can't because my throat is clogged and I don't even know what to say.

His hand closes around mine. "You don't abandon the people you love just because you're scared."

"I know. I know. I'm sorry—"

"No, no, Skillet. I'm scared. You fucking terrify me. But I get it. I know why you're scared too. And I—I want to be beside you while we both face our fears. Stronger together. Better together. You make me—you brought me back to life, and you make me want to live. So I want to do the same for you. However you need."

I don't have the words for what I need.

But I have arms that work to wrap around his neck.

A body that works to scoot as close to him as humanly possible.

A nose that can smell his tobacco-and-pine scent.

Fingers that can grip his hair and hold him close when he sucks in a fast breath as he buries his head in my neck.

"I'm so sorry." My voice breaks as a sob slips out. "I don't—I'm so afraid—you deserve—I want—I want you."

"I love you," he whispers. "I love you, and I won't give up on you."

Love.

Yes, love.

Not friend-love.

Not settling-love.

Bigger-than-me, bigger-than-him, bigger-than-the-world love.

The kind that makes it hard to breathe when he's not with me, and the kind that's so big inside that I don't know how my chest isn't cracking open with all the power of it that wants to spill out.

"I can't love you as big as you know how to love," I whisper into his neck, "but I want to. God, I want to learn—to practice—loving you."

"I can't live as big as you know how to live," he whispers back. "I want to practice living with you."

"I'm so sorry—"

"Shh, Margot. It's okay. Just tell me—just tell me you want me as badly as I want you."

"More. I want you more."

He shudders as he hugs me tighter, his lips pressed to my neck.

"I love you, Rhys," I whisper. "I love you with everything I have to love you with. It's not enough—"

"You are so much more than enough. You're everything."

I'm not.

He is.

But if that's the biggest thing we have to work out—who means more to whom—then maybe, just maybe, this man who was supposed to be only a fling could become everything I've ever wanted and needed in this life.

And maybe, just maybe, I can rise to the challenge of being everything he deserves.

Not because I enjoy a challenge.

But because this man—he deserves the very best.

And it will be the privilege of my lifetime to spend every day being that best for him.

33

Our kind of happily ever after

Rhys

"I'm going to marry you one day," I say to Margot as I sink into the soaking tub in the bathroom off her bedroom. There's a view of the New York skyline from here. Could get used to it, even if I'll miss the mountains.

The triplets and Daphne and Oliver followed us here, and now, after Margot and Oliver gave the triplets initial debriefings about what to say to the press and when meetings with lawyers will happen and what to expect there, and after we've all watched some of the online reactions to the leaked news that Margot's leaving Aurora Gardens because of a private rift with her father, they've all departed again.

She strips out of her shirt, and I suddenly forget anything else exists in the world beyond her.

Her and my suddenly aching cock.

"Not if I marry you first," she says, dropping her pants too. "How're the bubbles?"

"Lonely. Take your panties off."

She peels them off slowly, first over one hip, then the other, teasing me before baring her whole pussy.

"I love you for more than how much I love having sex with you," I tell her while I reach up and unhook her bra.

Her eyes get shiny. "I know," she whispers.

I pull her closer to the bathtub. "And I'm going to love teaching you every day how lovable you are."

She lowers herself into the warm water too, straddling my hips and leaning into me. "I don't ever want to hurt you again."

"You will. And I'll hurt you. And we'll work through it."

"How are you so perfect?"

"Grief, life, trauma, and good genes." It's my line, and it's the truth.

She's smiling as she holds me by the cheeks and leans in for a kiss. "I'm going to deserve you one day. It's my new life mission."

"You already deserve me."

"I don't."

"You're a pain in the ass."

She laughs, and then she's kissing me, her pussy cradling my dick in the warm water, and it doesn't matter who wins this argument.

We've both won.

I hook my hand behind her neck and kiss her harder. We're surrounded by bubbles, which keeps making me smile.

"I hope we always have bubbles in our lives," I murmur against her lips.

She smiles and kisses me again, her hands exploring my chest like she's discovering me for the first time.

I drag my fingers down her spine to her ass, giving it a squeeze, and she shifts in the water, bubbles sloshing around us as she lowers herself on my aching hard-on.

I shudder. "Fuck, you feel so good."

"You feel like everything I've never known I could want," she whispers back.

She holds my gaze while she lifts nearly off of me, then sinks back down on me again.

My eyes cross.

I love the way she feels.

The way she touches me.

The way she puts me first without even realizing she's doing it.

The way she loves me without even realizing she's doing it.

"Thank you for coming after me," she says as she rides me in the bathtub.

"Only you, Margot. I would only ever come after you."

"I thought—you'd be better—without me."

"It's okay to be wrong, Skillet."

She huffs out a laugh that has her inner walls squeezing my cock, and then she's kissing me once more, her movements more frantic, hands settling on my shoulders and squeezing hard as she rides me harder and faster, my hips flexing to meet her, everything inside me coiling hard and tight and ready, not like this is the last time I ever get to make love to this woman, but like it's the best time.

"No more secrets," I pant as she slams down on me again.

"Never secrets," she agrees.

"Fuck, Margot, I love you so much."

She groans and grinds down on me, spasms squeezing my cock as she starts coming, and I let myself go too, her name on my lips, her fingers in my hair, her ass in my hands.

"I love you, I love you, I love you," she chants.

It's music.

It's music and home and the promise of sunrise and the beauty of sunset, all wrapped up in this one complex, kind, strong, smart, compassionate woman whom I intend to love without reservation, without fear, without regrets, for the rest of my life.

She sags against me, spent, her chest rising and falling against mine as the last of my orgasm leaves me too.

"I love you," she whispers again. "And I'm going to do everything I can to deserve you."

"Just breathe, Margot," I whisper back. "That's all you have to do. Ever."

She sucks in a shaky breath, kisses my shoulder, and then snuggles back into me while the bubbles softly pop and fizz around us, the world going on below us. I drop my head back into the perfect headrest at the edge of the bathtub and hold her.

This.

This is peace.

Clarity.

Happiness.

"So I'm unemployed," she murmurs after a while.

I bark out an unexpected laugh at that. "I'm sure you'll find something to do with your time."

She kisses my neck. "Maybe we can find something that'll scratch both of our itches."

I crack up. "I thought we just did that."

"When we're not doing that."

"Have something in mind?"

"Yes."

It's utterly impossible to not smile broader at that.

Of course she does.

"Tell me," I murmur.

"So, I'm a billionaire…"

She's a fucking hilarious billionaire. "Yes, you are," I say through a roll of laughter.

"And my favorite people on this planet are people who are using their resources to do good in the world. So…I think I should use my resources to do good too. In ways that I can do good."

"Such as?"

She giggles.

God, I love her giggle.

"You're thinking something bad, aren't you?" I murmur.

"I'm thinking I can start my own hotel chain, not care if it makes money, and competitively price my father out of the market." She giggles again. Clears her throat like she's trying to be serious. Giggles once more.

"Not because I need revenge. More revenge. It's a nice side effect, but if I can make it more affordable for families to stay at our hotels, more affordable for businesspeople to have a comfortable spot to rest so that they can do what they need to do better, and if I can personally sacrifice profits because I don't need them, and invest in paying my staff well instead—that would make me happy."

I hug her tighter. "You're fucking amazing, do you know that?"

"And…just listen, okay?"

"Always."

"I want the hotel restaurant to be affordable and delicious too. A place for guests and locals alike to come and have a good meal. And I was thinking, you seem to love cooking, and so many of the recipes are your mom's—"

"You'd put my mom's recipes on the menu."

"Only if you're okay with it."

"Fuck, Margot." My voice gets thick. "Of course I'm okay with it."

"You can have as much or as little involvement as you want. I know—I know there are things you wanted—"

"You. I want you. I want to be by your side. The rest of what I do—I'll be happy doing anything as long as I'm with you."

She presses a kiss to my neck. "Bea has some family recipes too. I'd ask her—"

"Fuck yes, Margot. She loves you like a sister too, you know. Embrace all of your family. You deserve it."

She sucks in an uneven breath. "Why does love make me cry so much?"

"You're still getting used to how big it can be."

"It's the best, isn't it?"

I squeeze her tighter and bury my face in her hair. "The absolute best when it's real. And, Skillet, this is real."

Real and the absolute best.

"It was worth all of the pain to get here," she whispers.

I can't hug her tightly enough. "And if I have my way, you'll never hurt like that again."

"I love you so much, Rhys," she whispers through tears.

I kiss her hair again. "I love you forever."

Epilogue

And there's the oops

Margot

Snaggletooth Creek at the end of September is a beautiful place. Rhys, Daphne, Oliver, Bea, Simon, and I spent all afternoon at a local art festival, and now we're back at the cabin.

With the triplets, of course.

And, to my utter surprise, their parents too.

"Don't be so loud or the moose won't come back," Lucky says to Daphne, who just snort-laughed at a very terrible joke Oliver told as we sit around in lawn chairs while the sun sinks low in the sky.

"You don't want the moose to come back," Rhys says. He has an arm around the back of my chair, and both of us keep inching our chairs closer together, which is only mildly bothering Bandit, who's decided my feet are his favorite place to lie. "It's a wild animal."

"It likes Margot," Lucky says.

"It hates Margot," I correct. "It's rushed me twice."

"I think it was trying to give you a hug."

"Are you for real?" Decker says. "Dude. Moose don't hug."

"How do you know? Have you ever been a moose?" Lucky fires back.

"Definitely not," Jack says. He's been letting his hair grow out, and he's also been getting crap about it all night. "None of my previous lives were as a moose, and you've both shared all of my previous lives with me, therefore, Decker's never been a moose either." He glances at Daphne. "What about you though? Were you a moose in any previous lives?"

"Not according to Madame Petty," Daph replies.

"Oh my god, stop talking about Madame Petty," Bea mutters, which makes both Simon and Oliver crack up.

I smile.

Rhys leans over and kisses my cheek. "You're even prettier when you're happy."

"I apparently have Lucky's sparkly vibe," I reply.

Oliver chokes on a bottle of kombucha.

I throw a stick at him. "Just because you don't appreciate my sparkle anymore doesn't mean it's not still there."

"This should be so delightfully awkward, and yet it's disappointingly comfortable," Simon says.

Bea's laughing as she shakes her head at him. "Do not be the troublemaker."

"Everyone else has got a turn. When's mine?"

Simon's still shooting a movie in LA, but he was able to fly in for the day as a halfway point to meet Bea before he has to be back on set tomorrow. Getting all the way to New York wasn't possible, but Denver was a short enough flight for this to work.

"We'll see them often?" Rhys asks me as Daphne and Simon start debating if he should get a turn being a troublemaker.

I nod to him. "At least twice a month. It's already on my calendar."

"Good."

"Best kind of family?"

"Best kind of family."

"I was wrong about you," Mrs. Sullivan says to me as she takes the open seat on my other side. "I'm sorry."

"No apology necessary," I tell her. "Completely understandable."

"I—" She pauses and looks across the circle at Lucky and Jack, who have joined the argument about who gets to cause the most trouble. And then she smiles softly. "More family is never a bad thing, is it?"

"So long as it's this kind of family."

"You didn't have this growing up."

"I had Daphne."

Mrs. Sullivan tilts her head at me. "And it's really—it's safe? For my boys knowing...what they know?"

If anyone else asked me, I'd smirk.

But I don't smirk at my half brothers' mom.

"It's safe," I tell her. "And it wasn't just me. Jonas and Grey both pitched in with even more layers of lawyers triple- and quadruple-checking that everything's airtight and my father can't cause problems for anyone. Your sons are good people with good friends."

My father has been placed on leave at Aurora Gardens because of the questionable circumstances surrounding my departure and the departure of ninety percent of my staff, and my parents are headed toward a divorce.

Someone supplied my mother with all of the evidence of my father's affairs over the years, and it's likely she'll take him to the cleaners.

And it wasn't me.

Or Rhys.

I honestly hope I never think about my parents again in my life, but watching the triplets' parents tonight, knowing they're navigating through some secrets they've each kept from the other over the years, though none as big as the triplets' lineage, makes me suspect I won't ever fully succeed.

Someone else's parents will always remind me of mine.

It's fascinating to discover I can be happy, sad, bloodthirsty, tired, fulfilled, content, and ready to wash my hands of something all at the same time.

But the one constant—no matter my mood? Rhys is there.

Poking me to talk about it.

Listening without judgment.

Rewarding me for good behavior afterward.

I love him.

I love him so much, in ways I never thought I could love another person.

A loud sneeze shatters the evening, and while half of us startle, the triplets all grin as one.

"Oh, good, the rest of the party's here," Jack says.

"What was that?" Daph asks on a gasp.

"You've never heard a loud sneezer before?" Decker says.

"Have you even lived if you've never met a loud sneezer?"

Theo and Laney round the corner of the cabin to join us, followed by Sabrina and Grey and Emma and Jonas and all of their collective kids.

Bandit barks once, then settles back at my feet.

"Bless one of you?" Daphne says.

"Thanks," Theo replies.

She squints at him.

Then squints again.

And then nearly falls out of her chair laughing.

"Did your sister—" Rhys starts, then shakes his head. "Never mind. Don't want to know."

I meet Daphne's gaze, and I double over laughing too.

She did.

She subscribed to Theo's GrippaPeen channel.

"My life used to be really hard, you guys," Daphne says to the triplets as they all stare at her in horror like they, too, are catching on.

"Now we're getting to awkward," Bea murmurs to Simon.

"Marvelous," he replies with a grin.

I can't stop giggling.

Even Rhys is chuckling.

It's one of my favorite sounds in the world. I've made a point to try to make him laugh at least once a day, which I'm always rewarded for, one way or another.

Hearing him happy is reward enough, but I love the extra rewards that tend to start with him throwing me over his shoulder and pulling me into the nearest private place.

We eat, we drink, we laugh, and we all get to know each other a little better until it's too cold, and then everyone slowly packs up to leave.

Simon and Bea are headed to Denver so that he can catch an early flight back to LA tomorrow.

Daphne and Oliver are staying in a supposedly haunted hotel in a nearby town. "We're doing your research for you in case you decide to add haunted hotels to your new portfolio," Daphne tells me as she hugs me goodbye.

Oliver lingers a little longer, making one of his exaggerated you people made me do something I don't want to do anymore faces.

"Archie's such an asshole," he says.

"Who's Archie?" Rhys asks.

"Other brother from another mother," Oliver replies, which honestly cracks me up.

"Do I need to punch him for you?" Rhys asks.

"No, Daphne's got it when the time comes."

This is not where I saw my life taking me, but I don't hate it. "So what's Archie done this time?" I ask.

Oliver heaves another of his exaggerated sighs that Daphne finds charming. "He went and had some security company investigated, and now they're being charged with tax fraud. What a fucknugget."

Rhys grabs my hand and sucks in a loud breath.

"Fascinating," I murmur.

"Who cares?" Oliver adds with a twinkle in his eye. "Not like anyone we know has ever been in private security working for a company run by dickweeds."

The next thing I know, Rhys is gripping Oliver in a massive hug.

Oliver looks at me over Rhys's shoulder.

I give him a thumbs-up instead of coming to his rescue.

I'm good with my boyfriend getting along with my ex.

Especially when my ex makes my sister so happy and this mountain of a man who holds my heart has shown me that Daphne was right all along.

I did need someone like Rhys.

Or rather, exactly Rhys.

"What's going on?" Daph sticks her head back out of their rental car. "What did I miss?"

Rhys sets Oliver down—seriously, he was dangling a little—and swipes his eyes as I slip an arm around his waist and hug him.

"Boring business stuff," I tell her.

"I fucking hate business stuff," Oliver says. "Especially when people hug me because of it."

"Then get in the car and away from the people who keep sucking you in," Daph replies with a grin.

I blow her a kiss. "Be happy and don't take any shit from this guy."

She blows one right back. "Right back at you."

Rhys and I will see them in Athena's Rest again soon.

But for tonight, we're staying in the cabin.

Like old times.

The triplets' parents and their friends have all left, so when Rhys and I return to the backyard, it's just my half brothers.

They're whispering and snickering.

Well, Jack and Lucky are snickering.

Decker's just whispering.

Rhys and I share a look.

He grins, and that happy expression on him makes my heart flutter.

"What are you three plotting now?" he asks the triplets.

"Nothing," all three of them answer.

I crack up. "Sure you're not."

Rhys makes a noise that has me looking up at him, and I realize he's suppressing laughter.

Or possibly he's annoyed.

This is a new expression.

I lift a brow at him.

"You getting ready to play Lucky or Decker?" he asks Jack.

"I have no idea what you're talking about." Jack's words don't match his tone or his guilty expression.

"Are you serious?" Rhys looks at Decker, who won't make eye contact. "Dude."

I think I'm catching on. "Is this about that convention Nell talked you into doing?"

One thing I've learned about the triplets in the past few weeks—they've been tempering their personalities.

They're even more fun than Daphne, who's taking this as a personal challenge to top them.

"I don't people well," Decker mutters.

"You people great," Lucky replies. "You just have to trust that people outside our circles will see you for the amazing person you are."

Jack coughs.

Rhys pinches his lips together like he's trying not to smile.

"It'll be fine," Jack tells Rhys and me. "We've all been playing each other for decades."

"Nell's gonna make you in five seconds flat." Lucky grins. "I can't wait to see how much of a raise Decker has to give her this time."

Jack rolls his eyes. "She won't make me. I'm a much better Decker than you are."

"Bad idea," Rhys says.

"It's a brilliant idea," Jack replies. "I get to see LA. Decker gets to avoid people and probably end up with an even better reputation with his readers than he'd have if he played himself. What's the worst thing that could possibly happen?"

Rhys and I share a look.

"Daphne thinks it's a great idea," Jack adds.

"Okay then," I murmur. "I'll get on board. Sure. This is a great idea. I'm sure nothing will go sideways, and you'll have everything under full control the entire time."

Decker, Lucky, and Jack all do their silent communication thing again.

Lucky breaks it first. "Dude. That's almost as bad as trying to curse us again," he whispers.

"It'll be fine," Jack insists.

I have a gut-level feeling that it will not, in fact, be fine.

Based on the look Rhys is giving me, he agrees.

"At least it'll be entertaining," I murmur to him.

Something will definitely go wrong with this plan.

Rhys smiles at me. "Truer words. Want me to kick these guys out so we can enjoy their cabin?"

"Ew," Decker says.

"Hey. That's my sister you're talking about," Lucky says.

Jack holds out a fist for Rhys to bump. "Let the record show that I, the smart one, support you two doing whatever adult activities you want to do."

I wasn't sure what to expect when I found out I had triplet brothers. But this?

The way they've opened their hearts and their homes, welcoming me and introducing me to the most perfect man?

This is what life's supposed to be.

And I'll never want it any other way.

Bonus Epilogue

The other side of the story from a few weeks ago...

Sir Rodney Mooselwait the third, aka a moose with the unfortunate affliction of occasional boredom

Humans are so dumb.

I've been watching this one for a week now, and not only are his balls a lot smaller than mine, I'm starting to think he doesn't have any.

He's single.

He's sharing a cabin with what humans would call a hottie.

And he hasn't made a single fucking move.

Except—oh.

Oh.

I munch on grass and peer through the trees.

Is this it? Is he gonna get jiggy with it finally?

I inch closer and watch while he taps on the cabin window. "You want a swing?" he says to it.

Probably not talking to the window though.

Probably talking to the woman inside.

"Saw you staring at my...axe," he adds to the window. "Looked like you wanted to use it."

I crack up in my head at the idea of him flirting with the window.

Humans really are that dumb.

Wouldn't surprise me if he asked a pane of glass out on a date for all of the courage he's shown in flirting with the woman.

See?

Now he's grunting.

And humans think they're so evolved and advanced.

I settle down onto the ground where I have a good vantage point for watching while still having enough grass and shrubs around me to munch on my dinner, and a few moments later, after the guy with no balls has turned on some lights, the hottie comes into view too.

He hands her a pair of gloves.

Seriously.

Humans.

They're so fucking delicate.

She looks at the gloves, then back at him.

"Only other pair," he says when she puts them on. "Here. Put on safety glasses too. Then grab a log."

Safety glasses.

I almost snort, but I keep it in check.

Can't spy if they freak out and go inside like she did when I was watching her yesterday morning.

"Not that one," the grumpy ball-less human says.

"What's wrong with this one?" the smarter and prettier one replies.

"See the knots? Harder to split."

Once again, I almost snort.

Has he met this chick?

She could take him out with one hand behind her back. She just gives badass vibes on top of being, as they say, a catch.

And she's watching him like she's amused while he digs into the log pile and picks her log for her.

"Ever do this before?" he asks her.

"Nope," she replies.

"Harder than it looks."

Doubt that, if he's talking about his penis.

"Is that a challenge?" she says.

The dumbass makes a face at her. "Of course not."

She nods at the tool.

And I mean the actual wooden tool, not the dude. "Any tips or tricks I should know before I start swinging?"

Aim for his head, I think as I munch more grass.

He shows off how he can toss the tool around. "Don't hit yourself with this part."

"Don't maim myself," she replies. "Got it."

"Don't get cocky."

He's clearly not.

"Have to log a few hours at the chopping block first?" she says, and I almost spit out my grass.

That was fucking funny.

I'm telling you, dude's a moron if he doesn't make his move.

He stares at her. "Did you just—"

"I'm smart, I'm pretty, I'm rich, and I'm funny," she says.

Like, duh.

Even the squirrels have picked up on that, and they're not smart, pretty, rich, or funny.

Pretty much like this dumbass, who's—oh.

Oh, wait.

He's moving behind her.

I lean in and watch as he lines his body up with hers and puts his arms around her shoulders and slides his hands down her arms to help her grip the tool.

There's contact, people.

There is human contact.

This might end up being entertaining after all.

He's saying something to her, but I can't hear it, which is annoying as hell.

I'm a goddamn moose.

I'm supposed to have good hearing.

But can I hear what's probably the juiciest thing said at this cabin in mooooonths?

No.

No, I fucking can't.

And now that he's shown her the technique or whatever, he's letting her go.

Jesus.

Why am I even watching this?

He's not going to throw her on the log pile and do her like a rabbit.

He's not even going to throw her on the log pile and do her like a human.

Especially not with her handing over her phone thing now.

She doesn't strike me as the type to record anyone doing her like a rabbit. Or like a human.

And they're talking again.

Booooring.

She starts splitting their firewood, him watching her, not trying to paw her or anything, and I start to snooze.

Like, seriously?

Where's the entertainment, people?

When do the amusing people get here?

She hands the tool back to him, and he starts attacking more wood now.

I wish I was encouraged by this beefy display of human muscle, but the guy's already proven he's got no follow-through.

And now he's leaving.

Fucking figures.

Leaving her to stack the wood he split while he barely takes any of it with him.

Say it with me—humans are so dumb.

It's truly a wonder that the species has survived.

I snort softly to myself and rise back to my feet, and that's when I realize the lady's realized I'm here.

Huh.

Huh.

What if—no.

No, he's too dumb. That wouldn't work.

But would it?

What if it did?

Then I could watch.

For research. Science. Whatever excuse those humans give when they watch it on their televisions too.

Don't tell me they don't.

I have seen things.

But you know what?

I'm bored.

Why don't we see where this goes?

I stretch my back legs, and then I do the one thing I hate doing most, and I walk into an open clearing where I know a human will see me.

Yeah, yeah, I'm here, go on, gape at me, I think as the woman makes eye contact with me.

Her mouth goes as round as her eyeballs.

Like I'm an alien or something.

Jesus.

If they ever saw an alien like the one I saw a few weeks ago, they wouldn't stare at me like this.

I chew at that last bite of food I took and watch her.

She goggles at me.

I snort at her, just for fun.

Narrow my eyes.

Lower my head.

Once more—humans are so dumb.

Something clatters, and I look up in time to see the dude reaching out the window.

Finally.

Maybe.

Huh.

Probably need to sell this.

I lower my head again, and I charge.

Relax, relax, I'm not going to maul them.

Just scare them.

Scare them into—yeah, that's right, buddy.

Pull your woman into the house through the window.

Slam that window shut on me.

I keep running until I stop short right at the window, looking inside, and—

You're fucking welcome, buddy.

Finally.

Finally.

Finally, they're on the bed.

This might go somewhere interesting.

If he can't close the deal this time, though—truly, humanity has no hope.

I've teed her up.

Their adrenaline is running.

Fucking kiss her already.

I glare at them through the window as they don't get it on.

What the fuck is wrong with these two?

Are they defective?

If this was a Nora Dawn book, they'd be tearing each other's clothes off already.

Jesus fuck, seriously?

He's not even on top of her on the bed anymore.

Now they're—oh, hell yes.

She's touching his arm.

He has a boo-boo.

Sound the alarm, he has a boo-boo, kissing must be imminent.

Ooh.
Ooooh, we have eye contact.
We have eye contact!
And—
And WE HAVE KISSING!
They're doing it.
They're kissing.
Fucking finally.
Also, you're welcome, stupid humans.
Now, take her clothes off.
Take her—
"Hello?" someone new calls. "You guys here?"
Dammit.
I give up.
He's just gonna have to figure this one out on his own.
Stupid, stupid human.

ABOUT THE AUTHOR

Pippa Grant wanted to write books, so she did.

Before she became a USA Today and #1 Amazon bestselling romantic comedy author, she was a young military spouse who got into writing as self-therapy. That happened around the time she discovered reading romance novels, and the two eventually merged into a career. Today, she has more than fifty knee-slapping titles available.

When she's not writing romantic comedies, she's fumbling through being a mom, wife, and mountain woman, and sometimes tries to find hobbies. Her crowning achievement? Having impeccable timing for telling stories that will make people snort beverages out of their noses. Consider yourself warned.

FIND PIPPA AT…
www.pippagrant.com

www.ingramcontent.com/pod-product-compliance
Lightning Source LLC
LaVergne TN
LVHW011213120226
831287LV00006B/16